When the Dead Remember

LELIA A PIET

When the Dead Remember

A HAUNTING DOMESTIC SUSPENSE NOVEL OF MEMORY AND BETRAYAL

LELIA A PIET

Library of Congress Control Number:

ISBN: 979-8-9882545-5-3 [Paperback]

ISBN: 979-8-9882545-4-6 [Ebook]

Cover designed by Miblart.

Published by Origins First Press, Nolensville, Tennessee 37135.

Prologue

MAY 28, 11:08 AM —31 seconds

"Um… good morning. This is Eileen from the skilled nursing care facility. I hate to leave this sort of information via voicemail, but time is crucial. Based on our previous experience with hospice patients, we don't believe Cherri will be with us much longer. I thought, perhaps, you might like to be with her when she passes."

May 28, 11:47 AM —18 seconds

"Hey, honey. I thought I'd make it home at lunch today to take care of the dogs, but something's come up at work. Let them out for me—please. Love you."

May 28, 2:14 PM —45 seconds

"She's gone." —Ahem. Ahem—"Cherri's gone. She went peacefully."

"I… I held her hand. You know… so, she wouldn't be alone." —Ahem—"Okay, so…, I'm going to begin making arrangements for her service. Give me a call back. Okay? I love you."

· · ·

June 1, 3:22 AM —1 minute 48 seconds

"Oh my God. I can't believe this. I can't... can't believe it. How could he? How could he do this to me? Cherri's service—we just buried her... this afternoon. And now, he does this to me? And in our... our bed?

"I think she's young—younger than me. Thin. She has thick, dark hair hanging down her back. I can't see her face. I can't see her face! How can he do this to me? Should I take a photo for proof? I should take a picture.

"Oh. Oh, no. I think they heard me. I don't want them to know I've seen them. I'm going back downstairs. I can't deal with this right now; I'm a wreck after the funeral—my hair. I still have my makeup on... God, what am I even wearing?

"Please. Please call me back. I'm going to wait for you to call me back. You have to help me. You have to help me figure out what to do. Please.

"Please hurry."

ALL I HAVE LEFT in this world sits on either side of me—Roni and Alok, pillars propping me up, keeping me stable. The room's lighting is bright, harsh, too much so for such a somber occasion. The pew is hard and unforgiving, offering no sympathy during the moments of grief. Sniffles and whispers drift through the air behind me. At some point, I will have to acknowledge the presence of the people who have come to pay their respects, accept their condolences.

Straight ahead of our seat, a slightly built man arranges his notes, readying to begin the service. To the left of the podium, Cherri's portrait is displayed. On the right, a huge wreath of festive flowers—every color of the rainbow, every variety imaginable has been woven together in a hodgepodge to represent the way in which my mother lived her life.

The preacher, the minister—no, he called himself a reverend, I think—is otherworldly looking. Delicate features under snow blond hair, pouty pink lips poised to speak the moment the music ends. Two days earlier, the elfin man questioned Roni and me, hoping to honor Cherri during the service better.

"Her full name, please."

"Cheryl Ann Barnes Walder," I'd answered.

Roni jumped in, "But do not call her that. My grandmother,

Cherri, she would never have answered to Cheryl." The intensity of the demand falls away as Roni tries to explain her vehemence. "Cherri said the name was… unimaginative."

"Maybe it would be better for you all to complete this form; her date and place of birth, last residence. Perhaps there are some details of her sickness and death that you'd be comfortable sharing," said the man from the Metaphysical Church.

Cherri shared little in terms of what she wanted upon her death. Her sickness came on so suddenly that there was little time in which Cherri was actually coherent enough to have such conversations. The rapid deterioration of her mind left Roni and me to guess at what Cherri would have planned for herself. Cherri identified as a spiritualist, though she never attended formal services anywhere. And so now, the man from the Metaphysical Church of West Palm Beach, Florida, refers to the answers Roni and I jotted down for him as he prepares to speak about my mother's life.

Roni insists that Cherri wanted this, but I believe Cherri would have hated such a scripted ceremony. I may be Cherri's daughter, but I am in no position to argue with my own daughter about what Cherri may or may not have wanted. The two of them had always shared everything.

It may have stung early on, but it certainly came as no surprise when Cherri appointed Roni as her agent in the healthcare proxy. It was hard not to interpret it as a snub, but at the same time, it was a relief not to have the pressure of such responsibility. Besides, Roni is a healthcare professional and understands far more about the ins and outs of the decisions and treatments and medical jargon than I ever will. Still, I can feel in my heart that this theatrical performance is not how Cherri would've wanted to be remembered.

As the last chord of the hymn is hit, the reverend steadies himself at the podium. I lower my head as he begins.

"Thank you all for being here today, to honor the memory of Cherri Walder, to comfort her family in their time of grief. Cherri is survived by her beloved daughter, Juniper Walder; her cherished granddaughter, Roni Walder; and Cherri's adored son-in-law, Alok Prasad. They welcome you and have asked me to express their appreciation that you all have taken the time to be here, to share in the joyous remembrance of Cherri's life and the sorrow of her passing."

Eyes focusing on the tissue in my hands, words float through the room with no coherence. Tissue tatters cover the black skirt stretched across my lap. I can't recall dressing in this suit. Hair pulled tight at the base of my neck in a neat ponytail—when did I do that?

Twisting, squeezing, wringing my hands in my lap, Alok reaches to take them into his grasp, reassuring and affirming, then brushing away the tissue mess from my skirt. I look up at him and offer a small, thin smile. Alok joined our little group of three, the Walder women, fifteen years ago. Now, I can't imagine my life without him. My husband is hurting too; I know this. He and Cherri shared a special bond. Cherri was Alok's surrogate mother after his family disowned him in the name of religion for having married me.

On the other side of me, Roni sits staring straight ahead, shoulders pulled tall, the small of her back flush against the church pew. We are the only two left. It wasn't supposed to be like this. First, Luna, my younger sister, then my older brother, Dusk—both died years before our mother, years too young. Cherri hadn't forgotten them. In the end, she couldn't recall my name or Roni's, yet she was frequently calling out to my dead siblings. Are they with her now? Has Cherri joined them as she always believed she would?

Sounds of commotion rouse me from my thoughts. Beside me, Roni stands. She's speaking with someone. Alok tugs my hand, urging me onto my feet.

"What's wrong? What's going on?"

Alok runs his hand down my arm, soothing. "The service is over."

"It's done? Already?" We just sat down. How can it be over?

Alok nods, watching me, concern and sadness glazing his brown eyes.

At the front of the room, the man gathers his notes, collects his things—he's done. How can he be done? He didn't speak about Cherri's love of life, her zest for adventure, her zany wardrobe.

I grab Roni's elbow, turning her to face me. "Did the reverend say everything? Did he relay what we asked him to?"

"Yes, Mom. All of it."

"Juniper, people are waiting for us." Alok places his arm around my waist, turning me, gently prodding me up the aisle where the faces of our neighbors and friends of Cherri wait to express their sympathies.

SOMETHING ABOUT THE MOMENT, the experience, feels right. Seems familiar somehow, yet Cherri finds it odd. Odd in that the pain has subsided, the constant discomfort gone. Oh, but the absence is what makes it feel right. How long has she been living with the pain? The question, however, doesn't seem to matter much at this point in time, as even stranger and more unsettling is the view of the room Cherri now observes. From her vantage point, floating above the scene, Cherri takes in the whole of the enclosed space. She sees herself below, lying motionless, breathless.

And she understands.

Cherri's soul lingers near the shell she has donned throughout this lifetime. She is examining, contemplating, regarding. The body is tired and worn out, wrinkled and droopy, though Cherri never minded it—a comfortable broken-in shoe. The unruly red hair she never dared let go gray. The tall, lanky frame often moved in an awkward fashion and tended to embarrass Cherri during moments of nervousness and anxiety. It all suited her before, though now, as she takes in the details of her old shell, Cherri believes it is wrong somehow. She is weary, she determines. Weary and depleted. Cherri lets go, fully slipping from the weight of the body.

She is finally passing on.

The weight of her past lifetime is gone. Surging to the surface are new feelings: contentment, a sense of accomplishment for the feat completed. Cherri turns, readying herself to go, to move beyond.

No, wait. She turns back, seeing them, witnessing their pain, the grief they hold onto—Cherri's loved ones are struggling with her death. Their faces wear signs of distress and sorrow. Cherri, however, feels only the warmth of love, like the sun on her skin after a long, cold, dark winter or skinny dipping on hot summer nights. Cherri is fully immersed in a pool of love. She wants to reach out, to spread this amazing feeling of completeness among them, to console those she loves.

Cherri surveys each of them in turn, putting names to the faces of those she holds dear, recalling the relationships they shared. Her daughter, Juniper; her granddaughter, Roni; Alok; and all the friends who mourned her passing. She remembers. How incredible! She suddenly recalls every moment shared with each of these loved ones. What an unexpected and wonderful gift. For so long, her mind couldn't process who these people were to her, what it was she should feel for them, but now the haze has lifted. She wants to tell them, but to do so means she would have to reenter the body that forgot these special people in the first place.

Torn by mixed emotions—stay so as to give comfort to her loved ones or leave behind the exhausting lifetime she has completed—Cherri swivels her attention between the two options. Behind her are those she loves. Ahead is a bright, beautiful, magnificent light beckoning to Cherri. The joy, an immense amount of joy, radiates alongside the sense of calm and peacefulness. Cherri glances back at the body, taking in the heartbreak of her loved ones. The pull to comfort them, smooth away their grief, is strong. Cherri wants to tell them not to be sad but to be happy for her. She wants them to know she's not gone. She's here with them, and one day they will all be together again. Cherri knows this is her time; she knows she cannot go back.

Cherri understands what she must do.

Excitedly, Cherri moves on, leaving the pain and suffering she experienced in this last existence for the embrace of love awaiting her. The journey takes time, but Cherri is in no rush. The sense of urgency, the uneasy anxiety she used to bear in her physical state, have all fallen away. Wrapped in peace, euphoria flowing through her, Cherri steps farther into the gleaming brilliance. In the distance, figures stand, waiting, anticipating her arrival. The figures, this place, somehow it all seems familiar too, like stepping over the threshold of your front door.

Suddenly, Cherri is aware of a presence at her side, another being. Confusion strikes first, though absent is the fear or the startle, then comes the understanding. It is Cherri's guardian spirit, come to escort her through to the light source, bring her back to this dimension, welcome her home.

"You've returned from the physical state, and now it is time for your renewal period," the guardian spirit explains.

"My renewal?"

"Yes, you've completed the lessons you set out to learn within this past lifetime. Now, we will review your accomplishments, after which you will set goals for the lessons to be completed during your next lifetime. But I get ahead of myself. First, you need to re-energize, reinvigorate your soul, and then we will review."

"I feel so happy and calm, so at peace," Cherri relays.

"Soon, you will remember. You will recall your time here from before, before you were Cherri Barnes Walder."

"How is it possible that I would have forgotten such a wonderful place?"

"In the physical form, infants recall where home is, but they do not possess the capability to relay such information. As the physical body matures, mannerisms and expectations are learned, programmed, and the knowledge of this dimension fades. Although the soul never wholly forgets, fear is a strong influencer in the physical state. Fear causes the soul in physical form to forget it is, and has always been, loved and protected."

"Love erases fear. Love is all-encompassing and dissolves fear," Cherri says. The knowledge of the statement comes from deep within her, a place of inherent understanding.

"And now you are remembering. Your soul family is waiting. Are you ready to see them?"

Ahead, Cherri recognizes the souls of Luna and Dusk, her children from this past life. Her mother and father are also there. Love and joy swell to bursting within her. How long has she waited to reunite with these special souls? Suddenly, a new thought breaks through, and Cherri recalls that time means nothing in this dimension. This past lifetime may have spanned a period of seventy-four human years, but the concept of years and time does not exist in this realm.

Cherri is finally remembering.

CHAPTER THREE

Juniper

PRICKING sensations tap dance over the surface of my eyelids. Hollow thudding reverberates between my ears. A voice booms from above, demanding. Commanding? Through a tight squint, I understand Roni stands over me. Sunlight beams brightly through the open shades across the room, haloing my daughter's form. What time is it? And why is Roni yelling at me?

"Wake up. What the hell are you doing, Mom?"

I manage to roll from my side to my back, shielding my eyes from the light. "Sleeping." Why am I on the living room sofa? Where's Alok?

"Yeah, I see that," Roni says, placing a cup of coffee on the table in front of me. "The question is—why are you sleeping? You should be getting your shit together so you can get out of here."

The dogs circle Roni's ankles, begging for recognition. Have they been out? As if answering my silent question, Roni walks through the kitchen to let Boswell and Dash out of the door and into the backyard.

Searing pain shoots through my skull as I work to push myself into an upright position. The skirt I wore to Cherri's funeral bunches uncomfortably at mid-thigh. As I yank it down, my gaze falls to the coffee table. The remnants of last night's fuzzy happenings—an empty wine bottle, a half glass of red, a prescription bottle of sleeping pills—lend clues to the condition of my head. Fingertips to my forehead, I pull them through my hair as Roni returns to the living room.

"Well?"

"Well, what?" I gratefully sip the warm coffee. "What am I missing here, Roni? What is it that has you so riled up? And why are you here so early?" I lean back into the sofa's cushions and study my daughter's face for answers. "I thought you had to work today?"

Regardless of whether Roni has to get to work or not, Wellington is at least a thirty-minute drive in rush hour traffic from downtown West Palm Beach. Cherri, Roni, and I moved into Alok's home after he and I married, but when Cherri went into the skilled nursing care facility, Roni moved to be closer to Cherri. Roni hates making the drive all the way out here anymore.

"You're kidding me? You're totally fucking with me, right?"

"No. I'm not, and can we cut the language? It's too early for one of your foul-mouthed rants."

"You really don't remember?"

"Remember what?"

Roni plops down in the chair positioned on the other side of the coffee table. She fixes her dark eyes on me, blowing the heavy, black bangs from her brows. "Calling me last night? The voicemail?"

"Is that what this is about? I woke you up in the middle of the night, and now you're here to get even with me? Cut me a bit of slack, Roni. I buried my mother yesterday." Tears well at the spoken reminder.

"And Cherri meant nothing to me?"

"I didn't mean it that way, Roni. I was simply asking for a little understanding." I drop my forehead into an open palm, trying again to get my bearings before addressing Roni. "Even though we knew the outcome of Cherri's disease was inevitable,

I still wasn't ready, and by no means did I believe you were ready for her death either."

"I know, Mom. I get it—I do. And I'm not trying to blast you, but you need to address what happened here last night. You can't let this go because you're grief-stricken and don't want to deal with it. This is serious shit."

"What is so serious? You're being ridiculously cryptic." Annoyed, I stand abruptly, sway, and fall back to the sofa, grasping for equilibrium.

"Are you okay?" Roni leans to pick up the bottle of sleeping pills from the table and shakes. "Are these the ones I gave you? How many did you take?"

"I don't know. I don't remember taking anything. You know I don't like medications. I'm not sure how that bottle even made it to the living room unless Alok brought them to me. The last I recall, I shoved those into the back of my medicine cabinet."

Roni eyes me suspiciously. "And you don't remember calling me at three o'clock in the morning, leaving me a play-by-play voicemail of what went on in this house last night?"

"No. That doesn't even sound remotely familiar." The ache in my head worms into the base of my neck. Working fingertips to massage the area, I ask. "I left you a voicemail last night? At three?" I scan the surface of the coffee table. "Are you sure? I don't even know where my phone is."

Roni points to the open space below the sofa. I look down and retrieve my cell phone from the floor.

"Check your call log." Roni sits back in the chair, crossing legs, folding arms across her chest. Her foot flicks back and forth, waiting for me to comply.

The device lights up as it recognizes my face and springs open. The green phone icon brings up the recent call list. There, at the top of the screen, is Roni's name, call time 3:22 AM, outgoing, length 1 minute 48 seconds. Below the first entry, I see where I made several other attempts to contact her. I shake my head, hoping for some sense to knock free, something to give me an inkling of why I was so desperate to speak with Roni during the wee hours of this morning.

"You found it," Roni states, knowing I would, knowing the message I left.

"All right. I give. I did it. I left a message. What did I say?"

"Okay, so, if you really don't remember, I don't know that I want to be the one to relay this information." Roni sits up, leaning over her knees, looking at me, concern etching her features. "Think. Think hard. What's the last thing you remember?"

"I, um… Alok drove us home after the funeral. He wanted me to eat. I said I couldn't. I opened some wine." Concentrating, digging for recall, I look at my hands, pick at my fingernails. "I scrolled through some old photos on my phone. And then—then I guess I fell asleep."

My face feels tight and grimy with yesterday's makeup I didn't wash away last night. I look to the left and right of where I sit, then down at my clothing. A red wine stain trails along the placket of the blouse.

"So you fell asleep there, and Alok did what?" Roni asks.

"I suppose he went to bed and left me here—he was pretty upset too."

Roni reaches for her cell phone. She taps the screen, then holds the phone out as the voicemail begins to play on speaker.

"Oh my God. I can't believe this. I can't… can't believe it."

Whispers. Histrionics. The voicemail message is almost incoherent. I lean in to better hear.

"How could he? How could he do this to me? Cherri's service—we just buried her… this afternoon. And now, he does this to me? And in our… our bed?

The voice coming from the phone's speaker is mine, but I have zero recollection of ever saying those words.

"I think she's young—younger than me. Thin. She has thick, dark hair hanging down her back. I can't see her face. I can't see her face!

How can he do this to me? Should I take a photo for proof? I should take a picture."

"Stop. Stop it," I demand. "What is that?"

"It's you, Mom. Calling me for help this morning."

"No. No, it can't be. It sounds like I'm telling you Alok had an affair."

"You don't say? Because that's exactly what you said, Mom. You were hysterical and all the details… what else would you be saying?" Roni pushes the play button to finish out the message.

"Oh. Oh, no. I think they heard me. I don't want them to know I've seen them. I'm going back downstairs. I can't deal with this right now; I'm a wreck after the funeral—my hair. I still have my makeup on… God, what am I even wearing? Please. Please call me back. I'm going to wait for you to call me back. You have to help me. You have to help me figure out what to do. Please.

"Please hurry."

The message ends. I stare at the device in Roni's outstretched hand. The blaze of my daughter's glare heats my skin. The words I heard myself string together on Roni's voicemail run through my mind. Though slurred and barely coherent, the accusation was clear—I claimed I saw Alok in our bed with another woman. Could I really have witnessed such a thing? Why wouldn't I remember something so horrible if I had seen the whole sordid thing go down?

"There has to be some explanation for this. Nothing I heard on that voicemail is even close to familiar. Is there a picture?"

"No."

"See. We have no proof. Maybe I was hallucinating or something."

"Mom, did you hear the voicemail you left me?"

"Where is Alok?"

"Here. Listen again." Before I can protest, Roni hits play. The volume, as loud as it will go, my voice rings through the room, repeating the nightmare I can't recall, one I don't believe.

My cheeks burn under the hot stream of tears. "I need to see him."

"Before I found you sleeping on the sofa, I looked for Alok to confront him. He's not here; his car is gone." Roni's eyes are unwavering.

"This doesn't make any sense. I mean," I choke back a sob and continue. "Alok would never have an affair, and he most certainly wouldn't bring another woman into our home while I'm here."

"You passed out, Mom. He obviously thought you'd never know. Cocky, fucking bastard."

"Roni!" The pounding in my head gathers speed and force.

"Seriously? You're going to take his side after you witnessed him pumping another woman? Figures." Roni stands, snatching her keys and wallet from the coffee table. "You call me up in the middle of the night, begging for help. I drive all the way out here, and now you don't believe me? Don't believe your own words? Be careful. You're going to end up all alone, Mom." Roni turns to leave.

"Please, Roni. Don't go. I'm just… confused. Let me think for a minute. Maybe…" Hanging my head, focusing on the floor, I try to gather the thoughts, the memories. Why would I want to remember something so horrible? I don't. But I certainly don't want Roni all worked up over this either, thinking I've chosen Alok over her, a longstanding argument between the two of us. I've lost my mother. If this is true, I may have already lost my husband. I can not lose my daughter.

Roni eases back into the chair, waiting, scrutinizing, calculating.

Her voice softens. "Let me help," Roni says, understanding and compassion framing the offer. "We can try one of the exercises I use with my patients to help with memory recall." I lift my eyes to meet hers. "I've had a lot of success with this particular technique, but you have to be willing and receptive to the process."

I nod my consent.

"We can use the voicemail to recount what we know happened last night, hopefully triggering your memory about the actual occurrence."

Still uncertain of what I really want at this point, whether to remember, forget, or sweep the whole thing away, I concede, settling back into the sofa, making myself more comfortable and open to the exercise.

"Close your eyes," Roni begins. "You've arrived home after Cherri's funeral. Alok urged you to eat, but you declined. See yourself as you were on the couch last night. Tell me what you were doing."

"I was tired. All I wanted to do was sleep, but I couldn't."

"Where was Alok?"

"In the kitchen, cleaning."

"You couldn't sleep, so what did you do?"

"I got up and walked to the kitchen. I told Alok I was going to have a glass of wine. He offered to open it for me, said he'd bring it to me in the living room."

"That's good, Mom. What did you do next?"

"I returned to the living room and lay back on the sofa. My phone was on the coffee table. I grabbed it and opened it up."

"And what did you see on your phone screen? What app did you open?"

"The photos app—pictures of Cherri. I was missing her and wanted to remember some of the times we shared."

"What about the wine?"

"Alok brought it to me and said he was going to bed. He asked me to go with him, but I wasn't ready. I needed more time."

"Good. Now, what else can you remember?"

"Nothing. After I kissed Alok goodnight, I don't remember anything. I must have fallen asleep."

"Okay, so now we'll use the voicemail to help us fill in the rest of the night's events. Close your eyes again."

I squeeze my eyes, viewing the scene behind the closed lids. I don't want to see what the voicemail suggests.

"See yourself as you make your way up the stairs. Did you decide to go to bed? Were you hunting for your sleeping pills?"

Eyes open, I shake my head. "I don't know."

"Try, Mom. You *need* to try."

The breath I pull fills my lungs to bursting as I close my eyes and begin again. "I must have woken up and realized I wasn't in bed. Alok would be worried. Maybe. I guess. So, I suppose, I made my way upstairs."

"You're at the door of your bedroom. Do you see yourself? What are you wearing?"

"My black skirt—the one I'm wearing now, and the blouse I wore to the funeral."

I pause, but Roni picks up the scene again.

"You didn't want to disturb Alok, to wake him. You were being quiet. You eased open the door and saw Alok in bed. Did you see the woman with him?"

"I… I guess." The vision forms in my mind, becoming clearer, growing more focused. "Yes. I saw her. She had long, dark hair."

"What about her face?"

"No, she was turned away from me."

The voicemail loops through my mind; on continuous repeat, I can't shut it off.

"What are some of the woman's characteristics? Is there anything familiar about her?"

"No, nothing. I think she's younger, thin."

I open my eyes to erase the memory, but I can't. The nightmare scene has wormed its way into my head, and I can't unsee it now.

Tears fall faster. They may never stop. I've lost so much, so quickly. I look at Roni. "What am I going to do?"

"I can tell you what you're not going to do."

CHAPTER FOUR

THE ROOM IS small and unassuming. A dirt-streaked window on the left, a fake plant in the far corner coated in a thick layer of dust, rises unsteadily toward the popcorn ceiling tiles. In the center of the room, a couple of industrial chairs have been arranged for a face-to-face conversation between the two beings meant to occupy them. The room is completely void of any personal items—nothing set about to trigger negative emotions of a patient, no items that might give rise to provocations.

That might well be an unseasoned patient's assessment. However, this being my profession, I understand this room is for traveling therapists in need of space for their sessions. And like the locations in which they dole out their therapy, traveling therapists do not choose their patients, just as patients do not choose their therapists. Everyone is assigned to the situation.

I'm being watched—the assessment is underway, it seems.

The therapist, a middle-aged woman, sits in the chair facing the entrance to the room. It is, for the record, the seat I prefer, the position I am most comfortable and used to being in when I hold a therapy session with my clients. Reluctantly, I start toward the empty chair.

Waiting, even-tempered and forcibly agreeable, the woman crosses her legs, folds her hands. I know the routine: gain the patient's trust, give them time to connect with you. But that's hard to do when the patient doesn't want to be there in the first place, and I don't have a choice. The therapy sessions have been deemed mandatory by some higher-up whose identity has yet to be made known.

"Hello. My name is Donna," the woman begins as I situate myself across from her. "How are you today, Veronica?" A bland, staged, forced opening. Great. I've got a real professional on my hands.

"Roni."

The woman, Donna, looks at me as if I've sprouted a bushy red beard in the last twenty seconds. She doesn't pick up on the obvious name correction. Obtuse. How am I to get anything out of therapy sessions with this person?

"No one calls me Veronica," I explain. "It's Roni," I add once again, trying to curb the terseness of tone.

Donna holds a crumpled yellow legal pad on her lap, pen poised, ready to jot down any interesting tidbits I share. "Okay. Roni, it is." Donna makes the note on the pad, then begins again. "How are you feeling today, Roni?"

"Peachy." I press my back to the chair, pulling my spine straight. I may be sullen and unconvinced of the necessity of these sessions, but I refuse to convey the fact through posture cues.

"I'm detecting sarcasm in your response. Would you agree with that observation?"

"Sure."

"Okay. Let's delve a bit deeper. Explore that sentiment, if you will. Do you think your sarcasm stems from frustration or rather anger?" Donna pauses. When I do not readily reply, she tries again. "Perhaps another emotion?"

"Bitterness."

Donna writes the word on the notepad, looks up, and tilts her head—an attempt to exhibit concern while digging for clarification. "For your situation?" Again, she holds for my comment before pressing on. "For someone or something?"

"Look, can we at least acknowledge that I know how this game works?" Donna's head bobs in agreement, knowing I, too, have extensive experience as a traveling therapist. "And, I feel it only fair to inform you, I'm in no mood to play." This is obviously a total waste of everyone's time.

"Roni, you know as well as I do, we must comply with this directive. Why not make the best of these sessions, maybe even accomplish something, okay?"

Donna is right, of course, but the fact is, I'm not ready to do this yet. I don't want to be analyzed or fixed, and, if I'm honest, I don't see the need for this directive. I am not at fault for what happened. Quite the opposite, I am the victim. Bringing this fact to Donna's attention, however, is going to take some time. More time than I really want to relinquish.

"Fine, I get it. Let's just cut the bullshit and get to your point."

"Okay. Let's start with what I've learned from your records," Donna tries again. "I read you have been struggling with the loss of your grandmother. I take it the two of you were close?" She twirls her pen, watching for my reaction to her statement.

"Yes. To me, Cherri was more like a mother than a grandmother."

"Did you spend a lot of time with Cherri during your childhood?"

"Yes." I study my hands, avert eye contact. "I lived with her."

"And what about your mother? Did you spend time with her while you were living with your grandmother?"

"We all lived together… until I left for college at eighteen."

Donna observes me, trying to pick up cues, mannerisms, symptoms, anything that might tell her more about my mindset. While it is unnerving, I expect nothing less than her scrutiny. In the profession, we all do it, so I alleviate my discomfort by watching this woman at work. Donna is being assessed as a therapist in the same manner she evaluates me as a patient.

"What about your father?" She asks. "Did he live with you, and your mom, and grandmother?"

"I didn't know my father, and he's long dead now." His name was rarely spoken in our house. Cherri bristled at the mention of the man. I don't relay any of that to Donna. The information isn't applicable to this situation.

"That must have been hard on you—not having a father."

"It wasn't that bad. It was always the three of us. Cherri called us the Walder women. And then Juniper married Alok."

"How old were you when your mom married Alok?"

"Fifteen. Sixteen. Somewhere around then."

"That must have been an adjustment for you."

"Not really." I had gotten into the habit of not giving Juniper much of my time by that point. "I was too focused on my own life—high school, college entrance exams, applications to schools." Trying to deal with the fact that I was different than all my girlfriends who were vying for the attention of guys.

"Let's go back to your grandmother. From your intake form, I read that Cherri's death deeply affected you. That you were her caregiver in the end?"

"No. That's not true."

"What's not true?"

"That I was her caregiver in the end—it had become too much for any of us to handle. Cherri was in a skilled nursing care facility when she passed away."

"Tell me about her cause of death. Was she sick?"

"Yes."

"Was the illness terminal, something she had lived with for long?"

"When the doctors diagnosed Cherri, we were all aware she would have no opportunity to heal or come out of it. We knew Cherri would eventually lose all recall of family and friends, that she would forget how to care for herself. The progression was fast, though, faster than any of us had planned for. We had to find care for Cherri that would be consistent with her deteriorating condition."

"You used the term 'we.' 'We had to find care.' Were you speaking of you and your mother?"

"It was all of us: me, Juniper, Alok. We even consulted Cherri, tried to give her a voice in the matter." I clear my throat and add, "Not that she really had an opinion by that point."

"Because you all were in charge at that point? Due to her waning cognitive ability?"

"Because her condition had rapidly declined to the degree that she couldn't voice a coherent position on the matter. We wanted Cherri to be at home with us, in her own bedroom, for as long as possible. But as it turned out, we were unable to provide the proper care. The situation became dangerous."

"It's good that you and your family members were able to agree on the situation collectively. Often in these types of healthcare scenarios, conflict arises within the family unit as to the ideals of how and what kind of care to arrange for their sick loved one."

"Oh no, you've got it wrong. We didn't agree. Juniper wanted Cherri to be in a facility in Wellington, close to where we all lived at the time. However, that facility was not the best. The best care for Cherri was in downtown West Palm Beach."

"So, you and your mother disagreed. What was the outcome of the disagreement then?"

"Cherri was placed in the facility downtown."

"So your mother went with your advice?"

"No. Juniper had no say in the matter. I was the agent named in Cherri's healthcare proxy. The decision was always mine. Cherri appointed me because she understood I was the family member best fit for the role."

"Did this cause discord between you and your mother?"

"Juniper has always done whatever Cherri and I suggested. I wanted the highest quality of care for Cherri. Juniper certainly couldn't argue with that. Juniper was more concerned that I moved out of the house when Cherri did, leaving her and Alok alone for the first time in their marriage."

Donna makes a quick note on her yellow pad, then asks, "What drove your decision to move out of your mother's home when your grandmother left?"

"I wanted to be near Cherri, so I could be there whenever she needed me." Donna's gaze is steady, waiting for me to continue. "A new apartment building had recently opened a block away from the care facility."

Donna maintains focus, studying me, calculating, surmising. I'm sure Donna is making her own judgments, but her thoughts and summations do not concern me. Confidence in my actions has never been something I lack. It is the difference between me and so many others. Not only do I have great instincts for what is right and what is wrong, but I have the tenacity to follow through on my decisions.

"The whole of my life, Cherri put me first. She was always there when I needed her, and I was damn sure going to do the same for her."

"Is this why your mother decided to move downtown, as well? So she could put Cherri first?"

"No. Juniper's move was spurred by a completely different issue."

CHAPTER FIVE

Juniper

THE GARAGE DOOR squeals as it lifts to open. Alok planned to have the thing serviced, but he seems to have been busy with other endeavors. From the upstairs office window, I watch Alok's car disappear under the house. The door screeches closed, signaling the impending altercation. The tingle of a thousand needles stings the skin covering my arms and torso. How? How did I get to this place in my life?

"Juniper," Alok calls from the living room.

I refuse to answer. Childish? Perhaps. But what am I supposed to do? I am furious with him. He's crushed me. Tears threaten. No. You will hold it together. Roni insists I buck up, pull it together. She says I need to learn to take care of myself. She's right, of course. I'm almost fifty years old.

"Juniper."

He's at the base of the stairwell.

Bracing, fists clenching at my sides, heart pounding inside my chest, I listen for his footfall on each stair. How does one tell her husband that she saw him screwing another woman in their bed the night before? Where does one start with relaying the message that she is moving out immediately? Head back, eyes to the ceiling—*oh, Cherri, I miss you*—I lower my eyelids, seeking answers to the questions scrolling through my mind. The action does not disclose solutions but rather triggers mental footage of the voicemail, looping over and over. I shake the vision away as the door to the office pops open.

The dogs trot in, unconcerned, proudly leading Alok into the room. They each take the side of their favorite human—Dash on Alok's heels and Boswell at mine.

"Hey. Are you okay?" Alok asks, approaching me. "I've been calling you all afternoon. Why didn't you answer?"

Keeping my focus on the box before me, I reach inside to re-situate some previously packed items. Alok steps closer, his large hands settling on my waist—a gesture that only yesterday seemed so normal, so familiar, so personal and comforting, now causes every muscle in my body to tauten.

Alok's grip strengthens with concern. "Juniper. Honey?" Alok slips his arms through mine to fold around my midsection. More than anything, I want to let him hold me. "Tell me what I can do to help you through this. I understand you're hurting, but Cherri isn't suffering anymore. That should be of some comfort," he says, tightening his embrace. "Is there anything, anything I can do?"

"Get off." I peel Alok's hands from my body, throwing them off of me, stepping away.

"What is it? What's wrong? Is this because I left without saying goodbye this morning?"

"Why don't you tell me what's wrong?" I ask, not bothering to face him. "I think you owe me an explanation. You need to tell me what I did that was so awful, you could somehow justify cheating on me."

"What?"

I spin around to face him, furious. "Don't. DO. NOT. Treat me like I'm not worthy of an explanation. Like I'm stupid and will simply turn a blind eye to your infidelity." Pressure crushing my chest, I struggle to keep the flow of air pumping into my lungs.

"Infidelity? Juniper, what are you talking about? I'm not having an affair. You know I'd never do that to you. I love you."

"Stop it." To hide the tears threatening to spill, belying the strength I need to convey, I turn away. "On top of everything else —" I take a breath to help swallow down the lump in my throat. "I can't take you lying to me," I say, holding the side flaps of the moving box. "Please, it will be much more dignifying if you admit what's done is done, and we move on." I stumble over my words, wondering if what has spilled forth was even coherent.

"There is nothing that is done, Juniper. I've no idea what you're talking about. Where is this even coming from?"

"I saw you, Alok."

"You saw me what?"

"You've been caught. Game's up. I… I saw you. With another. Woman. In our bed. Last night." The statement comes out broken, stuttered, the way I feel. I don't know if I'm making any sense, and I'm too exhausted to care.

"That's not true. No one was here last night except the two of us."

Twisting my head over my shoulder, I look the bastard in the eye to deliver the damning blow. "I saw her, Alok. I saw the two of you together with my own eyes. Roni has proof." I turn back to the box and begin throwing the other items from my desk inside, not taking the time to wrap them properly for transit.

"This is absurd, Juniper. What do you mean, Roni has proof? What does she have to do with this? Roni wasn't even here last night."

"No, she wasn't here, but I called her in the middle of the night. She has the voicemail I left her, a play-by-play of everything I witnessed."

"Seriously, Juniper? You do get how crazy this sounds, right? A voicemail? Me with another woman in our bed while you're downstairs asleep?"

I whip around to face him, pointer finger jabbing the air. "Don't you dare do that."

"Do what? Tell you how ridiculous this accusation is? That this is insane?"

"I'm not insane. I told you I have proof." A wave of anger rolls over the length of my body, fury chokes off the falling tears.

"A voicemail? In the middle of the night, on the same day, you bury your mother? This has got to be some sort of grief-induced hallucination. Let's sit and…"

"I'm not crazy. The image is burned into my brain, Alok. She was young. And thin. Long, dark hair… hanging down her back… while you *fucked* her on our bed." I gasp through the sobs. Knees threatening to buckle beneath me, I can't—I can't repeat it again.

"Look, I believe you think you saw this, but you didn't. Juniper. Honey. None of what you have made up in your head happened."

"In my head? Are you for real, Alok? I am NOT crazy. I am not going insane. Roni and I have gone over this and over this, and I know what happened here last night."

"I never said you were crazy, Juniper."

"My mother lost her mind, and you're playing the insane card against me? You just said this whole thing was crazy."

"First off, I said this whole thing *sounds* crazy, not that you were crazy. I'm speaking the truth, Juniper. You want me to tell you I did something that I didn't."

I don't want to do this anymore. This confrontation needs to be over, right now. I need to get out of here. There is nothing left to say, nothing I want to continue dwelling on, nothing good that can come from this.

"Juniper…"

"Nothing you say will make what you have done to me any easier to accept, Alok. But for God's sake, you owe it to me to be honest, after all these years."

Alok places his hands on my shoulders. "Juniper, please."

I rip out of his grip before he can pull me into his arms. "I can't do this with you. I can't take any more of your blatant deceit." I walk away, heading to the door, Boswell following close behind.

"Juniper, where are you going?"

"I'm done, Alok. I'll send for my things."

CHAPTER SIX

Cherri

BASKING in the serenity and tranquility her soul family radiates, Cherri continues to be in awe. How could she have forgotten what she now experiences—the peace, the love, the joy? She spent seventy-four years on a plane where heartbreak, disappointment, and fear reign ruthlessly indifferent. How could Cherri have possibly feared death? Grieved the loss of a loved one, selfishly longing to have them back in her realm?

Cherri's guardian spirit returns to her side. She doesn't need a voice behind the words to know what her guardian relays. It is time to move on.

Distress replaces Cherri's feelings of contentment, the soft silence. "Move where?"

"To your life review, of course. Now that you have returned to this plane and connected with your soul family, it is essential to move onward to the next step in the process."

Cherri swings her attention from the guardian to the souls huddled around her. She isn't ready to leave them—she's only just been reunited.

"Soon. You will all be together again. Right now, there is work to be done."

Cherri is confused. She can feel this is the place her soul has been leading her back to all along. After the toil she has completed, this is to be her reward. It is all so clear. She is supposed to be here, and Cherri doesn't want to waste another moment without her loved ones. Yet, the guardian tells her they must move on; the reflection must commence.

As Cherri's loved ones take leave, confusion and disorientation shroud Cherri once again. The joy and peace and love exit with her soul family.

She moves, intending to follow them, to never let them go again, but the guardian spirit gently tugs her back. Gentle though it may have been, the act is jolting to Cherri's consciousness.

"I do not intend to startle you. It is difficult, after all the heartache you have recently endured, to believe you will be together with your soul family again. I understand this. The process, however, is critical to the betterment of your soul. Therefore, why would you have wasted this time away from your loved ones to enlighten your soul? You see? We must begin your review."

Though the guardian spirit's words and wisdom ring true, Cherri wants to feel the calm, the grace, again. All she feels at the moment, however, is disorientation.

As her guardian spirit wishes, Cherri focuses her attention on the other plane, viewing herself in the shell, seeing the body she has vacated. She recognizes the loved ones she left behind. Juniper and Roni, their journeys yet to be completed.

Juniper. Her daughter seems distraught, sad, deeply affected by Cherri's death. Juniper. Her daughter's name tugs at Cherri's memory. There is something… something Cherri must do, must tell Juniper. But what?

Cherri looks at Roni. She's close by Juniper, perhaps comforting her. No, something about Roni seems wrong. Is it the grief, as it is with Juniper? Cherri can't be certain of Roni's emotions, but Juniper's angst and distress wrench Cherri.

Cherri loved all her children equally, but her relationship with Juniper was stronger. Possibly, it was all Juniper and Cherri had endured together over the years—the shared strife they persevered through—that made them so close.

"We never lived apart, Juniper and me—other than Juniper's first semester of college," Cherri relays. "Of course, there were times I suspected Juniper might have thought I was in her way, especially after she married Alok. But Juniper always insisted that I had a place in her home for as long as I lived. 'We are all the family we have,' Juniper would say, 'and family takes care of family.' Juniper always said she wanted to be there for me like I had always been there for her."

Cherri's guardian spirit urges her to start the review from the beginning, properly. Cherri complies, though a nagging feeling persists, an unsettling tickle that makes Cherri believe there's something she's forgotten, something she should have done before passing over.

The anxious unease fades as suddenly, Cherri is witnessing her birth, experiencing the joy her arrival bestows on her parents. The scene changes, skipping along merrily through Cherri's childhood years, replaying early relationships, correspondences, and encounters. Each instance brings about the varying emotions Cherri stirs in others during her contact with them. The process is both enlightening and discouraging, learning about how her actions affected others, positively and negatively.

Cherri looks to her guardian in astonishment. "It feels so real. It's like I'm reliving every moment. It's like I am there with them."

"Yes. The review process takes you back to the specific time and place where it occurred so that you can witness and feel every sensation of a particular transaction."

Cherri nods and turns back to the review, which moves into Cherri's older childhood years. There are her parents—happy, loving, and strict, so religiously strict. She witnesses the point at which she begins to buck their authority, acting out in defiance. Not only does Cherri observe, but she must also endure the sensations of her parents' growing disappointment in their only child as she transitions into her teenage years. Each of Cherri's actions propels an emotional charge for all the players involved. The arguments, the battles, the ugly struggles between a willful teen and disgruntled parents.

By seventeen, Cherri can no longer live under their roof, abide by their rules, excuse away her daddy's heavy hand. Cherri watches, feeling the excitement of adventure as she leaves her childhood home in the darkest hour of night. Then comes the headlong hurtle into pain as her parents' heartbreak is thrust upon her when they learn Cherri has run away from home.

"I didn't mean to hurt them," Cherri tells her guardian. "At the time, I thought I was doing what was best for all of us."

"Your intentions are of no concern in this review. Our purpose is to explore the manner in which you conducted relationships while in your physical body so as to understand how you made others feel."

Relationships, encounters, emotions, babies, children, interactions. A jarring revelation from Cherri's past lifetime explodes into her consciousness. The review jumps several years into the future. The disruption leaves Cherri vulnerable and frightened.

"I have to go back. I've done something terrible."

"We all would like a chance to go back and right our wrongs," the guardian says.

"No, I need to tell her. I was supposed to tell her before it was too late. She must know what I've done."

"The opportunity for righting our actions on the physical plane is over upon our exit."

"There must be some exception. There has to be some way I can go back, some way that I can tell her before it is too late."

"You must accept responsibility for your actions long done and strive to do better in your next existence on the physical plane."

"But this won't matter in the next lifetime. It must be settled now. See? Look. Look at what I've done."

"You've leaped ahead. Best practice for the process states that we progress through your review chronologically. Let's begin where we left off." The guardian spirit attempts to comfort and settle Cherri. "Remember, time means nothing here. Time is precious only to the mortals on the physical plane."

But the only thing Cherri remembers is what she forgot.

CHAPTER SEVEN

Juniper

T HE REARVIEW MIRROR reflects the building where Cherri took her last breath. I pull my gaze from the reflection, blink away the pooling of tears, and turn my attention forward to the apartment building.

Towering twenty stories, the building's white exterior gleams against the bright blue skies of the downtown skyline. The contemporary design of the facade boasts sleek lines and seductive curves. The Grabell is one of the newer buildings in the historic business district of West Palm Beach. Though in the last few years, several sparkling, high-rise, luxury apartment buildings have sprouted up in the area. Roni chose the Grabell over other buildings because of its proximity to Cherri's nursing care facility. Now, I have chosen the Grabell because Roni dictated it so—to the point of *'I've secured you a furnished unit in my building, Mom; it's available immediately.'*

I step out of the car, load the parking meter, walk to the passenger side, and click Boswell into his leash. As we make our way to the building's entrance, Boswell's tail wags, his demeanor happy, ready, eager. The poor dog has no idea of the loss he has suffered: His home—gone. His buddy, Dash—gone. Fenced backyard—gone.

I am all too aware of what I have lost—the weight of it

pressing firmly on my shoulders, slowing my forward progress. Cherri's death was a devastating blow, but Alok too? Both gone, and now, I do what must be done. Yes, I nod in affirmation, approaching the double doors of the Grabell, tugging Boswell along.

Oddly enough, I've never been inside the building, even though Roni has lived here for almost two years. Whenever I made the trip downtown to visit Cherri, Roni was always present at Cherri's bedside. When it came time for the two of us to leave, I would suggest that Roni give me a tour of her apartment, but she always had other commitments she needed to get to.

Boswell and I approach the front door just as a resident waves a key fob in front of the panel to unlock the doors. I step in behind the person, offering a quick thank you as I scope out the lobby.

Boswell's nails click-clack along the gray hardwood flooring. High ceilings, art deco lighting, and shades of blue and foamy green greet us. To my left, a sitting area holds a low-back sofa and acrylic-armed chairs. On the right, a young woman sits behind a concierge desk.

"Welcome home," she says.

Home?

"Well. I, yes—I mean, I suppose we are," I mumble.

"Excuse me, I didn't catch that," she says politely.

"Oh, I'm talking to myself again. I'm actually just moving in. This afternoon. Juniper Walder. Unit 715."

"Welcome to the building, then. I'm Clara, one of the building's concierges. Do you need to see the leasing office? I'm afraid they're all out on property right now, but maybe they left keys for you. I can check." Clara stands, ready to head out in search of the keys.

"Oh no. Don't do that," I sputter, then hurry to clarify. "What I mean to say is, my daughter arranged the apartment and lease for me. Roni said she left the keys with the concierge, but if you don't have them…"

"Hmmm," Clara begins. She shuffles through items in her drawers, scans her notes. "Okay, yes. Here is the move-in note, and…" Clara searches the back area of her desk. "Here are the keys," she says, pulling them from an envelope labeled *Walder/715*.

"Thank you," I say, accepting the fob and keys.

"So, you've never toured the building?" Clara asks.

"No. I haven't seen the apartment either. Like I said, my daughter arranged everything. Roni. Roni Walder? Maybe you know her."

"Yes, of course—she's on the fourteenth floor. I know the name and unit, but I can't quite picture her face at the moment. Would you like me to show you around?"

"That would be most welcome, thank you."

Clara places a sign on top of her desk stating that the concierge has stepped away and directs me to follow her down a corridor off to the right side of the lobby area.

"The leasing offices are just here," she points, "off the residence lounge in this alcove. So, if you happen to need Savannah or Sybilla, the leasing specialists, one of them is usually available." Clara comes to a stop in front of a wall displaying two flat-screen televisions. Another low-back sea-green sofa and a communal desk fill the alcove, illuminated by dangling, eclectic light fixtures.

Clara looks at me, bobs her head, then continues down the hallway—restrooms on the left, a meeting room directly ahead.

"This is the conference room," Clara explains. "You'll need to make a reservation, but we do have another workspace on the seventh floor that's available on a first-come, first-served basis. "Next to it—here," she pauses as we turn the corner, "is the gym. You'll have to use your fob to gain entry."

Clara rotates to head back in the direction of the lobby. Boswell and I dutifully follow, double-stepping to each of Clara's long strides so as to keep up with her. In the lobby, she stops again.

"We have a complimentary coffee station here," she says, pointing to the left. "Shoot, sorry. We're supposed to use the term 'cybercafe.'" Clara swings her directive to the mail area, continuing, "And our mail and package hub is in this area."

Clara holds, looking at me for confirmation of understanding. As I nod, she turns and heads to the back of the lobby. We stop once more beside a round, marble-topped table. Clara presses the up arrow to summon one of the two elevators.

"We'll head up now. The only other common area is the club-room, which I mentioned earlier, and, of course, the pool, but both are on your floor. You said 715, right?"

I nod another affirmation, unwilling to trust my voice to work around the lump in my throat. Clara is terribly nice, and the building is beautiful, but this whole scenario is surreal at best. Everything is happening so quickly, too quickly.

The elevator carries us to the seventh floor, doors sliding open to reveal the elegant clubroom straight ahead. Behind the glass enclosure, the same sleek contemporary decor adorns the space—white sofas and chairs, chrome-accented bar stools, orchid centerpieces topping scattered tables.

"Again, you'll use your fob for entry into this area. You'll need to go through the clubroom to get to the pool. Although your unit is one of the few that has direct access to the pool. So you probably won't even use this entrance. Would you like me to take you through to see the pool?" Clara asks.

"No, it's fine. I'll take a look later on."

"Okay then, I'm off. Your apartment is to the right. Follow the hallway to the end and make another right—it's dog-legged. Your unit is the last door, right next to the service elevator. You'll also find the trash shoot there."

"Thank you, Clara. I appreciate you taking the time to show me around."

Clara presses the down arrow for the elevator. "Okay, then."

While she waits, Clara bends to pet Boswell. "And who is this guy?"

"Boswell."

"You'll have lots of friends here, you handsome boy," Clara says to Boz, then addresses me. "Best part of my job—all the dogs in the building." Clara stands as the elevator arrives and steps inside.

"I'll see you around then," she calls as the doors slide to whisk her back downstairs.

CHAPTER EIGHT

TINKLING NOISES SOUND outside my door. I hurry through the living room, past the kitchen, pressing an eye to the peephole. The jingle of a dog collar as the animal trots beside a woman dressed in jeans and a white T-shirt. She approaches unit 715—the apartment directly across the hall. It was a fully furnished show unit until about a month or so ago. Lots of comings and goings over there throughout the last few weeks—tools, equipment, ladders, banging, drilling—and finally, now, the new neighbor has arrived. Five-six/seven, lean. Sleek, blonde hair falls over her shoulders.

The woman fumbles inside a large handbag. The dog sits quietly beside her, watching, waiting. The woman huffs in frustration and squats on the hallway floor, dumping the contents of her bag. I study her profile as she rifles through her things. She's older than I thought. From behind, she appears to be in her thirties, but her face is etched. I'm guessing mid-forties or older.

The woman locates an envelope and pulls out a key, laying it aside as she returns the other items to her handbag. I want to tell her the door probably isn't locked; it hasn't been for a while now. But I don't. I'm not ready to introduce myself just yet.

The woman stands, key in hand, bag draped across her arm. She turns slightly and cocks her head. Something has caught her attention. The dog notes the change in his owner's demeanor and stands. The woman eases three steps back. The dog follows obediently.

I hear it then. The noises come from the apartment between our two units, 714—the two-bedroom unit occupied by Grant Carson. Grant works from home, is in his last years of midlife, and likes to prove his *stud-hood* with women half his age. Judging from the depth of the moans coming from the unit, I'd say he's having something more than a sandwich for lunch.

The realization of what is going on behind the door hits the woman. She raises her hand to cover her mouth as she leans closer toward the door. Proves there's a bit of a voyeur in all of us.

The woman shakes her head and steps back toward her apartment. She slips the key into the lock, turns the handle, and disappears behind the door.

CHAPTER NINE

Juniper

ON THE OTHER side of the door marked 715, a long hallway extends toward the unit's living area. Locking the door behind me, I unhook Boswell from his harness and leash, then lay his things on the long, marble-topped console table. Modern artwork hangs on each side of the hall. Boswell runs ahead to explore his new home while I take a moment to let the idea of a new *home* sink in before undertaking the task.

Roni explained the unit was the building's show apartment and, as such, has been professionally decorated. A small favor, I suppose, as I cannot fathom trying to pull together furniture for an apartment at this moment in my life.

Ahead on the right is a closed doorway. I swing open the door to reveal a bedroom with a full ensuite bathroom. The queen bed, taking the center spot of the room, is flanked by two double-drawer nightstands. The bathroom decor, in muted grays and blues, matches the hues of the bedroom. Sliding glass doors open to a small porch wrapped in lush vegetation. Through the door, a small porch area is secured by a gate leading to the pool area. This must be the pool access Clara spoke of.

Continuing the tour, I make my way along the hallway, finding a half bath on the right and a set of double doors on the left housing the washer and dryer stack. A small office area marks the end of the corridor. Inside the small space, a long, sleek desk lines one wall while a reading chair and a bookshelf take the opposite wall.

Carrying on, the apartment opens up into the main living area—kitchen, dining, living room all in one. Glass and metal and white, everything gleams. The living area is cordoned off to the left, and the kitchen is on the right. The wall across the room is lined with windows, allowing natural light to flood the space.

Drawn to the view in the distance, I step toward the windows where a white sectional sofa butts up to the low wall. The intercoastal waterway, dotted with anchored boats, gently ripples two streets away. Palm Beach Island is in the distance, the ocean lapping at the eastern shoreline. It would be a gorgeous, glorious view if not for the fact that the building where Cherri died stands on showcase, mere feet away from the building of my new home, a reminder with each passing gaze.

Rotating from the windows, I survey the kitchen. An island bar with a sink separates the living room from the kitchen. Pendant lamps dangle above white quartz countertops. Dark cabinets, accented in stainless steel hardware, line the back of the area, which houses the refrigerator, oven, and microwave.

Boswell trots out of another room—the primary bedroom, I assume. I head over to find out for myself. Passing the dining area set up with a glass-top table for four, I take a quick peek at the balcony to find that it, too, has been furnished and accessorized. The lovely retreat outside the sliding doors exudes an ethereal quality that beckons me to relaxation. Instead, I carry on with the task at hand.

An upholstered platform bed takes the space under the room's ceiling fan. My tour takes me past the two chairs and a small table situated as a sitting area on the wall opposite the bed. Another set of sliding doors leads to the balcony on the left side of the room. At the far end of the room, I find a bathroom and an impressive, oversized walk-in closet. I retrace my steps through the primary suite to examine a long, deep, and dark alcove at the far corner. The strange, awkward space is several feet long and barely wide enough to accommodate a full-length standing mirror and vanity table.

Grateful as I am for the convenience and elegance of the furnished rental, I don't have the energy to truly appreciate it and slump to the edge of the bed. Falling back onto the plush pile of pillows, I stare at the ceiling, wondering how in the hell I got to this place. Not this *place* necessarily, but the *whole of my life place*. How has it come to this? I've never lived alone, and I don't want to. As if he knows I need the companionship, Boswell jumps up onto the bed and rests his head across my midsection.

On the precipice of fifty—aren't you supposed to have life figured out by fifty?—and I'm scared. It all boils down to fear; fear of being alone, fear of losing my mind, my memories. I may not know how I got *here*, but I do know Cherri never imagined she'd forget her entire life. Is this how it starts? Forgetting, completely erasing the recall of your husband with another woman? And how is it that my daughter has to remind me of the things my mother did and said? Am I genetically predisposed to the same disease that took Cherri's life? Will I die in the same manner? Forget all those I love, all the memories I've cultivated throughout my life, lose the ability to take care of myself, no longer remember how to do the most mundane of everyday tasks? I don't want to live like that. Cherri wouldn't have wanted to finish out her days in that manner either, but she did. My mother never saw her disease coming—she didn't have a choice, and now she's gone.

Breaths grow shallow. Heart rate increases. Muscles seize. I gasp for air, for control. What if everything I ever did was wrong? What if I were meant to have done my life differently? I worked so hard to prove myself, to establish a professional persona. Yet, in doing so, I've allowed everyone else to manage all other aspects of my life, and now, I have no one. Except Roni. I cannot, I will not lose my daughter. The wheezing turns to heaves in a battle to breathe normally. Boswell startles. Inside my head, pounding—forceful and urgent—bolts me upright.

I search the room, realizing the pounding is actually coming from somewhere inside the apartment.

"Yoo-hoo."

Tiptoeing back through the apartment, Boswell on my heels, I follow the female voice.

"Hel-loooo?" The voice rings louder. The hallway? The guest room? Oh, God, please tell me I'm not in someone else's apartment. No, I can't be. The key worked.

As I round the corner to the kitchen, I run into a petite, older woman. Yelping, bumping, startling one another, we both shriek. What the… This woman is the intruder. Why is she frightened?

"Can I…"

"Oh, you scared the daylights out of me!" She exclaims. "I thought I saw someone in here, and then when you didn't answer the door, I thought maybe my eyes were playing tricks on me, so I talked myself out of seeing anybody, and then boom, there you are."

The woman yammers on without so much as a breath. "I heard there was a new tenant moving in, and about time too; this unit's been empty for the last two years, so I guess they just decided to rent it—been using it for media spreads and as a show unit; it is beautifully decorated, don't you think?" She walks through to the living room, leaving me standing in the office area, mouth agape.

"Of course, I'm still flabbergasted they finally rented this one out. I mean, after what happened in here during the construction of the building—the death and all—I didn't think anyone would ever move in. Oh, but I shouldn't bother you with all that right now."

Who is this person? Readying to answer that question, I step toward the kitchen, opening my mouth to speak, but another voice calls through the apartment.

"Mom? You here yet? You know you should probably get in the habit of locking your door around here." Roni rounds the corner and sees the woman standing in the center of the living room. "Oh, hi, Noreen."

"Hi there, Roni. This is your mom? Well, of course it is—you just called her Mom. But she certainly doesn't look old enough to be your mother. Not that you look old, Roni—goodness, I just realized how that must have sounded. No, I mean—she just looks so young, that's all."

"It's fine, Noreen. Everyone says that right before they tell us how we look nothing alike."

The two continue to carry on a conversation as if I'm not in the room.

"Look at that." The woman (Noreen?) glances back and forth between Roni and me. "You're right, different as salt and pepper the two of you are—literally though, right?

"So, this is your mom's apartment? That's wonderful. I'm sure it will be wonderful to have your mom nearby," Noreen says to Roni.

The countertop is cool under the grip of my sweating palms.

"Mom?"

The summons sounds as if it comes from underwater.

"Mom?"

I shake away the disorientation, turning my attention to Roni. How did she get in here?

"When are the movers supposed to be here, Mom? Did they say? You were able to get all your things from Alok's house, right? It took some strategic negotiating, but I had a client who owed me a favor and was able to arrange for them to do the pickup and then drop here straightaway."

Pushing the hair away from my face to catch behind my ears, I find my voice. "They called on my way here." I check my watch and add, "Should be here any minute now. I don't know what I'm going to do with all those boxes, though. Maybe the guest room? But there are so many."

"What boxes? I thought you were only going to bring your personal items and let Alok have everything else."

"I am—I did. It's all of Cherri's things. I didn't want to leave her stuff there. You know what a pack rat she was."

"Okay, well, I'm sure there's a storage unit open in the building somewhere. I will go down to management and look into renting one. It'll have to wait until tomorrow, though. I have to be in Boca Raton in an hour, and I won't be done until much later this evening. There's a group session down there I have to oversee tonight."

I nod, digesting all the new in my life right now.

"All right, I've gotta go. I only stopped by to make sure you got in okay."

"I'm good. Thanks for everything, honey."

Keys and phone in hand, Roni turns to leave, throwing up a hand as she walks toward the door.

My gaze shifts to the woman who has watched our entire private exchange without uttering a single vowel, which seems odd even given the short amount of time I've been in contact with her. Who is this woman? This intruder? And how did she get in here?

"So… you're Noreen?"

"Oh, yes, I'm Noreen Flemming. I came by to welcome you to the building, but here I am interrupting time with your daughter. I didn't catch your name—you are…?"

"Juniper Walder."

Noreen walks over, hand thrust forward. I accept her handshake, studying her presumptuous confidence. Her dark brown hair, styled in an inverted bob, gives her a stylish edge that her outfit doesn't quite support—knee-length shorts topped with an oversized, turquoise tunic.

Noreen firmly holds the grasp of our handshake while her eyes travel to my left hand. "So, will your husband be along soon? I'd love to meet him, as well, oh goodness, there I go again. I guess these days, I'm supposed to use the term significant other or is it partner, maybe?"

I glance down at the wedding and engagement bands circling my ring finger. Yanking free of Noreen's hold, I tell her, "He's not living here. We're," the word sticks in my throat, "separated."

"Oh, I see. Well, this must be terribly new to you, then. Living alone, I mean. I assume you'll be living alone since Roni already has a place here. Unless, of course, you have other children or family that will be joining you."

"No, it's only me."

"There is not a thing wrong with having an apartment for one. I know; I'm a solo dweller myself, and I'm happy to keep you company if you ever get lonely."

"I'm sure I'll be fine. But, thank you for the offer, Noreen."

"It's no problem if you change your mind—we're neighbors. Floor neighbors, is what I'm trying to say. Seven-eleven, that's me—just around the corner."

Nodding a slight consent, I will this conversation over.

"And if there is anything you need help with—getting to know the area, recommendations, information on the building— I am a bountiful resource."

"Um, actually, I do have one question for you. How did you get into my apartment? I'm sure I latched the deadbolt."

"No, dear, it was open; I just let myself right in."

I know I locked the door. At least, I thought I was certain. Is that how Roni entered the apartment as well? Did I just have another memory lapse? Have I forgotten something else?

"Are you okay, Juniper? You look a bit pale, dear."

"No. I'm fine. I… I was certain I locked the door when I arrived before I took the leash off Boswell."

"Oh, I wasn't speaking of the hallway door. I came through the sliding glass door in the bedroom." Noreen starts toward the guest room. With little choice, I follow.

"See, this porch," Noreen slides the door open as she continues, "has a gate to the pool." Noreen takes off through the gate and out to the pool deck. She stops, pointing to the next gated entrance along the building's exterior. "This one is mine, told you we are close neighbors. Isn't that fun?" She claps her hands for effect.

I can't pin down the exact moment my head started spinning, but the motion compares to that of the tilt-a-whirl ride at a county fair. Slowly, measuring each step, I absently return to the gate leading into my apartment. Noreen, oblivious that I might need a moment to myself, follows me back through the sliding doors of the guest room, pulling them shut behind us, clicking the lock.

"You'll need to be careful about remembering to lock this door because anyone could just walk in on you; that's one of the disadvantages of being on this floor; not only do we have the noise of the pool, but we have the added danger of accessibility, and you have more danger than I do, of course."

"I do?" I plop onto the bed to ease the dizziness.

Noreen, taking the action as an invite, joins me. "Yes, you see, you have two other sets of doors which lead to your balcony. Being on the seventh floor, anyone can simply jump over the low railing of your porch and step onto your deck. Most people don't have to worry about locking their balcony doors because no one can gain access to the private porch. You'll need to be sure yours are secured because both of your balconies are wide open."

Her words skip through the air, barely registering as sensible. Running fingertips through my hair, I notice the loud pounding that now reverberates inside my head. What is wrong with me?

Noreen stands and walks out of the bedroom door. Where is she going, and what is with this woman?

The pounding isn't in my head; someone is at the door. I hear the door open, Noreen greeting the caller. Callers? Unsettling, confusing, the flurry of activity continues without me. Ordinarily, I wouldn't see anyone other than Alok during my days. Hours spent in front of a computer screen, my only communication is generally digital. Yet, here, within only thirty minutes, I've been in direct contact with more people than I normally associate with throughout a week's time.

Closing my eyes in the hope of edging the dizziness to darkness, I stand. On the other side of the doorframe, Noreen is speaking with the movers who have brought my things over from Wellington.

"Yes, come in. Juniper said she was expecting you."

Did I? I did. I said that to Roni only a moment ago.

Noreen is speaking with the movers again. Head heavy, my chin dips. Noreen takes it as an affirmation of the question she's posed, but I don't know what she asked of me.

People move throughout the apartment. Noreen speaks, points, directs. I glide across the gray flooring of the unit, never feeling my footfalls land. Boswell runs busily alongside the strangers, supervising as they place boxes in various rooms according to their labels. I can hardly tell if I'm dreaming or watching the happenings of someone else's life.

Without reason, without purpose or direction, I move through the rooms in a fugue state. I find myself back in the guest room, boxes stacked along the perimeter. Noreen enters as I pull tape from a sealed box. She is speaking. To me. She relays that the movers are finished; they need my signature on the shipping invoice. My lips move, forming the words, I'll be right there while studying something of interest inside the box, head tilting from side to side.

Noreen asks if I'm all right, moving to stand beside me. As she lays her hand on my forearm, I hear her yelp. What has provoked her reaction? What have I done? The questions swirl in my mind, unanswered.

And then I see it. The vision shocks me out of the dream state, jolting me back into reality, back into being an active participant in my own life. The metal in my hand is cold and heavy and unfamiliar.

I've never owned a gun—and, yet, I've come to be holding this one…

CHAPTER TEN

MONTHS OF PLANNING have gone into preparing for this day. That said, I was once told, 'good things come to those who wait,' and today, my *good* has arrived. The thud in my chest picks up speed in anticipation and excitement. It's time to tune in, to try out the equipment, to witness The Grabell's newest tenant settling into her apartment.

Unit seven-fifteen hasn't been considered suitable for lease since the building opened. Speculation has it that the unit wasn't rented out due to the tragedy. Who would want to live within the confines of the place where a person took their last breath? Murmurs from the cleaning staff floated through the building, claiming the unit haunted. Maintenance relayed strange noises coming from inside the apartment.

It was all bullshit, of course, but the leasing agents had to give it enough time so that the tragic demise would be forgotten. Until that time, management had the unit professionally decorated for photography spreads, media blitzes, and as a show unit for potential renters. Just my opinion, of course, what do I know? Whatever the reason they waited to rent the apartment, it gave me more time to properly get the equipment into place.

A few strokes on the keyboard, and her face fills the monitor. A couple more taps to focus the camera lens reveal she is standing in the middle of the living room, appearing lost and confused. The dog at her heels watches her as I do, waiting for her next move. She lifts the manila envelope she holds for inspection. Hand-printed block letters spell out Juniper Walder 715.

Juniper turns her attention to the kitchen, eyeing the boxes on the countertop. She steps forward, tossing the envelope aside, running her hand over the surface of a box. I zoom in to read the box's label—Kitchen/Boswell. She uses a fingernail to loosen the edge of the tape that secures the box and then rips it off to open the flaps.

From inside the container, Juniper pulls out one dog bowl, then another, followed by a stand to hold the bowls securely. Tossing paper to the floor, Juniper roots through the remaining contents and seemingly finds what she is looking for. Lifting the dog food bag from the box, she opens it, fills the bowl, places it into the bowl holder, and then moves to fill the remaining bowl with water.

A storm is moving inland off the ocean. The clouds race in quickly, darkening the skies. Juniper studies their movement through the balcony doors, crossing arms over her midsection, bracing for impact. A bolt of lightning streaks the sky to the south. She jumps at the sight and again as the thunderclap booms.

She walks to the edge of the room, studying the wall plate of toggle switches. Juniper flips one, then another, committing the function of each switch to memory, it appears. After testing each one, she flips on the two that illuminate the kitchen lighting—one commands the track above the center of the workspace, the other controls the dangling pendants over the sink.

As she sets about to unpack more boxes in the kitchen, I deem this the perfect opportunity to test some of the equipment's functions. Splitting the screen of my monitor, I open the application for the remote light switch control. One stroke and the track lights extinguish. Juniper looks above to view the light fixture. She walks back to the switch plate, pressing the toggle to illuminate the four bulbs along the track.

Juniper moves back to the box she works to unpack.

Another stroke takes out the pendants, and another snuffs out the track bulbs.

A wicked grin crawls my face as I watch Juniper's confused expression grow trepidatious.

Chin raised to the ceiling, she studies the dark bulbs. Juniper returns to the switch plate and presses the toggles again to illuminate the room. She plants herself at the edge of the room, watching the bulbs, waiting to see that they will remain lit. Satisfied that the lighting is now working properly, Juniper returns to the task of unpacking.

I watch as she unpacks several boxes, carefully placing the various items around the new space. The activity takes some time as Juniper is quite particular about where an object is situated. Conscientious, some might say. Maddening is more like it.

Still, while most people would find her actions banal and tedious, I know her every move is calculated and measured, and I intend to respond in kind.

CHAPTER ELEVEN

Juniper

ONE MORE MILE, and you can check this workout off your list. Just one more, Juniper. You can do it. You can do it. I bump up the speed on the treadmill and dig in, get it done. Sweat drips into my right eye, stinging. I grab the towel, wipe my face, keep going.

Right when I begin to think all is feeling normal again, the unsettling scenes—complete with an endless array of disastrous outcomes—worm their way into my head. Creeping, inching, spreading, attaching to each thought. The scenarios worsen, each leading to possibilities far more perilous than the previous. The only way I am able to control them anymore is on the treadmill.

Music loud in my ears, I rev up the belt and run, run, run as fast as I can, leaving the obsessive worry far behind. I run until I'm too tired to conjure the distressing thoughts and images anymore, and they finally slough off, waiting for the right time to return. The problem of late is that it's getting harder and harder to outrun my anxiety.

I was never one for sports or athletics throughout my school years, and then once I began my career, I didn't have the time to devote to exercise. When I met Alok, I began going to the gym with him. After some time, I began to see the results of hard work and soon found the act therapeutic. Now, I never go a day without some type of physical activity. It keeps the demons away, helps me sleep at night.

The treadmill is where I take time to work things out, to problem-solve. My head clears, my mind works more efficiently. In the past, working out eased my worries and apprehension. These days, I can't run far enough to even make a dent in my angst.

Alok and I always worked out in our small home gym without interruption or worry. Living at the Grabell, however, I now share workout space with others, which only further promotes the worry, the obsessiveness. Did I get the machine sterilized after the person who used it before me? Am I sweating too much? Maybe I've spent too much time on the machine? I can let the last worry fade, though, as at least one machine has remained empty and open for use throughout my seven-mile run this morning. Different people have been hopping on and off for the last hour. But the treadmills on either side of me are currently empty, leading me to hope I can finally run off these anxieties now that I am alone.

Ironic that I should want to be alone when all I've felt of late is isolated. I didn't expect to be so lonely living by myself. Of course, I was prepared for the loneliness; I'd never lived alone before. But, because of my working situation, I'm used to spending a lot of time solo, so I never dreamed this isolation would bother me as much as it does. Too much time to think— that's the issue. And then, there is the fear. Hard as it is to admit, I'm constantly afraid. All the noises, and the silence, I don't know which is worse, or better, or preferred.

I've invited Roni over on multiple occasions: dinner, coffee before work, wine after work, to walk along the waterfront. Roni is always busy, it seems, though I believe a big part of her excuses is just that, they're excuses. I understand we've never been close, not like Roni was with Cherri. Now that Cherri is gone, I was hoping Roni would lean on me more, share what's going on in her world. And yet, if I'm honest with myself, when

I do spend time with Roni, it can be disconcerting. She's constantly reminding me of how much I forget nowadays. Every incident she fills me in on leaves me spiraling in self-doubt.

Constantly, obsessively, I worry about the moments and incidents I fail to recall. So much so, I think maybe the constant attention to forgetfulness is promoting more lapses in memory. Is that possible? And then, the losses are more than I can bear—my mother, my husband—it's all taking a toll on my confidence. My mother, I was somewhat prepared for, my husband I was not, and I've never lacked confidence in myself, so I never dreamed I would lose it.

How can I possibly hold on to confidence any longer, when the one thing—the one person—I believed with my whole heart would never hurt me… betrayed me? Did I not appreciate Alok enough? Did I not give him enough of myself? My time? Is it because I'm getting old? Fat? Soft?

At least my career hasn't suffered, but my time is coming. This I know. The financial blog I started twenty years ago was one of the first of its kind. Nowadays, however, there are more advisors on the internet than one can possibly sort through. It is a matter of being seen first, staying trendy, being techie, edgy. The era of simply putting out good, solid advice is over. I'm behind the times, a dinosaur, so say some of the competing millennials. I don't podcast or, God forbid, VLOG. I'm simply not comfortable with having my face front and center, or my voice, for that matter.

Perhaps it's time I put myself out to pasture. I've made more money than one person really needs, particularly a frugal one such as myself. Stepping aside would give me more time to focus on Roni, make things right for a change. But would that be considered quitting? Giving up? I've never been a quitter. I've never let myself quit anything. Yet, it is all I can think about lately, this desire to quit, to run back to how my life used to be.

In some instances, I am the most self-controlled, self-disciplined person you will ever meet. Diet. Exercise regimen. Sleep schedule, work schedule, habits. But admittedly, I am also weak. I've vowed to myself, to my daughter, to become a more independent person, and yet, there are many moments when I am ready to forgive, forget, and move back to Alok. I know it is fear and anxiety eating away at me, chip, chip, chipping away at me, testing my resolve. God, it's so exhausting.

I grab the towel and swipe at the perspiration on my face again. As I toss the towel back to the machine, I glance at the monitor. Eight and a half miles. Whether the worry is still niggling or at bay, I must get off this treadmill and head back to my lonely apartment.

CHAPTER TWELVE

It's all intriguing, this new pastime of mine—consuming the hours of my day, trailing late into the night—studying her expressions, her actions, and inactions. Since she took occupancy of the apartment, Juniper has actually done very little. What I have discerned is that I am learning more about Juniper by what she doesn't do than by what she does.

No friends, or family, or even neighbors come to visit. Juniper appears lonely for it, for some sort of companionship. The dog at her heels, she pads aimlessly through the rooms as if looking for someone. Sometimes she will stand, staring at an object for several minutes, then move to straighten or reposition the piece. She'll stand back, eye on the object once more, considering the placement. The procedure repeats until, presumably, she's satisfied. Her lips move, forming words that float into the air, unanswered, unheard. While I can see her, I cannot hear what she says. Getting that equipment in place prior to Juniper's move-in was not possible due to a shipment delay, and sadly, I cannot read lips.

Clearly, she's deep in the throes of sorrow and anguish. The proof is playing out in front of me, and not only in the obvious hours upon hours of weeping I've witnessed. One doesn't take on such an endeavor without completing the necessary research, and I've done my homework.

In terms of grief, there are as many forms and types of the affliction as there are ways in which people cope with it. In Juniper's case, she is not sleeping—up in the middle of the night, pacing the floors, flipping lights on, then off. She makes herself food, studies it, then picks at it before dumping it into the trash. The way she'll suddenly stop in the center of the room to steady herself against something solid as she sways ever so slightly.

Exercise seems to be her way of coping. Juniper doesn't miss a day. Before the sun rises, she's dressed for the gym. Two cups of coffee—with cream, no sugar—and then she's out the door to walk her dog. Upon return, she makes the bed, fills her water bottle, and heads to the gym. She's gone for a couple of hours, then heads straight to the shower. This last part is not witnessed. I'm not a pervert—no cameras were installed in her bathroom. I know she showers because of the time elapsed. It takes Juniper an hour to dress for the day. She exits the bathroom fully dressed, hair done, makeup applied. Though, as of yet, I've been unable to ascertain why she bothers.

Most of her time is spent lying on the sofa, one hand on the dog, the other sliding the charm on her necklace back and forth, back and forth. Zoom functions have revealed the gold charm is the initial A, threaded onto a delicate chain. I watch and wonder what is going through her mind. Of course, I get no answers, but still, I continue to observe.

The only other activity Juniper practices regularly is walking her dog. She calls him Boswell and tells others when they ask that Boswell is a miniature golden doodle. Three times a day, she'll leash him up for walks. Riding the elevator down, Juniper exits the building through the front doors then follows the route as dictated by the time of day.

In the morning, she's out the door at 7:00, walking Dixie north to Clematis, then turning onto Narcissus before returning to the building via Evernia. At 1:00, the pair takes Dixie south to

Hibiscus, makes a left on Quadrille, and then returns using Fern to reach the building. In the evening, the walk is at 8:00, but they never veer far. Juniper only allows little Boswell to use the park across from the building at night, trekking from one lamppost to the next. While some might liken her actions to the common moth, I note, Juniper is afraid of the dark.

CHAPTER THIRTEEN

LITTLE OF THE cuticle around my left thumb remains. I inspect the other fingers while I wait for my therapist to arrive. Even though I can ascertain no benefit (much less a good reason to continue this process), I wait. In the same sparsely decorated room we met last session: two chairs, table, fake plant, nothing to hold my interest, I sit in petulant anticipation of Donna's arrival.

I can't change my feelings on this. I don't want to be here, and that point alone is a sure sign therapy will fail. I'm aware of how cliché it sounds, but you can't help a person who doesn't want to be helped. I've always been a firm believer in that philosophy. Still, here I am, on time and ready, unlike my therapist.

"Hello," she singsongs behind me, breezing into the room, kicking the door closed with her foot. "How are you today, Roni?" She continues, rushing to situate herself in the chair across from me as if some sense of urgency has been spurred at the last possible second.

"Dandy."

"Oh, good," she mumbles absently, digging through her briefcase, pulling out her notebook. "Ah, here we are." Donna reaches for the glasses perched atop her head, drags them to her face, then takes some time to glance through the notes from our last session.

The act is unprofessional. A therapist—a good therapist—would have taken the time to refresh their recall of a patient's case prior to the start of the session. Honestly, though, now that I have a solid moment to observe this woman, I understand there is not much about Donna that is professional. Aside from Donna's obvious ill-preparedness, her briefcase is a wreck, and she's unkempt. Stray, unruly strands fly from the hair barrette holding long bangs off her forehead, her slacks wrinkled, the cuff of her blouse sports some sort of food stain.

Donna looks up, removes her reading glasses, and makes direct eye contact—time to get serious.

"When we last spoke, you told me your grandmother was more like a mother than a grandmother." Donna glances back at her scribblings on the yellow pad. "But all three of you lived under the same roof. Today, I would like for you to explore why you believed your grandmother to be your mother figure, to examine the relationship you and your grandmother had a bit more intently."

"We're just jumping right in there, are we? No foreplay today?"

"I apologize for getting straight to the point, but as you are well aware, our time is limited."

Before I say something I will regret, I break the stare-off with a blink, cut my eyes to the plant across the room. The greens are fading, or perhaps it is only a thick coat of dust causing the discoloration.

Donna continues. "I also got the impression during our last meeting that you prefer to get things moving. I believe your instructions were, 'cut the bullshit and get to your point.'"

Score one for Donna. She listened and took note during our previous session.

"Cherri."

"Excuse me," Donna eyes me questioningly, then glances at her notes. "Oh, that's right. Your grandmother's name."

"Yes. Cherri. Cherri didn't like labels. She believed that being labeled took away from her person, her identity. She wasn't just a mother or grandmother. She was Cherri."

"I see. So, what made you identify Cherri as a mother figure rather than a grandmother?"

I don't see much of a point in hashing through this, but given the other topics we could explore, this one actually appeals to me more, so I oblige.

"Cherri was always there. Juniper might have been around, but she was never *there*."

Donna scribbles another note as she asks, "Where do you believe Juniper was if she wasn't around? If she wasn't, as you say, *there*?"

"Juniper was always working."

"So, she traveled for work quite a bit then?"

"No. She just worked a lot. Cherri managed everything at home, which included watching out for me, and Juniper made the money to support all of us."

"Is this to say your mother has a demanding job?"

"I suppose the job is demanding, but more so, it's that Juniper is obsessed with work. Always has been. It's an addiction."

"That's a strong word, addiction."

"In Juniper's case, it is appropriate. She put work above everything and everyone in her life. We would have a family event scheduled, and Juniper would sneak away for some work situation that always seemed to be floating on the periphery. Promises to attend functions I had for school or extracurricular hobbies were only seen through if some work issue didn't arise."

"So, you resented your mother's commitment to her work?"

"No. The one thing I actually admire about Juniper is her work ethic. Once she makes up her mind to do something,

Juniper gives it her hundred and nine percent. I was just never the *something* she made a commitment to."

"Okay, so while you admire your mother's commitment to work, you resent her lack of attention toward you?"

"Not really. I didn't lack for attention. I had Cherri. Cherri never had anything more important to do than whatever it was she and I were doing together."

"That's quite a gift."

"Yes, it was. I was fortunate, and I always understood that."

"Still, it must have been hard from time to time—not to have the attention of your mother."

"Look, I get why you keep steering this back to Juniper, but…"

Donna watches as I shift in my seat. She's studying my body language, and I don't like what I am allowing to be said right now, but I can't seem to control it either.

I start again. "Yes. Of course, I always wanted to be closer to my mom. I mean, all the girls at school would talk about how great their moms were, how close they were with their mothers. 'My mom is my best friend.' God. How many times did I hear that one? I couldn't help that Juniper and I never had that. Besides, I had Cherri, so I didn't feel too slighted. I could say right back to those nitwits that my grandmother was my best friend. But, yes, I did sometimes wonder what it must be like to have that kind of relationship with your mother. Was I missing out on something? What kind of friend would Juniper be?"

Donna leaves me to mull on my last thought, watching me pick at another cuticle. I will myself to stop, to not give Donna too many nonverbal cues to decipher.

"Would you say your mom has a lot of friends?"

"No. I'd say my mom has no friends."

"Because of her addiction to work?"

"Because of the way she looks, the way she carries herself."

"What do you mean by that statement?"

"Juniper is beautiful—not pretty, not attractive, but beautiful. People don't connect with Juniper because of her looks."

Donna tilts her head in question. "So it's an aesthetic issue?"

"Juniper is like this golden goddess. All thin and blonde and athletic, yet effortlessly feminine. People get one glimpse of her, and their defenses shoot to the sky. I've witnessed it time and again. People don't give her a chance. They think because Juniper is attractive, she is, therefore, a major bitch when in actuality, Juniper is one of the nicest people you will ever meet. Juniper would do anything for anyone and never complain about it. She smiles and speaks to everyone, regardless of what a dick they are. But because she's tall, has great bone structure, and a BMI two-thirds of the country can't achieve, people automatically hate her."

"But you don't *like* your mother. You've said it has nothing to do with her work, and you understand that she is a good, decent person. So what is it exactly that makes you harbor this disdain for your mother?"

"I never said I 'harbor disdain for my mother.' I haven't said anything at all about how I feel about my mother. Jesus, Donna, don't put words in my mouth."

"Then tell me, Roni, how do you feel about your mother?"

"How can I tell you how I feel about somebody I don't even know?"

"So then, tell me about her. We can explore who Juniper is as a person. Let's work this out together."

This woman is dense. Dense Donna. I glance at the clock on the far wall.

"Look at that. Our time is up." I stand, turn back to face Donna, and place my hands on the back of the chair. "You'll want to be preparing for your next appointment so that you don't have to catch up while your patient sits here and waits for you to do so."

CHAPTER FOURTEEN

BOSWELL'S LEASH almost slips from my grip as I recheck the time. Roni said twelve-thirty, I'm sure of it. Were we supposed to meet at the restaurant? No, she said she'd be in front of the Grabell. Did she forget? Roni's been through a lot as well, and sometimes I forget that during my moments of self-wallowing. My daughter is grieving too, and I need to try harder to be there for Roni. I should text her, check on her.

—*I'm outside the Grabell. Shall I go ahead and grab a table for us at Johan's?*

Immediately, I see the dots indicating Roni is responding.

—*Already here. Where r u? Have to get back to work soon.*

I hurry, guiding Boswell across the street to peek inside the windows of Johan's Coffee House and Cafe. There's Roni, sitting at a table in the center of the room, studying her phone. I look down at Boswell and back inside the cafe.

—*I'm outside. Look up.*

She lifts her head—motions for me to come inside. I shake my head, but the message doesn't convey.

—*I have Boswell.*

Roni stands, grabbing her drink and table flag to make her way outside.

"Hey," she says, scoping out the options for outdoor seating. "I sat inside because you told me you weren't bringing Boswell."

"No. I didn't."

"Mom. You did. You said you had an errand to run after lunch. And you're late. We said noon."

"No, you said, twelve-thirty."

"Mom. Seriously? We had a whole discussion before I went to work this morning. Remember?"

"Yes," I place my phone on the table as I drag a chair out, then sit and situate Boswell. "You came by for coffee before work, and we agreed to meet for lunch at twelve-thirty in front of the building. I didn't say anything about errands."

"Mom... I specifically said twelve because I have a group session in Lake Worth this afternoon. You said you were leaving Boswell because you wanted to walk up to City Place to visit the salon there and talk with someone about your hair." She uses her pointer finger to circle the part in her hair at the top of her head. "Your roots... remember?"

I do remember telling Roni I needed to get something done with my hair—all the stress has been wreaking havoc on my color.

"Right, you told me not to use my regular stylist in Wellington."

"Yes. Because if you go back to Wellington, you're likely to drive by the house, and get out, and visit Alok, and then God knows what comes next. Go order. I'll stay with Boswell."

Inside, I peruse the menu, though nothing is appealing. The knowledge that I have forgotten yet another piece of pertinent information seems to have robbed me of my appetite. Still, I place an order for a salad I don't particularly want, grab my table flag and iced tea, then join Roni and Boz outside.

Roni works to chew a bite of her sandwich delivered in my absence. The look on her face strikes me as odd. I return a word-less questioning peer as Roni picks up my phone from the table. "Why is Bonnie calling you?"

"Bonnie? From Cherri's care facility, Bonnie?"

"Do we know another Bonnie?"

"Did you go through my phone while I was gone?"

"Your phone rang while you were inside. I looked to see who was calling, but it was clearly a robocall. I went to block the number for you and then delete it. While I was in your call history doing that, I saw where Bonnie had called. So sorry to have been trying to save you the hassle of a robocall. Jesus, Mom. Paranoid?"

"I didn't mean it like that, Roni. I certainly didn't intend for you to think I was snippy about it. I'm sorry." I apologize, even though I don't believe I came across as accusatory.

"So, why is Bonnie calling you?"

"She boxed up some of Cherri's things and was calling to let me know she was leaving them at the front reception desk for us to pick up."

"Why didn't she call me? I'm listed as Cherri's first contact."

I ignore the sting of Roni's statement. I need to be there for my daughter instead of being concerned about my own hurt feelings. "I don't know. Maybe she did call and couldn't reach you, then rang me. We're both on the list."

Roni looks away, making it impossible to read her thoughts.

"Thank you," I say to the waitperson, who drops off my salad and grabs the table flag.

"Are you okay?" I ask as the man exits. "I know you don't like to talk about Cherri's passing, but I think it might be helpful if you did. It might help both of us. Other than you, I have no one to confide in. Do you? Do you have someone you feel comfortable talking with about your feelings?"

"I'm fine, Mom. So, I'll swing by the care facility after my meeting this afternoon and pick up Cherri's things."

"I already took care of it." I manage a piece of kale into my mouth, chewing slowly.

"I don't know why you'd bother. I still have to settle Cherri's account—pay up the remainder of the bill."

I poke through my salad, averting my eyes from Roni's. "I did that too."

"Why? I have all of Cherri's accounts in my name. You weren't listed as the responsible party. Why are you paying for something you don't owe?"

"Because she was *my mother*, Roni. I can afford to take care of it. You shouldn't have to do that."

"You do recall the conversation we had when Cherri went into that facility?" Roni asks, her lips stretched tight. "You told me that if Cherri was placed into that particular facility, I was responsible for taking care of every last detail."

"Roni, I was upset that you wanted Cherri to be so far away from Wellington. It was one heated conversation. I was wrong. I shouldn't have put that on your shoulders; I was emotional and irrational…"

"Just stop. I'm not doing this. So what was in the box?"

I poke through the contents of my salad bowl. "Some nightgowns, a hairbrush, the photos we placed in her room."

"I have to run." Roni tosses a crumpled napkin onto her plate as she pushes back the chair and rises.

I choke down my last bite. "Already?" Did I say something to make her mad?

"I said twelve. I can't help it that you were late."

"But…"

"Later, Mom."

Boswell watches me as I watch Roni hurry across the street toward the Grabell's parking garage and disappear inside.

"Well, you're out and about," a voice calls behind me. It takes a moment, but I realize the greeting is meant for me and turn to see who approaches. "Does this mean you've settled in?"

The woman who turned up uninvited inside my apartment on the day I moved into The Grabell speaks to me as she waves down the waitperson who dropped off my salad earlier. She asks him to clear away the dirty things from Roni's recently vacated seat. As he swipes away the crumbs, the woman orders a coffee drink, ignoring the establishment's thoughtfully designed ordering system.

"It's nice to see you, Juniper. I was going to stop by again and see if you needed anything, but wanted to give you a bit of time to get established."

So much about the day we met remains a blur, be it memory loss or a traumatic block, I'm unsure. But I know I can't recall this woman's name, no matter how deep I dig.

"You don't remember my name, and that's perfectly okay. You've only just moved into a building full of new neighbors. Of course, you're having a difficult time recalling everyone's name. I'm Noreen Flemming. I live on the seventh floor too."

"Yes, I remember," I say, not bothering to relay that she's the *only* neighbor I've met.

"I saw Roni hightailing it across the street a minute ago. Everything okay?"

"She had to get back to work."

"You know, Roni and I have never had the opportunity to get to know one another. What is it that she does?" Noreen asks, scooting back into the seat, making herself comfortable.

"Roni's a clinical psychologist specializing in substance abuse treatment. She works with patients going through rehabilitation in various treatment centers throughout Palm Beach County."

"My goodness, that's a hefty job. I think I'd be looking to abuse some sort of substance after a long day in that line of work." Noreen laughs at her own joke.

I push the salad aside, faking a smile so as not to be rude.

"Is everything okay, Juniper? You seem upset. We can talk about it if you like."

"It's nothing—mother/daughter stuff." I pick up my tea and sip.

"I'm a good listener," Noreen offers.

How many times have I said to myself lately that I'm lonely, that I wish I had someone to confide in? And now, across from me, sits a person who is interested in my life. What could it hurt to talk, to take a chance on opening up to Noreen?

"We've been at odds about my mother." I keep the answer brief.

"But, you told me your mother had passed on?"

"I did?"

"Yes, the day I met you. You were unpacking and told me all about your mother. Cherri."

Something else I've forgotten? Not only is Roni unnerving me with recounts of details I can't recall, but now a neighbor I've met only once is doing the same. Have we had more than one encounter? I'm afraid to ask.

"Yes, you're correct. Please forgive me, Noreen. I've had a lot on my mind."

"Well, of course, you have, and to be honest, you didn't look to be feeling so well the afternoon you moved in." That whole day was surreal. Thinking back on it, it seems to have happened to someone else. "And then there was the gun," Noreen adds. "Did you ever figure out who it belonged to?"

"No, it's still a mystery. I've never owned a gun—don't know the first thing about them, really."

"What you didn't say was how your mother died. Do you mind me asking?"

"Of course not," I say, shaking my head, absently dragging my fingers down the iced tea glass to clear away the condensation.

"Cherri began showing signs of memory loss a few years back. I didn't think much of it. We all forget things now and then, especially as we age. I was busy: with my husband, my work, the dogs. I just didn't have time to help her look for everything she kept misplacing. Cherri was always unorganized—her life was led by chaos, and she preferred it that way. I figured it was more of the same with her.

God, I feel so guilty now." I rub a palm over my cheek, dry the tears. "Maybe if I had listened or taken notice of her symptoms, we could have gotten a diagnosis earlier, extended her life."

Across from me, Noreen remains quiet.

"Gosh, I can't believe I spilled all that on you. I apologize. I'm not generally so forthcoming." I pull the napkin from my lap, dabbing at my face.

"It's good to get these things out," Noreen says as the waitperson returns with her drink. She thanks the man, lifts the cup, and blows over the edge. "Have you spoken your feelings to anyone else?" She asks, then carefully sips the hot coffee.

"No. Honestly, I'm not a big talker, which is why it is unlike me to dump all that information onto someone I've only just met."

"Well, you have a lot to process. Your mother's death, your recent separation…"

"How did you know that?" I ask, cutting Noreen's last thought short.

"You told me, dear."

I've no recollection of this, but I refuse to show my confusion. "Of course. Sorry."

"Perhaps it was the stress of your mother's illness that caused your breakup? Do you think there's any chance you might reconcile?"

Shoulders slumping, exhaustion heavy in my limbs, I sink back into my seat."I don't know what to think. On the night of Cherri's funeral, I saw Alok in bed with another woman."

"How awful for you," Noreen exclaims, returning her cup to the table.

"It would be if I remembered it."

"You don't remember finding your husband in bed with another woman? I would think seeing something like that would be burned into your memory, something you would want to forget but couldn't."

Eyes lowered, I confess. "After the funeral, I had wine… and… evidently, I took a sleeping pill."

"So how do you know he had an affair? Maybe you dreamed the whole thing."

"If only that were possible. No. From what we've pieced together, I hid around the corner, too shaken to confront them, and called Roni, leaving her a voicemail saying I had witnessed Alok's infidelity. Then, I guess I blanked the whole thing out. I can only assume my mind couldn't handle it and wiped the scenario away."

"It's amazing, isn't it, how on some inherent level we know to protect ourselves—self-sooth." She sips her coffee.

"Self-sabotage, maybe. I think it would be better for me, in my case, to recall every detail. Maybe then, I wouldn't even consider forgiving or running back to Alok every fifteen minutes. It's another contentious point with my daughter."

"The affair or the possibility of forgiveness?"

"There is not one bone in Roni's body that understands the possibility of forgiving Alok for adultery."

"But you want to? Because you don't remember?"

"I'm so hurt, but I don't know where my feelings about Cherri's passing end and Alok's affair begin. Everything's all mangled together. Everything hurts. Nothing feels real anymore."

"It sounds like you're having doubts about leaving your marriage."

"Well, yes, I am having doubts because I would never, ever, NEVER have thought Alok would cheat on me. Roni says I'm naive, and she's probably right. I mean, I heard myself, heard my voice, on the message I left for her."

"Have you talked to Alok about this? Asked him why he would do this to you?"

"When I confronted him, he denied the whole thing, said I was crazy. But we haven't spoken since I moved out. Roni doesn't think it's a good idea for us to communicate right now.

As a matter of fact, I'm fairly certain Roni blocked his number from my phone."

"Did you ask her to do that? Do you want to block his number?"

"I didn't ask her, but I admit, it does make it easier. If Alok called, I know I would answer—so I left it that way."

"You don't have to block him forever. I'm sure there will come a time when you'll be ready to talk again after the wounds have healed."

"You're right. I may not know much for certain right now, but I know I don't want Alok permanently blocked for my life, no matter what ends up happening between us."

The waitperson returns to our table with a bowl of water. "Thought your little guy might like a drink of water," the young man says, placing the bowl in front of Boswell, taking a moment to rub his ears. "What's his name?"

"Boswell."

"You sure are a good little fellow," he says to Boz, then looks at me. "He hasn't barked once at any other dogs coming and going."

"Well, one, he's been a bit depressed lately. We recently moved, and his live-in companion, Dash, stayed behind with his owner. But two, Boswell's vocal cords have been removed—he doesn't have the ability to bark or even growl."

The man studies me, not bothering to hide the look of disgust marking his features.

"It wasn't me," I counter. "I would *never* do that to *any* animal. I rescued Boswell when he was three after his previous owner died."

"Why would anyone do that to a poor, defenseless animal?" Noreen asks, watching the server soothe Boswell with quiet sympathy for his tortured past.

"Boswell's previous owner was an older gentleman living in an assisted living facility. After multiple complaints about Boz's barking, the staff told him he'd have to either get rid of the dog or move out. He had no family who could take Boswell, and he couldn't afford to live anywhere else. His solution? Find a vet willing to perform the procedure — and I can tell you, most won't do that to a dog."

"So, Boswell doesn't make any sounds?" Noreen asks.

"No, he can't even whimper. Not only was the vet disreputable, but unskilled as well. "

"Poor little buddy. Guess he's not much of a guard dog, huh?" The waitperson asks.

"No, but he's a great lap dog."

The young man reaches to take my dirty dishes and exits.

"I need to get along," I tell Noreen. "I'm heading inside to pick up the keys to the storage unit I rented. I want to get all of Cherri's boxes put away. I'm not ready to go through them yet, and seeing them in the middle of the guest room is dredging up memories I'm not ready to face yet either."

"Sounds like you've got quite the project ahead of you."

I stand, rouse Boswell, and push the chair under the table. "Thanks for the chat, Noreen. It's been nice to talk to somebody."

"I just so happen to love gabbing. Please feel free to knock on my door anytime. I'm happy to listen."

"I appreciate that. See you around the building."

CHAPTER FIFTEEN

SHE'S in a better mood today. Headphones firmly planted in her ear cavities, she flings open the door to her unit, dancing down the long hallway, dog jumping at her heels. His tail wags happily as she moves to the music only she hears. As Juniper sways, she begins peeling away the sweaty workout clothes. Tossing her hat onto the counter, tank top falling to the floor, Juniper picks up her cell phone, checking for messages received while she was busy working out.

Juniper has been out of the apartment and in the gym for the last hour and fifty minutes. I didn't follow her to the gym today. I've done that enough over the prior days to get a sense of her regime.

Today is Thursday. On Thursdays, Juniper wears her flower print leggings, mauve tank, and purple sports bra. She runs for an hour, cools down for five minutes, then retreats to the weight room to work on her back muscles. Mondays, it is purple leggings and a black tank, and after the run, she's onto biceps and triceps. Tuesdays, orange tank, multi-colored leggings; it's leg day after her run. Wednesdays, she only runs, but on Fridays, she adds a chest workout at the end of her treadmill stint.

Do you want to know what she wears on Fridays and Wednesdays? I can tell you, but it seems tedious at this point.

Juniper is tedious, however. Routine is hardly the word for her actions. Repetitive to a bore, perhaps. I, on the other hand, appreciate her monotonous habits. It means I know exactly what to expect and how to plan.

One other thing going in my favor—the dog—no vocal cords, can't bark. Lucky me. The dog has seen me inside the apartment, sorting through her computer, checking out a drawer I want to get a better look inside, tinkering with a camera angle. He's suspicious and watchful, while I'm careful.

Everything gone but for her leggings, Juniper removes the earbuds, grabs her cell, and heads into her bedroom closet. When she steps out again, she is wearing only a long t-shirt.

At the kitchen sink, she fills a container with water, then pads out to the balcony to water the new plants she purchased from last Saturday's trip to the green market. (I forgot about her latest acquisitions and tripped over the damn things the other night— almost gave myself away.) This is a new addition to her morning ritual. When she's completed this chore, she'll head to her office to check email before showering.

But Thursday is an exciting day—for me anyway. On Thursdays, Juniper does something Juniper rarely does. She leaves her apartment. Juniper travels to Lake Worth on Thursday afternoons to visit her mother's gravesite. Afterward, she'll stop at the deli she likes, order their everything salmon entree, eat half, box half, and return home to walk Boswell before turning in for the evening. On Thursdays, I have extra time to explore.

Today, I'm hoping to get the sound equipment installed finally. But I really need to find out what she's done with that damn gun. Regardless, I have a lot to do this afternoon.

CHAPTER SIXTEEN

EVERYTHING about this day has been off. Blue skies turned gray—billowy, white puffs chased away by ominous, heavy rain clouds. The day that started out so promising, after an exhilarating workout, quickly turned inauspicious, and it began with the content of one email from one man.

Alok.

He's been trying to call. He says he needs to speak with me in person. Why am I being so immature, ignoring him? We're adults—we talk things out, we work through our problems… when there are problems, according to him. The man continues to maintain his innocence, the denials droning on and on.

The truth is, I've wanted to speak with Alok, have even gone so far as to bring up his contact card, but haven't been able to bring myself to press the button. I keep thinking, believing, that if Alok wants to speak with me to work through this, he will be the one to initiate contact, not me. I didn't have an affair. I didn't sleep with another person in *our* bed.

I began the response email with the truth. I haven't been ignoring Alok's calls. I simply have not been getting them. Roni blocked his number (although I did not include it in the email because, for some reason, I don't want him to be hurt by the fact that Roni has taken my side in all this). Before sending the response whooshing off into the ether, I tapped through on my cell phone to reverse the block on Alok's number.

Sitting in the office, struggling with the simple actions of pressing a couple of buttons, Roni's familiar knock sounded at the door. I stood, tugged at the hem of the t-shirt I threw on after changing my workout clothes, and headed to the door.

As is always the case with my daughter, Roni knew something was wrong right away. And of course, when I explained about Alok's email and unblocking of his number, Roni had many thoughts on the matter. Namely, everything I do and think is wrong.

Over coffee, Roni walked me through my feelings of guilt, of loneliness, of depression, helping me to understand this is all part of the grieving process. She reminded me that I must stay strong to finally get through this slump. And though she hugged me and told me what a great job I was doing before she left, I still felt her words of encouragement lacked sincerity.

But insincere; why? Because I don't believe my daughter? Because I can't believe myself? I can't believe myself, a fact I must accept. I keep forgetting, misplacing, confusing—people, objects, dates, memories. It's a horrible feeling—to believe you've done something, bought something, said something, and yet be told that 'something' was fabricated—by yourself, no less. I've spent hours going over and over in my head what I thought I knew but didn't. Trying to undo someone else's claim that my belief is only that, a belief, and not reality. It's grueling. My head spins and aches; everything becomes uncertain when I find myself in this state. I can't trust any of what I thought, what I felt in my bones. What's worse is that it only compounds and spirals, leading me to believe I'm wrong about other things. What have I done that I'm unaware of? What will I learn about later? It's time to admit I have a problem.

I expressed the idea to Roni that perhaps I should see a doctor, get a professional opinion about what is going on with my mind. See about doing some early testing for signs of memory issues. Cherri died from complications of dementia. Therefore reason stands that I'm at some risk for the disease. Roni was clearly offended, quick to remind me that she's a doctor and, as such, believes my issues are symptoms of grief. Worse, she hinted they're psychosomatic—or that I'm inventing the chaos in my mind to avoid facing the problems in my marriage.

And so, after an uplifting workout, I was thrown right back into my dark hole, where I've spent the rest of my Thursday.

Thursdays have become my designated day to check on Cherri's gravesite. Afterward, I treat myself to dinner. Today, that routine has been interrupted. At least I made it to Cherri's resting place, put out fresh flowers. But almost as soon as I arrived, the rain began, and the darkness of the evening rolled in early.

My visit with Cherri cut short, my words with Roni earlier, Alok's email had all compounded, and I didn't have the energy, much less the appetite, for dinner out.

Now, I pull into The Grabell's parking garage and wonder how on earth I even got home. I can't remember the drive; my head is so full of other thoughts that I can only assume muscle memory got me here.

The service elevator doors slide open and close, whisking me up to my apartment. As the key slips into the door lock, I shake my head, still flabbergasted at the idea of saying *my apartment*. One minute I'm a daughter, a wife, a mother; the next I'm all alone bearing just one title, mother, and it seems, only by term. Roni has been the one mothering me, not the other way around.

Inside the door, I twist the deadbolt into place, resolve to change the way things have become. Roni needs me to step up and be her mother. I've got to quit leaning on her so much.

The apartment, eerily quiet and still, I set my handbag on the console table and make my way down the dark hallway. I suppose I simply am not used to the idea of living by myself. At the end of the hall, I grope for the panel of toggle switches to light the kitchen area. As the room illuminates, I realize Boswell is missing. Since we moved in here, my sweet pup has been waiting for me at the door while I'm out. Even my poor dog isn't used to being left solo. Now that Dash is with Alok, Boz has been experiencing some separation anxiety. Again, I sigh—the action heavy with resignation—my dog and I are nothing but two head cases.

I kick off my shoes and switch on the living room lamps, open the blinds to view the life happening outside my windows. The lights of the buildings across the way, the vehicles driving the streets, the boats bobbing in the intercoastal—make me feel somewhat a part of the city, even if I'm not an active participant. It's nice, though, to see people going about their lives. The rain has cleared away for the time being, and now people stroll the sidewalks in search of dinner from one of the many downtown restaurants.

Flopping onto the sofa, I remove my shoes, peeking around the arm of the couch to check Boswell's pillow. No Boswell.

"Boz," I call in the direction of the darkened bedroom. Something is wrong. He always comes at my call.

The tiny hairs along the back of my neck rise. Eyes widen as my breathing becomes shallow—the strong sensation of someone else being inside my apartment sends my heart rate soaring.

"Boswell," I try again, my throat tight, voice constrained.

Still, no sign of my constant companion. The clench of worry grips my midsection. Standing, easing toward the bedroom, my face flushes with heat, panic gripping my forehead. If something were to happen to Boswell, I don't think I could handle it.

Inside the doorway of my room, I feel for the lamp on the bedside table. The twisting knob rotates but produces no light. I try again and again. Nothing. What the hell? The lamp worked fine just this morning. None of the rooms in the apartment offers overhead lighting. Without the aid of that lamp, I'll have to walk through a dark room to get to the other side of the bed and turn on the lamp there.

I stand silent, mustering the courage to go further into the room. The whir of the ceiling fan blades circulates the air in the room. The flesh along my arms rises with bumps—from fear or fan, I can't be certain.

"Boswell," I call, just above a whisper. Sometimes he'll nap in the back corner of the closet. Maybe he's fallen asleep and didn't hear me come in. Slowly, I step around the edge of the bed, eyes focusing on the bathroom and closet, readying to run if someone or something emerges from one of those areas.

"Boswell," I try once more, making my way toward the over-sized closet.

At the foot of the bed, I stop short, breath catching in my throat. Boswell is posted at the alcove in the room. He sits, staring into the darkness, gaze never leaving the long, deep offset area. The decorators used that area for the standing mirror and vanity. Perhaps it was intended to create a sitting area off the bedroom, but the space feels awkward and almost separate from the room. No windows, no lighting, it's like the architects forgot to pencil in the door on another closet.

"Boswell."

I step closer, cautiously, tentatively. I don't want to spook him, yet his determined focus unnerves me. Something commands Boswell's attention, something he cannot and will not look away from. The knocking in my chest quickens. Tension tightens every muscle in my body as I study him, easing down beside him. My outstretched hand—for scent, for acknowledgment, for comfort—shakes despite best efforts to control it. I start at Boswell's head, offer a wary stroke along his spine. Boswell slowly rotates his head toward me as if to say, *'Yes, I know you're here,'* then turns his attention back to the dark recesses of the room.

My eyes follow his gaze, but I can see nothing. I move to illuminate the other bedside lamp, careful not to bump into the bed.

Twisting the knob produces no lighting from this lamp either. I know these lamps worked earlier. Before I have time to consider the consequences or weigh potential outcomes, I rush to flip on the closet and bathroom lights. They do little to light up the bedroom, though, and still not enough to light the alcove. There is no way for me to light up the area and see what has Boswell's attention other than by flashlight.

My phone is still in my handbag, but there's a flashlight in the kitchen, under the sink.

Throat thick with anxiety, I ease back toward the kitchen area, following the lights outside the bedroom door, head swiveling, checking for the presence of an intruder.

In the kitchen, I find the flashlight and press the button to test the battery. The light is dim, but it is mobile, at least.

The noise of something crashing breaks through the stillness.

My head jerks upright. The beat in my chest responds with increasing speed. Was that my imagination, or did a noise just come from the bedroom? Boswell is still in there. Is someone in there with him? How can someone be in the apartment? I locked all the doors before I left. Or did I? Looping through the day's events, my mind works to conjure the memory of me locking up before I left the apartment.

Another noise—the clanging of the vertical blinds covering the sliding glass doors that lead to the balcony. Heart pounding. Breathing suspended. That's not my imagination.

Boswell.

Boswell is in there. I have to get him out. On tiptoes, I start toward the bedroom door, careful not to make a sound. As I reach the doorway, Boswell tears through, tripping me. I lose my balance and catch myself inside the doorframe. My eyes dart to the balcony door. The blinds dance in the breeze, the door partially open. A thundercloud cracks in the distance. Appearing through the curtain of dangling, vertical panels, the cat from unit 703, which wanders through the neighboring balconies, saunters into the bedroom. The animal steps in and around the broken glass of the decorative vase, now in shards on the bedroom floor. From behind me, Boswell rips into the room, scaring the cat back out the way it came. I notice Boswell doesn't chase the cat onto the balcony. I walk toward the door and find he couldn't fit through the opening if he tried, and knowing how Boswell feels about cats, I'm sure he tried.

I don't understand. I didn't leave this door unlocked, much less open for all the local wildlife. I took Noreen's warning to heart about keeping the balcony doors locked. Anyone could hop the low boundary wall of the balcony and be at my back door via the pool deck.

Mind racing through the day's sequence of events, I look for a possible explanation. This morning, I watered the plants, didn't I? Typically, I use the living room entrance to the balcony for watering, though. I wouldn't have gone through the bedroom, or would I? Did I? Boswell and I sat outside yesterday, but not today, not that I recall. When was it that I stepped outside to follow the sounds of the emergency sirens blaring through the streets? Today? Yesterday? The day before?

I don't know, and trying to dredge it up is giving me a splitting headache. I pull the door closed, flip the latch to lock it, then head to the spare room to ensure the balcony door is locked.

CHAPTER SEVENTEEN

Cherri

Cherri's guardian spirit gently reminds her of the task at hand. The nudge releases her from the spiral of thoughts. Cherri can no longer recall what it was that seemed so urgent, so necessary, yet the sense of unease the memory called up still lingers.

"It is natural to cling to the final echoes of physical life, but your learning lies ahead, not behind. The tether is strongest right after crossing over. We must sever the tie and move on with your life review."

Cherri turns her attention back toward the light. As she does so, the blanket of calm, warmth, and love envelops Cherri once again. Whatever seemed so terribly important is now gone, leaving Cherri to wonder how she even considered departing this peaceful place. The life Cherri has just exited was full of happy times, but also pain and strife. The afflictions of the physical plane do not exist here.

"But the pain and conflict were important to your learning process," Cherri's guardian spirit explains.

Cherri experiences momentary confusion. She has not conveyed her thoughts regarding the feelings of pain, or at least doesn't believe she spoke of them.

Her guardian spirit responds in reference to Cherri's concern. "We have many forms of communication here."

Cherri nods because she understands. She recalls, instinctively, that interactions in the spiritual form are different from those in the physical world—thoughts and emotions drifting freely across the astral plane, unbound, finding their way without voice or touch.

"And now we must return to your life review to assess the knowledge you garnered while on the physical plane. This is an integral part of your soul-actualization. We must examine the relationships you participated in throughout this past lifetime. Relationships in the physical form provide the means for your personal growth and learning. To fully acquire the knowledge of love from all angles, you must understand it through the emotions of joy and pain, the emotions that dominate physical relationships."

Cherri, again, confirms her understanding.

"We'll return now to where we left off, to your young adult years."

Cherri experiences the days and months following the abrupt departure from her parents' home. The sensations and transactions are so real, it takes a moment for Cherri to adjust. As she does, Cherri feels the heartache, the worry, the doubt both of her parents carry because of her actions. Cherri gave no indications of where she might go or when she could possibly return. The angst her mother and father suffer, imagining one horrible scenario after another, the fear for their only child, cripples Cherri. As a result of her actions, the physical conditions of Cherri's parents steadily deteriorate.

Traveling away from Lucedale, Mississippi, the only town she has ever known, Cherri sees and feels the emotions of the current moment. In the company of like-minded friends, Cherri lives freely, lives boldly, protesting politics of the time, bucking societal norms. Cherri feels the love and happiness that she and her friends collectively experience during their young, carefree years.

For two years, Cherri and her band of counterparts travel through the country, locating communes of others who understand them, accept them. Cherri and her group of friends chip in to help with the daily chores, doing their part to support the cooperatives that have invited them to stay for as long as they desire. When the time comes for them to move on, Cherri and her friends do so without reservation or guilt. There are no steadfast rules to adhere to. Everyone is free to do as they wish.

And then comes the fated meeting. Cherri watches as she meets Dennis Walder, the man she believes will make her even happier, the man who will make her life complete.

Their courtship is brief if indeed it can be called such a thing. The two marry quickly so that Dennis can avoid the draft. Cherri is nineteen. Dennis is twenty-one. And while they both pledge commitment to one another, the union means more to Cherri than it does to Dennis. Cherri mulls over her new circumstance, telling herself this doesn't matter. Ultimately, they belong to one another. It is a time of loving freely, of acting against what society deems acceptable. And as such, Cherri and Dennis do not place boundaries on love. If you feel love, you show love, you give love, you receive love.

Cherri and Dennis have been married less than two months when Cherri learns she is pregnant. Scared and uncertain, Cherri relays the news to Dennis. Cherri is scared because she doesn't know the first thing about babies. Cherri is uncertain because she can't be sure Dennis is the baby's father.

Dusk is born as the sun sinks into the western sky on a warm, mid-summer day. Cherri thanks the women of her community for assisting her beautiful boy into the world. No hospitals, no doctors or nurses necessary—her boy is perfect. Cherri studies her son and knows in her heart Dennis is Dusk's father. Dennis isn't convinced, but as far as he is concerned, he now has another dependent in the government's eyes. Dennis is certain he is free of the draft threat now.

The three of them move through their days traveling the country, picking up odd jobs here and there, meeting new and interesting people in the cooperatives they stay at along the way. The trio stays within a community until Dennis grows restless and finds reason for them to move on. And Dennis always finds one excuse or another for them to head out, to find a new group.

Dusk is four years old when Juniper is born. Dennis says there is absolutely no way Juniper is his child, though Cherri can't understand why he wouldn't claim her as his own. Juniper is the very image of Dennis—blonde hair, blue eyes, same cleft chin. Within Juniper's first year of life, Cherri is pregnant again. As Cherri's belly expands for the third time, Dennis's sullen moods grow more pronounced. His agitated nature keeps the family moving on, never staying longer than a month at a time in any one place. Dennis shows no shame in revealing his true feelings towards Cherri and the children. Though he may not think much of them, he stays on when Luna enters their lives so as to avoid the Vietnam War.

Shortly after Luna arrives, however, the draft calls come to an end, and when the draft is officially over, so too is the marriage of Dennis and Cherri Walder.

CHAPTER EIGHTEEN

Juniper

WHY AM I DOING THIS? Roni would disapprove. She knew I couldn't be trusted, and now I know it too.

I can't help myself.

It's right around the corner.

Who am I kidding? Roni would not support even one of the decisions I've made this morning. I'm a disappointment to my daughter.

I know this, and yet, I need this.

The doctor's office I left moments ago is only a few miles from where I lived with Alok. Inside my car, the air conditioner struggled to cool the interior as I attempted to talk myself out of a drive-by. Staring out the dark-tinted windows at the parking lot of the medical facility, the heat rising from the pavement, I felt my own temperature soar with every new question that popped into my head. Would Alok be home? Was our neighbor, Mrs. Hinckley, back from visiting her daughter in Maine? Were the ducklings still following their mother through the streets of our neighborhood to the lake, or had they gone their own ways? Does *she* visit him freely now that I am no longer living there?

The doctor had no definitive answers, so I might as well seek out the answers to all the other questions looping through my head. Right or wrong, that's how I justified my actions. Roni, of course, would never legitimize, much less approve, of any of it, no matter how convincing my argument might be. A drive by… definitely not. And then, she's already stated her opinion multiple times that my memory lapses are most likely due to grief. I didn't need a doctor's examination to determine that. Me? I had to know something more concrete. However, after bloodwork, a battery of tests, and a litany of embarrassing questions, I am no closer to getting answers about my deteriorating memory than I was prior to my appointment. So now, I've set my intentions to gain some clarity about my personal situation—or rather, Alok's personal situation.

Decision made, knuckles white atop the steering wheel, I maneuver the car along the familiar path I've taken for years to get home. No longer can I call it home. I moved out, moved on. Was it too soon? Should I have tried to work things out or at least given Alok a chance to explain his actions? No. Roni's right. The deal was made before we wed. No affairs, no lies. Roni has been suspicious of Alok's actions for a while, ever since she moved to downtown West Palm to be near Cherri. Roni told me that on a few separate occasions, she had caught him in lies, had witnessed his wandering eye. Why didn't I listen to her then? Maybe this situation would be easier to accept if I had.

The problem, however, is that I've never imagined or even considered a life without Alok. Once he became part of my world, I couldn't see one in which we both existed, if not together. Daily, I counted my lucky stars and thanked the heavens above for bringing that man into my life. I believed I was so fortunate to have found the kind of love that few others ever experienced. When Cherri got sick, I knew I would be able to handle whatever life threw at me because I had Alok. When Cherri died, I lost part of myself, but I knew I would be able to go on because I had Alok. And now, I don't.

I creep through the right-hand turn, leading me to my destination. In case Alok is home and by chance staring out one of the house's many windows, I stay a good distance away. The home two doors down from where Alok lives is for sale and far enough away that I can see what is happening at my old house without being seen. Pulling tight against the curb, I put the car in park, studying the house for signs of change. Nope. It stands as grand and proud and forlorn as it did the day I drove away.

The house is huge, too big for the two of us. After Cherri and Roni moved out, Alok and I would often lose one another, running from room to room, calling out for the other. Four thousand square feet behind the French Country chateau facade. Double front doors open to a two-story foyer, floor-to-ceiling windows on the backside of the house looking out over the pool, in the distance, the man-made lake. Five bedrooms and six bathrooms—the Walder women had never before seen the likes of something so stately. But it became our home, a happy place for the four of us.

Is Alok lonely in that big house? Has he invited her to move in with him?

My phone rings, startling me out of disturbing thoughts. From the passenger's seat, I pick it up to see Roni's name on the screen.

Inhaling deeply, clearing the swelling lump in the back of my throat, I click the vehicle's Bluetooth speaker to answer her call. "Hi, Honey. What's up?"

"Just checking in. I stopped by your apartment, and you weren't there. What are you up to?"

I shift in the bucket seat, straightening my spine. Roni cannot know where I am. I'm not in the right frame of mind for one of her lectures. I do the next best thing, "I went to the doctor this morning," though I know this response will not go over well either.

"You didn't mention a doctor's appointment. Is everything okay?"

I hadn't planned to tell Roni I was seeking medical advice

about the problems I've been having with my memory. Grief and stress are causing my lapses in recall, according to Roni's assessment. How can I not worry that it is something more, though, especially given Cherri's diagnosis that took her from us too soon?

"I've been feeling…" Pitiful, that's what I am. Afraid of my own daughter and what she will think of me, how she will see me as neurotic, paranoid, a hypochondriac. Roni is already disappointed in me for not being strong enough to let go of a man who cheated on me. Here I go, adding to her reasons to view me as weak. "I've just been so discombobulated lately. I need confirmation that I don't have the same disease that killed Cherri." There, I said it, and now Roni can do what she will with my confession.

"What did the doctor say? Are you ill?"

"The test results are going to take some time, but the doctor says she thinks it may be 'perimenopause symptoms exacerbated by angst and mental strain.'"

"I told you it was most likely depression and grief. Geez, Mom. Well. Do you *feel* better now that you have a *professional* opinion?"

This is a dig, of course. I didn't accept Roni's diagnosis, even though she has a PhD in clinical psychology.

"Before I can feel at ease with what's happening, I need to learn more about Cherri's illness." Because Roni was Cherri's health proxy, I've had little access or face time with my mother's doctors. Roni insisted she accompany Cherri to all her appointments alone, relaying that the doctors believed it would be tedious to have more than one family member in attendance. Roni gave me updates after each exam, but we never discussed the technical terms of Cherri's disease. "Until I can give the doctor the specifics of Cherri's diagnosis, I won't know for sure if I am hereditarily impacted. Do you have…"

Roni cuts me off before I can finish the question. "Hang on a sec, Mom. I'm getting another call. It's work."

The air conditioner is finally catching up to the heat outside. I shift the vents—once aimed straight at me—so they now circulate air through the cabin. Outside the window, life moves forward: moms pushing strollers, kids riding bikes, landscapers wielding yard tools. Everyone seems to be moving on except me. And I don't want to.

The lining of my stomach is a ring of fire, nerve endings tingling, skin itching, head tight with thoughts and feelings and memories and questions. Memories play in my mind's eye. Countless hours have been lost to playing, rewinding, replaying the moments of recall, trying to find some sort of clue, a sign of what I missed on the front side of Alok's betrayal. Something— anything—so I might be able to say, Oh, I see now; how did I miss that when it happened? Would I feel more at ease if I found the answers I'm searching for, the telltale signs I overlooked? I doubt it. Still, I keep dissecting conversations, combing through interactions, hoping to recall the look in Alok's eyes, some twitch of his face I failed to see in the moment.

Will I ever be the same again? At the risk of proving my daughter right—that I am, in fact, whining—I don't want any of this to be true. Roni says, "We can't have…" No, that's not it. "We don't always get what we want, Mom." I know this, of course, but it doesn't change what I feel, the ache deep in my chest. Roni also said the hurt would ebb soon, but it hasn't. I'm not sure it will, honestly. My heart still feels as if it is being ripped apart. The lump that has settled at the back of my throat refuses to dissolve, no matter how much water I swallow over it, day after day.

Surfacing from the pool of pity I've been wallowing around in, I realize Roni's work call is running long. I hope everything's okay. I retrieve my phone from the passenger's seat, checking the screen to see if I'm still connected to the car's Bluetooth. The symbol denoting I am currently on the phone is not displayed. I tap the phone icon and understand Roni is no longer on the line. I tap through to text her and find the message she has sent to me.

—Sorry. Had to hang up. Work emergency.

It's just as well. Now I don't have to hear the disappointment in her voice when Roni politely discusses the doctor's diagnosis, the very same prognosis she previously doled out. I scroll backward, perusing the texts Roni and I have shared of late. My mind drifts back to the moments when the correspondences were made, what I was doing at the time. The texted conversations when we sorted through the planning of Cherri's funeral fill my screen. Scrolling further, I find messages regarding her deteriorating last days at the care facility. A tear slides over my cheek.

Lost in reverie, all sense of time and place lost, I stare at the phone screen. Pounding on the driver's side window shatters the silence. The jarring noise startles me, sending the phone flying through the compartment of the car. It lands with a heavy thud on the floorboard at my feet. I dive beneath the dashboard to retrieve it and hide.

Please don't let it be Alok.

The fact I'm hiding is ridiculous, given the tint on the car windows is so dark that no one can see inside the vehicle. Reflexes—that's all it was. My first instinct was to locate my phone. Right? Of course.

Please don't let it be Alok.

I run my palm across the floorboard in search of my phone, holding to the steering wheel with the other hand. Maybe if I stretch out the recovery of my phone long enough, the person outside the window will go away. The pounding starts again; this time, a voice accompanies.

A female voice.

Mrs. Abernathy.

Phone recovered, I pull myself upright and press the power button to lower the driver's window.

"Hello there, Mrs. Abernathy. How are you?" Falling somewhere between the ages of eighty and one-hundred-twenty-five —none of our neighbors know for sure—Mrs. Abernathy has appointed herself the neighborhood watch leader of the gated community. I was so concerned about staying out of Alok's sight that I completely forgot about the woman and her watchful eye.

"Peachy. And why is it you are sitting in your car so far down the street from your house?" The woman gets straight to the point.

"Oh, you know, I like to get different views of the house." It's the first thing that pops into my head and doesn't ring true somehow. I keep going to cover the flub. "You know, sometimes being right in the middle of something, you miss the details, just overlook something glaring. I find it helps to step back and study from different angles."

"That's right smart of you, Juniper. You'd be surprised how many aspects of life that particular philosophy applies to."

Wouldn't I, though? Every aspect of my life right now.

"Where have you been, anyway, missy?" the woman presses, unwilling to let my lie stand without more. "Haven't seen much of you lately."

Nothing escapes Mrs. Abernathy's attention. Has she seen Alok's new fling coming and going? Though I'm half tempted to ask her outright, I don't want word of our separation circulating the neighborhood. The fact that Mrs. Abernathy is inquiring about my whereabouts of late suggests she has no knowledge of what Alok and I are going through.

"I've been staying in downtown West Palm Beach with Roni since Cherri passed away." It's not entirely the truth, but it does come close.

"I'm surprised that husband of yours hasn't been spending more time downtown himself, for different reasons, of course. Seen him working out of the house most days of late. With that big contract of his getting shredded by the city's new mayor, one would assume Alok would be riding that man's backside."

What's going on with Alok's company? Did I miss something?

"You know, our communication has been lacking since Cherri passed. We've been so busy, and Alok hasn't wanted to bother me with his work issues. What's wrong with the contract in downtown West Palm?"

"Juniper, now I ain't one to tell a person how to conduct their marriage, but honey, you two need to talk more if you're going to make it work. I should know. Al and I were married fifty-seven years when he passed on. We told each other everything."

"You're right, Mrs. Abernathy; I know you're right. It's just with my mother passing so recently."

"Oh, I know how hard that has been. On all of you. I was sure sorry to hear she'd gone on, but she's in a better place."

I nod in response, struggling to keep back my true feelings on her words. It is possibly my most hated phrase in the realm of condolence offerings. However, I want to find out what is going on with Alok, so I play the part and act like she's given me a thought I'd not yet considered. "I'm sure you're right. It's hard to remember that when I miss her so much."

"I'm sure you do, dear. That's why you need to be leaning on your husband during all this. I'm sure he's missing Cherri, too, and then going through all the hoopla with that new mayor." She's mentioned it again. What is going on?

Alok is the owner of a large security guard firm, offering armed and unarmed services for its clients. He has several contracts throughout the state. It's how we met, actually. His firm was bidding on a security project at the investment company I worked for in Tampa. We began dating and knew almost immediately we were meant for one another.

When Alok proposed, the decision to move to West Palm Beach came easily. My blog had grown and was really taking off. I had been contemplating quitting my day job, and with only the blog to maintain, it didn't matter where I lived. Cherri was happy to be included and loved the idea of change, considering how long she had lived in Tampa. Roni was the only concern I had about moving—her being fifteen, having recently come out to all her friends. I thought she wouldn't want to leave her school, but as it turned out, she was looking for a fresh start herself.

"Would you mind filling me in on what's happening with that contract? It might help me be more supportive when he tells me about it."

"You're right, and I'm sure that's what your good-looking man needs right now. Some support."

I bet he does. Little does Mrs. Abernathy know that my husband has been getting support elsewhere.

"Well, it's been all over the Palm Beach Post." Mrs. Abernathy continues, "So if you want more details, I'm sure you can search their archives. But, as soon as that new mayor took oath, he turned around and gave Alok's security contract for the downtown area to another company."

"Last I heard, Alok was putting together his bid package. That process takes months. The city was going to let Alok's company work month to month during the bidding process."

"Nope. The new mayor came in and canceled that process. Said he was going forward with a no-bid contract—giving it to one of his buddies."

"Well, that's not fair." An overwhelming wave of allegiance washes over me, making me forget how angry I am with Alok, forget what he has done to me.

"Ain't right at all. That mayor has ruffled more than a few feathers since he stepped in. From what I understand, the transition is supposed to happen next week."

Alok must be furious. I can only imagine how frustrated he is. "Thank you so much for the information, Mrs. Abernathy. I'll be sure to ask Alok about it when I see him."

"Well, he isn't home right now, left before the rooster got up this morning."

"It's just as well. I forgot an errand on my to-do list, so I'm going to head back out and get that done. Maybe he'll be home when I get back."

"Maybe. Yeah. I'm gonna run on inside myself, hotter than a witch's caldron out here this morning."

"You definitely need to get out of this heat," I agree. "I'm going to shoot off a quick email and get on my way. You take care, Mrs. Abernathy."

The woman throws up her hand and takes leave as I raise the window to shut out the heat.

I pretend to be engrossed with my phone while keeping one eye on Mrs. Abernathy's progress up the sidewalk. Once she's locked safely away, I turn my attention back to the house I love and miss. I need to get out of the neighborhood. Alok could return at any time. Explaining to him my reasoning for sitting down the street wouldn't be as easy as it was with Mrs. Abernathy.

My peripheral vision catches sight of a figure in motion.

Oh my God. Who is that? Through the car's windshield, I see a tall woman with dark hair—it's long. She's trim. I can't determine her age as I can only see her from behind. Why is she approaching my house? Okay, so not my house anymore. Why is she heading to Alok's house?

I twist inside the bucket seat to look through the car's rear window, trying to locate the vehicle she must have arrived in. I don't see a parked car anywhere. My heart speeds—faster and faster, I think it might burst through my chest. Darkness surges through my body, giving way to a rage unlike anything I've ever felt before.

Is she the one? Is she the woman I saw Alok with? The one I called Roni about? Surely, she's not a neighbor. I would have known, right?

I'll take a picture. Maybe I can blow up the image, enlarge it, get a closer view. My hands shaking, I accidentally hit the Photos app and furiously poke at the screen to close it and open the Camera app as intended.

Raising the camera lens to the windshield, I aim at the house to see the woman disappearing through the back gate—before I can capture her image.

CHAPTER NINETEEN

Someone is watching me. I can feel it—the uncomfortable sensation jerking my attention from the smartphone in my hand to the resident standing before the concierge desk. She smiles. Is it the smile of someone who's caught me, or is it sincere? I acknowledge her with a nod meant to speak for me: *Yes, I've seen you. Do you need something?* Or perhaps: *Yes, you caught me—what do you need?* Either way, her presence has been acknowledged.

"I have a package to pick up," she says, the smile flowing through her words.

I guess she's just nice. *Weird.* Most of the people who live here treat me like the hired help I am, or even worse, like they're paying my wages straight out of their pockets. It's not my fault they chose to live in a place that charges exorbitant rent fees, like it gives them the right to be pompous assholes.

"Unit?" I ask the woman.

"Excuse me?" She asks, tilting her blonde head to one side.

"You're apartment number." I clarify. She must be new—that's got to be why I don't recognize her.

"Oh. Um, seven-fifteen?"

Reflexively, my eyebrows raise at her question. Does she not know what apartment she lives in? I mean, yeah, she's old, but not old, like *'I sometimes forget where I live'* kind of old. Maybe fifties, but she's in good shape—better than me—so she might be in her forties.

"Yes, seven-fifteen, Juniper Walder. Sorry, I only recently moved in."

Slipping my phone underneath the piece of paper on my desk, I reach to pull out the drawer on my left. I locate the keys, stand, and push the rolling chair back behind me. Under the woman's—Juniper Walder's—intense scrutiny, I make my way through the door that encloses me inside the concierge area and step toward the package closet. I fumble to find the key that fits the lock, glancing down at the uniform trousers I am wearing as I do so. I probably should have ironed these before I wore them to work. No doubt the woman behind me notices. Whatever.

Inside the package closet, I search the shelves for a package marked with her apartment number.

"I'm not seeing anything for you. Are you sure it was delivered?"

"Yes, I got delivery confirmation from the sender earlier today."

"I don't see anything here for you. Sorry."

"It would be a large box and probably wouldn't fit on the shelves. Is it one of these on the floor, maybe?" The woman steps inside the storage room with me, examining the packages on the floor.

The room grows small. My breathing shallows in response.

"It's probably in the other closet," I say. The statement comes out too quickly, too harshly; I can't help the sound of my delivery. I've got to get out of here. Now. I flip the light off and close the door, locking the residents' packages safely away.

"Are you okay? You look a bit peaked," the Juniper woman says.

"I'm fine," I lie. "We're not supposed to have residents in the package closet." Another lie, but it's better than relaying my claustrophobia issues. I learned in my last building (before they let me go) that oversharing with residents is considered unprofessional. What was it my superior said, exactly? You're not paid to make friends with the residents. They're not looking for friends; they're looking for someone to do their grunt work.

"I apologize," Juniper Walder says, taking a step back, waiting for me to lead the way to the other holding area.

She stays close as we cross the lobby to the closet used to house dry cleaning and larger packages.

"Again, I apologize because I should have led with the fact that it would be an oversized box. I'm still getting used to living in a multi-unit building. Besides one semester in college, I've never had any experience in communal living, and I must admit I'm finding all of this odd and difficult to get used to."

Juniper Walder continues to ramble on, but I quit listening when my phone rings across the way. I forgot to silence the ringer. Shit. Is she the type who'll tell? One of those who will complain to management?

"Is that your phone ringing?" Juniper Walder asks. "Do you need to get it?"

"No," I respond, forgetting to emphasize whether I mean, 'No, it's not my phone,' or 'No, you are my priority at the moment.'

As I slide the key into the storage closet door, the buzzer sounds at the front door.

"Well, you're popular. Would you like me to get the door while you check on my package?" Juniper offers.

"No, thanks. Your box is on the floor there. It looks heavy. Do you want to use the valet cart?"

The buzzer rings again. "Sorry, I need to get that." I crouch and push the package out the door of the closet.

"Go ahead," she says sweetly. "I can get it from here."

"Okay," I say, unable to hide the tentativeness in my voice. "You're sure?"

"Absolutely. You've got other things to do than coddle me. Go ahead."

"Thank you," I throw over my shoulder, hurrying to the front door.

"No, thank you," she casts back. I feel bad about being so indifferent to this woman earlier. Juniper Walder doesn't seem to be like the other people who live here.

I push open one of the glass double doors for a tall, handsome man, explaining he has an appointment with the leasing office. He follows me to the desk so I can check my agenda for his name and confirm his meeting.

As I lean over the desk to retrieve the clipboard, a sharp noise ricochets through the lobby behind me. My first thought: someone's animal is in pain. Did a dog get caught in the elevator doors? Then comes the crash—the splintering of glass. I twist around, ready to make a dash to help. It's Juniper. She's dropped her package and stands frozen, jaw slack, eyes wide—with fright? surprise?—at the man who has an appointment with leasing.

"What the hell are you doing here, Alok?"

CHAPTER TWENTY

Juniper

He stands in front of me, gaze dark and cool, clearly unruffled by this chance meeting. Or is it by chance? Alok still has yet to answer me as to what he is doing in this building. Surely, it can't be that he has come to pay Roni or me a friendly visit. My blood heats, flushing my extremities—the nerve of this man. Until a few days ago, I had held onto the hope that perhaps this whole mess was something I had fabricated, that it was all some product of my dark imagination. But then, as I sat in my car, an outcast in my own neighborhood, and watched *her* enter the house we had called *our* home, I knew it was real—I *know* what a lying bastard Alok really is.

The same red rage I felt while watching that woman enter our house last week swells once more. Jealousy? Anger? Anguish? I don't know what to call it. I only know it is a feeling I've never experienced before. A feeling so intense it overtook all of my senses and stole away the remainder of my day. By the time I arrived back at the apartment that afternoon, I couldn't account for where my last hours had gone, or how I'd gotten back to the apartment building, or even if I'd really held a conversation with Mrs. Abernathy.

The concierge moves toward me, Alok close behind. The poor girl regards me with muddled confusion—should she help me with the dropped package or run from the madwoman standing before her? The look jolts me back into reality, into motion.

"Alok, I asked you a question. What are you doing here?" Firm and solid, I hold my ground, no fidgeting, no insecure actions, only strength and conviction. I do not move to put the box I dropped upright. I do not inch back, although I am desperate to put more distance between us.

Alok takes a step forward, positioning himself in front of the concierge. The girl understands the confrontation is personal and moves to her desk, saying, "I'll check you in with the leasing agent whenever you are ready, Mr. Prasad."

Alok looks over his shoulder, no doubt throwing off one of his dazzling flirtatious smiles, thanking the girl. His hair is longer; a dark curl laps at his neck. Turning his attention back to me, he looks to the floor, contemplating another step closer, but the box holds the space between us. Instead, he pulls his gaze up to meet mine. Those eyes, do they not see what he has done to me? I thought I knew those eyes, the heart behind them. Though pain courses through my entire body, I will not break the stare.

Alok lowers his voice. "Juniper, let's not make a scene." He reaches for my hand, but I snatch it before he can grab me. Still, he manages to brush the skin along the inside of my wrist, the sensation raising the flesh along my arm into rigid bumps—visible, telling.

Huffing, hoping to emanate exasperation for this exchange— I simply don't have time for this, nor do I want to see you—I slip the arm behind my back to conceal the effect his touch has on me.

"Why are you here, Alok? Just answer the damn question," I demand, yet match his voice level. I live here now, and I have no desire to be fodder for building gossip.

"I'm here to sign my lease."

"What?" I shake my head, feel my shoulders slump, betraying my resolve. Certain I have misunderstood, I jerk my spine straight.

"You don't need an apartment. You have our... I mean your house." The frustration with this ridiculous conversation raises the sound of my voice. The concierge glances in our direction, letting me know she has heard me. "What kind of game are you playing, Alok?" I ask, more aware and careful with how far my voice will carry through the open lobby.

"It's not a game. Look, I had no idea you moved into this building." His hands cut through the air, accenting his words. "It's not like you left a forwarding address. Hell, you don't even answer phone calls or reply to my emails. How am I supposed to know this is where you would play out this absurd ruse?"

"Because Roni lives here, Alok. It wouldn't be difficult to surmise."

"I wasn't aware Roni lived here. Have you forgotten Roni's disregard for me since Cherri was diagnosed?"

"Roni does not disregard you," I spit back, then add in my best snarky tone, "Well, now she does. She has little respect for cheaters."

"I'm not a cheater. Jesus, Juniper. Let it go."

"Do. Not. 'Let it go' to me, Alok. I'm not an idiot. I have eyes."

"You have an overactive, twisted imagination. I have not cheated on you."

"We are not doing this in the lobby of *my* apartment building."

"I agree. It looks like we both have to live here. Maybe I can come to your apartment after taking care of my lease."

"Absolutely not. I refuse to be behind closed doors with you. I know perfectly well what you are capable of."

Alok narrows his focus, veiling the storm brewing behind his eyes.

"I don't know what reason you could possibly have for letting an apartment here. I've already told you I have no intentions of taking the house from you, Alok. You owned it when we got married. It is yours, not mine. That's why I left instead of kicking your ass out," I reply, folding arms across my chest.

Another thought occurs to me. "Does your moving in here have anything to do with the fact that you lost the downtown security contract?" I throw out the question without considering it first. Yes, I want to know what happened, of course, but the way I have posed the question comes off as snide and contemptuous.

"You heard?"

"Yes, Alok, and while I think what the mayor is doing to your company is terrible, it doesn't change how I personally feel about you. And, I don't think you're going to change the man's mind simply by living downtown; that's assuming you really didn't know I was living here. Though come to think of it, why would I believe anything you say? You've already proved yourself a liar."

Alok places his hands on hips, squaring off. "I'm not living downtown to try and recoup the contract. I'm renting here because the house sustained so much damage that it is unlivable. Renovations will take some time, and I don't want to stay at the hotel any longer." He raises his right hand to rub his brow and run fingers through his hair. He's stressed. I see it and know it to be fact, having lived with him for fifteen years.

"What do you mean, unlivable? I drove by last week, and the house was fine."

"Yes, I know. Mrs. Abernathy filled me in on your *visit*."

I should have known that nosy woman would say something to Alok about seeing me last week. "Of course, she did. Mrs. Abernathy sees everything."

"Well, not everything. She didn't see who tried to burn down our house last week."

CHAPTER TWENTY-ONE

AFTER I DROP the package off at my apartment, I take the elevator to the fourteenth floor. I knock. Wait. Shift my weight from one foot to the other. Behind the door, I hear the shuffle of feet, silence, then the click of the deadbolt turning. The door eases open to reveal a large room sectioned off into a kitchen, a bedroom, a living area—all allotted into one wide space. This must be one of the studio units. I thought Roni said she had a one-bedroom/office unit?

A skittish man emerges from behind the pulled door. He pushes the centerpiece of his glasses to sit higher on his nose as he looks up at me. He can't be much more than five feet tall, sporting nothing but a pair of basketball shorts on his thin frame. While my daughter may be somewhat of a mystery to me lately, it's unlikely Roni has developed a penchant for men.

"Hi," I say. Delivery tentative, hesitant. "I'm looking for Roni."

"You got him."

"No. I mean, my Roni."

Hands coming to rest on hips, the man squints, raises one brow.

"My daughter, Roni Walder," I clarify.

"Oh yeah, Roni, sure. Sorry, some of my friends call me Ronny."

It's my turn to offer a puzzled expression.

"I'm Ron, but the Roni you want lives down the hall," he says, pointing left.

"Really? I was sure she told me her unit number was four-teen-o-four." Why I am standing here arguing with a half-dressed man about whether this is indeed his apartment or my daughter's is ridiculous.

Why do I do such things?

Because you're tired of being corrected.

Whatever the reason, it isn't this man's fault. "I'm so sorry. Of course, this is your apartment. Obviously. Which unit is Roni's, then?"

"She's the last one on the right—her place overlooks the pool. I don't think they're home right now, though."

Shaking my head, I form a response but decide against giving it voice. This man is confused, it seems. Roni lives alone; she's never been one for roommates. If Roni wasn't living with her family, then she wasn't going to live with anyone. My daughter has always been too fiercely private to share space with another person, and she rarely, if ever, shares her personal feelings or thoughts with anyone. Actually, the trait gave me pause when Roni announced her decision to pursue a career in psychology. At one point during her teenage years—after I had begged Roni to talk to me, or Cherri, maybe a close friend—I offered to find her someone to talk to, a therapist. Roni was adamantly against the idea.

"Is everything okay?" Ron asks.

"Fine, fine. It's all good. Again, I apologize for disturbing you, Ron. Next time, I will double-check that I have my informa-tion correct."

"So you're Roni's mom, eh?"

"I am. I'm Juniper. I should have mentioned that already."

"It's nice to know you, Juniper. Roni never mentioned her mom was hot." He glances at my ring finger. I've been unable to bring myself to remove the wedding bands, which works to my benefit in this situation. "You and Roni look nothing alike."

Face flushing, sweat pools at the back of my neck. "Okay, well, I should get going. See if I can get a hold of Roni." I throw up my hand, back away from his door.

"See you around the building," Ron says, closing himself behind the door.

I turn and head back toward the service elevator. At the last apartment on the right, I stop outside the door, readying to knock, then think better of the idea. No. I am not going to put myself through that again. I pull out my phone and call Roni. It rings twice.

"Hey, Mom. What's up?"

"Where are you?"

"Working. I'm on the road, headed to the next center. Why?"

"I needed to talk to you, and so I went to your apartment, only to find out it wasn't your apartment. It's another Ronny's apartment. A male Ronny. Ron. Whatever."

"You went to Ron's apartment? Why? Why are you bothering him, Mom?"

"No, I went to your apartment, and some man named Ron answered the door to tell me you didn't live there."

"No, I don't live there."

"Well, I know that now. What I don't know is where you *do* live. Because you told me one thing when it is obviously another." I'm aggravated and tired of these ridiculous dances I must participate in just to get to the truth of the matter—first, Alok in the lobby, and now my daughter.

"Mom, I specifically remember telling you I live in unit fourteen-eleven."

"No, you told me your apartment was fourteen-o-four."

"No, I said my friend Ron lived in fourteen-o-four, just down the hall from me. Remember? We had a conversation about how he's a counselor for one of the rehab centers I service. And you said, 'It's wonderful you have such close working relationships.' Any of this ring a bell?" The exasperation in Roni's tone is all that rings loud and clear to me.

Roni catches herself, takes a breath, and continues in a more tolerant voice. "Okay, so what is it you needed me for?" she asks. And though I know she's trying, I can still hear the underlying annoyance in her question.

"Mom, are you there?"

"Yes, I'm here. I'm just thinking. I don't understand how I got that so mixed up, and now I've gone and bothered that man. What is wrong with me?"

"Mom, why did you go to my apartment? Why are you hunting me down when you know you can just call me? Is everything all right? Are you okay?"

"I'm fine. I just got some disturbing news and…"

"Hang on, Mom. It's my other line. The Ft. Lauderdale center."

Pacing the short leg of the L-shaped hallway, I stop and check the number of the apartment Ron pointed out to me a few minutes ago. The unit number reads fourteen-eleven. Seems Ron was correct. My daughter *does* live at the end of the hall—the last apartment on the right. But she doesn't have a roommate. That much I know.

I'm anxious to head back to my apartment, but cell service in the building's elevators is nonexistent, so I'll have to wait until Roni and I finish our conversation. Leaning against the wall, I search my memory for the recent exchange Roni claims we had about Ron, about the two of them working together. In no corner of my mind does the history of this discussion dwell. Something must be wrong with me, even though the doctor states the contrary. All my bloodwork came back fine, within range for a typical fifty-year-old female—actually better than average, thanks to all the exercise. Still, there has to be something overlooked, something missed. You hear about it all the time: patients who dismiss their first doctor's opinion because of doubts about their condition, only to learn from another caregiver that their health is in dire straits.

Down the hallway, the door next to Ron's opens. A young woman locks the deadbolt, then heads toward the main elevator bank, never bothering to look my way, to know someone is watching her. As she disappears from view, my phone beeps with the notification of a text message received. I pull the phone from my ear to read the message.

—*Had to take another call. Talk soon.*

It seems Roni has left me hanging.

Again.

Hurrying out of the service elevator as the door slides open on the seventh floor, I turn the corner and bump into Noreen.

"Hello, neighbor," she says, clasping my forearms for balance.

"I'm so sorry, Noreen. I almost knocked you down—I need to watch where I'm going."

"You're fine. I'm fine. No harm done, but you're in a hurry, I see," she says, releasing me, taking a step back. "I was just checking to see if you were home. When you didn't answer, I figured maybe you took Boswell to the park. I was just headed downstairs to see if you might be outside."

"No, but not a bad guess. Boswell and I went out earlier. We need to exchange phone numbers, so you don't have to run the building to find me."

We move from the elevator room to stand outside the door of my apartment. Boswell gently scratches from inside as if to let me know he's there, waiting, wanting to join the fun. I slip my key into the lock and twist, letting him into the hallway. Noreen bends down to greet him, speaking in doggy gibberish.

"So, you were looking for me?"

Noreen stands. "I was in the mood to visit."

As I open my mouth to respond, Noreen interrupts with an abrupt, "No," then shakes her head, prompting me to wonder if someone other than me is also having memory issues. "No," she repeats. "I'm just going to say it. I met your husband."

Since the night of Cherri's funeral, any reference to Alok sends my heart into a blowout sprint, triggers the tingling of the nerve endings under my skin. "Where?"

"He was moving in, and I introduced myself. I recognized his name and told him I knew you."

Why is he doing this to me? I'm trying as best I can to move on, to forget. I certainly can't accomplish that if he pops up around every corner of my new living situation. "You didn't tell him where I live, did you?"

"No. Well… this is what I said. I told him you lived on my floor, the seventh floor, at the end of the hall."

Unable to give voice to the thoughts thrashing about my mind, I turn, open the door, and usher Boswell inside. Noreen takes my silence as a dismissal and turns to head back to her apartment.

I look over my shoulder, calling to her. "I thought you wanted to talk."

"I do. But you seem upset."

"No. I mean, I *am* upset, but the crux of the matter is that I'm just not having a great day." Noreen has become a trusted friend —a confidant. She has been so generous, letting me lean on her. And it helps too that Noreen's an outsider. She doesn't have established opinions on the situation because she doesn't know anyone other than me involved in it.

Until now.

Alok is inserting himself into my new life, ingratiating himself with my new friends and neighbors.

Instead of the frustrated scream clawing to be released from the back of my throat, I breathe and confess. "I could use someone to talk to."

Noreen scoots inside the apartment behind me, latching the deadbolt, then moving to follow me down the hall.

"Would you like some coffee or water?"

"No, I'm fine, thank you." Noreen slips onto a barstool, folding her arms to lean atop the kitchen counter. "So tell me about your day. What's not been so *great* about it?"

From the cabinet, I pull out a glass and begin filling it with water from the fridge. I pull a long draw, swallow it down, and walk around the counter to take a seat on the stool next to Noreen.

"I ran into Alok in the lobby earlier, where he informed me of his intent to move into the building."

"So, this came as a surprise to you?"

"This came as an electric shock to the base of my spine. I had no idea Alok had taken an apartment here."

"Alok mentioned he had just come from signing his lease." Crinkles form above Noreen's brow as she scratches her head. "But you said you all have a house in Wellington and that you moved out, and he kept the house?"

I take in a long breath. "We do." I release the breath. "He does. But evidently, the house has sustained fire damage and is now uninhabitable. So, Alok decided to rent an apartment downtown while the repairs are being done."

"Wow, the damage must have been significant then?"

"It seems so. And, it seems, as if the fire department is ruling it arson."

Astonishment colors Noreen's cheeks. "Oh no. Who would set fire to your house?"

"Savannah from the leasing office interrupted us and pulled Alok away before I could ask who the authorities think is responsible for starting the fire. I have no idea how something like this could have happened and won't unless I go looking for Alok."

"Do either of you have enemies, maybe someone harboring resentment?"

"I didn't think so. But then, what do I know?" Alok may have pissed off some sidepiece for all I'm aware of; maybe said sidepiece has a vindictive spouse. I don't mention those theories to Noreen, though. No reason for her to think I'm jealous, in addition to the fact that I'm going crazy and quite possibly losing my mind.

"Maybe Roni knows something. Has she stayed in touch with Alok? Have you spoken to her about it?"

"Given how furious Roni is with Alok about the affair, I doubt that. However, I did try to speak to her. I went to her apartment before I ran into you—at least, I *thought* it was her apartment. Apparently, I had her apartment number wrong and ended up on the other side of another Ronny's door—who, by the way, is actually Ron—he told me where to find *my* Roni." Taking another sip of water, I think about the man's claim that Roni lives with someone. He was right about the apartment number. Is it possible he's correct about the roommate, too?

"Ron, okay, yes. I know Ron," Noreen says, bobbing her head, letting me know she's listening.

Cognizant of the fact that Noreen is waiting on me to continue, I nod while trying to convince myself I know more about my daughter than some half-naked man who lives down the hallway from her. I want to ask Noreen if she's heard anything around the building about Roni having a roommate, but it's hard to admit my daughter is withholding details of her personal life. From me. Her mother. Isn't it enough that I have to choke down the understanding that I have no idea who my husband is? Now my daughter wants to conceal her true self as well?

"Juniper? Juniper? You okay?" The words float through the air, struggling to cut through a heavy fog. I shake my head, blink my eyes, feeling as if I've just woken from a deep sleep.

I look at Noreen—pull myself back into the moment.

"You're a million miles away."

Elbows resting on the countertop, I drop my forehead into steepled fingertips. "There is so much running through my mind. I'm having a difficult time sorting through it all. If I could just dig it out somehow and organize it."

Patiently considering my dilemma, Noreen swivels the barstool, angling her seated position toward my slumping figure. "You can start by talking to me. Maybe I can help you work through some of these thoughts. I don't want to pry, so if you aren't comfortable…"

"It's not that I don't trust you, Noreen, but I don't know where to start. That's the real issue." Lifting my focus to the oven's digital display across the kitchen, I let myself expel all I've kept bottled up the last few weeks.

"Honestly, I find myself wondering if I've woken up on another tangent of my life, one that could have happened if I had done one thing versus what I actually did that led me to this timeline because everything happened so quickly, so unexpectedly, I'm in a tailspin with no ability to right myself, and I think I might be losing my mind, and I'm not being overly dramatic, or a hypochondriac, or looking for sympathy or attention, but my memory is full of holes these days, forgetting where I placed something, losing full-blown conversations, looking around to find myself in a place but having no recollection as to how I got there."

My hands fly through the air, adding an unwanted flare to the gushing anxiety. Not only do I sound crazy, I'm certain I must appear that way as well, but I can't stop. Barely taking a breath, I continue to ramble on whether Noreen is listening or wants to or not.

"I truly believe I might be losing control—just like Cherri did —which is why I keep trying to remember (without dwelling on it the way Roni insists I am) the very first signs of Cherri's disease, like when it started and how she was acting, because yes, Cherri was forgetful, but I always thought that was from the alcohol, from the fact that my mother was a heavy drinker her entire life and was always forgetting one thing or another."

"Multiple times I've tried to talk to Roni, which is difficult for me to do anymore considering that each time I pose a subject, she has to walk me through what I've said or done on a previous occasion, and I understand it must be exhausting for her to even try and have a conversation with me anymore because if I'm being *really* honest with myself, I think she's trying to find ways to put me off. Every time I try to reach out to Roni, she has an excuse for why she needs to end the conversation, and more often than not, before the conversation has even gotten started, so it seems that Roni might be *over* her mother, or probably, more like she is tired of *mothering* her mother."

I can't help myself. Everything comes tumbling out, a big mess spilling out before me. Noreen sits, taking it all in, but I can't look her in the eye, or I might quit, and I need to get this out.

"And then, come to find out, I think Roni might have a roommate, possibly even a new girlfriend, and if it's a girlfriend, then Roni must be serious about her, considering Roni's never shared space with anyone—our house was so big, she practically had the back half to herself all throughout her teens, but even in college, after she moved into the dorm, Roni couldn't handle cohabitating with anyone, so she moved back home and commuted. And, *if* Roni is in a serious relationship, why has she not mentioned this woman to me? The other Ron is aware of this significant person in my daughter's life, but her own mother can't be trusted with that information. Oh my God." My eyes find Noreen's wide stare over tautly clamped lips. "Oh my God, what if Roni has told me about this girlfriend, and I've forgotten?"

I brush fingertips over my cheeks, not realizing until I feel the wet heat that I am crying. What must Noreen think of me? The same thing everyone else does, I suppose—that I've lost my mind, that I'm going crazy.

"I'm sorry," I tell Noreen. "I didn't mean to blurt all that out and certainly don't expect you to fix my issues."

Now that I've given voice to the doubts racing the looping course of my mind, exhaustion settles into my bones. A lighter, freer feeling was what I had hoped would happen after expelling all that, but instead, I now experience a sense of deflation.

"You do have a lot on your mind—a lot to sort through," Noreen starts.

I nod, staring at my hands clasped firmly in front of me.

"Let me start by saying, I don't think you're crazy, Juniper. I think you're under a great deal of stress. Losing a parent is a major life change for anyone, but to top it off, you find out your husband is cheating on you. You need to cut yourself some slack.

"And as for Roni, well, she, too, is going through a significant life event. I doubt your daughter is trying to cut her mother out of her life right now when she, too, has lost the one other person she considered a parent. And let's assume Roni does have a serious girlfriend. *Maybe* Roni is being sensitive to your feelings."

"I'm not sure I follow."

"Well, your marriage is on the rocks; you've recently learned Alok is having an affair. What? Roni's going to come prancing in with a girlfriend? Albeit, I don't know Roni well, but given everything you've told me about her, she seems to be a considerate, thoughtful adult."

My mind works over Noreen's viewpoints—her thoughts about my stress level being the reason for my forgetfulness are on point with Roni's observations and the doctor's diagnosis. And as far as her perspective on Roni, it does seem plausible. Of course, Roni knows how upset I've been over Cherri's illness, her death, and now losing Alok. My daughter is looking out for my best interests, and here I am thinking the worst of her— imagining Roni's ignoring me, shutting me out of her life because of my whining. God, I'm so self-centered.

Well, I certainly know how to fix things with Roni. I will give her some space and, moreover, the benefit of the doubt. I'm so ashamed of myself. Now, how to deal with the problem of alleviating some stress for both my mental and physical well-being?

Noreen breaks through the heavy silence. "You okay? I didn't overstep, did I?"

"Goodness, no. I can't tell you how much getting your interpretation of this situation means to me. For the first time in weeks, I have some clarity about what's going on in my life. I may not know how to handle it yet, but at least I have a better grasp."

"I'm so glad I can help. It's been a while since I felt useful. Retirement has left me with a lot of time on my hands and no one other than myself to give it to."

Again, I feel shame for having made everything about me. Noreen confided she was finding it difficult to adjust to the post-employment life. She has no family of her own to lean on, having given her life to the rich families of the Palm Beach islanders. She helped raise their children, ran their households, kept their secrets. Noreen won't say which families she worked for throughout the years—only that she worked her way up the ladder from millionaires to billionaires and is still bound to strict non-disclosure agreements from her past employers. Having time for herself was something of a rarity during her career, and now time is all she has.

"I've been so wrapped up in my woes, I haven't even asked how lunch with your old employer went."

"It was nice to get out. Good to see Mrs. X again," she says, offering no further distinctions. All Noreen's previous employers are Mr. and Mrs. X. "Silly me, however, thought we would be going out for lunch, but to do so would mean Mrs. X would have to be seen dining with the help. Some things will never change." Noreen smiles, sadness etching the corners of her mouth and eyes. "Nevertheless, her new chef prepared a lovely lunch, and Mrs. X caught me up on all the island gossip."

"Anything good?" I sip from my water, thinking this is a

good distraction for me. I haven't had a simple social chat in weeks.

"Not much I can share, but she did fill me in on the ransomware attack."

"Ransomware attack?"

Noreen eyes me, her features marked in disbelief.

"Sorry, I've no idea what you are speaking of, Noreen."

"It's been all over the news."

"My personal life is the only news I've kept up with. I've barely been through my email in the last few days."

"West Palm Beach is under a ransomware attack. It's gotten serious, from what I understand. The mayor continues to decline the cyber attacker's demands, prompting the attacker to react more aggressively with each slight. Every time the mayor denies the aggressor, another city system goes down."

"Sounds personal."

"It does, doesn't it? Evidently, the new mayor is to blame for the aggression."

"I don't understand. Why would the mayor assault his own city?"

"No. Not the mayor committing the assault on his city, but the mayor's city is under assault because of something he's done, maybe even someone the mayor has personally offended. Who knows? I can tell you the man doesn't have many fans on the island, though."

"The island has its own mayor. Why would they care about what the West Palm Beach mayor does?"

"Because some of the islanders have invested heavily in real estate and businesses in West Palm Beach. Anyway, whoever it is has a heck of a grudge and a damn good tech geek on their side. This attack is picking off the city's functions, one by one. Only the city government buildings were affected at first, but the threats keep growing. Before long, we'll lose our emergency responders, according to Mrs. X's information about the most recent demands."

Thoughts race, scrambling to the dark place in the back recesses of my mind. I know someone who has a tremendous grievance with the mayor. I know someone who is a genius in all things technology. No. None of that meshes with the man I know. Alok wouldn't do something like that. He's not that man.

Or is he?

CHAPTER TWENTY-TWO

"WHY IS it I am sensing reluctance on your part to continue the review?" Cherri's guardian spirit probes. "You are of the understanding that once complete, you will be free to rejoin your spirit family, correct?"

Cherri doesn't answer but makes an inquiry of her own. "Is it mandatory we continue the life review chronologically?"

"It is customary."

"But not required?"

"No," Cherri's guardian spirit replies, then holds, offering Cherri the opportunity to elaborate. When Cherri adds nothing further, her guardian presses on. "What is fueling your apprehension? What is it you're trying to avoid?"

"The first part of my review… those years were difficult. More often than not, I felt lost and alone. I thought I knew what I wanted from life, who I was—and then I didn't. I had to start all over again. The only information to be garnered from reviewing this next portion of my life is heartache."

"You must keep in mind that it is not the feelings you experienced during the time period you should be concentrating upon, but rather how you reacted to those feelings. The actions you took in response to those feelings. It is not your emotions on which you should focus. The knowledge to be gained is from examining the emotions that others felt as a result of your actions. This is how you will solidify the lessons you previously chose for your soul to learn in this past lifetime."

Cherri remains in quiet contemplation. She is unconvinced that delving into the events of this next portion of her review will not cause her emotional suffering. She remembers all too well how wretched the years in the upcoming portion of the review were.

"You have already proved there was no circumstance you could not handle. Whether you passed the lesson or rather failed it, you made it through the situation presented to you. Disappointment and discouragement are unwarranted, as all lessons were achieved in one manner or another, no matter the outcome. We are not here to judge what you did or didn't learn, only to determine what lessons you will seek out in your next lifetime."

Cherri does not respond, letting the encouragement and guidance calm her.

"Your unease and fear indicate that you continue to allow your soul to be tethered to the physical plane. It is time to let go of that life, and all of the emotions you experienced will be just that, experiences long gone."

Cherri affirms her understanding, relays her willingness to place faith in her guardian spirit. She knows she needs to let go, yet—strangely—something, someone, still holds her back. Even so, the time has come to move forward with the review, and she gives herself over to the process.

Cherri's review moves into the days after Dennis's abrupt exit from her life. She clearly recalls, while in her physical form, how disappointed she'd been in herself—in her actions. Back then, the emotions were her own: despair, heartbreak, dejection. But now, it is Dennis's guilt and shame that she feels.

It never occurred to Cherri that Dennis might have felt anything other than relief when he decided to abandon her and their three children. Cherri certainly never had the opportunity to lash out or condemn him or even express her feelings to Dennis about his departure. As Cherri remembered it, Dennis claimed on more than one occasion that he was not taking on responsibility for three children who were most likely not his in the first place; he had better things to do with his life. 'Other plans,' he'd said. Then one day, he was simply gone. Dennis disappeared, leaving Cherri to believe she was the one at fault for all that went wrong in their marriage.

If Dennis harbored any other pangs of remorse in his lifetime, Cherri would never know. As soon as Dennis had stepped away from their lives, it was as if Cherri and the children ceased to exist for him. And just as was Dennis's swift exodus on the physical plane, so too, he is gone from this part of her review.

Cherri is not proud of what she must admit, but be truthful, she will. Cherri always held hope during her physical life that Dennis would seek her out, would return to be part of the children's lives. Dennis's connection to Cherri, to Dusk, and Juniper, and to Luna had been permanently severed when he deserted them. Cherri understands Dennis's time in her life review is over, and now she must move into the years that follow.

Dennis left Cherri and the children in a strange town—one they had only arrived in the night prior—miles upon miles away from any friends or family, no means to get home, to get anywhere. Without warning, Cherri is a single mother of three kids under the age of seven. She has no money, no transportation, no one to call upon. The only people she has left in the world are her parents. Cherri hasn't had contact with them in almost ten years. Will they even speak to her if she calls? After all this time, will they take her and three kids into their home? Even if they are willing, Lucedale, Mississippi, is a long way away from Indio, California.

Cherri has never been fully responsible for her own well-being. She has always done what she was told, whether in her parents' home or whatever community she and Dennis were living within. Cherri was never the one in charge; she simply carried out orders. And now she has three growling, little tummies relying on her to make the decisions, execute the plans, keep everyone safe and healthy.

Cherri comes to the conclusion that she must go home. Her mother will help; her mother will smooth things over with Cherri's father. Cherri's deeply religious father will not be happy to learn his only child is a single mother/divorcee (not that she and Dennis are legally divorced). She can at least tell her father truthfully, however, that his grandchildren were not born out of wedlock.

Cherri makes it to her hometown after a long and arduous trip. She doesn't have the gumption or the energy to fight with her parents, and so she doesn't. She swallows back their criticism and castigation. Cherri lives by their rules and sees to it that her children do the same. In time, her parents' bitterness is replaced with acceptance and gratefulness. Cherri does exactly as she is told, and, in the process, finally learns what it is to take care of herself and her kids. It is not long before Cherri is also caring for her ailing parents.

Not knowing if she was alive or dead or kidnapped or maimed, the years Cherri spent away took a toll on her parents. The pair have always been older than the parents of Cherri's friends due to the fertility issues they suffered early on in their marriage. Her mother and father had endured many years of unsuccessful pregnancies before finally being blessed with Cherri. To lose their only child to the world after they had tried so hard and for so long to have her impacted not only their psyches but also their physical well-being.

Cherri had always wondered about her parents' failing health when she had come home to people she hardly recognized. Now in the midst of her life review, to learn their deteriorating conditions were at her hand disturbs Cherri's peace, her calm.

"If only I had made other choices…" Cherri laments to her guardian spirit.

"Yes, you had choices—decisions—but you must keep in mind that the other souls you had relationships with also had planned lessons for their lifetimes. Your parents, as individuals, each did the same for themselves. The emotions of heartache and despair that your parents experienced were placed before them so that each would have the opportunity to learn whatever lessons they had personally deemed necessary."

"But if Mama and Daddy were going to feel those emotions one way or another, why do I feel so horrible about what I did to them?"

"Because you feel responsible for your parents' reactions. During your time, the choices you made were still yours, as were the choices your parents made. They, too, could have made different decisions, chosen to behave in an alternate manner."

Cherri allows a slight nod, though she is not sure she understands completely. If she did, surely, she would feel better about this portion of her life review than she does at the moment.

Nevertheless, the review moves on to the next years. And just as that time of her life had been a blur when she lived through the years on the physical plane, so too are they playing out in the same fashion before her now.

Cherri's young children, of course, depend on her, but given the poor health conditions of her parents, they too, need Cherri, and she is determined not to let any of them down. Everyone does their part to make it through the difficult, hectic span. Her parents watch after the children, providing Cherri and the kids with a place to live while Cherri fills in for her parents' physical limitations around the house. The children remain mindful and respectful of their elders. It is Cherri who carries the disproportionate burden for the family unit, however.

Cherri is the only member of the household capable of maintaining a job. Capable, yes, Cherri can lay claim to that attribute. But skilled? No. Cherri can not check that box. Cherri left home before she graduated from high school. And while Cherri had worked hard for the communities she participated in throughout the last years, she'd never had formal employment. In terms of hours and skill level, the only jobs feasible are in the service industry. Before long, Cherri realizes that working behind a bar makes her the most money and allows her to work at night while those she cares for during the day sleep away the dark hours.

The review continues, but Cherri realizes this portion is not moving as fluidly as the previous years—stilted, disjointed somehow. She and her spirit guardian examine her actions during this time period with more scrutiny. There must be something about this piece of her lifetime that Cherri is missing.

Cherri's spirit guardian replies to her musings. "Your days may have dragged into months, that hauled into years in a monotonous manner to you, to others; but, it is here during this time that you made the choice which placed your life onto another path—a path you did not intend to follow in this lifetime."

Cherri understands now. It is her shortcomings that are on full display. She may have been able to hide and conceal her issues with alcohol consumption on the physical plane, but there is nowhere to run from them here. "I wasn't able to overcome it," Cherri says, regret thick in the proclamation. "Again," she lets the word fall between them.

"No, you were unsuccessful, and you'll have to face the challenge again—during your next lifetime. Perhaps in that one, you will not succumb."

Cherri says nothing. There is nothing to say. She turns back to finish witnessing this portion of the review, to witness her weakness.

Ten long years, Cherri lives her days caring for all those in her life without time to consider her own welfare. She gets through each monotonous day, prepares for the one that follows, and then consoles herself with drink into the deep hours of the night—mulling over the mess she has made of her life, trying to forget.

CHAPTER TWENTY-THREE

Juniper

THE SHRILL SOUND OF AN ALARM—ONLY inches above the headboard of my bed—jerks me from a deep sleep. Unable to yap his displeasure at the loud, offensive noise, Boswell runs in circles beside the bed. It's all I can do to gather my thoughts, slough off the grogginess.

Is that the fire alarm?

From the nightstand, I grab my phone and check the time. Three-thirty. Roni mentioned the new building has had issues with false alarms in recent months. The alarm may be in error, but I'm not willing to take that chance with Boswell. Throwing back the duvet, I locate the clothing I peeled off a few hours ago, dress, and shove my feet into the flip-flops nearby. I run through the apartment, harness and leash Boswell, all the while hearing the commotion outside my door. People shouting, banging on doors. My heart keeps pace with the horrible scenarios flashing through my thoughts.

Calm down. This is probably a false alarm.

By the time Boswell and I get out of the apartment, the hallway is clear of residents. Panic surges through my extremities, frays the edges of my nerve endings. The loud trill roaring through the empty hallway further spurs the manic thoughts. Poor Boswell struggles to keep pace as I rush down the hall, following the exit signs, trying to recall where I've seen the stairwell.

An apartment door flies open several feet ahead of me. A woman scurries out of her unit.

She looks both ways down the hall. "Is this for real?" she yells over the noise.

"I've no idea. I only recently moved in. Stairs?"

The woman points left, turning her body in that direction and hurrying ahead. I pull Boswell along, following her. We find the doorway of the stairwell and rush down the seven flights to street level.

The night air is still and sticky. Pajama-clad residents spill into the park across the street and linger around the building's entrance, their conversations circling the same complaints.

"Do you know what's going on?"

"These alarms are getting old."

"Management needs to get its act together."

"Has the fire department gone in yet?"

Boswell and I make our way to the park, uncertain of where to go, what to expect. Scoping out the crowd, I look for Roni, spotting Noreen instead.

"Hey, have you seen Roni?" I ask as she approaches.

Turning and craning, Noreen scans the congregation. "I haven't, but she must be here somewhere. I have my phone if you want to call her, make sure she got out okay."

"Actually, I have mine," I say, shifting the leash to my other hand as I reach for my phone. My nerves take over, and the leash slips, bobbling before it drops to the ground.

"Here, let me take Boswell while you call Roni."

I pass Boswell's leash to Noreen as I press into my phone app and locate Roni's number on my favorites list. The phone rings several times and sends me to voicemail. Why doesn't Roni answer? Is she okay? She couldn't have slept through that alarm.

Pacing a small patch of grass, watching Noreen walk Boswell toward a group of residents, I try Roni again. Behind me, I hear a cell phone ring and twist to locate the phone's owner, thinking it may well belong to Roni. The noise stops, but the ringing on the other end of my call continues as I silently plead for her to answer.

"Mom," Roni says. My quiet appeal has been granted. *Thank you.* "Are you out of the building? Everything okay?"

"I'm fine. Where are you?" I ask, surveying the crowd again. "I don't see you anywhere?"

Roni doesn't answer but instead asks, "Are you at the park?"

"I'm near the art sculpture with Noreen and Boswell. What's going on? Do you know? Is this another false alarm?"

"Most likely, but you can never be sure. Someone said they saw smoke in the garage near the trash receptacles."

"So tell me where you are. Boswell and I will come wait it out with you."

"No. It's best you stay there, Mom. I'm at the back of the building—you probably wouldn't be able to find me in this crowd anyway. I'm in the middle of a conversation with some neighbors, but I'll come over when I'm done."

"Okay, honey. I'm just glad you're safe. See you soon." The phone pings to let me know the call has been disconnected. I stare at the screen.

Did Roni even hear me, or did she just hang up on me? Is her roommate (or perhaps girlfriend) with her? No. Stop it, Juniper. You're doing it again. I intend to keep the affirmations I made— give Roni some space, the benefit of the doubt.

I slip the phone into my back pocket once more and use the illumination of the park lamps to search the crowd for Noreen. She and Boswell have made their way to the far edge of the park. Noreen patiently follows Boswell while he sniffs through the foliage of bushes lining the perimeter. I make my way toward them.

"Did you get a hold of Roni?"

"Yes. She's around the back of the building chatting with some neighbors."

Noreen's brow lifts, pulling her eyes wide in question.

"What? Why are you looking at me like that?"

"Because it's written all over your face. You don't believe her. What are you thinking? Do you think Roni's lying?"

"Maybe not lying, but I don't think Roni's giving me the whole truth either. I can't help but wonder if it has anything to do with a girlfriend. Maybe Roni is with her and still isn't comfortable introducing us yet?"

"You could be right, but I'm proud of you for not grilling her about it."

"Thank you. I'm proud of myself, to be honest. This is taking tremendous reserve." I slap an unidentified insect nibbling on my arm. "Has the fire department arrived yet?" The muggy humidity gnaws at my patience level for this pre-dawn activity.

"Not that I've seen," Noreen says. "I was talking with some other residents while you were on the phone with Roni. Kennedy told me Grant asked the night concierge about it on his way out. The concierge said it might take a while—apparently, the ransomware attack is still ongoing.

"Ordinarily, when the alarm sounds, it alerts the fire department immediately. This time it had to be called in. And wouldn't you know it? They're having trouble getting a phone line to work since the building systems are internet-controlled.

"Someone finally had the good sense to use their cell phone, but they were told it may take longer than normal to get here— something about all the city traffic signals being down."

"Good grief, what a nightmare. We could be out here for hours." I smack my forearm, where another nibbler has latched on. Sirens sound in the distance. My eyes travel in the direction of the noise. "Thank goodness. Maybe we'll get some answers soon."

Fear and panic suddenly shadow Noreen's features. "Boswell," she shouts, scrambling after him as his leash hits the concrete and drags. Boswell tears across the park.

"Noreen, stop," I yell to her. "It's okay. I'll get him."

Noreen slows her pace as I pass her, racing to catch up with Boswell. Boswell doesn't run much farther, though, as he finds what he's after—his buddy Dash, Alok's whippet.

◉

Tails wagging, the two dance and prance around each other, hopping and playfully nipping at the air. Alok is at the other end of Dash's leash, but I am not quite as keen to see him as Boswell is to see his old friend.

"Boswell," Alok calls out, bending to scratch behind Boz's ears. Boswell gives Alok a happy lap with his tongue. I swallow the feelings of betrayal and remind myself that Boswell is just a dog—*my* dog.

Dash, sweetheart that he is, takes his turn at smothering me with kisses, tail wags, and playful yips. I lavish him with coos. "Good boy." "Oh, I've missed you." "My goodness, how sweet you are." It's true; I have missed this adorable animal and didn't realize how much until now, as tears begin to well up.

Alok breaks into my thoughts. "These two are excited to see one another."

"Indeed." I give Dash another rub and stand from the squat, which is starting to cramp. I turn my attention to Alok and see that he stands next to a man donning a security uniform. The man is younger than Alok. Long braids hang over the back of his shirt. "Hello," I acknowledge, noting the man's uniform is not the one Alok's men wear. The emblem on the sleeve reveals that this man works for one of Alok's competitors.

"Juniper, this is Steven. Steven, Juniper." Alok relays the pleasantries, although not entirely pleasant in the delivery, and he definitely offers no details to convey how the two know one another. Is Alok uncomfortable with this companion? Or is Alok uncomfortable with me? Have I pushed him away so often that he no longer wants to be around me?

"Juniper, you got Boswell?" I hear Noreen ask, coming up

behind me. I snap out of the useless, agonizing thoughts, turning toward Noreen at the moment she spies Alok and Steven. The look she wears is one I can't quite read. Noreen runs a palm over her forehead to wipe away the perspiration, quietly assessing the group.

"Hey, Noreen," Steven says, his voice carrying the lilting cadence of a Jamaican accent.

"Steven," Noreen addresses. "How are you?" She asks him, though I get the impression it is only to be polite, as I watch the slight shake of her head. It's almost as if she is trying to tell Steven not to say anything more.

Curious about the relationship, I keep an eye on Steven to see him nod, then pull his focus to take in something across the park. It's obvious I'm the only one here who doesn't know Steven, although something about him is familiar. I fix my gaze on Steven, trying to recall how I would know him, but nothing comes to mind. Standing next to Alok, Steven shuffles his weight between his feet. Is he as uncomfortable with this meetup as Alok and Noreen both seem to be?

Noreen breaks the awkward silence in our small circle. "Hello, Alok. It's nice to see you again." She pauses, then adds, almost as an afterthought, "Well, the circumstances could be better—and at a more convenient hour, of course." She lets the comment fade and wipes her forehead again.

"Noreen." Alok addresses her. "This is a hassle, I agree. Steven and I were just discussing the situation." Alok slips his hands into the pockets of his shorts, rocking onto his heels. Back and forth, he goes, a nervous tick I know well.

Why is he so edgy?

"Yeah, this cyber attack has all the city systems running slow," Steven adds.

Across the street, flashing lights of the emergency response vehicles, two fire engines, and an ambulance dance through the morning's dark hour.

"We should know something soon," Alok says.

The four of us look in the direction of the building as fire-fighters dressed in heavy gear stomp inside.

"I'll check in with headquarters, see if I can find something out," Steven says, stepping away from the circle as he pulls a cell phone from his pocket.

As I watch Steven from the corner of my eye, the realization of how I know him clicks. Steven used to work for Alok.

Or is he still working for him?

The fire in the garage was contained. A dumpster fire. At 5:00 a.m., firefighters deem it safe for tenants to return to their apartments.

Through the throng of residents waiting for one of the two elevators to arrive in the lobby, I spy Roni next in the queue. Beside her is a woman, standing close. Shoulder to shoulder, the two lean toward one another, speaking in whispers. The gesture is intimate. I watch the pair, willing the woman next to my daughter to turn her head. Even from behind, something is so striking about her—the curve of her spine, the way her dark hair cascades over her shoulders. The woman lifts her arm, running her palm down the length of Roni's back, then up. Her hand stops at the base of Roni's neck and gently massages the area, letting her thumb graze the spot behind Roni's right ear.

I continue to watch the exchange, though I feel terribly uncomfortable in doing so. The answer to my unease is not forthcoming. Maybe it's because I've never seen Roni with a significant other. Or because the moment feels so personal, so private. Or, more likely, because I now know for certain she's keeping this important person in her life from me.

The bay of an elevator door slides open. Residents eager to return to their beds hurry to claim their spot in the carriage, calling out floor number requests to the person wedged by the panel. Roni and her partner squeeze into the last remaining space. Roni pivots first, spotting me across the lobby. The look shading her features is one I've never seen her wear before. I maintain eye contact with Roni, keeping my peripheral vision on the woman next to her, waiting for the woman to turn, hoping to catch a glimpse of her face. But when the woman twists toward Roni, her profile is masked by the length of her hair, and then the doors slide closed.

Something in her manner cools the blood surging beneath my skin. I can't tell if it's the striking sense of familiarity or the most intense déjà vu I've ever experienced, but in the stale heat of the humid night, a knowing chill runs straight to my core.

CHAPTER TWENTY-FOUR

Guess Who

OUTSIDE UNIT SEVEN-FIFTEEN, I knock, adding more force behind my knuckles than necessary. I know this woman isn't home, but I have to play the game. The strap of the tool bag digs into my shoulder. I switch the satchel from one side to the other, waiting the required length of time per company policy before entering an unoccupied apartment—just in case someone's watching. And around here, someone is always watching.

I recheck the work order. "Leak under the kitchen sink. Priority: High. Permission to enter if the tenant is not home."

I check my watch—three minutes since the initial knock. From my belt, I unclip the clunky ring of keys and find the one for the unit's door. Behind it, a dog. He doesn't bark, but he doesn't wag his tail either. He plants himself in the middle of the hallway, as if to say, *Do not go any farther.* I take my chances and step around him. He doesn't bite, but he stays tight on my heels. Jesus. Animals…

In the kitchen, I toss the tool bag to the floor, calling through the apartment, "Hello. Anyone home? Maintenance. I'm here about your sink."

As I thought, no answer. The tenant isn't home.

On the floor by the sink cabinet, blocking the walkway, chemicals have been neatly arranged by size and color. She cleaned it out as requested.

I turn to walk through the apartment, check things out—the dog's practically another fucking appendage at this point. If I liked animals, I'd say he's cute, looks cuddly. The dog's owner, though, that woman is fine. Lucky dog gets cuddles from her—Juniper, Juniper Walder. She's some sort of financial wizard. I head into the office, tap the keyboard to bring her computer screen to life. Damn. It's locked. I was hoping to get a look at some of her files. Thought maybe since she lived alone, she wouldn't bother keeping it password-protected.

Moving into the guest room, I find little of interest and head toward the master bedroom. Standing at the threshold, eyeing her bed, I hear the unit's front door open and halt.

"Mom," a female voice calls from the hallway.

Roni.

"Maintenance here," I call back, hurrying to step over the hurdle of chemicals blocking the path. Shit. I knock over some of the chemicals, right them, and ease the counter door under the kitchen sink open just as Roni rounds the corner to find me peering inside the cabinet's dark hole.

"What are you doing here?"

I stand and tap the work order on the counter. "Request to fix a leak under the sink." From the bag of tools, I pull out a flashlight. "Nice to see you too, Roni."

"Mom didn't say anything about having a leak, Martin. How am I supposed to know you're not in here snooping through her shit?"

"Because it's company policy—we don't do that. Go ahead, take a look around if you don't believe me. I ain't touched nothing." The dog has finally taken leave from me and hangs out next to Roni, wearing a look on his face that says, *Don't believe that fucker.*

"Whatever, Martin. Just get it done. I'll text Mom and let her know you're here."

I snatch the directive from the countertop and shake it at Roni. "I got the work order right here, Roni. Your mom gave permission for maintenance to enter when she's not home."

"Don't have a coronary, Martin. I believe you. I don't want Mom walking in and thinking someone's been invading her space. Knowing Mom, she's probably already forgotten she requested to have the issue fixed."

Roni situates herself on one of the barstools around the other side of the counter. She pulls out her phone and begins to tap, making it obvious she has no intention of leaving while I'm in the unit. I bend down, shining the flashlight into the empty cabinet, running fingertips over the bottom surface to determine where there is moisture. Evidently, Juniper wiped away any pooling water, then discontinued using the sink. That woman follows directions to the letter.

I stand and run water from the faucet, letting it drain. Waiting for a good amount to run through, I look out into the living room, up to the ceiling fan, spying the small black dot on the cover of the globe.

"Mom said thank you for getting here so quickly and asked me to hang out until you're finished. So how much longer is this going to take?"

I pull my eyes from the ceiling fan light and fix them on Roni. "I haven't found the problem yet. Can't say." I twist the nozzle to turn off the water and disappear beneath the cabinet again. The problem presents itself fast enough. This is an easy one. Lots of these renters hang brushes and shit from the nozzles under the sink, not realizing they're loosening them up for a leak. A quick twist to each of the knobs, wipe up the water that has leaked through, and I can mark this off the list.

Using the countertop for leverage, I pull into a standing position. "All done," I say, closing the cabinet doors.

"That was fast." Roni scrolls through her phone, not bothering to look up from what holds her attention.

"Common problem. Happens a lot."

She continues to ignore me.

"So, how's that girlfriend of yours?" I ask. "Hannah, right?"

That gets Roni's attention. Her head pops up, glare finding me. "My private life is just that—private. Not for discussion."

Geez, guess I hit a nerve. "Hey," I pull my hands up to show I mean no harm. "I was just making conversation. Sorry."

The sharp, cold look clears her face almost as fast as it appeared. "No. I should apologize. For snapping, I mean."

Weird. I'm sure she can see the look on my face—like what the fuck just happened to you?

"No, really. I know I've been snippy since the minute I walked in here, and you're only here to do your job. I can't fault you for that."

Hell no, I think, but don't dare say in front of this crazy woman. Talk about cold and hot. She ain't nothing like her mama. Not only do they not look a thing alike, but Juniper is as nice as Roni is bitchy, from what I can tell.

When I say nothing in response, she continues. "I've had a really shitty week. That fire alarm that kept us up all night, this ransomware attack on the city—causing chaos left and right in the streets, and I won't even start on my work situation right now."

"Yeah, I get it." I gather up the satchel, sign off on the work order, and ready myself to get out of here. Roni hops off the stool, hurrying around to the side of the counter to block me from the path to the door.

"Hey, listen. I know I was totally bitchy about Hannah. It's just... in my line of work, clients tell me personal things about their lives, and then they think they're entitled to personal stuff about me. You know—quid pro quo crap."

I listen, reposition the strap of the bag over my shoulder. She goes on.

"That's my standard line to them. 'My private life is just that—private. Not for discussion.' So when you asked the question I get all the time, I snapped. It's not your fault. So. Sorry."

"Okay, sure 'pology accepted." I wait for Roni to step aside, but she's not finished yet.

"About Hannah," she starts, pauses, then continues. "The thing is, I haven't introduced her to my mom. So, I would really appreciate it if you wouldn't bring the topic up with my mother. We've had so much happening in our family recently, and my mom is going through a lot. It's not a great time for me to bring somebody new into the equation."

"Like you said, it's none of my business. I'm just here to do a job."

Roni steps aside, leaving me room to scoot around her and head toward the door. The dog escorts me all the way down the fucking hallway like, *Yeah, get the hell outta here, asshole.* Jesus.

I pull open the door, turning back to take one more look at the light fixture in the hallway's ceiling, and find Roni is standing right behind me. I jump. Christ, I didn't even hear her walk up.

"Figured I'd see you out. I didn't mean to scare you, Martin. You know what they say about people who startle easily…"

I twist toward the doorway and hurry through, making a quick left into the waiting area for the service elevator.

Roni leans out, poking her head around. "Hey, Martin. I'll be sure Mom leaves a good review for your prompt and efficient service."

The elevator door opens, and the automated voice relays that the car is going down.

"Okay. Sure. Thanks," I say, stepping inside the elevator and punching the close door button.

CHAPTER TWENTY-FIVE

Entering the room, I see her across the way, Dense Donna. She's early—unusual. I'm early—not unusual. Concentrated focus on the open file folder she holds, Donna doesn't bother to address me as I move to sit directly in front of her. A glance at the clock in the corner reveals the session isn't scheduled to begin for another five minutes. And so, I wait. I get it. Donna's lack of action conveys (loud and clear, I might add) that she has control.

She's the therapist.

I'm the patient.

Fuck. Her.

Look at her. I'm not the one who needs help; she is. From here, I can see the reading glasses perched at the tip of her nose are filthy—all filmy and fingerprinted. The better question, however, is how she can see (much less read) anything through them. Donna licks a finger and flicks to the next page. Her flippancy causes my body temperature to rise. I concentrate on keeping my eyes out of the narrowed glare they want to pull.

As the tick of the minute hand lands on the hour, Donna closes the manila panels and slips the file folder into the bag sitting next to her chair. She digs inside the bag, retrieving a pen and a yellow legal pad. Donna scratches a note, removes her reading glasses, and shifts her focus in my direction.

"Good to see you again, Roni."

"Good of you to notice me sitting here, Donna."

"Ahh, I see." She steeples her fingers, holding the pen between them. "I apologize for making you wait, Roni."

"That's mighty professional of you, Donna." Pursing my lips for effect, I add, "Perhaps it would have been more professional of you to put other client files away the moment I arrived. I've never let a patient believe they were less important to me than another of my patients."

"What makes you think the file belongs to another patient?"

"Because, again, it isn't professional to prep for a client while they are present. Unless, of course, you have actually engaged with said client and are referring to the patient's notes as pertaining to the current counseling session."

"You've set some rigid guidelines for yourself, Roni. That's commendable."

"I don't need your commendations, Donna. I need you to sign off on these sessions so I can move on. Obviously, you as well believe this mandate is bullshit; otherwise, you wouldn't be catching up on patient files while I sit here."

"As it happens, I was reading your file, and I must say I found it rather fascinating; so much so, I thought it necessary to get through all the information before you and I began today's meeting."

"You're telling me you've only now decided to read through the file? We've already had two full sessions."

"I admit, at the onset of our initial session, I had briefly glanced at the material. Prior to our second meeting, I was caught off guard by an emergency and was unable to prepare as I should have. So no, I hadn't perused all the information inside your file when we started your sessions."

"Shame on you, Donna."

Donna looks at her lap. She shifts in her chair and switches up the way her legs are crossed, the act hiking up her pant leg. I notice her socks have slipped around her ankles. I want her to yank them up—contemplate telling her to do so. Instead, I keep my mouth shut, wait her out.

"This topic is doing little to promote your well-being. Let's move on."

"Good idea." I smile—allow Donna to believe I have taken on a more conciliatory mood. "So, what's on the agenda today?" I ask, aiming for congeniality. "What do you want to know?"

Fuck, I think I just confused myself with that little performance. I sounded practically perky. From the look on Donna's face, she's also confused by the delivery. Donna needs to believe I am willing and ready to delve into my innermost thoughts and feelings. It's the only way to get this shit over with, and the sooner, the better, in my opinion. This is such a waste of everyone's time.

"Well, actually, I'd like to ask you about something I read in your file."

"Okay. Ask away. That's what we're here for." I offer a tight, closed-lip smile. It's as much as I can give; I doubt it came off as genuine, although it looks as if Dense Donna bought it.

"I want to talk about someone you haven't spoken about, someone who seems to play a rather large role in your life. I want to talk about Hannah."

Hearing her name roll off Donna's tongue sends me onto my feet, fists pressing against my thighs. "Hannah is off-limits." I turn away from Donna and head toward the door.

"Roni, please, come back. Sit down. Let's talk this out."

"I am not talking about her." With my back to Donna, hand on the doorknob, I draw in a breath—a nice, big, dramatic one— while planning my next move.

"You've made that clear. We'll take up a different subject, but let's not cast away this meeting. We don't get a lot of time together."

Donna's got me. She knows I'm in a difficult situation and that if I'm to get out of it, she's going to be the one to assist me. My future depends on what happens in this hideous room with this ridiculous, heinous person. And to compound matters of this atrocious situation—if Donna has indeed read that file as she claims to have—this witless, dim woman knows more about me than any other human on earth. Not even I know the full extent of what's in that file—who was interviewed on my behalf, the little anecdotes others thought worth sharing about me, or which incidents they deemed necessary to report.

Inhaling, I pivot and return to my seat. Donna begins as I settle in.

"We ended our last session speaking about Juniper," she says tentatively—waiting, I assume, for me to explode again. I won't. I'll keep control this time. I just wasn't expecting to hear Hannah's name before. Donna caught me off guard, that's all. But she won't do it again.

"Tell me, Donna, do you have children?"

"Yes. As a matter of fact, I do." Donna maintains direct eye contact as she answers my question.

"How many?"

"Two."

"Boys? Girls? One of each?"

"This session is about you, Roni. Details of my private life are not part of this discussion."

Bitch. God, she's frustrating.

I nod for Donna to continue.

"During our previous sessions, you've described your upbringing as normal." Donna glances at her notes. "You relayed that although Juniper was addicted to her work and had little free time to spend with you, you never felt disregarded because of your relationship with Cherri."

"I recall what I said, Donna. Is there something new you would like to inquire about?"

"Yes, I would like to address the fact that your file contains a more colorful account of your upbringing. Perhaps not quite as tidy and rosy as the one you fabricated during our previous discussions."

"Fabricated? Are you fucking serious? Now, I'm lying, Donna?" The nerve of this woman is beyond my good nature.

"Bad choice of words. I should have used the term *communicated*. However, given what you know I have read in your file, I'm sure you can understand why I might have chosen that particular verb."

"I do not need a goddamn English lesson. For fuck's sake. Fine. Okay, so my childhood was not normal. Is that what you want me to say? You want me to focus on the negative. Is that what you're getting at, Donna? Is that what I need to do to get you to leave me the fuck alone? Focus on the negative, disregard the positive? You mean the cup's *NOT* half full?"

"I've read your file, Roni. In an earlier session, you suggested your childhood was within typical realms. However, the narrative presented inside your report portrays quite a different tale."

"You're right. Is that what you need to hear? No, Donna, I didn't have a normal childhood. How could I possibly have had a normal childhood? You've read the full file. You're privy to my history. So, why ask me such an absurd question?"

"In Juniper's interview, she reported coming across several documents while sorting through Cherri's things. The account goes on to state that Juniper was surprised to find a full stack of write-ups from the schools you attended throughout your youth. Several were from school counselors, reporting multiple incidents of lying and theft. Juniper claims she had no knowledge of these indiscretions—that Cherri had withheld the information from her."

"And that surprises you, Donna?" I keep my tone even, edging out the defensive disposition gnawing at me. "I've already told you Juniper wasn't around for the ins and outs of my upbringing. You just repeated the statement I gave about Juniper being addicted to her work."

Donna rolls the pen between the flats of her palms, pensive. She continues.

"Let's talk about the incident reports. While Juniper spoke of their existence, she gave no specifics about these conduct reports, only a broad overview, relaying that you lied and stole throughout your school years. Do you feel comfortable expanding on some of those instances?"

It takes every bit of restraint I can muster not to shift in my seat, not to act in any way flustered, not to lash back at her bullshit inquiries. I've *therapy-ed* myself to death throughout my professional training. I think I know plenty well what the hell happened to me, why I've acted the way I have, why I've done the things I've done. I do not see a reason for rehashing them with Dense Donna. Nevertheless, I must give her something.

"I don't recall the exact moment I came to the realization, but at some point, I realized Juniper wasn't like other parents. She was much younger than my friends' parents, and then she wasn't married—I had no father to speak of. Today, a single mother, seventeen years older than her child, isn't seen as a big deal, but society hadn't quite gotten there yet during my youthful years.

"I do recall being young and embarrassed when people— parents, teachers, and later, other kids—asked me about Juniper, about our home life. The probes began with polite remarks on Juniper's appearance, almost as if to butter me up for the real information they sought. I would express thanks for their compliments, knowing that having a beautiful mother had nothing to do with me, knowing that I looked nothing like her, waiting for the next query, which was inevitably always the same fucking thing. *Your mom looks so young. How old is she?*

Watching the expressions as they calculated the age difference between Juniper and me became comical. At first, I didn't understand—Juniper seemed old to me. But then I began to register the disapproval, the judgment shadowing the features of these inquisitors. The next question was always about Juniper's marital status. *Oh, so your mom is not married?* Then—*Do you know your dad? So, that's why your grandma lives with you.*

"I soon understood that my family situation was not the norm, that it was something I should be ashamed of, and so it— the shame—grew and festered.

"As I made my way through elementary school, I began to understand the dynamics, the workings of my friends' families. It was then I realized Juniper didn't just look different from other mothers—she didn't act like them either. My grandmother, Cherri, played that role. But then my friends didn't call their grandparents by name either. We, the Walder women, were all fucked up. There was nothing normal about my family or my upbringing. And so I began to *fabricate* stories for those bold enough to question me about my family, about what went on in our house."

Donna sits across from me, unmoving, unblinking. She's afraid I won't go on if she draws attention to her presence. I let her sweat it out a minute before I proceed.

"The stealing phase was born from my frustration." I pause, thinking about how to deliver this next bit.

Donna grows impatient with the delay and prods. "Explain what you mean by frustration. Frustration with a situation? Frustration with someone?"

"Cherri was good to me. There was nothing I couldn't ask for that she wouldn't deliver, except when she couldn't recall what it was I'd requested. It wasn't as if this happened a time or two. It wasn't that I was asking for outlandish stuff, just small things: snacks, a backpack like the ones my friends had, a special book I'd been waiting for, supplies for a school project. Cherri and I would have these conversations, and she would promise me the moon, but then not deliver it because she couldn't remember making that commitment.

"Later, when Cherri realized she had let me down, she'd pull me into a tight hug, promise she'd be better. She wasn't going to do to me what she had done to the others."

"The others?" Donna asks.

"Yeah, I had that same question. Cherri never explained what she meant by the statement, though. I assumed Cherri was speaking about her kids, their childhoods. I didn't really understand and simply took her at her word, but then Cherri would slip, and we'd repeat the whole scenario again. It wasn't until my teen years that I recognized this pattern, and then, being a person's most selfish years of life, those teen years, I took advantage of Cherri's disease. I learned to use it to my benefit."

Lost in memory, I almost forget Donna is sitting across from me. I haven't thought about Cherri like this since before she passed away. The memories swirl into a mush of sadness and loss, thick and mucky at the center of my chest—an ache I'm not comfortable experiencing. A pain I don't want to reveal, especially to Donna.

"This is difficult for you," Donna states, so matter-of-fact, so knowing it pisses me off.

"I miss my grandmother. I'm not the first or last person who has lost someone they were close to."

"We haven't discussed Cherri's illness. Do you believe these instances you are speaking of were the onset of her dementia?"

"No," I state, contemplating clarification, considering how much more to disclose. I can determine no harm in letting Dense Donna in on the truth of the matter, though. Maybe she'll cease with this line of questioning about my family.

"Juniper likes to tell people Cherri was a heavy drinker. The truth is, Cherri was an alcoholic. I attribute the reason I decided to specialize in substance abuse treatment to the issues Cherri battled throughout her life. Maybe if she'd had someone to help her—maybe if Juniper had pushed Cherri to seek assistance— Cherri would have overcome her addiction."

"So, during these instances when Cherri would make grand

promises and forget about them, those were due to overconsumption?"

"Yes."

"And when you didn't get what you wanted, you stole from your friends and teachers?"

"Yes."

"Did you ever speak to Juniper about Cherri forgetting the items you needed because of her indulgences with alcohol?"

"No."

Donna shifts, recrosses her legs, studies the scribble she has made on the yellow pad. It is so blatantly slathered across her face—a particular question she is trying to reach without leading me. I consider telling her she's doing a shitty job with the process anyway, just ask the damn question, but instead decide to let her squirm it out a bit.

"So, when these incident reports would come home from school, were you afraid Juniper might find out about them, that she would be upset with you, perhaps show disappointment in your behavior?"

"It never occurred to me what Juniper might think of my improprieties. They were between Cherri and me, no one else."

"Did Cherri ever ask you not to tell Juniper about the incident reports?"

"No," I blurt with more abruptness than I intended. I can't take it anymore; all this dancing about is causing a terrible pounding at the back of my head.

"Do you have a specific question you would like to ask, Donna? Your tiptoe, tapping bullshit, is taking up time."

"Fine. As you like, I'll be more direct. Why do you think Cherri didn't tell Juniper about these issues you were having in school? After all, your mother has a right to know. I'm sure, regardless of how busy Juniper was with work, she would have wanted to know about the difficulties her daughter was suffering."

"Cherri didn't speak about the incidents to my mother because she doesn't know my mother."

There it is again—that dumb ass, blank stare on her face.

"I don't follow, Roni. Is there something you're not telling me?"

The aha moment hits me with blunt force. Donna is a hypocritical twit.

"And look who is lying now. You sit there, judging me for the lies I told as a *child*, and you flagrantly lied to me at the beginning of our session."

Donna tilts her head to one side, narrowing her eyes in question.

"You told me at the opening of our time today that you had read my file, which is an obvious lie. If you had read through the entirety of that file, you would know—Juniper is not my mother."

CHAPTER TWENTY-SIX

'I haven't been completely honest.' Before Noreen stopped her, those were the last words to come out of Juniper's mouth.

What was she about to confess?

I've been sitting in front of this computer screen, watching, waiting for something of substance to be relayed—something I can use. The pair has been planted at Juniper's kitchen counter for well over an hour, sipping wine, chit-chatting, sharing, reminiscing. The more they drink, the better the possibility of getting what I want.

Or so I thought.

They were draining a bottle of red, and I was about to give up when Juniper laid out the desire to be truthful. And then, that damn Noreen ruined it. Juniper was ready to divulge some sort of sensitive information until Noreen hopped off her stool and headed to the front door, calling over her shoulder that she'd be right back.

Now, I wait. Now, I wonder. Will Juniper continue? What was so important that Noreen felt she needed to interrupt Juniper and leave the apartment?

The attempt to finish up the sound equipment installation while Juniper visited the cemetery on Thursday evening had been botched. However, I finally got the last of the listening devices inside the apartment during Juniper's ritualized trips to the gym. While watching is of great interest, being able to put sound with her actions is better—especially since Juniper has been disappearing for hours at a time with no indication of where she has gone. I try to determine some sort of information from Juniper's computer, but I've come up with nothing. Maybe she'll let Noreen in on where she has been going and what she has been doing.

As Juniper waits for Noreen to return, she licks her pointer finger and rings the rim of the glass. The low hum fills the silence. Then, a door slams in the hallway. I click a button and change cameras to view Noreen heading into the kitchen, another bottle of wine in hand.

Ah, very good, Noreen. I like the way you think.

Rounding the corner, Noreen holds up the bottle. "You got the last one; this one's on me. Corkscrew?"

"How sweet of you, Noreen. You didn't have to do that." Juniper points behind Noreen, directing her. "Top drawer to your left."

"I figured," Noreen says, using the knife to cut away the foil topper, "if we're getting into confessions, we'll definitely need more wine." She laughs as she twists the cork from the bottle.

Juniper finishes the last sip in her glass. "You might be right, but if we finish that bottle, you may hear more than you anticipated."

Well, there's something to hope for.

Juniper stands and grabs her wine glass. "It's so nice out this evening; let's sit on the balcony."

"Oh, I like that idea," Noreen concurs.

Great. The only way I'll hear Juniper's confession now is from the other side of her balcony. This confession could be exactly what I am looking for, and I need something I can use. Time is running out.

All the south-facing balconies on the seventh floor are accessible from the pool deck. The unit Juniper is in has a second porch-like balcony off the guest bedroom. If I use it, I can get inside and hear them from the door in Juniper's bedroom.

Can I do it? Can I get inside without either of them knowing I'm there?

They are on their second bottle of wine, and the sun has set. The dog shouldn't be an issue—he's comfortable with me being in the apartment. I will, however, need to be extra careful not to be seen. In this place, someone, somewhere, is always watching.

CHAPTER TWENTY-SEVEN

Juniper

A SOFT, warm breeze blows off the intercoastal, a nice change from the gusty winds that whipped through last week. At street level, seven floors down, the hum of car engines, the laughter of friends strolling, and an occasional bark from a dog fill the night air with sounds of life. Noreen settles into the chair arranged on the other side of the low table while I situate myself on one end of the patio sofa.

"I love this view," Noreen says, placing her wineglass on the table, gazing at the water in the distance. Several boats anchored in the intercoastal rock gently in response to the wake of a passing vessel.

"It is the best perk of living here," I agree.

A loud crash from inside steals the peacefulness of the moment.

I twist toward the open balcony door. "What on earth?" Jumping to my feet, I head through the doorway to see from where the noise has come. Noreen follows close behind.

Off the hallway, at the entrance to my office, Boswell stands wagging his tail, his focus on something inside the room. I step around him and see several books scattered about on the floor.

"Geez, guess I stacked those too high, and they all fell over," I tell Noreen, stooping to collect the books and re-stack them in a more stable manner.

Problem solved, we move back to the balcony, Boswell accompanying. Outside, we retake our seats as Boswell stands sentry at the open door.

"Boswell seems out of sorts," Noreen says.

"He's probably still riled over the books falling. He's never cared for loud noises."

"I'm with Boswell." Noreen takes her glass of wine from the table and sips. "So, you were about to tell me something before I ran out to get the wine. Something about not being honest?"

"Well," I begin, then sip my wine, letting it roll over my tongue, and swallowing. "I suppose that sounded rather dramatic. The truth is, we'd be here all night if I decided to be honest about everything going on in my mind. Sometimes, my head feels so full that I think it might fly to pieces if one more thing is shoved in there. The first thing I need to be honest about, though, is us. I can't tell you how much your friendship has come to mean to me." Noreen smiles as I continue. "When I first met you, I didn't want a friend. I wanted to be left alone. Truth be told, I figured you for the resident busybody."

Noreen chuckles. "I understand how you might have thought that. I did come off a bit strong during our initial meeting, but I'm glad I did. Because of it, I have a new friend."

"I've never had many friends. I don't think I even know how to behave in a friendship, really," I admit. "I've never had time—you know, time to share with other people, even my family. I let work schedule my hours, steal time from my loved ones. Work has always been my priority. And now, because of my ambition, I've let down those I care about most."

"You must cut yourself a bit of slack, Juniper. I'm sure you did the best you could for your family, and I think you make a wonderful friend. Do you know how hard it is to find someone who listens to what another has to say? You give yourself, your time, and considerate thought to each conversation we have.

You're present and dwell in the moment. That is a gift most people can't give of themselves."

The compliment is nice to hear. It isn't often I receive them, especially now that Alok is no longer part of my life. I suppose if I care to admit it, I've always looked for commendations, accolades. Cherri was never one to acknowledge accomplishments, instead believing that we should look for gratification from within, not from others.

"What made you so driven? Where did your ambition stem from, do you think?" Noreen asks.

"You know, many people may not be able to answer that question, but I can tell you the day and hour it happened to me. I was at Chris's house."

"And Chris is?"

"Chris Anderson. Roni's father."

"Oh. I don't believe you've spoken about him before. I take it he wasn't part of Roni's upbringing."

"No, he wasn't, although I would have liked that." Thinking of Chris and my feelings for him makes me feel as if I am being unfaithful to Alok. It's ridiculous, of course, especially given the fact that Alok is the one who proved to be a cheater.

Noreen reroutes the topic back to where we started the conversation. "So, you were at Chris's house when you found your ambition?"

"I was. Chris and I were juniors in high school. We were your typical school nerds—studious, fastidious, rule-followers—who shared a lot of the same classes and AP courses. Chris's parents didn't allow him to drive, so it became routine for me to drive Chris home after school, then complete homework together.

"We were setting up our study session in the Andersons' living room. Chris went to grab snacks for us before we got started, while I took the opportunity to use the restroom. On my way back to the living room, the path took me past the kitchen. That's when I overheard Chris's mother. Mrs. Anderson was livid, laying into Chris. I shouldn't have—I knew it was wrong–

but I stopped to stand behind the door, to listen to what she said.

"'You're wasting your time with that hussy, Chris,' Mrs. Anderson said. 'I don't understand it. You're a good-looking boy —smart, a bright future ahead. That girl is nothing like you, Chris. The whole family's good-for-nothing gypsies, living off the government, using drugs, whoring around. You want to know what Juniper will look like—be like—in twenty years? Take a look at her mother, Cherri. Three kids, no stable employment, a revolving door for the men in her life.'

"It's funny—I still remember her every word. Time and again, I've replayed that conversation in my head.

"Anyway, it was at that exact moment that I vowed never to become the awful prophecy Mrs. Anderson foretold. I would make something of my life. I was intelligent and capable, driven even. But then I got pregnant with Chris's baby. It seemed that Mrs. Anderson had placed a curse on me rather than a prophecy."

"But it wasn't. You got Roni out of the relationship, and you proved that hateful old biddy wrong. Look at how successful you are!"

A sad smile tugs at the understanding of Noreen's sweet loyalty to me. I wonder if Cherri would have had the same reaction, if anyone would have—I've never told anybody that story. To relay it conveys I'm imperfect when all I have ever wanted to be is perfect. Though now, after all these years, I understand that the need for perfection has stolen so much of my life from me. Whereas I thought others would be more attracted to me for my perfection, it was quite the opposite. Achieving such a goal makes a person more unapproachable.

"I shouldn't have called Mrs. Anderson that. I don't know what type of relationship you all have with them nowadays."

"We don't, never have. The Andersons blame me for their son's death."

"That's an awful guilt to place on someone."

"It is, but there is a fair amount of truth to the Andersons' claims. Chris had been visiting me the night he was killed. He died in a car accident on his way home from our house."

"I'm so sorry. So that's why Roni has never known her father, then?"

I nod and stare into the glass I hold. The wine is disappearing quickly. The more I drink, the easier the old secrets pour out. Noreen reads the situation and offers to refill my glass. I accept the offer and watch as she tops off her own.

"So, you've told me about your mother. I know Roni is your only child, and you've been married once—to Alok. Do you have any siblings? A brother or sister you can talk to?" I'm grateful to Noreen for changing the subject. It's hard to think of Chris, to remember how much I cared for him, to feel that I am betraying Alok by doing so.

"I do have siblings—or rather, had—one of each, an older brother, Dusk, and a younger sister, Luna. Cherri and I never talked about their deaths, but I can't imagine what it must have been like for her to lose two children. I guess that's why I never harped on her about drinking so much—I figured that was how she dealt with the pain. Who was I to say how she should or shouldn't handle a heartache I couldn't and didn't want to understand?"

"I'm so sorry for your loss, Juniper. Losses. You've had so much death in your life."

Again, I nod in affirmation. Noreen's observation is difficult to process. I have lost so many of the ones I love, and now, although he is very much alive, I am losing Alok as well.

"Do you mind if I ask how they died?"

"Dusk overdosed on heroin. He started dabbling with drugs early on, but his experimentation became more extensive after we settled in Bainbridge, Georgia. We moved from town to town after my grandparents died. The transitions—to new locations, new schools, new friends—were tough on all three of us, but more so on Dusk. He got in with the wrong crowd. Somehow, he managed to graduate, but then he took off. We wouldn't hear from him for years at a time. It was right around the time I met Alok that we found out Dusk had died. Gosh, it's been fourteen, fifteen years now."

"Did your sister pass before Dusk or after?"

"Luna. Luna was my best friend. We were only fifteen months apart, and too, we were the only constant in each other's lives.

"She and Chris died together in a car accident. Luna was driving over a bridge when she swerved into the lane of oncoming traffic. Luna overcorrected, and the car went into the water. The impact of the crash killed both of them immediately." I swallow back a mouthful of the wine, inhale, and continue. "It was my fault. I'm responsible for their deaths. And that rant, the one I heard Chris's mother dole out on him regarding me that afternoon, was nothing compared to the one I received when I arrived at Chris's funeral."

"Oh, Juniper, just because a grief-stricken mother placed the blame for her son's death on you does not mean it's true."

"It is, though, Noreen. I was supposed to drive Chris home that night, not Luna. Luna didn't even have her driver's license yet."

"So why was Luna driving?"

"I was sick. I thought I was too sick to drive. Rather than call Chris's parents—who had no idea he was at our house—and have Chris face their wrath, Luna said she would drive him home. I should have stopped her. I should have driven; I could have pulled over, thrown up, and then carried on. They would be alive today if I had stopped them from doing something I knew was wrong."

A blaring siren approaches from the south. I stand and walk to the balcony railing to see where the emergency vehicle is headed. Noreen joins me as the noise grows louder. The ambulance passes our apartment building and stops in front of the nursing care facility where Cherri spent her final days. I can't help thinking someone else just lost a loved one residing at the facility.

"I hope the response time for this emergency responder wasn't as long as our wait on the fire department the other night," I say.

"I doubt it," Noreen answers. "If anything, the ransomware on the city is getting more intense. The mayor continues to refuse the hacker's demands, and with each denial, another attack occurs."

"Doesn't this attacker understand what is happening to innocent people due to their actions?"

"Doesn't the mayor?" Noreen huffs. "This seems personal to me, though. I suspect whoever is controlling the city's systems has a score to settle with the mayor, not the citizens of West Palm Beach."

I know someone who has a personal issue with the mayor of West Palm Beach. Having the new mayor strip away your company's security contract with the city and then give it to a *friend* would indeed cause contention. Alok does have the technological know-how to pull off a cyberattack, but the Alok I know would be opposed to vengeance, no matter the amount of money at stake. Then again, we've established I don't know the real Alok.

I breathe deeply and turn away from the scene at street level. The red lights of the ambulance bounce off the sliding glass doors. My eyes drop to the floor, move to take in the area around the sofa, around the back of the chair. Where's Boswell? Normally, he sits with me no matter where I am. It's odd for him not to be glued to my side, especially since it's almost time for our evening walk.

"Have you seen Boswell?"

"No, not since we came outside to sit," Noreen answers, turning back to watch the scene playing out across the street.

Concern churns in the pit of my stomach. All this talk of loss, and now Boswell goes missing. He's fine. Of course, he's fine. This is another anxiety moment gnawing at your sanity. Boswell's probably asleep in his bed.

Despite the inner conversation, I hurry through the door to check Boswell's usual hangouts. I call out to him, expecting him to run around the corner at any moment. Nothing. I rush back through the apartment to check my bedroom, the only place left he could possibly be.

Inside the threshold, I switch on the lamp by the bed, stepping through the room toward the bathroom and closet. Startled, I stop suddenly. Boswell sits at the alcove, staring into the dark corner of the room. The same thing he did the night I came home from visiting Cherri's gravesite.

"Boswell," I whisper. No response. Does he hear me?

Using caution not to alarm him, I step around to illuminate the other bedside lamp. The corner he's fixed on remains dark, frustratingly so. I have got to get a lamp for that area.

Noreen pops her head inside the door of my bedroom. "Did you find him?"

The back of my neck prickles with unease. "Yes, but he's acting strange. Boswell won't move. He's fixed on this corner of the room. He's done this before, but it's beginning to creep me out. It's almost as if there is something back there, hiding in that area."

"He would growl if there were something back there, though, wouldn't he?"

"He can't. No vocal cords."

"That's right. I forgot he can't growl either."

I kneel next to Boswell, slowly bringing my hand up to stroke the back of his head and neck. "Are you ready for a walk, buddy?" I ask him. Boswell's tail begins to wag as he stands, answering my question.

Standing, I look at Noreen. "He seems fine. I guess I'm taking him for a walk."

"Would you mind a bit more company?" Noreen asks. "I could use a little stroll myself."

I collect Boswell's leash and harness, strapping him up for our nightly routine. Noreen waits for us by the front door while I grab my keys and cell phone. I turn to walk down the hall toward the front door. Light extinguishes behind me. I twist quickly around just in time to see the light illuminate again.

"Everything okay?" Noreen asks.

"Yeah," I answer, turning to look again. "I thought I saw the lights flicker on and off."

"I think all these deep conversations about your past are beginning to mess with your mind," Noreen laughs.

"You're probably right," I agree, heading out the door and locking up the apartment.

Boswell and I mosey through the park. He sniffs and explores, in no hurry to head back inside. My head is so packed with thoughts of our conversations tonight, I'm shocked when I check my watch and learn we've been in the park for twenty-five minutes now.

I urge Boswell along, reaching inside my pocket for keys, only to remember I gave them to Noreen. We were in the park for only a few minutes when Noreen realized she had left her cell phone in my apartment. I gave her my keys and told her to leave the door unlocked—Boswell and I would be up in a few minutes.

At the front door of the building, I knock on the glass to get the concierge's attention since the entry fob is on my keys. I don't recognize this person, nor does he recognize me. I go into a full explanation as to why I don't have my keys, rattling off my name and unit number so the man can check the picture on file with the person standing in front of him.

Cleared for entry, Boswell and I take the elevator up to our home. Inside, I find the keys Noreen left on the countertop. Evidently, Noreen decided to clean up a bit before returning to her apartment. A clean wineglass drains on the rack next to the sink, and the other holds the last bit of wine we didn't finish. The Post-it note beneath the glass reads, "Nightcap!"

I smile, thinking how nice it is to have a friend, and I pick up the glass, taking it with me to the bedroom.

CHAPTER TWENTY-EIGHT

Cherri

CHERRI'S guardian spirit takes a step back, allowing Cherri a moment to process all she has witnessed from her life thus far. The task, though necessary, can be grueling for some souls, depending on how their time was spent on the physical plane. Many souls have called the chore of reviewing their past lives hell. Cherri believes she may have found her fiery inferno… in all she has reviewed, in all she has yet to witness.

Keenly aware of what the upcoming portion of her life review holds, Cherri longs for a reprieve from the exercise. She recalls with vivid clarity the feelings she experienced during that time of her physical existence. Knowing how painfully intense those moments were for her, Cherri certainly has no desire to understand the emotions others suffered because of her actions. Cherri can't possibly excuse what she has done. Still, she tries to explain her decisions, her conduct, if only to herself.

The years Cherri spent with her parents may have marked the onset of her unhealthy relationship with alcohol, but during that time, Cherri was a fully functional and responsible adult. It was the death of Cherri's parents that unraveled her, took an unexpected toll on her. Cherri's father was the first to depart, and then six months later, her mother passed over. While their deaths were expected, it didn't ease Cherri's grief.

Cherri's relationship with her parents was complicated and fraught, to say the least. Her childhood was challenging (according to both parties); her adolescent years, intolerable (as Cherri recalls); and her disappearance, unforgivable (her parents maintained).

After Cherri's return—three children in tow—something in her parents had shifted, softened perhaps. Even though their health had deteriorated, they were a tremendous help with the children, providing the stability and safety the kids needed, and the support and guidance Cherri needed. Looking back on that time in her life, Cherri realizes she, too, saw her parents in a different light. She was open and accepting of the lessons they instilled, learning from them how to be a better parent and a responsible adult.

Of course, as Cherri reminisces now, she understands what she failed to realize at the time she was living out those days on the physical plane. No, she was simply too busy trying to provide for and raise three children on her own, as well as care for her ailing parents. It pains Cherri to understand now that she never gave any of her moments to gratitude. Instead, her free time was spent wallowing in self-pity and drink.

After her parents passed, Cherri was forced to come to terms with the fact that she was the only adult left. This proved difficult as Cherri had never genuinely felt like an adult. Cherri may have been the only physically able-bodied grown-up in the house for the last ten years, but in her parents' presence, Cherri still envisioned herself as their child. While living with her parents under their roof and by their rules, Cherri didn't have to accept full accountability for her own children.

When Cherri lost her parents, she finally realized the wonderful support system she'd been gifted was gone. She had leaned heavily on her mother for advice and reassurance, and she knew her father had provided the stern presence she couldn't bring herself to give her own children. Only after their passing did she understand just how grateful she was for their help. Dennis certainly hadn't been around to lend a hand in raising their children or to lean on when times were tough. And now, there was no one to fill that role. Cherri had to move forward alone.

Fueled by grief and 'adulting overwhelm,' Cherri would throw herself pity parties—*bottle of vodka for one, please*—allowing herself to think about Dennis. Think about what a shit he was for leaving her, leaving them.

And then her thoughts would turn sad, and she would feel sorry for him, fat sympathetic tears trailing her cheeks. Dennis wasn't seeing his children grow up, grow into their own personalities. He missed everything about them, everything wonderful and amazing, and they *were* wonderful and amazing. Dusk was becoming a man. Juniper was whip-smart, the top of her class. Luna was the most precious, caring child anyone had ever met— everyone said so. It would be Dennis's loss not to know his children. Another sip of vodka, another provoking thought, and then Cherri would think, would know, it was her children who were at a loss, a loss of a father.

Cherri had never considered how her actions affected her children. Earlier in the review, however, she'd been forced to confront exactly how they felt about their mother's reprehensible behavior—and she'd been revolted by it herself. No matter how deeply she longed to shake sense into her physical self, the self-pity, self-doubt, and waning confidence persisted. It was at this point in her life that the drinking became excessive, growing into a beast she could no longer control.

Cherri continues to witness her past, watching on as she comes to a conclusion—she could be in control since she was finally on her own. Cherri's parents were gone, yes. She was sad and missed them. Yes. But, Cherri was once more free of their reign. The children were older, more manageable, capable of taking on the responsibility of their own self-care. It was time, Cherri determined, time to take back her life, be the person Dennis took from her. She had made it through some tough years, and finally, Cherri was free to make choices without condemnation from anyone.

Cherri put her childhood home on the market and began selling off the items she and the kids no longer needed. Lucedale, Mississippi, had too many ghosts and too many watchful eyes behind loose lips. Cherri was tired of it. She was moving on. She would take the opportunity to show her children other places, other ways of life. Cherri missed moving from town to town. Cherri missed men. Now that Cherri had no one to answer to, she would live the life she had been missing the last ten years.

Their first stop had been Daphne, Alabama, another small town that held Cherri's appeal, until it didn't, and they moved on. The kids were good with the moves until they weren't. Six schools in as many cities within a two-year time span proved more than Dusk, Juniper, and Luna could handle. Cherri had given in, and they settled in Brunswick, Georgia. Dusk only had a year left in school, and the girls had high school to get through, then Cherri would begin her gypsy lifestyle again. Cherri could handle four years in one town. She had no intention of giving up the drink or of being entertained by gentleman callers, though. No reason for a girl to restrict herself in all areas of enjoyment.

As it turned out, Dusk also had issues with addiction. Still in his teens, Dusk didn't know how to handle or cope with substance abuse—and there were so many substances to experience—but he did know his mother couldn't help him. She couldn't help herself.

The year Dusk got his diploma, he disappeared. No word of where he was going or what his plans were, but it didn't come as a surprise to Cherri and the girls. Dusk had quit filling them in on his days long before his disappearance. It was difficult for Cherri to discipline her son when she couldn't get a handle on her own issues. Though, to be honest—and the life review was about facing your truths—Cherri had never disciplined Dusk, even when she wasn't battling her own demons. Dusk could do no wrong. Cherri knew she shouldn't have a favorite, but it wasn't something she could help.

Although now, in the midst of her life review, having recently witnessed how the girls felt about Cherri's obvious affections for Dusk, Cherri is disappointed in her actions. She had never meant for her girls to believe they were any less than the beautiful souls they were.

Dusk's unanticipated exit should have made Cherri focus on being a better parent to the children she had left to attend, but no. Cherri, as selfish as she had always been, cloaked herself in self-pity once more and left Juniper and Luna to take care of themselves.

As they had before Dusk left, the girls went on with their days. They had school and friends, and were busy being teenage girls. Juniper had a serious boyfriend. Luna was learning to drive. Cherri was grateful her daughters were close. Cherri never had siblings, so watching Juniper and Luna together gave her a kind of absolution for the fact that her attention was often elsewhere—the girls had each other.

The moment has arrived, however. Cherri's guardian spirit allows her the comfort of bathing in the love of her young girls, but the time has come to face the history Cherri wishes only to erase.

The evening proceeds in the same manner as the many nights before it. Cherri is home after a long day of waiting on customers, throbbing feet propped up, drink in hand, washing down the bitterness of being left by a husband and now a son. The girls have put together dinner for themselves and Juniper's boyfriend, Chris Anderson.

Cherri likes Chris. He is a responsible, courteous young man, unlike his parents. The elder Andersons have no qualms about displaying their prejudices against others, particularly those who do not meet their social or economic standards. Cherri understands Juniper's feelings for Chris are strong, strong enough to endure the judgmental glares and snide remarks the Andersons often make about Juniper and other Walder family members.

Luna pops into Cherri's room, checks on her mother, asks if she would like something to eat. Cherri declines. The alcohol often robs Cherri of her appetite, and when she does eat, the act makes her queasy.

Cherri isn't sure when, but at some point in the evening, Luna returns. "Juniper is sick, throwing up," Luna relays.

"It's probably something she ate," Cherri slurs.

"Maybe," Luna agrees, "but Juniper is too sick to take Chris home. Can you drive him?"

Cherri may not be smart enough to quit drinking, but she is wise enough to understand she has consumed too much alcohol to drive. "Chris's mother, have that bitch come pick him up," Cherri spouts by way of solution.

"Chris can't call his parents," Luna informs. "Chris didn't tell them he was having dinner with us. His mom will be furious, probably ground him when she finds out he is here."

"What a pain in my ass these people are." The Andersons have yet to teach their only child how to drive, holding back the rite of passage until they decide their son is mature enough to be behind the wheel of a car.

"If Juniper is too sick, then you drive him."

"But I don't have my license yet," Luna reminds.

"You're a good driver. What difference does a couple of months make?"

"If you think it will be okay," Luna agrees, then adds, "but I haven't driven at night yet."

"It's just like driving during the day. Go slow, though; don't draw attention to yourself."

Cherri looks to her guardian spirit, imploring for a stop in the review. Cherri's heart is breaking all over again.

She feels Luna's insecurities, Luna's whole body filling with tension at hearing her mother's solution to the evening's problem. Luna's last few moments are spent in agonizing panic about committing an act she knows is wrong, yet Luna is unwilling to defy her mother's directive because she is such a good girl. Cherri is responsible for Luna's apprehension, for her fear.

"Luna is fine," Cherri's guardian spirit reminds her. "You were just reunited."

"I know she is fine now. I know everything turned out as it should, that our lives played out as planned. Knowing how I made Luna feel, how scared she was in the moments before her death, though, is unbearable. Even more so... than knowing I was responsible for my daughter's death."

CHAPTER TWENTY-NINE

Juniper

Standing in front of the single-serve coffee maker, I chastise myself for drinking that final glass of wine Noreen left for me last night. My body feels like it has been on an all-out bender, but I don't recall drinking that much, especially given it was over a four-hour time frame.

I jump as a loud pounding noise reverberates from the hallway. The knocking grows louder and more forceful as I near the entryway.

"There you are," Roni says as I open the door to let her in. "Why aren't you answering your phone?"

After waking, I typically remove my phone from the charger and disable the 'Do Not Disturb' mode. I realize I've done neither of those this morning. My whole routine is off today. The fact that it's seven o'clock when I've ordinarily been up for an hour and a half by now might have something to do with it.

"I just got out of bed. For some strange reason, I overslept."

"Well, you did have a late night after all. You probably needed some extra sleep." Roni slides onto the barstool across the counter.

I stir a bit of cream into my coffee, take a sip, and turn to face Roni. "What are you talking about? I had some wine with

Noreen, walked Boswell, read for a bit, then called it a night. I couldn't have gotten to bed any later than ten-thirty."

"Seriously, Mom?"

"Seriously, Mom—what?" I step around the counter and take the other barstool as Roni stands to make herself some coffee. "Sorry, honey, I should've offered to make you a cup. I'm not quite all here this morning."

"We've established that already."

"Why are you being so snarky?" I take a big sip of coffee, eager to get the caffeine pumping through my veins. I close my eyes, swallowing the hot gulp, mentally kicking myself for doing something I know is careless, feeling the heat trail painfully down the length of my esophagus.

"Because you kept me up half the night."

"I didn't even see you last night." I sip with caution and ask. "Are you feeling okay, honey?"

Roni pulls her cup from under the machine and blows over the top of her coffee mug. "I really don't feel like getting into this with you right now, but fuck, Mom. Like really? You really don't remember seeing me last night?"

"What are you talking about, Roni? I didn't see you last night. I haven't seen you since Monday afternoon when you dropped by to return the phone charger you borrowed."

"Mom, you called me at eleven-thirty, begging me to come down here because you had something to tell me. You said it couldn't wait."

"I called you last night? At eleven-thirty? No." There's no way I did that. I would remember if I did that. Wouldn't I? What if I did? What does that mean? Now I'm sleepwalking? Or, am I really losing my mind? "Is this a joke? If it is, it isn't funny, Roni."

"No, Mom, it's not funny. It wasn't funny last night, either. You were going on and on…"

"About what?" I ask, not giving her time to finish her sentence. I need to get to the bottom of this. Did I really lose entire chunks of an evening? It can't be the wine; I didn't drink that much.

Roni sits motionless, watching my face, my movements, studying me—I find it incredibly unnerving.

"Please don't look at me like that. Just tell me. What do you think happened?" I ask, focusing on keeping the tremor out of my words.

Roni twists the stool so her body faces me. "Like I said, you called me at eleven-thirty, pleading, '*Come see me.*' You said you had something important to tell me. I tried reasoning with you— that it could wait until morning—but you were adamant."

She pauses, crosses her arms over her middle, then continues. "The only way I could appease you was to agree to come. You even insisted I stay on the phone until I got here, which you know is impossible, since reception cuts out in the elevators. When I arrived, you were at the door, about to come to my apartment because I hadn't answered when you tried to call me back."

"Well, what was it?"

"What was what?"

"What was so imperative for you to know that I couldn't wait to tell you?"

"That's exactly what I asked you when I got you settled back inside the apartment, but you couldn't remember."

"I called you down here in the middle of the night and then couldn't recall what I needed to tell you?" A squeak escapes, accenting the need to know certainties. I find this all difficult to believe. I find it hard to breathe. I find it impossible to keep the tears from rolling down my cheek.

"Mom. Don't."

I shake my head, turn my face away from her. Determined not to give in to self-pity, I draw a deep breath and bring my gaze to view Roni's. "So that was it? Nothing else happened?"

"No. I mean, yes. You finally remembered what it was as I put you into bed."

"You put me into bed? Jesus." That does it. This was not an overconsumption incident. "First, you took care of your grandmother, and now, you're burdened to do the same with me? I won't put you through that, Roni. It's not fair to you."

"Mom. Don't."

Roni continuously tries to ease the fear I carry—of losing my mind, becoming the invalid Cherri never knew she'd become. She has tried to convince me that my fears are unfounded. *'It's only peri-menopause, it's only stress,'* she claims. But after what she witnessed last night, Roni must be drawing the same conclusion I am. Roni's so strong, so committed to her family. The exhaustion, the toll this is taking—I can see it all in her eyes, etched in her features.

"So, what was it? What did I finally remember to tell you?" I sit straighter, pulling my spine to rest against the back of the barstool. Reaching for my coffee, steeling myself, preparing for what comes next.

"It was about Luna. About Chris, my father. About ghosts haunting you, being in the apartment with you." Roni stops. Her eyes search my face for signs of recall, or perhaps, the inability to handle this conversation.

"You said it was your fault—that the reason they died was because of you. You said that you killed your sister and my father."

CHAPTER THIRTY

Guess Who

WHAT THE FUCK, man? Where is this fucking elevator? I've been standing in this lobby at least five minutes, waiting for one of the two resident elevators. Movers shut down the service elevator, so I have no choice but to wait or climb twenty flights of fucking stairs. Once I get in an elevator, it's a different story.

After each elevator inspection, I have to tweak my program, but it's worth it to be able to control how fast, how slow, to be able to expedite the ride if needed—nothing but another computer to hack. Now, if I could figure out how to control it from outside the elevator box. Then I wouldn't have to wait, and I don't like to wait, especially not after the morning I've had.

Facing the elevators, my back is to the concierge desk. I hear the girl behind the desk speak to someone who has entered the building. A woman replies. The click-clack of dog paws approaches. I slip the headphone buds hanging around my neck into my ears. No way I'm doing the polite chit-chat thing right now.

I look at the phone in my hand, think about finding some music to pipe through the headphones, but I'm not in the mood for that either. This day can't get much worse, but I'm sure as shit not going to chance it by striking up a conversation with whoever stands behind me. First, parking patrol issues me a citation right as the damn meter ticks over expired, and then I run straight into the chick I slept with last week, who happens to be on the arm of a guy from my office, a coworker. Fucking females. That bitch acted like she didn't even know me. Fine. I like her boyfriend. Nice guy. Hate thinking I did that to him.

I turn my head, pretend to be searching for something in the mail hub area so I can get a look at the woman behind me. Out of the corner of my eye, I see her. Looks like she finished a workout then took her dog for a walk. I've seen her in the gym. Multiple times, actually. Juniper. She's in good shape and should be for all the time she spends in that gym. Even if I hadn't seen Juniper around—or know what I've personally ascertained about her—Roni has made sure to inform all the renters in the building about her mother's state of mind. Telling everyone *Juniper is fragile right now, treat her with 'kid gloves'*, saying we shouldn't be upset if Juniper doesn't remember who we are.

Finally. The door of the left elevator slides open. I move fast, but have to wait while at least six people file out of that damn box.

Once they clear, I move inside, push twenty, and lean against the back panel. I tap into the app on my phone, which I use to control the elevator's speed, as Juniper steps inside.

She moves to stand in the opposite corner, then asks, "Do you mind hitting seven for me?"

I pretend I don't hear her 'cause I'm supposed to be listening to something come through the headphones, and I'm not engaging with this woman. Number one, I don't feel like it. Number two, God only knows what I'd let slip, knowing as much as I do about Juniper Walder.

She gets the point and reaches over to hit the button for her floor. The doors begin to slide. Suddenly, a big brown hand breaks the plane, causing the door to open once more. Good God, man. I just want to get to my apartment.

The doors open, allowing the owner of the hand to step inside the box. I've seen this guy before, but not around here. I had no idea he lived here. Juniper and the man exchange tense glances. Not sure what that's about, but the two don't seem friendly. The man punches eighteen and situates himself in the center of the elevator, between Juniper and me.

The doors shut without any other passengers piling on. I tap a couple of connections on my app as we take off. Think I'll slow this ride down a bit. Yeah, I'm anxious to get home, but I want to see what happens with these two.

Out of the corner of my eye, I see Juniper eyeballing the man. It isn't a flirty affair. It's the squinty look women give men when they're pissed. I look up from my phone to the display above the elevator doors. We haven't registered the second floor yet. Head down, using peripheral vision, I check to see if either of them notices the slow crawl upward. Neither seems concerned nor even notices that the elevator's progress barely registers as movement.

Juniper leans toward the man, speaking in a low voice she doesn't think I can hear. "What are you doing, Alok?"

Ah, this is the husband. I've heard her mention his name. Weird. I saw him with someone else the other day. Maybe they weren't involved, but their discussion did look intense.

"Riding the elevator to my apartment—same as you."

I catch the guy glance my way to see if I am listening.

"Don't be coy with me, Alok. It was a rhetorical question, asshole."

"So, if I'm supposed to read your mind, can you at least give me a hint? Is this about something I was doing before or after our house almost burned down—right around the same time you were spotted snooping through the neighborhood, interestingly enough."

What the hell? Did he just accuse her of arson? Dude…

"Are you kidding me? You think I had something to do with the house fire?" she asks.

I decide to buy some more time and stop the elevator on the third floor. The two of them hush until they understand that no one waits to get on with us. As soon as the doors shut, though, she's laying into him again.

"You might want to check with that floozy I saw going around the back of the house the day I was *supposedly* snooping around my *own* neighborhood. And, oh, by the way, that woman looked a lot like the woman I caught you with in our bed."

Oh shit, did you cheat on her, dude?

"Juniper, you're losing it. You know I didn't cheat on you, so now you're conjuring up another woman sneaking around our house? I've tried to be patient with you, but this is ridiculous."

Now he's calling her crazy?

"You're smooth, Alok. I'll give you that. You almost had me; I almost forgot what I started with the *mastermind of deflection*. You never answered my question."

I need to stop this ride again.

The two of them keep going this time, unconcerned if someone else might be getting on the elevator, which, of course, no one does.

"Great, and what is that I'm deflecting, Juniper? You mean the question of 'what am I doing?' I'm fairly certain I asked you to clarify your question so I could provide an answer. It's difficult to answer a question when I have no idea what you're talking about."

At the risk of getting caught up in this, I take a chance and glance up at the floor count display. They don't even notice we've basically stalled out between the fourth and fifth floors.

"I'm talking about the city, Alok. I'm talking about the security contract the mayor jerked away from you. What kind of game are you playing? A few strokes on the keyboard, and you're going to show him. Shut down this. Shut down that. You need to realize other people are being hurt because of this vendetta you're pursuing."

That's where I saw him, at the Cyber Cafe. Every hacker in town knows the wi-fi in that joint is super encrypted. Yeah, I remember him because it's mostly just us regulars in there. It's the kind of place where there's this unspoken code—you didn't see me, I didn't see you. What stood out about him wasn't that he was the new guy in the room but that the guy actually held a meeting there. None of us ever talks to anyone else when we're there. You want coffee and chit-chat, you go to Johan's.

"You have truly lost it. I think you might need a doctor, Juniper."

"And I saw you with Steven. I know who he is. Steven may work for this new security company, but I know he used to work for your company. The two of y'all were looking awfully chummy the other night. What is he—like your inside source or something?"

What the fuck is she talking about? I gotta give it to this guy, Alok. Juniper does sound like a wack-a-doodle.

"I have no idea what you're implying, Juniper. Steven's a good guy. I always liked him. I'm not going to hold a grudge against the man because he's working for the competition. Steven has a family to take care of."

"Well, the mayor has a city to take care of."

"Yeah, and he's doing a piss-poor job."

"So you've decided to show the residents of the city how inept he is? It isn't your place to do that, Alok."

"This conspiracy theorizing seems to be taking a toll on you, Juniper. Seriously, though, you look tired. Is everything okay?"

"Gee, thanks. Your sincere concern is touching."

Damn, Juniper. The man seems genuinely concerned, and you keep on doling out sarcasm. I check on the progress of the elevator. It's creeping towards five right now. Let's stop this thing one more time. I keep my focus on the phone in my hand so as not to draw attention to myself or the slow ascent.

"I'm only inquiring as to how you're doing, Juniper?" Alok reaches down to pet the dog. "Shoot me for caring about you."

"If you must know, I didn't sleep well last night. Roni and I were up late."

"How is Roni—she doing all right?"

What's really crazy is how different Roni and her mother are. They don't look alike. They don't act alike.

"You don't get to pretend you care, Alok. You gave away that privilege when you slept with that tramp."

She's stuck on that idea, dude. If you did it, you might as well own up to it. I think it's time I put this guy out of his misery. I tap a few times on my phone, and the elevator lands on the seventh floor. The doors slide open.

"Juniper, for God's sake. How many…"

"Whatever, Alok." Juniper tugs the dog out of the elevator.

As the doors close, Alok leans back on the rail that runs the perimeter of the box. Through a side glance, I see his chest fill with air, head shaking from side to side as he drops his eyes to the floor.

A couple more taps around the app on my phone, and I send us racing upward, leaving the lunatic behind.

My good deed for the day is done. You're welcome, dude.

CHAPTER THIRTY-ONE

TODAY, I will give her something. Donna wants more, and so I will tell her what she wants to hear—actually, I should say, what *I* want her to hear. As a peer psychologist, I am aware of the information Donna needs to ascertain before moving forward with my case, and so, my intentions are to cooperate.

I've had some time to think and have realized that I may not want to—and I certainly will not enjoy doing it—but the sooner I tell Donna what she is waiting for me to say, the sooner we can move on from this ridiculous charade.

Rounding the corner of the hallway then stepping through the threshold, I see Donna sitting there, punctual for a second time. Seems I may have made an impression on her with regard to promptness. Then, as I enter, I understand she will not be bothered to acknowledge me. It seems I didn't get through to her on that point. Dense, rude, disrespectful, fucking Donna. Why change now? Right as I decide to play nice with you, Donna, you can't even be bothered to recognize my presence.

I plop down into the chair across from her, mulling the situation, waiting for her to take notice of another being in the room, doing what I can to cool the flush climbing my neck, trying to slow the furious pounding inside my chest. And yet, time ticks away—precious minutes I need to be using to get this inquisition checked off the list of things I must accomplish so that my life might return to normal.

The overhead fluorescent bulbs burn bright and loud—the buzz an annoying reminder that the spotlight is on me again. As much as I am ready to get this over with, I can't hurdle the unease I have for being the one analyzed instead of the one analyzing. Breathe. Relax your muscles. You're better than the woman across from you, I coax myself. This has to be done—and done properly.

As if she's just caught sight of me, Donna looks up from the notepad she's been scratching away on.

"Oh, Roni. Forgive me. I didn't hear you come in."

The startled act she delivers is convincing. She's either truly dense or a fabulous actor. It is difficult to give any type of accolade to this woman, though, so I'll simply go with dense. Besides, I am all too familiar with this game and shall happily take her down at it.

"You seemed so engrossed in your work, I didn't want to disturb you." Though I would have if much more time had passed.

"That was very thoughtful of you, Roni."

Is this woman patronizing me? She's patronizing me. My blood heats. I breathe.

"So, let's look at where we left off." Donna flips through her notepad, searching, unprepared—like I said, disrespectful and rude, condescending. Never have I had such a lack of respect for a patient.

"Actually, I'd like to speak about a question you posed last session. One that, at the time, I wasn't ready to discuss."

Donna eyes me over the top of her reading glasses, eyebrows rising into her hairline. "Yes, yes. Of course." She smooths the papers on her lap, resting her pen on the pad. "So, what is it you want to talk about today?"

"Hannah."

Look at the gleam in Donna's eyes. She thinks she's getting

somewhere. "By all means, please share as you feel comfortable."

I clasp hands in my lap, lowering my gaze. "When I met Hannah, my whole life changed." I look up at Donna, an action I hope will be seen as genuine. "I know—I mean, I get—how theatrical that sounds, but in this case, there is no other way to express it. My life changed forever when I met her, and in so many more ways than just the one."

"Would you like to expand on some of those ways?"

Oh my God. Does this woman need to hear herself speak? Donna should not be interrupting me right now. Clients have a tendency to shut down when interrupted. Lucky for Dense Donna, I have an agenda I intend to keep today.

"I do," I answer. I draw in a deep, dramatic breath and continue. "First off, I didn't believe in love—never have, never thought I ever would. I thought it was just something people said to one another, about one another, but I didn't think it was real. That's not to say I thought they were lying—only that they were under some societal pressure to buy into the emotion."

"But you loved Cherri; therefore, you had experienced the emotion firsthand," Donna states, tilting her head to the side in question.

Does this woman have any clue what she is doing? I want to scream at her—shut the fuck up, Donna! Try listening for a change. Instead, I answer her.

"Yes, I did. But that was different. Cherri was my grandmother, my family. You *have* to love family."

"Did you, *do you*, love your mother? Do you love Juniper?"

Donna is trying to steer me back to the end of our last session. This is what Donna wants, what she has planned for our session today. Breaking news, Donna, this is my time, and I will not let you hijack this discussion. We will talk about what I want to talk about, not what Donna wants, and I'm not ready to expand on that subject yet. I choke back the anger and continue.

"Love was different with Hannah is what I am trying to say.

It was so… all-encompassing. Once I felt love for Hannah, I couldn't *unfeel* it, and I didn't want to lose it. The very thought of losing her hurt beyond any pain I'd ever experienced. But the most wondrous part was that Hannah loved me back. Until that point, I wasn't even sure I was lovable. You've read the file; you know what a bad kid I was. I still find it hard to believe Cherri could love me after all I put her through."

"How did you come to make the decision not to tell Juniper about Hannah?"

Christ. Seriously? Again? This woman. "I wasn't ready, okay. Now, can I finish?" The loss of control is unprofessional, but Donna, dense, or dumb, or dimwitted, is responsible for my inability to control my impulses.

"I apologize. Take your time, Roni. It's important we go at your speed." Finally, Donna says something intelligent.

I take a moment, letting Donna sweat—wondering will she or won't she continue now—before I start again. I decide maybe Donna is right. Maybe I'll move forward with some of the reasons I didn't disclose my relationship with Hannah.

"If I told my family about Hannah, they would have insisted on meeting Hannah, then Hannah would know my handful of relatives, and like I said, I wasn't ready for that. I wasn't ready to share this wonderful woman who changed my life and the way I saw the world."

"So apprehension led you to keep Hannah's existence to yourself?"

Unh, unh, unh. Donna is trying to pivot again. Not happening.

"I suppose you might call it fear. Fear that if Hannah knew the truth about my family, it would scare her away. She wouldn't love me anymore, and I couldn't have that happen. As you and I have discussed in previous sessions, our small clan is not normal. I wasn't ready for Hannah to know about them, about our history. Hannah's family was solid, boringly predictable. Mother, father, only child—stable contributors to society, well respected among their community—everything the Walder women were not.

"It was a fluke that Hannah and I even met, or maybe a twist of fate. Straightaway, though, I knew our relationship would be difficult. The more I thought, the more the reasons mounted as to why a relationship between the two of us would never work. I actually tried to convince Hannah that we had to stop whatever it was we were doing, that we needed to end whatever it was that we were beginning. Because eventually, we would end up having to break things off. But Hannah was more optimistic, determined that we would find a way—that's how much she loved me, wanted to be with me."

"And you wanted it too?"

I nod, blinking away the sting of threatening tears. In no situation will I display the clichéd emotional reaction for Donna's voyeuristic pleasure. Instead, I focus on the happy occasions Hannah and I spent together.

Hannah made me feel special, adored. I was never one for public displays of affection, but with Hannah, my inhibitions took leave. When I was with her, no matter what circumstances we were in the midst of, it seemed as if it was just the two of us. I recall the day I became cognizant of my open, outward exhibitions of emotion for her.

We had decided to spend some time at the pool, Hannah's idea. We were not the only ones seeking out a cool swim. There wasn't a sun chaise left to share, but the pergola-covered sofa was open for use. We claimed the space, leaving our towels and bags to mark our place while we swam. We lolled along the edge of the pool, sharing how much we enjoyed being together, tossing out dreams of living in the same city, perhaps under the same roof. Were we ready for that? Ready or not, we both wanted it.

Waterlogged and sun-tinged, we returned to the sofa to dry off and relax. Hannah stretched out along the longer segment of the L-shaped sectional while I took the shorter leg. To my surprise, Hannah lay her head in my lap, unconcerned with what anyone else around the pool deck thought of the two of us.

It wasn't that I was ashamed of my sexuality or cared what anyone thought about my orientation. I know I am exactly who I should be, who I want to be. Outsiders witnessing our private moments and affection for one another was what I had an issue with. But with Hannah's head in my lap, her gaze on me, her fingertips trailing my arm in an easy back and forth motion, I could give two fucks what anyone else thought of us. All I could think of was Hannah.

My throat thickens with emotion. I miss her.

Donna readjusts her seated position, uncrosses then recrosses her legs. She's growing restless, unable to interpret my reverie, and I will not be sharing those thoughts with her. After what she considers a reasonable amount of time, Donna inquires. "Did you tell Cherri about Hannah?"

"I tried. I wanted to share my happiness with someone, but it wasn't the right time to bring an outsider into the family. With Cherri, though… I decided it was safe to tell her. For one, Cherri couldn't put together a string of words to form a coherent sentence, even if she did recall what I told her. Moreover, Cherri understood the importance of a secret, and better yet, how to keep one."

Donna tilts her head to one side, seemingly her signature, *see how well I listen posture.* "So Cherri did understand you had found love, you think?"

Pulling my spine straighter against the back of the chair, pressing my forearms against the chair arms, fingertips numbing under my grip, I buy a bit of time to determine how far I want to go with this revelation.

"The way Cherri's eyes shone, I believe I got through to her, although Cherri's utterances on the matter were unclear." I release my grip on the chair arms, folding my hands in my lap, and add, "It was just the same old ramblings if I'm honest with myself." Hearing the words fall from my mouth, I feel my chest seize, air no longer flowing in and out of my lungs.

Calm down. You have the control.

"So, you're saying Cherri was prone to prattle, or is it that there was more to these 'same old ramblings' as you call them?"

"I've told you—and, in no uncertain terms, I might add—of Cherri's alcohol addiction. You may not be aware, but alcoholics are prone to babble, even spew drunken tirades on occasion."

Donna is losing patience. I can see it in her facial expressions. She wipes all signs of frustration from view and tries again.

"How do you feel about continuing our discussion regarding Hannah?"

I really don't want Donna to know anything more about Hannah, but that was my intention for this session. I need Donna to check off on this portion of the interview so we can move on, so I can finally be done with these mandated sessions. When I resolved to go through with this, however, I didn't understand how painful it would be to talk about Hannah. I miss her so much more than I thought.

"I'm not sure what else you want to know about Hannah, but sure, okay. Let's get this done."

Donna sits across from me, studying my expression, twirling the pen between her fingers. "You said that, unlike you, Hannah had a normal"—she flips through the pages of her pad—"boringly predictable family life. But that's not entirely true, is it?"

This bitch. It takes all the constraint I can muster not to jump out of my seat, to hold my tongue behind clenched teeth, not to tell Donna what I really think about her. She wants everything her way! Donna is going to make me say it.

"I never met Hannah's family."

"I understand that, and I am aware Hannah's family has all passed on. That is not what I asked, though, is it?"

I close my eyes, shake my head. Fucking bitch. She wins.

"Hannah was just as fucked up as I was because Hannah was part of our family."

JUNIPER STEPS through the entrance of her apartment. Dancing. She's dancing? Again? Why? What's happened to put her in such a celebratory mood? What the hell is going on?

It's been a couple of days since I've actually had a chance to check in on her. That has to change. I must make time for this project because *time* is running out.

Judging by her appearance, Juniper came from the gym—water, workout attire, towel. A few strokes on the computer keyboard bring up the sound inside the unit. Silence. I zoom in on her face. Closer inspection reveals headphones nestled inside her ears.

Of course.

She was listening to music in the gym and now brings the dance party back to her abode. She gyrates and punches at the air, not much of a dancer. What is it they say? 'Dance like nobody's watching.' Except that around here, you never know who might be keeping tabs.

She always seems to be in a better mood after exercise, but this is different. The look she wears is pleasant, content. Juniper is pleased with herself? Is she happy? Inspection of her body language, the silent lip-syncing of the words to the song playing only for Juniper, relays a certain cheeriness in her demeanor.

Shit. I've let this go too long.

The last time I looked in on her, she was miserable, questioning her every thought, every action. Now, watching Juniper, she seems a different person. Taking in her moves from the middle of the living room floor, Boswell cocks his head to one side. He also appears to be in question about what has put Juniper in such a chipper state of mind. Juniper spins into her living room, crosses her arms at her waist, and rips off the sweaty tank top. She twirls it over her head, then flings it playfully at Boswell. What the hell? What has changed in a week's time?

Juniper reaches behind her back to unclip the sports bra as she heads to the bedroom to finish disrobing. Having no interest in witnessing the remainder of the post-workout routine, I let her be. I sit back in the chair, staring mindlessly at the computer screen, Juniper's living room still on display. Something is different about her living space.

There.

I zoom in on one of the sofa's side tables. Photographs? She's placed framed photos around her living room. Who? Who is it she wants daily visual reminders of? Expanding the camera angle reveals that the photo portrays three generations of the Walder women. The image behind it features Boswell and Dash. And who will I find in the picture across the way? I maneuver the mouse to obtain my answer. It's an older photo, grainy, looks a bit yellowed with age. Three people smile broadly for the photographer, two girls and a boy, all appearing to be in their teens. A right-click, grab, and magnification reveals one of the teens to be Juniper. Undoubtedly, the other two are the dead siblings, Luna and Dusk.

Nothing about this scene is okay. Juniper is settling into her life, accepting the upheaval of her world, and moving on.

Three clicks of the mouse and the screen darkens; I've seen enough.

I sit back in the desk chair, shoulders slouching in defeat.

Behind my forehead, the pounding grows fiercer with each thought. Then it hits me, my next move.

And, it's brilliant.

CHAPTER THIRTY-THREE

Juniper

"CALL RONI WALDER, MOBILE," I command the mobile aide feature.

The automated female voice responds, doing exactly as I ask. Why can't I have people in my life as accommodating and amenable as my vehicle's voice assistant?

As I sit inside the car, waiting for the drawbridge to lower once all boat traffic has passed through, I listen to Roni's phone ringing through the speakers.

"Hey, Mom, listen—hang on a sec. I need to finish this call I'm on. Be right back."

"O…" Is she still there? "'Kay."

Outside the passenger window, a large sailboat glides through the water toward the open bridge. Lined up and waiting to proceed are at least four more seaworthy vessels. I settle back into the bucket seat, taking advantage of the headrest. This might take a while. I could have used another grocery store that didn't involve the bridge's scheduled openings, but that store is farther distance than the one on the island of Palm Beach.

Roni must be on a work call; otherwise, she would have already clicked back to answer me. Any other time, I would disconnect and let her work. Today, I have an ulterior motive.

That sounds terrible for a mother to say, but Roni has never really treated me like her mother, per se. She always put Cherri in that role. How could I argue the point? The first six years of Roni's life, I was absorbed in academia, and then the years after, in building my career. Now that Roni and I no longer have Cherri, I want Roni to come to me, to count on me to fill the void, to need me. I want to be there for her. I want my daughter to let me in on the big moments of her life, on the important people in her life.

Yes, I admit it. It has become somewhat of an obsession to learn the identity of Roni's love interest. Her happiness is important to me, and I would be honored to share it with her. This question of whether or not my own child trusts me is gnawing a terrible hole in my confidence. Roni is busy with her career and this new person. She has too much going on right now to think about where our relationship stands. As her mother, I am going to make this easier for Roni, easier for her to lean on me, trusting enough to confide in me.

"Mom? You there?"

"Hey, I'm here. Sorry to bother, I know you're busy, but I just left the grocery store and picked up those items you said you needed. I am on my way home now. Are you in your apartment? I can drop them off for you."

"No. I'm on the road again, headed to another facility."

"I could get the office, or Martin the maintenance guy, to let me into your unit and put them away for you if you like."

"No," she snaps, then more calmly, "No. I mean, there's no need to go through all that and bother Martin. Just stick the stuff in your fridge—I'll grab them on my way in from work later."

Shuffling multiple bags to hang on one arm, I slip the key into the lock and dislodge the deadbolt. Boswell's snout appears through the crack of the door I prop open with my foot. Pushing forward, stepping through the threshold, Boswell dances at my feet, circling, twirling as I make my way down the hall.

"Boswell, what has gotten into you, silly boy? I wasn't even gone that long." I drop the bags onto the counter and bend to scratch under his ears to reassure him.

Pulling myself upright, I work to put away the grocery items, placing Roni's things to the side for easy transfer once she gets home from work. Boswell stays close at my heels, still out of sorts. This transition must be getting to him. Thinking on it, he was never left alone before. Boswell always had his buddy Dash to hang out with when Alok and I were away from the house. Maybe that's the issue—Boz is anxious about being home alone and missing his friend. Would Alok object to letting Dash visit my sweet little guy?

Before I can talk myself out of the idea, I reach for my handbag to retrieve my phone. From the dark confines, I pull it free and walk across the room to take a seat on the sofa, tapping into the messaging app and locating Alok's contact.

Composing what I think to be a *non-solicitous* invitation for Dash's (and only Dash's) company, I glance across the way to get a glimpse of Boswell before re-reading the message. Boswell lies in the middle of the floor, his head between his paws, looking lonely and dejected.

Even though the message reads to the point, frank, and distinct, something about reaching out to Alok feels wrong. It's Roni. I know she won't approve. Roni would be disappointed in me if she knew I was voluntarily contacting a man who had the gall to cheat on me in our house, in our bed. *How pathetic is that, Mom? Have more self-respect for yourself.* I can hear her; she's right. I need to be stronger.

But I am being stronger, though perhaps not in the specific manner Roni would prefer. Would Roni approve of my decision to learn how to stand up for myself, to protect myself? I've wanted to tell her, and it's not that I am withholding this information from Roni. But honestly, when have we had time for a proper discussion on the matter? We can't have a two-minute phone chat without Roni pushing me off to her hold button.

Taking in a deep draw of air, I sink back into the sofa, head falling back into the cushions. Thumb on the screen of my phone, I delete letter by letter the carefully composed message for Alok.

"Come here, Boswell. Come see me." His eyes flick in my direction, then back to the floor in front of his snout. My dog clearly has no intention of allowing me to soothe him. If I reach out to Alok about Dash, Roni will be mad. If I don't make an attempt to organize a playdate with Dash, Boswell will continue to mope.

Huffing in frustration, my gaze falls to the photo frame on the end table across the room. What? Wait—I didn't… Did I? No. I know I didn't.

From the depths of the sofa cushions, I push myself upright. My head spins with the abrupt movement, my balance unsteady as I stand. Gripping the edge of the sofa, I make my way over to inspect the frame more closely.

This picture was not placed here. I remember. I remember that I put this particular photograph on the climbing shelf in the hallway. Clutching the frame to my chest, I hurry to the hall. The shelf has been rearranged.

"What? How did…?" The unsteadiness has made its way to my voice. My head shakes slowly in the motion of no—no, this is not right. All of the photos I set out so meticulously have been repositioned.

I may have forgotten a few things recently, but I didn't do this. Time and careful consideration were put into the placement of these photographs. They were color-coordinated. I recall doing it—how long the activity took me to complete. I must have moved them five times before settling on the arrangement and placement of the photos.

Roni. Could she have come along and rearranged them to her liking? No. Roni hasn't been in the apartment since I decided to put out the family photos; she doesn't have access. I tried to convince her we should swap extra keys for emergencies, but Roni insisted it wasn't necessary.

The pressure in my chest builds. Is it fear? Fear of what? Myself? Or is it that someone has been inside my apartment? That someone has been in my personal space? Chills race over my arms, up my spine. Could someone still be here? Head flipping left then right, lack of air making it into my lungs, my vision begins to fade from the sides.

No.

Stop.

There is no one here. If an intruder were in the apartment, Boswell would surely have alerted me to their whereabouts. Wouldn't he? I force oxygen down my throat once, twice, three times. But what else is wrong? Has anything else been tampered with?

I rush through the rooms, checking each one for signs that my items have been altered in some way or other. Along the way, I check that the doors are locked securely—no way for a trespasser to enter. Each room, each space appears the same. Nothing out of place, everything as I left it before I went to the store.

Everything except the picture frames.

I return to the hallway to examine the shelf again, looking for some clue that I could have done this, rather than an intruder going through my personal things. Boswell stays close on my heels, circling in the manner he did when I arrived home. His head nudges my shins, pushing, prodding. I can't tell what he's doing. Is he trying to alert me?

I bend, taking Boswell's head into my hands, looking into his eyes. "Did a stranger come in here, Bozi? Are you trying to tell me about it?"

Boswell watches me intently. Vision blurring with welling tears, I slide down along the wall to sit on the floor of the hallway. Boswell hops onto my lap. What if Boswell had been hurt? I don't think I could handle it if something happened to my sweet boy right now.

Boswell and I camp out in the hallway. Relishing the attention of his favorite human, Boswell calms as if nothing ever happened. Did I read the situation wrong? Was Boswell upset by the presence of an intruder, or was he reacting to me and my apprehension of something I fabricated?

The confidence, the certainty of my actions, wanes. All doors proved secure, nothing else out of place or missing. No one else has a key to the apartment, and not since the leak under the sink have I requested maintenance to enter for any services. Is it possible that at some point, I rearranged the frames? I must have. It's the only plausible explanation.

Still, I can be so absurdly conscientious about positioning my things. I've always been that way. But then again, I haven't felt like myself lately either. Through my nose, I inhale deeply, an attempt to calm nerves, to accept culpability for actions I seemingly buried in my mind. Again.

Inner interrogations and suspicions, making excuses, concessions, time stolen—I no longer know what to believe anymore. Is it all in my head? Is someone trying to tell me something? Or is someone interfering with my sanity?

I don't have the answers. However, I can claim I've been proactive—taking precautions for my own safety now that I am forced to live alone as a single woman. Yes, I should be proud of myself. Cherri would be proud of my initiative—of stepping up to take control, whether this is all in my head or really, frighteningly happening. And though she may not like that I acted without discussing it first, Roni will eventually approve—and be proud, too.

One thing I know for sure—if I sit here much longer, I am going to be late for my next lesson.

JUNIPER EASES her car out of The Grabell's parking garage and pulls into traffic, signaling a right onto Fern Street. Keeping up with her lately has proved difficult. She just disappears with no indication of where she is going. I've searched her calendar, checked her phone log, combed the search history on her computer. But today, I'm going to figure this out.

As the cameras rolled live feed, I watched her charge through the apartment, checking doors were locked, dark closets void of intruders. The placement of the photographs—that's what sent her deliriously darting from one displayed frame to another.

For a good twenty minutes, she sat in her hallway, confusion clouding her features. While I could see her lips move and hear a mumble as she talked to herself, I, unfortunately, couldn't make out any of what she said. Was it mad mumbo jumbo, or is she coming to a more indisputable understanding of what is really happening to her?

From the observer's perspective, Juniper seemed to have come to some sort of conclusion. She jumped from her seated position next to the climbing shelf, startled Boswell out of sleep, hurried straight to her handbag, checked the contents, then ran out of her apartment door.

It's a risky undertaking, but I have to figure out what

Juniper's doing when she disappears without notice. This is the first time I've followed her, and I remind myself to keep a safe distance. Onto Australian, then to Southern Boulevard, Juniper weaves in and around other cars. Her driving is reckless and out of character for a woman who's so careful and meticulous in her actions.

Where is she going, and why the urgency? Is Juniper on her way to Wellington again? When I checked her calendar app earlier this morning, I didn't find any scheduled appointments for this afternoon.

Four cars back, I maneuver through the intersection for the Florida Turnpike and see Juniper signal a right-hand turn ahead. STRAIGHT SHOT, a gun range and weapons store, reads the sign rising above the establishment's entrance.

The gun. I thought she got rid of that thing. What is she doing?

While the gun made her visibly squeamish the day she found it, Juniper displays no qualms about firearms now. No hesitation whatsoever, she hops out of the car, hiking her purse high on her shoulder, and zips through the front door of this store specializing in weapons. I wait until she enters the store, then step out of my car. I can't afford for Juniper to see me, to recognize me.

Scanning the inside layout through the glass door, I spot her at the back counter, waiting in line to speak with the attendant posted there. Her attention diverted for the moment, I slip through the entrance, checking left and right. The store is set up in a series of low-rise rows, housing a variety of weapon-related products. I dart around to an aisle a good distance away from where Juniper waits for the man in front of her to finish up with the store clerk.

A woman moves to stand behind Juniper and taps her shoulder. The two exchange words casually as they await their turns with the clerk. I watch the pair chit-chat as I pretend to study gun safes on the shelf in front of me. Does Juniper know this woman, or are they making polite conversation?

The man steps away, and it's Juniper's turn to carry the clerk's attention. She speaks. Her request spurs the attendant to pull a clipboard from the wall behind him. He flips through some papers, ticks something on the page, and asks Juniper a question I can't make out. Juniper responds, shaking her head in a no fashion, then reaches inside her handbag and pulls out the gun. No hemming or hawing, so self-assured, Juniper checks the safety and the cartridge chamber, then places it on the counter-top. The attendant picks up the weapon, turns it over in his hand, and sets it to the side. He reaches under the counter, pulling out what looks to be a box of ammunition, then moves to the register on his right.

Behind me, a voice booms, startling me from the concentrated observation activity.

"Finding everything okay, here? Something I can help with?"

The sales associate is young, tall, and lanky. A large, angry pimple marks the center of his chin. He barely looks old enough to drive, much less handle guns. The name badge pinned to his red vest announces his name is Peter.

Stuffing my hands into my pants pockets, I turn back toward the shelf housing the handgun lock boxes. "I was just checking out the safes. Thinking about getting a gun, and I want to make sure I have somewhere to keep it out of a child's reach," I relay. It's the first thing that comes to mind, but it seems to make sense to the young man.

"Can't ever be too careful," Peter agrees.

"Hmmm," I mutter, studying the kid in front of me, keeping an eye on Juniper at the back of the store.

"So you don't have a gun now?" Peter asks.

I look over the kid's shoulder to see Juniper heading down a long hallway behind the sales counter. Her hand goes up to wave at someone in the distance. I turn my attention back to Peter, ready to pump for information.

"No, not yet. But it I decide to go ahead with one of these

safes, do I purchase it at that back counter?" I point to the area Juniper has just vacated.

"No. Our checkout registers are at the front of the store," the young man says, turning his body to point to the sales registers.

"Oh, I thought I saw a woman purchasing ammunition at the back counter."

Peter's face lights up in understanding. "Yeah. Probably. That's where customers check in for the gun range and scheduled classes," he nods.

"Classes? You mean like to learn how to use a gun?"

"Yeah, absolutely. We always have some sort of program in place. If you're interested, I can get you a brochure, or you can check out the various class offerings on our website."

"You have classes going on back there right now?"

"Well, you'd have to register in advance. There's paperwork and all."

"Yeah, but there's a class going on now? That's where those people were going down the hall back there?" I question turning to point, to confirm, Juniper is headed for a lesson.

The kid nods, shuffling from foot to foot. He's ready to move on, and I don't want to draw any more attention to myself.

"Sorry, I was just curious."

"No need to apologize. Happy to answer any of your questions. I'm here to help." He pulls his mouth into a big goofy grin. Is this kid for real? He pulls his hands into fists at his hips authoritatively and continues, "We got a class back there getting ready to start." He nods in the direction of the hallway Juniper followed moments earlier. "It's our weekly women's group lesson."

"Group lessons?" I mumble, the understanding of Juniper's actions coming into focus.

Peter determines he needs to clarify. "Yep. We offer group and solo lessons. Either of those something you might be interested in?"

It's time to shake this kid now that I've got what I came for.

With feigned urgency, I pull my hands from my pockets, patting around to my backside, and snatch the phone from my pocket. I hold up a finger to Peter as I fake a phone tap to answer a call, then lift the device to my ear. Turning away, I pretend to be in a deep conversation. Before heading out the store's front door, I turn to Peter and wave thanks.

CHAPTER THIRTY-FIVE
Cherri

THE PORTION of her life review that Cherri had dreaded the most is complete. She effectively sentenced her daughter, Luna, to die and has had to bear the weight of her actions twice. Witnessing it during the review on the astral level proves just as difficult as it was to live through on the physical plane.

Still, Cherri knows even more of her shameful actions are yet to come—actions to which she has never given a voice, much less confessed to another soul. Her guardian spirit had informed her that all must be addressed, and thus far, she's been given no reprieve, regardless of how difficult facing her life lessons has been. Cherri has no reason to believe she will be allowed to breeze past these next acts. She has to face what she has done to those she loves, even if the effects of all her transgressions haven't yet been recognized by those they will eventually come to affect.

"This is not punishment," Cherri's guardian spirit tells her, reminding Cherri that her thoughts are not hers alone during this process. "Every soul experiences a life review upon returning to this plane."

"I realize and understand the purpose of the review, the learning garnered as such. Still, it was bad enough to have lived through some of these moments during the first go-around. I assumed that once I got through the challenges, I would be done with them, and now to have to relive them… It's hell."

"And yet, it will all be over in due time, at which point you will be prepared and more equipped to make the choices for your next lifetime, for your next life lessons."

While Cherri understands the necessity of the process, she is still reluctant. If only she had been able to remember, to recall what needed to be said when she was still part of the earth plane, then maybe this process would be easier, the guilt more bearable.

"But that is not the case, is it?" the guide asks, in reference to Cherri's unspoken thoughts.

Cherri does not reply. No answer is needed.

Knowing she must continue, Cherri turns, readying to face her past actions.

Luna is dead. Dusk is gone. It is only Juniper and Cherri now. The two are wracked with grief and disbelief. Each of them takes responsibility for Luna's untimely passing, though they never speak to one another about their culpability. It is a silent burden, heavy with shame and self-reproach, for both mother and daughter as they navigate their days.

Without the other two family members, Cherri and Juniper are but shadows of themselves. The pair tries to remain positive, maintain hope that Dusk will return home soon. But the ugly truth hangs thick and choking in each breath they take—Luna will never come back to them. Dusk doesn't even know his youngest sister has died. Maybe he is the one who is best off; surely, not knowing would be better.

Juniper continues to suffer the same sickness she had on that fated night Luna and Chris died. Juniper and Cherri both assume the grief is causing the illness to linger. But as the days roll into weeks, Cherri suspects the matter with Juniper is something else entirely.

The discussion is awkward. As Cherri witnesses the exchange, from the astral plane, between her daughter and herself, she feels Juniper's discomfort. It hadn't occurred to her on the physical plane, but now, as Cherri watches on, she wonders why she found it so difficult to talk about sex with her children. For such a free thinker and woman who had been so comfortable with her own sexuality, it is beyond Cherri's comprehension why she hadn't taught her kids more about their bodies. Nevertheless, Juniper is pregnant. Pregnant with Chris Anderson's child; Chris Anderson, who died in the passenger's seat of the car Luna illegally drove; Chris Anderson, whose parents boisterously blame the Walders for the death of their only child.

The idea of bringing a baby into the world when Cherri and Juniper are struggling simply to balance on two feet is not a thought either of them can muddle through. However, once they discover Juniper is pregnant, there isn't time to flounder in making a decision. Obviously, for Juniper to carry to term, there is no rush, but if she is going to terminate her pregnancy, she will need to do so with the utmost urgency.

Of course, the decision is never Cherri's to make, but every ounce of her is against the idea of Juniper going through with an abortion. It seems to Cherri that they are being handed a gift. Luna has been taken from them, but now they have a chance to know and foster a new life, a new chance…

For Juniper, a baby doesn't fall into her plans. Juniper has always been an organized and methodical planner, unlike her go-with-the-flow siblings. Any deviations from what Juniper has lined up wreck her disposition, overwhelming her to the point of inaction. Juniper has long planned to attend college after high school. Cherri's other two had no desire to further their educations, and Cherri wasn't one to pressure her children into doing what she envisioned. Cherri has her own life, and her children each have theirs. Juniper is determined, however, to educate herself, have a career that is fulfilling and monetarily rewarding. Yet, Juniper finds herself pregnant at sixteen, her senior year of high school still to complete. She is devastated by the thought of having to scrap all those dreams, but at the same time, Juniper can't possibly take the life of an unborn child. The decision locks Juniper down.

Cherri realizes Juniper is still a child herself. She needs guidance from a parent, but Cherri has never exercised that particular parenting technique. She believes her children need to make their own decisions, have an opportunity to make mistakes, and learn from them. For the first time in her life, Cherri steps in to handle this issue for Juniper. In addition to having just lost her sister and her boyfriend, this situation is too much for Juniper to cope with.

Witnessing this portion of her life review, Cherri experiences Juniper's relief, the gratefulness Juniper has for Cherri's help, and that her mother is there for her to lean on and get Juniper through the difficult time. Cherri now sees that it was a turning point in their mother-daughter partnership. Their relationship would have taken a much different path had Cherri not stepped in to assist her daughter. At least, Cherri has something to claim as having done right in her recent lifetime. While it pleases Cherri to have brought these feelings to Juniper, this portion of the review also proffers the insight that Cherri's other children never knew a situation in which their mother did the same for them.

Shrouded in shame, Cherri looks at her guardian spirit. Cherri's guardian gives a nod and signals for the review to continue.

Cherri understands that she will have to help Juniper lay a new plan, one that will benefit all of them, particularly the new life growing inside of Juniper. First, Juniper needs to keep her pregnancy hidden as much as possible. Of course, she won't be able to conceal her growing midsection completely, but Juniper doesn't need to tell her classmates everything going on in her life. While Juniper's condition is nothing to be ashamed of, there are those who will judge the situation unfavorably. More importantly, they must keep the gossip to a minimum.

Brunswick, Georgia, might be a bigger city than Lucedale, Mississippi, but the Andersons know everyone in Brunswick, and they cannot learn that Juniper is carrying their grandchild. Those people will make both of their lives a living hell if they know a piece of their son lives on inside Juniper.

During Juniper's first trimester, which honestly goes by quickly given that Juniper was already so far along when they learned of her pregnancy, Juniper seems to forget she is with child. Wrapped up in completing college applications, writing essays, and finishing up her coursework, Juniper has little time to dwell on the baby's inevitable arrival. But, when there is a spare moment, Juniper touches her belly and wonders how she will get through her college education while caring for an infant. Cherri knows that is her cue. During the doubting moments, Cherri jumps in immediately, soothing Juniper's nerves, offering words of reassurance.

Cherri and Juniper are a team—they are all each other has left. The two of them will get through this together, Cherri reassures Juniper. Cherri will take care of the baby while Juniper takes care of her education. Yes, they will both have to work harder than in the past, but this new little life will be worth it. Juniper believes Cherri. Everything will turn out fine. Juniper just has to lean in. With diligence, Juniper will achieve her goals and ambitions.

As the due date draws near, Cherri and Juniper's apprehension swells—Cherri about the Andersons learning of Juniper's imminent expectancy, Juniper about the uncertainty of her future. Juniper also expresses concern to Cherri that she has yet to see a doctor throughout her pregnancy. Cherri has taken charge of Juniper's healthcare, and while Juniper feels confident under her mother's careful eye, she knows most women deliver babies in a hospital under a doctor's care.

Cherri explains to Juniper that in years past, she attended more than her fair share of childbirths, assisting in more births than she could count. Back in the days when Cherri and Dennis were touring the country, doctors were not to be trusted. No one had babies in hospitals. Women helped women with the labor and delivery of their babies. None of Cherri's children were born in hospitals, and they turned out just fine.

The more prickly matter Cherri doesn't share with Juniper is the fact that they can't afford doctors and hospitals. Luna's unexpected death brought on the costs of a funeral Cherri hadn't prepared for. As it is, Cherri and Juniper barely get by day to day. Even beyond those reasonings, though, is the real reason Cherri keeps Juniper out of a doctor's office. The Andersons. The accident that killed Luna and Chris was highly publicized. There can't be a soul in the town who hasn't heard of the tragedy. The connection would easily be made, and before long, someone would inform the Andersons of Juniper's condition.

The baby comes mere days before Juniper's high school graduation ceremonies. The timing couldn't be more perfect, as Juniper, just that same morning, finished the last of her exams. On a glorious day early in June, in the basement of their rented home, Veronica Walder is born into the world. Cherri wants to name her June, but Juniper insists the name is too similar to her own.

Cherri places the baby into Juniper's arms and watches Juniper survey her perfect little girl—dark complexion, hair, and eyes; she obviously has more of her father's traits than she does of Juniper's. Cherri is witnessing the moment Juniper falls in love with her baby—a moment that will often gnaw at Cherri in the years after whenever she recalls the memory. Juniper claims she will never love anything more than her baby girl. She is more determined than ever to establish herself in a solid career so that she can give Roni everything she ever wants. But then, Juniper's resolve begins to teeter.

The problem turns out to be that Juniper loves Roni so much

she can't possibly imagine going away to school and leaving her baby behind as she and Cherri have planned. She will never be able to concentrate on school if she is missing and worrying about Roni.

Cherri can't let that happen. Juniper can't give up her dreams. Too many plans have been made, too much time invested. Juniper worked hard to earn a full scholarship at Stetson University in DeLand, Florida. She has always been determined to have a real job in a real office, not slog her way through life slinging drinks and burgers like Cherri has done. And Cherri wants this for her daughter. Sweet Luna is gone. Dusk has deserted them. Cherri will help Juniper get what she wants.

Moreover, Cherri can't let Juniper raise Roni in Brunswick. Throughout her pregnancy, Juniper floated the idea of perhaps letting the Andersons know about the baby rather than trying to hide it. Juniper reasoned the baby wasn't going to have much family. How bad could it be for the child to have Chris's side of the family for support? Cherri knows what the Andersons are capable of, even if Juniper is too young and naive to understand. If they find out Juniper gave birth to Chris's child, they will never allow her to be Roni's mother. The couple has clout and status in the community. Chris's father is Judge Anderson— Superior Court Judge Anderson, in fact—and there is not one doubt in Cherri's mind that the Andersons will take Roni away from them.

Cherri will raise Roni. Juniper is too young to be responsible for a baby and will be far too busy pursuing her degree, building her career. Cherri will find a way to convince Juniper that, in order to be the best mother to Roni she can be, Juniper needs to carry out the plans she has made.

And though Cherri has long looked forward to the years when her own children would be leaving the nest, Cherri now welcomes the idea of raising Roni. Roni is another opportunity for Cherri to get parenting right—finally.

CHAPTER THIRTY-SIX

Juniper

From a deep sleep, I jolt upright. Limbs heavy, mind stumbling over the most recent timeline I can produce. Nothing clear or forthcoming, a noise slams through the night. Crashing, tumbling—outside on the balcony—then silence, the quiet proving louder than the chaos. Adjusting my vision to the dark, I scan the room. Boswell stands by the sliding glass door, intent, concentrated. Someone is out there.

Long tentacles of fear cinch every part of my body, crushing, pushing me further into the depths of the bed as I wait for what comes next. The sound of something breaking shatters the silence of the room. Boswell uses his nose to poke at the vertical blinds.

The knocking inside my chest grows in fierce intensity. The room moves into a slow spin. I lower my eyelids to close, ease them back open, and realize I'm not breathing. Releasing the pressure from my lungs, I resolve to take control of myself, of this threatening situation, mere feet from my supposed refuge. I toss back the duvet, sliding my legs over the edge of the bed, gently placing my feet on the floor.

One foot in front of another, I move to stand at Boswell's side. Easing back one of the slats of the vertical blinds, I'm careful not to alert whoever is on the other side of the door that I'm aware of their presence. From this vantage point, I see some of the patio furniture has been displaced, a potted plant smashed in the right corner of the balcony. I shift my view to the left.

Movement. A shadow, crouching, turning, pulling up to look over the edge of the balcony wall of my next-door neighbor's porch.

My cell phone is charging on the bedside table. I twist, hurrying across the room, shin finding the corner edge of the bed. Tears spring in response as my hands catch the weight of my body on the mattress. I right my balance and push up, then continue to the charger, yank the phone free, and tap to call the local authorities.

Three rings, a beep, the noise of a fax machine. Silence. An automated voice: 'Please hang up and try your call again.'

My chest rises and falls; the actions of pulling and releasing air grow heavier and more labored with each effort.

As advised, I tap the phone frantically, trying once more to reach the police, to inform them of the intruder. It's ringing. Another crashing noise from outside. I hurry to the bedroom door, flattening myself behind the edge of the doorway. Tugging. Yanking. The intruder tests the lock of the sliding glass door. Jiggling. Jiggling. Under every inch of my skin, I feel the prick, prick of needles. Please, I beg silently. My prayer is answered. It's locked. Thank God I remembered to secure it before retiring earlier in the evening. The person on the other side pulls with more force. Is it possible for the lock to be dislodged? The question raises the hair at the back of my neck.

In my ear, the words, 'Please leave your message after the tone.'

Again, I hurry around the end of the bed, heading into the pitch-black darkness of the closet, to the furthest point in the back, crouching.

"This is Juniper Walder," I manage in a breathy whisper. I use a hand to curve over my mouth, cupping the phone's microphone to amplify the words without raising my voice. "There's an intruder on my balcony. Someone is trying to get inside my apartment." I pause, listening, wondering—is the person still out there, or have they given up and moved on? I hear nothing from outside, yet in my ear, I hear the frustrating noise of a busy signal letting me know the call has been disconnected.

"Dammit." Evidently, the demands of the hackers responsible for the ransomware attack have yet to be met. What am I going to do? Anxiety swelling, I feel the emotion well behind my eyes, threatening to break.

Where's Boswell? I step toward the closet entrance and peek around the room.

Tap, tap, tap.

The noise comes from the direction of the balcony, from the glass door.

"Boswell," I call out in a low tone. I've left him out there with a madman on the loose. "Boswell, come here, boy. Boz."

I pull upright, shoulders hunching, trying to make myself smaller. Outside, the sound of metal dragging slowly across concrete—a loud, grating, screeching noise.

"Bos...well," I choke out. I see him by the door, unmoving, watching, attention unwavering. Outside the door, it's gone quiet again.

On tiptoes, I scurry to the kitchen countertop, grab my purse, and drop into a squat on the floor, concealing myself behind the cabinetry.

Tap, tap, tap.

The racket is unnerving. I dig furiously through the bag, feeling my way to find it—the gun. I just had it at my lesson. Where is it?

Tap. Tap. Tap.

My heart races, sending hot heat coursing through my body —breaths become shallower. I dump the contents of the bag onto the floor. Wallet, hairbrush, notepad, sunglasses, keys, nail file, hand sanitizer—everything but the gun. How can it not be here? I came straight home after my lesson and haven't been out of the apartment other than to take Boswell on his nightly walk. Am I forgetting something? Did I put it somewhere for safekeeping? Think, Juniper. Think.

TAP. TAP. TAP.

Something brushes against my leg, toppling me out of the squat. It's Boswell. He's left his post at the door, sniffing, searching, wondering what I am doing sitting on the floor. Boswell moves, positioning his body next to mine, nudging for comfort, solace. We hide. We sit. We wait for what comes next.

The air hangs heavy with silence—no more clanging, breaking, scraping.

No more tapping. Is the intruder gone?

Shoulders fall, legs sprawl out in front of me. I console Boswell, letting my head rest against the back of the cabinet. Crushing fatigue settles over my body, shutting down any further action, any further fear, as the night slips peacefully into dawn.

CHAPTER THIRTY-SEVEN

Juniper

"AND THE POLICE NEVER CALLED? Never came? Is it possible you fell asleep and didn't hear them at the door?" Noreen asks.

We walk Flagler Drive, following the waterfront. Boswell takes advantage of the slow stroll, frequently stopping to sniff along the route. "I was on the kitchen floor the rest of the night. Being that close to the front door, if someone had knocked, I would have heard them."

"This cyberattack has gotten out of hand. When emergency services can't be reached… It's unacceptable. The mayor has got to do something."

While I agree with Noreen, it's difficult to give much thought to her laments at this time. My concern at the moment is who tried to break in last night and why they would want to. Was this a random act of violence or something more targeted? Without these answers, Roni won't be the only one questioning my sanity.

I nod to show agreement but push the conversation in another direction. "The balcony is a wreck. Plants busted. Dirt everywhere. Furniture flipped upside down and out of place." Overhead, the chorus of birds conversing—on the street, people heading off to careers, school, appointments. Life is happening just like any other day.

"And next door? Grant? Did he have any damage to his balcony?"

"None that I could see. I actually knocked on Grant's door this morning before I went to your place and asked him if he had heard anything last night."

"What did he say?"

"That he spent the night with a friend on the nineteenth floor." I suck in a deep breath, shaking my head in judgment of my next-door neighbor's amorous activities.

Noreen rolls her eyes. "That Grant. He certainly has a way with the ladies. I'm surprised he hasn't tried his charms on you."

"Oh, he did. I told him I'm married."

"And that worked?" Noreen asks, disbelieving.

"Ahh, you didn't let me finish. I also told him I own a gun," I say, offering a side glance and half-smile.

Noreen claps her hands, laughing. Boswell throws her a look, wondering if there's something he needs to be aware of.

"It doesn't make sense, though," I continue. "I saw the shape of the person peering over the wall at Grant's balcony. Why destroy my things? Why look over at Grant's porch and then decide, 'Nah, I don't feel like wrecking that one?'"

"Don't take this wrong, Juniper, but you sound rather blasé about this."

"Not blasé, just exhausted."

"I'm assuming you called Roni last night. She knows, right?"

"I did, but her phone just rang and rang. I didn't want to go running up there, knocking on her door in the middle of the night, knowing she has a girlfriend she doesn't feel comfortable telling me about. Anyway, Roni said that somehow or other her ringer was switched off. She saw all my missed calls and checked in on her way to work."

"Let me guess. She likes Alok for it."

I nod, confirming her assumption. "His name was the first one she tossed out. But even Roni couldn't come up with valid reasons why Alok would do something like this. He might be a cheat, but I don't think Alok would intentionally try to scare me or be destructive. It's not in Alok's nature."

"And Roni agreed?"

"About Alok, yes." I pause, thinking about how to deliver this next bit of information or even if I should.

"Spill it. What are you not saying?"

"Have you heard the story about the construction worker killed while working on our building?"

"I have. I was still working for the last Mrs. X at the time. That story was all over the news. The man fell to his death from the fifteenth floor. Such a tragedy. His poor family." Noreen quiets, then stops walking and turns to me.

"No. Really? Roni doesn't strike me as someone who gives credit to ghost stories."

"She's not, not normally," I explain. It was the only other theory Roni had after she casually wondered if perhaps I had ransacked my own balcony."

"What? Why would you do that?"

I shrug, turning to head back toward the apartment building. "Roni thought it strange no one else heard all the commotion last night, that no other tenant on the seventh floor had any damage done to their balconies, that the police never showed up after I *supposedly* called them and left a message. It sounded like Roni was suggesting I wreaked havoc on my own balcony and then forgot I had anything to do with it. And when I insisted I didn't do it, she lobbed the ghost angle."

Left to our own thoughts, we make our way back to the apartment building in silence.

Noreen stands behind me as I unlock the door of my apartment. She's offered to help me with cleaning up the balcony. While I feel terrible about accepting her help, I'm so tired and still so worked up over last night's ordeal that I'm most grateful for her aid and company.

I unleash Boswell and lead Noreen into the apartment, tossing my keys to the kitchen counter next to my handbag.

"Would you like some water?" I ask Noreen.

"Sure," she answers, walking to the sliding glass door and peering out at the mess. Noreen turns, accepting the water. "I know what Roni said, but I don't know how you could have done all that." Noreen waves her arm toward the outside area.

"I didn't. I didn't do all that," I say, thankful to have someone in my corner, someone who doesn't believe I'm losing my mind. I twist to place my glass next to the sink, then turn back to Noreen. "I'm just glad I couldn't find my gun last night. To think about what might have happened… What did I think I was going to do? Shoot someone?"

"Well, isn't that why you are taking those lessons, to learn to protect yourself?"

"Yes, but obviously, I wasn't in any danger. The intruder left without forcing their way inside the apartment."

I work on gathering trash bags, a broom, a dustpan. "Even still, I need to figure out what I've done with my weapon," I say, closing the bi-fold doors over the utility closet.

Noreen crosses the room to stand at the kitchen countertop. "Juniper, your gun is right there." Noreen points to my handbag.

"I told you, I looked all through my purse last night. My gun wasn't in there."

"Not *in* your bag, *under* your bag." Noreen lifts up my purse to reveal the handgun.

"How did that get there?" My heart begins the familiar racing pattern. I rush to the counter, pick up the gun, and inspect it. "This was not here last night. It wasn't here this morning either."

Noreen watches with concern. "Are you certain, Juniper?"

I meet her gaze, registering the doubt behind her eyes.

CHAPTER THIRTY-EIGHT

I ENTER THE ROOM, reluctantly moving toward the empty chair. Donna sits in the opposite seat, spine pulled straight, notepad on a fresh page, pen in hand, attention focused on me. The intense stare is unnerving, tracking me as I walk into the room. What the fuck has she got planned for today?

I hold Donna's gaze as I lower myself into the seat, offering a slight nod to signal that I am ready for her first move.

Twisting the pen in her hands, Donna nods in response. She has her hair pulled away from her face, strands springing free from the confines of the long, fat barrette fixed tight to the top of her head. Even from my distance, I can tell the enamel is chipped and rusting—the clip as outdated as her hairstyle.

"Hello, Roni,"

"Hello, Donna."

"How have you been?" she asks, cocking her head to one side, her signature *I'm here and listening* maneuver.

Fine. Whatever. I can give her the kudos for being on time, being prepared, being present the moment I enter the room. But, seriously? What the hell game is she playing?

"Cut the shit, Donna. Let's get on with it." I've had enough experience with hypertension to understand the sensation flooding my face denotes rising blood pressure. Calm yourself down, Roni.

"As you wish," Donna says, slipping the reading glasses to rest on the bridge of her nose. She flips through the folded pages of her notepad, perusing the scrawl made during previous meetings. I wait. I shake my head. So much for being prepared. I gave her credit before credit was due.

Donna lays the pen atop the pad, then reaches up to remove the readers, folding the frame sides into an X, tapping them against her knee.

The eye roll is an involuntary impulse, over before I realize what I am doing. Jesus. Get on with it.

"Stop the fucking theatrics, Donna. Just tell me what it is you want to talk about today. I don't have time for this crap." I uncross my ankles, set my feet flat on the floor. Lay my arms to rest on the sides of the chair. I am here and ready to do the work, but I have no intention of placating this imbecilic woman.

"Fine. Let's begin where we left off last session." Of course, that's what Donna would say. How predictable she is. It must be boring to interact so deliberately, so formulaic.

With exaggerated emphasis, I use both hands to flick the hair back from my face—she wants a show. "As you wish, Donna," I hurl her words back at her.

Donna sets the glasses on the pad. I watch them slide into her lap as she says, "Then let's begin with family."

The air in the room is heavy and stale. I glance at the thermostat on the back wall of the room. Is Donna purposely manipulating the temperature of the room? Is she trying to trigger frustration, anger? It would be completely unethical for Donna to use such a method on a patient. Come on, Roni. Really? Dense Donna? She's not particularly intelligent, or even clever for that matter. No. It's the mechanical failures of this shitty facility; it's practically falling apart. I make a mental check to control my temper, not to give in to the side effects of a hot, stifling room.

220

"Family is a subjective term, don't you think?" I'm not going to willingly hand over what she wants. Not yet.

"Hmmm," she starts. She sits attentively as if actively prodding me.

Well, Donna, you will have to work harder than that. If she wants more, she will have to ask for it.

It seems Donna gets the message as she moves to cross her legs, get more comfortable, make me feel more ingratiated toward her. "Let's expand on that," Donna encourages, twirling that damn pen again.

"Let's," I agree, shifting my posture, arranging my legs one over another, mirroring Donna's stance. "Drawing on some of my own patient interactions, I've found the definition varies greatly from subject to subject. Some patients—or rather people —define family as those related by blood, perhaps marriage, and of course, adoption. I find that the interpretation, the so-called 'traditional family,' is the more widely objective definition. Wouldn't you agree, Donna?"

Donna's mouth opens, then shuts, as I move ahead without allowing time for her response. I don't give a shit if she agrees or not.

"However, there are some who are insistent—for one reason or another, typically due to events in their past—on making their own decisions about with whom they choose to be family. Maybe they see family as those who dwell in the same abode at the same time. Perhaps it is based on good friends or mentors who bear some semblance to a parental figure—or maybe a sibling persona."

Donna sits, a glazed look sliding over her face as if this conversation has flown straight over the top of her frizzy, outdated coif. (I did say she was dense...)

"All the specifications and restrictions—it's no wonder people have such a difficult time defining family. Do you find the topic controversial with your patients as well, Donna?"

Donna ignores my ploy, instead progressing with her own agenda. "How do you define family, Roni? Do you prefer the subjective ideals, or are you more in line with the traditionalists when it comes to defining family members?"

"Oh, but we haven't finished the ways in which to define family, Donna. Do you have to love someone to consider them family? Personally, I have many acquaintances who have spoken openly about disliking family members, some even who use the word hate."

"I think we should save the classic debate of family until another time," Donna says, scooting in her chair, repositioning weight distribution from one butt cheek to the other. "I think we need to focus on your personal definition of family."

"And do you have any other 'thinks' you'd like to share, Donna?"

Donna stares, her head does that cocking to the side thing again, waiting on me to continue as if I'm some surly teenager throwing a tantrum. It's infuriating, but I won't let her know how much she pisses me off, how unprofessional and inept I find her. I've got to get through these sessions.

"Forgive me, Donna. The manner in which I interact with my patients allows them the freedom to discuss what they are comfortable with, then I ease them into the difficult subjects. I'm not in the habit of dictating a client's therapy session in such an abrupt manner as you are so prone to do."

"Am I to understand you are uncomfortable discussing your feelings and beliefs regarding the term family?"

Tongue held between my teeth, I keep my gaze even. If I speak right now, I will say something I will come to regret. And yet, she continues to badger me.

"Or is it instead that you are uncomfortable discussing your family, the feelings you harbor for your family?"

"I'm not sure what you're getting at, Donna. You asked me to define family, and I did so to the best of my ability, given the constraints of time."

"Yes, I did ask you to discuss family. More specifically, I suggested we explore your individual definition of the term."

I'm going to give her this win simply for the sake of moving on. Besides, this family bullshit is starting to bore me. "In short, I have always been somewhat of the traditional camp, although my own 'gaggle' was not conventional."

"Yet your 'gaggle', as you say, small though it may have been by contrast to other families, fit the traditional definition in some sense: mother, grandmother, step-father. Did you ever contemplate looking for other family members?"

I can't with this bitch. Eyes roll. Body posture tenses. "You know I did, Donna. You read it in the damn file. I appreciate that therapists have different styles and techniques they each prefer to draw on with their patients, but you are inconsistent, Donna. If you wish to use a direct approach, then for fuck's sake, just do it and move on."

She sits, twisting that goddamn pen, silent, judging. "Then let's proceed with the DNA test."

"What about it?"

"How did it come about?"

"You want an anecdote? Fine. Here's a little story for you to report back to the supervisors." I hold, making Donna wait, wonder—will she or won't she? When I am ready, I shift to sit straight in the chair again, bring my hands together in my lap, and begin.

"A couple of years back, our family was celebrating Christmas together. We didn't know it at the time, but that would be Cherri's last Christmas at home. We followed the tradition of opening our presents on Christmas morning. Each of us would take turns distributing the gifts we had purchased.

"Those DNA kits were all the rage that year. Everyone wanted to find their ancestral origins, maybe locate long-lost family members. Alok had gotten Juniper a kit as part of her Christmas, thinking she might like to find out about any other family members we might have. Cherri was on a rapid decline. We all knew the opportunity for her to deliver an account of our family history, to fill in the many gaps (if she even wanted to do so) had long passed. Cherri never talked about family—not her parents, her husband, or his roots, and God forbid my father's name was ever uttered. Each time I posed a question about my paternity, Cherri would shut down.

"I assumed, as Alok had, that Juniper might want to know more about our background—origins, geographical regions, that sort of thing. Maybe we would finally get a few answers about who we were and where we came from. After Juniper unwrapped her gift, she thanked Alok and set the kit aside.

"A few months later, we were all having dinner, discussing the next moves for Cherri's healthcare. I was curious if Juniper had sent off her DNA sample and, if so, when she expected the results. To my surprise, Juniper said she wasn't comfortable learning more about her familial history."

"So, just to clarify," Donna interrupts, "Alok purchased the gift, but you were the one who confronted Juniper about the results—or rather, the lack thereof?"

"Not that it is particularly pertinent to this account, but yes, that's correct."

"Was there a specific trigger that led you to broach the topic with Juniper?"

Fingernails dragging across the chalkboard, that horrendous, body-clinching screech—that is the sensation I experience listening to Donna lob out these ridiculous queries.

"Cherri's babble," I throw out, hoping to shut her up.

"Cherri's babble?" Donna scrunches her face into a question mark. "Are you comfortable elaborating on that?"

"Jesus, Donna. You know, it's important, as a therapist, that is, that you listen to your patients and what they tell you."

Donna leans forward in her chair, closing some of the distance between us. My eyes narrow in reflex to her proximity.

"Actually, Roni, I am listening," Donna says. She plunks her readers onto her face and flips back a few pages in her notepad. "During our previous session, when we discussed Cherri's babble, you said, 'Alcoholics are prone to babble, even spew drunken tirades on occasion.' What I'm trying to clarify is whether this was a drunken tirade or something more significant."

"Something more significant, *which* I would have made clear had you given me the opportunity to do so."

Donna widens the distance again, sitting back in her chair, removing her glasses. "Do you need a break, Roni? We can conclude today's session early if you are not up to finishing."

"If you're asking whether I will cooperate, Donna, the answer is yes. We both understand the urgency of conducting these sessions. However, I cannot help how infuriating you are."

Donna nods. "If you prefer a different therapist, I will seek the transfer on your behalf. Believe it or not, Roni, your well-being is my only interest here."

The blood coursing underneath my skin is near the boiling point. Concealing the long draw of air I pull through my nose, I ease my composure, regain control, show this woman she will not get the best of me. Shrouded in smugness, Donna sits, watching me, believing she has the upper hand.

"Actually, Donna, I was going to suggest at the conclusion of our time today that we consider doubling up the effort, get these sessions over with. I'm sure both of us have other things to which we'd prefer to devote our energies."

"I didn't realize that was something you'd be interested in. I've been under the impression that you are not fond of our conversations. I can certainly take a look at my schedule to see if I can make the extra time for you."

Left, right, back, I twist my head to pop my neck. Another

dramatic action? Eh, maybe. But I am trying to relieve the tension caused by this woman. "Can we get on with this?"

"Of course. Before our side conversation, you were going to clarify for me, Cherri's babble versus her drunken tirades. Somehow Cherri's babble triggered your interest in Juniper's DNA results."

"Cherri's memory was getting worse by the day, yet some of the things she said made perfect sense. With so much clarity, in fact, I would almost think the doctors had gotten the diagnosis all wrong. Cherri continued to return to one subject, though. She would say Luna's name over and over, telling me it was all her fault—whose fault, Cherri's or Luna's, I'm not sure. Cherri was never coherent enough to explain what she meant by that statement. And strange as it was, after dredging up Luna, Cherri always went into the baby rant."

"Baby? Did Cherri have another baby?" Donna flips back into her notes, shaking her head, stating, "I thought you told me Luna was your grandmother's last child. Is that correct?"

"Dusk was Juniper's older brother, and Luna her younger sister. Cherri had no other children. Sometimes, I would think she was talking about me. I was the only other baby. But then Cherri would call out for Dennis. It almost sounded like she was stuck in mid-argument—'She's your child, Dennis. They're your kids.' Then Cherri would switch directions—'She's not capable of taking care of her baby. She's mine. She's our baby.' And then she'd circle back, calling for Dennis to come home, saying she could prove it to him.

"Babble. As I've been trying to explain, babble. Honestly, I was at a loss. I thought maybe I could figure out what Cherri was trying to tell me if I knew more about our family history. Had Juniper used it, the DNA kit would have perhaps answered some of those questions."

"Did you discuss Cherri's rambles with Juniper?"

"Juniper didn't understand them either, or so she said."

"So you believe Juniper knew what Cherri was saying and refused to share that knowledge with you?"

"I'm not ready for that part of the discussion; I'm not prepared."

Donna dips her head in understanding. "Let's go back to the DNA kit. You said Juniper was uncomfortable searching for her familial history?"

"That's what she said, but more likely, it was the fact that Juniper was afraid of rejection. Her father, Dennis, had rejected her once, and I think Juniper was afraid he would do the same again if she sought him out. Juniper claimed going forward with the test would be disloyal to Cherri. After all, Dennis had abandoned his wife and three children. I think Juniper couldn't bear the thought of learning he might have taken on another family— one he actually wanted. For all Juniper didn't say on the topic, she did wonder openly about whether or not Dennis might have had other children. They'd be Juniper's siblings, and she didn't know how she would feel about them. She didn't want to face making a decision about what she would do with that information—not while Cherri was so ill.

Then there was the question of the life Dusk had led. What had he done in the years after he deserted his mother and sister? Did he have children of his own—nieces or nephews Juniper never knew about? What if she learned Dusk's DNA was linked to an unsolved criminal act? Juniper claimed she already had enough to deal with, losing Cherri to the darkness of her mind. All of her attention, she said, had to go to her mother. Maybe in the future, she would perform the test."

"But you believed Juniper knew more than she let on, that she had other reasons for not going through with the test?"

My eyes dart back to Donna, delivering a look so piercing that even as dense as she is, Donna reads it clearly. She repositions her legs, jots a quick note on the pad, and looks at me with a pleasant, closed-lip smile.

Is Donna scared of me? Afraid of what I might do? How do I feel about that? I'll take the time to ponder these questions later.

"I wasn't sure what Juniper knew or if she was keeping information from me. What I did understand was that there was more than one way to conduct that research."

"So, because you and Juniper share DNA…"

I cut Donna off before she can finish.

"I took the test myself."

CHAPTER THIRTY-NINE

Juniper

THE DISPLAY on my cell phone flashes Roni's name.

"Hey, honey."

"Mom, answer the damn door. I've been knocking for over five fucking minutes."

With the phone still pressed to my ear, I hurry down the hallway. "Sorry, sweetie, I had no idea." I open the door and see Roni standing there, phone still to her ear, listening to me.

I laugh at the absurdity of the situation, though Roni clearly isn't amused. "That you were out here," I finish, disconnecting the call. As I hold the door open, the smile I've been wearing for the past hour slowly slips away.

Boswell and Dash dart around my ankles, then bolt out the apartment door, racing the length of the long hallway. Chasing and circling, nudging one another, Dash yaps for both of them.

"Mom, you need to get them under control," Roni scolds. "They're disturbing the neighbors."

Watching the dogs tumble and play, my heart swells, lips curving upward again. I can't bring myself to put a stop to their capers.

"Mom?" Roni presses, vying for my attention. "What is Alok's dog doing here?"

"Boswell. Dash." I call down the hallway. "Come here, boys." Stepping farther into the hall, I move toward them.

I was aware of the repercussions of following through with this playdate. I understood Roni would be displeased with my actions. But look at how happy the babies are. How can she stay angry with me when the dogs are having so much fun?

"Why is Dash here, Mom?" Roni asks, following me.

"Aren't they adorable? Come here, you silly boys." Boswell and Dash respond to my call and head back toward the apartment, chasing one another, continuing their game. The two beat us to the door, tongues out, panting, tails wagging, waiting for us to let them inside the unit.

"Mom," Roni snaps, slamming the door behind her.

"Lock it, please," I call back over my shoulder.

I hear the thunk of the deadbolt, then Roni's hurried stride. "Why is Dash here, Mom? Wait," Roni commands, stepping through the space, looking, searching, then turning back to face me. "Is Alok here, too? Tell me you haven't taken him back."

"No, honey. It's just Dash. Boswell has been so lonely without Dash that I arranged for them to spend a little time together. That's all." I bend to scratch the boys' heads, each one having posted themselves at either side of me.

"But only for the dogs? Not for you and Alok. You're not seeing him again, right?"

"No, I'm not *seeing* him again, although he's still my husband, I might remind you. No, we are cordial at best. Happy?" The words have a snippy edge to them. I'll tone it back.

"No, Mom. I'm not *happy*. Jesus. I just don't think it's a good idea for you to have contact with Alok yet. The situation is raw."

"You can't make me feel guilty about this, Roni." My tone slips from snappish to whiny. "The dogs don't understand why their worlds have been turned upside down. Hell, I barely understand it myself. But I can assure you—I never set out to upset you or make you unhappy with me. God knows I've done enough of that already."

"I'm not upset or *unhappy* about Dash being here, Mom, but *might I remind you*—since this question of happiness keeps rearing—Alok is the one who has made you unhappy."

"I don't need to have my memory refreshed. Just because I want the puppies to have some playtime together doesn't mean I'm crawling back to my cheating husband." I pull a bag of treats from the cabinet, open it, and stare inside. "It's not easy, though, Roni. I can't simply turn off my feelings for Alok after everything we've been through."

"I know, Mom, and I'm sorry you're going through this. That's exactly my point, though. It's going to be more difficult to make the break if you continue to have contact with Alok. It will muddle your feelings for him, make it easier for you to devise concessions for his bullshit explanations."

I take two treats from the bag and offer one to each dog. "The hardest part of this is that without notice, I lost the person I shared everything with every day. That's not easy to turn off."

I squat to put the bag away, stand, then twist to look Roni in the eyes. "Having stated how difficult this is for me, let me also say, I'm aware of how hard this is on you, too. Trying to stay strong for me, to be understanding and patient with everything happening in my marriage. But Alok is your stepfather. You obviously have your own feelings of betrayal to cope with. And then here I am, experiencing some of the very same symptoms Cherri exhibited prior to her diagnosis while you're still coming to terms with losing her so recently. This can't be easy for you either, honey."

"Thank you for your concern, Mom, but I'm fine. I'm dealing." Roni shrugs, turning to take a glass from the cabinet and fill it with water from the fridge.

"Well, if you ever want to talk about anything," I try.

Facing the refrigerator, Roni mumbles, "I've been talking to someone."

"Oh?" Maybe Roni is finally ready to open up about the woman living with her? "A co-worker? A friend?" I prod.

"Mom. My point is, I'm fine. *You're* the one who isn't dealing with this very well."

"I just wondered if maybe you have a new friend. You did say you have someone you're able to talk to." Roni stands at the countertop, staring at my new notebook, tracing her finger along the pattern adorning the cover. As she remains stubbornly silent on the matter, I continue, "And then, Alok did mention he thought he saw you out at dinner the other night."

Is it my imagination, or did I see Roni flinch at the last comment?

Roni lifts her gaze from the notebook, aiming it pointedly at me, her eyes narrow. "And when did Alok have all this to say? I thought you said you hadn't seen him?"

"I have not seen Alok—other than when he dropped Dash off this afternoon."

"So, you welcomed him into your new home, shot the shit, shared a bit of gossip about me?"

"Roni. No. It wasn't like that. If you must know, the moment was quite awkward. I think Alok was trying to find common ground to break the tension–not to gossip about you."

"Then exactly what did Alok have to say about me?"

"That he was having dinner on Clematis Street last week and thought he saw you having dinner with a friend, someone he didn't recognize."

"Was that it?"

"Well, yes, other than he said he didn't want to disturb you because it looked like the conversation was intense, so he decided not to say hello. Alok did ask me, though, to send you his best wishes before he left this afternoon. I think Alok misses you."

"Great. Alok doesn't get to fucking miss me, does he? Alok made his decision. And that decision"—Roni flicks her wrist, finger darting between us—"took both of us, you and me, right out of the equation. We were out the minute he concluded he needed a new piece of ass."

"Roni!"

"Mom!"

"Okay, let's take a moment. First, let me reiterate that Alok and I are not working things out. All I'm trying to say is that I think he regrets what he's done. He looks terrible. He's lost weight, and he's got those heavy dark circles under his eyes—the ones he gets when he's under a lot of stress."

"Do you hear yourself?" Roni says, her words dripping with disgust.

"You're right. I know you're right. Next time Dash and Boswell play, I'll have Alok leave Dash with Noreen. Then we won't have to see one another, and Boswell can still have his playdates."

"Great idea. Everybody wins." Roni lifts her water and sips.

I try a different tactic, knowing I'm at risk of starting another argument. "I want to be clear—I would never gossip about you, Roni. You're my daughter. All I want is your happiness. So when Alok mentioned he thought he saw you out on what looked like a date, of course I asked for more details. We both know"—now I point between us—"you've always kept your dating life to yourself. And I respect that," I add quickly. "But I want you to know you can talk to me, share with me, open up about anything...or anyone."

"Thank you, Mom." Roni sips her water again. "When there's something to share, I'll let you know."

The disappointment is heavy, pressing on my lungs. I tried, but Roni still doesn't believe she can trust me. I sink back into the sofa, allowing the dogs to join me, answering their nudges for attention. The energy I felt surging earlier is gone, sucked away by this exchange with Roni.

Roni pulls me from my wallowing. "What's this?" she asks, pointing at the notebook. "I like the pattern on the cover—and it's a good size. You could keep it in your handbag." She lifts it, testing its weight in her hand.

"Un-huh," I nod, "that's exactly what I thought."

"Are you keeping work notes again? Have you decided to end the hiatus on your blog?" Roni fans the pages.

"No," I answer, keeping up with the task of appeasing the dogs while trying to come up with a good response. Nothing comes to mind, however, and I'm tired. "I'm keeping memory notes," I admit, already dreading where this conversation will head next.

Roni looks from the notebook to me. "A memory notebook? Like a memoir?"

"No. It's… well…" Given her mood this afternoon, I should have lied. I should have said yes, that I was going back to the blog.

"What, Mom?"

"I know you don't like to talk about it," I start.

"Talk about what? For Christ's sake, Mom, spit it out." Roni walks around the counter to the chair across from the sofa and sits facing me.

"About how I am having issues with my memory."

"It's not that I don't want to talk about it, Mom. I just don't want you to obsess over it. I've said from the onset that your lapses in recall are most likely stemming from stress. Let's face it, you have had a lot going on in your life."

"You're right. I mean, of course, you're right. You're the health professional, and you can't imagine how much I appreciate you being so patient with me. But I think it's getting worse, Roni. It seems more and more often, I am unable to recall events with any clarity, and I can't live like that." I blink and close my eyes, willing myself stronger.

Roni leans forward in the chair, propping elbows on knees, clasping hands together under her chin. "Okay, number one—how can I help? Number two—what does this have to do with the notebook?"

"Remember the gun I found in Cherri's things?"

"Yeah… so, you're starting to worry me, Mom." Roni shakes her head. "And wait—hold on. Is this in response to number one, 'how can I help,' or number two, 'this has something to do with the notebook'?"

"Two, the notebook," I tell her. "See, I decided that if I was going to be a gun owner, and I was going to live alone, I needed to know how to use a gun properly."

"Mom, you hate guns."

"I did, in the past, but now I've learned how to handle one. I was frightened of guns before, but now that I know how to use it, the gun doesn't scare me."

Roni stares at me from across the way. Waiting, eyebrows tightly drawn together, she studies me.

"I've been taking lessons."

"Lessons? From who? When?"

"Straight Shot in Wellington has a class for women twice a week. They start with the basics—the parts of a gun, how to load a cartridge, clear the chamber, that kind of stuff. Then we learned about stance and dominant eye."

Roni raises her palm, signaling me to halt. "Fine, you're more comfortable with a gun now. I get it, but that still doesn't answer the question of the notebook."

"Well, here's the thing. During the class, I decided I didn't want to forget anything, especially when it came to something so important as operating a gun. One mistake with these weapons and… Anyway, I concluded I needed to take notes, to be certain I remembered correctly what I had been taught. After each lesson, I would check back over the notes I took during class and commit them to memory."

"Okay," Roni sits back in the chair, folding arms across the middle of her body.

"The act of taking those notes led me to think about keeping a record of my daily activities, things I don't want to forget, important conversations, accounts of meetings."

Roni eyes me, weighing my words. I can't read the look on her face. Doubt? Exasperation? Annoyance?

I try to alleviate the awkward silence. "Thus, the notebook."

"And is this working? Are you noticing a difference?"

"It's only been a few days, but I feel confident this is going to help me in my relationships and, more importantly, help to sort fact from fiction."

CHAPTER FORTY

"Cherri used to tell me, 'Good things come to those who wait.'" I reflect. Head down, picking at my nails, I am well aware of my body language signals. I glance through my lashes to see if Donna is watching, measuring.

No.

She sits across from me, elbow propped on the arm of the chair, leaning her head against fingertips, unbothered by what her body language signals. Donna is bored. What the fuck is going on with her? Donna's demeanor today is not what I've grown accustomed to and certainly not the level of interest a therapist is expected to display. Is the doubling up of our sessions responsible for the change in Donna? Whatever. I don't have time for her bullshit. We're in here to deal with my problems, not hash out her issues.

"Did they?" Donna asks, shattering my thoughts.

"Did they what?" I toss back. Could she be more unclear in her inquiry? I'm dealing with a goddamn amateur. So close—I'm *so* close to completing the required therapy. I've got to keep it together, not let her get to me.

"Did good things come to you, or were you unable to wait?"

"You know as well as I do, Donna, that this has nothing to do with what you and I are trying to accomplish here. This line of questioning is in no way related to my case."

"Then, why are you leading me down this path, Roni? In one of our previous sessions, you made it quite clear that I was to listen and respond in kind, thereby making you, the patient, more willing to discuss the topic freely. Is this topic—will this subject matter—lead us to a discussion that is viable to your case?"

She's goading me. This bitch is completely unprofessional. I may need her to sign off on my case, but I will not let her steamroll me.

I stand, running my hands down my thighs to smooth out the pants I wear.

"We can continue our discussion at our next session." I turn and exit the room.

JUNIPER,

YOU SHOULDN'T BE HERE. You don't deserve to be here—not after all you have done. Let me clarify that when I say *here*, I do not mean at The Grabell, or West Palm Beach, or even the state. No. I mean, *you* shouldn't be in existence.

I know what you're thinking, what's going through your mind. *Who? Why? This person doesn't know me.* Let me assure you, I know you well, Juniper—probably better than you know yourself at this point. I've watched you. I've followed you. I've been through your things, fed your dog, cradled your family photographs in my hands.

Still not convinced? Shaking your head? That welling in your eyes spilling over yet? If not, then allow me to assure you, what I'm telling you is real.

Three times a day, you leave the building, each time through a different exit. When you return, you use an entrance located in a different part of the building. I'm sure you can deduce that if I know the ways in which you enter and exit the building, I've also clocked the three different walking treks taken at the given time of the day. Is this to keep you from getting bored, or do you do it for your dog's benefit?

You often wear a look of depression. I know you're lonely. Your mother is dead. Your husband is a philanderer. Your daughter has a life you're rarely a part of, and you have no trusted friends. Indeed, most days, I watch you and wonder where your will to live comes from. What makes Juniper Walder believe life is still worth living?

I've watched you sleep. The way you kick the bedcovers off your body at one in the morning, then pull the sheet back over you at one-thirty. You need a bathroom visit at three, and on your way back from the bathroom, you drag Boswell into the bed with you.

You didn't think I knew your dog's name? It's right there on his pretty red collar, silly, right above your cell phone number. Boswell and I have become close over these last few weeks. Your dog likes to watch me in much the same way I watch you. Maybe that's the key to our bond: we both watch in silence. We're both consummate watchers with little to say. I guess I feel closer to him because the poor thing has no bark. He misses his friend, though. He was looking so sad until you arranged for his little buddy to visit. Shall we talk about Boswell's best friend, Dash?

Do you find yourself having a favorite between the two dogs? I know you do. I've seen how you react to both of them—bad dog mommy. Lucky for Roni, she's your only child. I think it's safe to say, given all I know about you, that if you had more than one child, you'd definitely play favorites. Perhaps it's your proclivities for favoritism that are the reason you have no true friends to speak of, no one to confide in about this horrendous situation you find yourself living through.

That's okay, though, right, Juniper? You can deal with all of this on your own—the death of your mother, the infidelity of your husband, the mistrust of your daughter—you'll just go take it out on the treadmill. Five, six, eight miles should do it. Don't you think? While I'm thinking about it, let me give you some advice. That sports bra you wear with the black leggings and multicolored tank—you know the one of which I speak; you wear it every Friday. You need to get rid of that. Orange really isn't your color.

Orange does look good on Alok, though, wouldn't you agree? It's a shame things haven't worked out with you two. He seems like a nice guy. Yes, I know him too, and I have to tell you, he doesn't seem the type to cheat on his wife. Are you sure this whole affair thing isn't something you've conjured? I mean, you aren't exactly a reliable witness in your own life. I'm not sure how you keep track of anything. I suppose that system you've devised to jog your memory must be helping some.

That new notebook you've been keeping, the one you take with you everywhere, drop everything you're doing to record thoughts, conversations, moments you've shared with others— you know that one? You should be more careful where you leave it. Really, you're just going to place it on the counter in the gym while you run? I'm not trying to tell you what to do, just offer a bit of advice. More than that, though, I wanted to make sure I mentioned how appreciative I am that you are taking the time to narrate your encounters in writing. It's much easier for me to know more about you—so many great details. Watching only offers so much information. I've often found myself wondering, "What's going through Juniper's head?" And now, I know.

While I find your thoughts intriguing, I must admit that it would be more beneficial for you to know what I'm thinking.

REGARDS,
FOR ME TO KNOW AND YOU TO—WELL, YOU KNOW...

CHAPTER FORTY-TWO

Juniper

THE PAPER BURNS MY FINGERTIPS—ITS content searing. I fling the letter to the countertop and step back, watching as it furls into the trifold creases the sender pressed into place.

Who wrote this? Someone has been watching me. Someone has been following me, is still watching me, still following me.

The details, the knowing comments—who, why?

Hyperventilation edges out the light. I drag in breaths, fighting to steady myself, to keep the darkness at bay.

I yank the workout hat from my head and release the elastic hair tie. The pressure continues to mount at the base of my neck, behind my forehead, despite my attempts.

I turn, twist—left, right, behind me—the phone. Where is my phone?

Boswell hovers protectively at my feet as I tap at the screen to call Roni.

No answer.

"Honey, it's Mom. Please. Please call me as soon as possible. Someone is watching me, Roni. Someone knows everything I do, my every move, how I sleep. They know about you and Cherri, about Alok. They've made friends with Boswell, read my memory journal.

"I found it stuck in the apartment door when I returned from the gym—a letter. I don't know what I should do, Roni. Should I call the police? No, I can't get through to emergency services with this ransomware attack. They didn't even answer the other night with the intruder. Dammit, Alok. It's Alok's fault. He's behind this cyberattack, Roni. I know he is.

"I'd call Noreen, but she told me she would be in and out of depositions for one of her old employers all day.

"Where are you, Roni? You told me your appointments were scheduled for this afternoon. You told me that, right? You did. I remember. I wrote it down in my memory journal, the one that the person who is watching me read. We talked about it—you and me. Remember? You commented about liking the pattern on the cover.

"I can't stay here. But, where else do I have to go? This person knows my every move. What if they're watching me now? I can't be here. I'm coming up to your apartment. I know someone lives with you. I know you don't want me to know about her, but I don't care, Roni. I want you to have a girlfriend, a partner to share things with. I want you to be happy.

"I'm scared, Roni. I know I'm not making any sense, but I will. I'll be right there. I'll explain everything. Okay?"

I press the button to disconnect the call and see that I never hit send. I've been talking to dead air. It's just as well. I'll tell her in person.

From the counter, I grab my keys, run through the hallway, out the door, and straight to the stairwell—too impatient to wait on the elevator, I begin the climb. Four floors of the seven complete, I round the next flight and realize Roni will never believe me. She'll think I've made this whole convoluted scenario up in some attempt to get inside her apartment to meet her girlfriend. Roni will accuse me of losing my mind again. But wait, I have proof now. I have the letter, verification that all this time, someone has been watching me, coming and going from my apartment. But I don't have the evidence in hand. Roni will insist on seeing the letter.

Get the letter, then go to Roni's. That's the new plan.

I turn, catching myself mid-trip as my left ankle twists underneath me. I use the stair railing to pull up from the stumble and continue. Going down requires less energy, yet my heart rate remains high, despite all the cardio training.

On the seventh floor, I whip open the door to the stairwell, dart to the door of my apartment, twisting the knob. It's locked. Of course, it's locked; you just locked it. I struggle to get the key steady in my grip, to slip it into the slot. Finally, it's in, and I twist, opening the apartment door, securing the deadbolt behind me. Boswell underfoot, I trip forward down the hallway and continue to the kitchen counter.

The water bottle I use during my workouts is on the countertop next to my gym towel, ear buds, and hat, but no letter. I left it right here.

I twist and turn, my hair stringy and uncombed, swinging around my face with the motion of my head. Did I drop it? Maybe it fell and got caught under the oven or refrigerator.

On hands and knees, I use the flashlight on my phone to search the dark spots for the lost letter. It's not lodged under either of the appliances. I jump up, blood rushing to my head. I hold to the kitchen sink while closing my eyes, willing equilibrium to return.

Lifting my eyelids, the motion measured and deliberate, the room comes into focus. I rotate in the same manner, expecting the letter to pop into view now that I've calmed myself. It's one big room—kitchen, dining, living room. Other than leaving the apartment with only my keys in hand, I did not move from this area after reading the letter. So what did I do with it?

I start throwing items off the counter. It's not hidden under any of the objects. I search the floor of the entire apartment. Though it makes no sense, I look inside the cabinets, the dishwasher, the oven, the refrigerator. I check to make sure I haven't stuck it inside my clothing somewhere. The letter is gone. It's not here.

Deflated, confused, frightened, I sink to the floor. Boswell crawls into my lap and licks away the tears rolling over my cheeks.

The letter is gone.

The pressure in my ears, muffling sound, feels as if I'm underwater. Covered in a damp, cold sweat, a clammy chill runs over my skin. The frantic energy that fueled me only moments ago is gone, leaving me powerless to move.

Was there ever a letter, Juniper, or did you make the whole thing up?

CHAPTER FORTY-THREE

"How are you this afternoon, Roni?"

"I'm doing well, Donna." I don't bother to ask about Donna's well-being. I don't give a shit.

"Shall we get started?"

"No time to waste," I say, pulling myself to sit straighter in the chair, ready to do the work, ready to get down to business. I made up my mind before this session. Regardless of how I feel about this imbecile sitting across from me, I will be cooperative. The only way to get rid of Donna at this point is to give over whatever information she requests.

"Then let's return to the DNA test."

Fuck her. She goes immediately to this topic. I knew we would get around to discussing it, but I wanted it done on my terms. It's not easy for me to admit wrongdoing because I'm rarely wrong. However, some of my actions regarding the DNA tests were admittedly a bit unethical.

"More specifically?" I prod, holding off to see what topic Donna wants to wrangle. This nitwit may not even want to know about the immoral act I committed.

"The results, Roni. What did you learn from the results of the test? It is my understanding that they were not as you expected."

Yeah, there really is no way around this. I huff and scoot to reposition myself in the chair.

"This topic makes you uncomfortable?" Donna asks.

"This whole mandated farce makes me uncomfortable, Donna. Are you just now realizing that? I thought I had made it clear that I'm not particularly thrilled sharing who I am with you."

Donna blinks her eyes and nods knowingly. She's twirling that damn pen again. Stress runs the length of my extremities, a stinging itch that makes me want to claw my skin off. Shake it off, Roni.

"You're correct. The DNA results did not come back with the information I anticipated. Even though my birth certificate lists my father as unknown, I knew from Cherri and Juniper that his name was Chris Anderson. I knew my father's involvement with Juniper took place in Bainbridge, Georgia, where his family resided. I expected, rather hoped, I could locate some of his family, maybe take a trip to Bainbridge to meet them."

"Had you entertained the idea of finding your father's family before?"

"No."

"So, what prompted you to do so?"

"I hadn't really thought about it before because my life was happening so fast—new stepdad on the scene, graduate from high school, attend college, graduate studies, start a career. I finally had the time to search them out, I guess."

Donna tilts her head to one side, her eyes locked onto mine. She doesn't believe me. The woman truly is infuriating.

"Okay, fine. It was Cherri's ramblings. I never cared about my father's family. Cherri had told me repeatedly how awful they were, how little they thought of Juniper, how hateful they were to any Walder they came in contact with. I had no desire to know them. Why would I even want to? But Cherri kept bringing up their names and babbling on and on about Juniper's baby."

"You've said this before, about Cherri's babbling in prior sessions. Are you now speaking about a different instance?"

"No, Donna." I draw a deep breath to keep myself from saying something unbecoming. "If you'd let me finish, you'd understand I am answering your question."

"Of course. I simply wanted to clarify."

Turning my head toward the window, I realize today is the first time the blinds have been open. I take in the view outside the window, calm myself, and begin again.

"I began to wonder if Cherri was trying to tell me something and couldn't get it out. Maybe she was finally giving me her blessing to search out the Anderson family. All I knew for certain was that she continued the same repertoire of babble. Surely, it meant something. Then I recalled the DNA kit Alok gave Juniper for Christmas and decided that would be the best way to seek out my father's family."

"But, if you had their name and location, why not simply search out Chris Anderson's family? Why the need for a DNA test?"

"Other than the man's name, Chris Anderson, I had nothing to go on. Cherri and Juniper never spoke the first names of Chris's parents, and both his first and last names were comically common. And too, I wasn't even positive Chris was his first name. Maybe he was Christopher with a C, or was it with a K?"

Donna's eyes narrow in doubt.

"You know, Donna, if you don't believe what I'm telling you, then why fucking ask me?" Once again, my resolve to remain calm has been hijacked by this maddening woman.

"What I think is that there's more to the explanation as to why you sought out the DNA test results than what you are conveying."

"Because I didn't trust what Juniper and Cherri had told me all my life—is that the answer you're looking for, Donna? There, you got it. Go ahead and jot the info into your notes. I'm sure that will look great on the report."

"Let's not worry about my report. The intent of our time together is to address the truth of the incident and work on your well-being, Roni."

Head down, staring at my lap, I pinch the bridge of my nose. There isn't a chance in hell this woman could contribute to my well-being. I won't say this. I will continue the sham and come to the conclusion of these sessions so that I can move forward—far, far away from this lunacy.

"I will try the best I can to explain this in terms that you will understand," I begin. "First, the name Chris Anderson is quite generic. I mean, how many Andersons are there in this country, and then to have the first name Chris? The two of them…"

"Now, by two of them, you are referring to Juniper and Cherri?" Donna interrupts.

"No, Donna. Dash and Boswell, the goddamn dogs. Who else would I be referring to?"

Donna nods for me to continue.

"Juniper and Cherri seemed to have some sort of pact when it came to my paternity. The *only* thing they would ever tell me about Chris Anderson or his family was his name. Given that Juniper and I look nothing alike, I asked Cherri about Chris's physical features, if perhaps she or Juniper had a photograph. What I got most of the time was, 'You look a lot like him.' Every now and then, one of them would say, 'Dark hair, dark eyes—a lot like yours.' So, when I finally was able to get around to searching out my father's family, I wanted something more concrete to go on. I couldn't just go knocking on doors: 'Hi, I think I'm the daughter of your long-dead son; I believe you are my grandparents.' It would sound crazy. I had to be able to offer some proof."

"But then you got the DNA results, and *that* was when you decided to make a trip to Bainbridge?"

"For fuck's sake, Donna. Have some patience."

Donna twirls her pen and nods.

"When I received the results, I got exactly what the test

promised—multiple generations of distant ancestry, relatives multiple times removed, ancestral history with migration paths. None of those results interested me, and besides, they were confusing, given that I didn't know much about my familial history. I skimmed over that information, thinking to go back and study it more in-depth later on, and moved on to the section on maternal relatives, only to find there were no names listed. This didn't concern me too much because Juniper and Cherri had never submitted their DNA to any such database. Therefore, there wouldn't be any information to offer. What really had me spinning was that the test results revealed my father's name. How was it possible that my father's DNA was in the database if he had been dead for over thirty years?"

"Because…"

"Donna, don't you fucking do it. Don't you dare answer for me."

Donna scoots around in her seat, lips taut with displeasure.

"The name of the man on my test results died only three years prior to my DNA submission. In my mind, there had been some kind of mistake in the process. My father's name was Chris Anderson, but the name listed on the results was Robert Ulrich." I hold here, gathering my thoughts, reining back the feelings that flog me each time I recall the events of learning the truth about who I am.

Donna takes my silence as a cue. "What did you do with the information?"

"I tried another testing kit—a different brand. I was convinced there was an error, but then the second test provided the same results."

"And yet, you still weren't convinced?"

"No, but this time, I bought two tests. I needed to see if a maternal match could be made."

"So you asked Juniper if she would submit her DNA?"

"No, Donna. If you would listen, as I have asked you to do on multiple occasions, you would recall I told you in a previous session that Juniper was against doing the DNA testing. She didn't want to know about any long-lost family members."

"I do remember you providing that information," Donna concedes, doing that little nod of her head that is starting to grate on my nerves. "So then, how did you go about obtaining her DNA?"

"Cherri."

"But Cherri wasn't in her right mind. How did she give you consent to perform a DNA test for her, or did you not bother with attaining her permission?" Donna's face relays the moment she makes the realization. "That would be illegal, would it not?"

"Illegal, no, unethical perhaps, but you are not here to judge me, Donna. I was Cherri's health proxy—she named me to make medical decisions on her behalf. This may not have been medical, but I did have the authority."

Lips pursed, Donna watches me. She is visibly flustered, but she keeps her mouth shut. Commendations for Donna—this is the most restraint she's displayed since our first unfortunate meeting. I continue before she has the pleasure of interrupting me again.

"I swabbed the two of us, sent the tests to the company, and probed Cherri during her lucid moments. It would take a miracle to learn the truth from Cherri, given the rate at which her mental capacity was deteriorating. Anxious for answers as I was, Cherri was simply never coherent enough to provide them.

"But then the results arrived. Cherri's came in first, and as I expected, there wasn't a lot of information listed. Her family was so much older and long passed on—none of them were in the DNA database. My test, test number three, same test kit as Cherri's, once again came back claiming my birth father's name to be Robert Ulrich."

I take a moment to breathe, staring out the window at the dark clouds of a quick-moving storm rolling in. "There was still no name listed under the maternal parent heading. Of course, there wouldn't be because Juniper had not submitted her DNA.

However, I did expect to find Cherri's name within my report. Her DNA was now in the database; therefore, Cherri and I should have been linked as relatives."

"But you weren't."

"No."

"How did that make you feel?"

"How the fuck do you think I felt, Donna. I was confused, dumbfounded, stunned. God, I was devastated. Cherri was the person I was closest to in the whole world, and then I found out we're not even related."

"Still, you determined it best *not* to confront Juniper with these test results?" Donna asks.

"I wanted the truth. For thirty-odd years, I lived under a lie— three DNA tests had proved as much. If I was ever going to have an answer, I'd have to find it myself."

Donna lets me sit for a moment. I suspect she's waiting for me to share some emotion. That's not happening. I will not give her the satisfaction of thinking she's sapped out a tear.

"Are you okay to continue, Roni, or would you like to pick this up in our next session?"

"I'm fine to continue, Donna. Is it you who needs a moment? A potty break, perhaps?" Yes, there is a snide edge to my tone. I'm in the middle of spilling my guts, and she wants to suggest taking a break?

"Then, if you're ready, Roni, please continue."

This time, I give her back one of her bullshit nods. Donna stares blankly, then throws out, "So then, how did you determine where to start your search for truth regarding the identity of your father?"

"I had a name, one that came up time and again as belonging to my father. That's where I started."

"Did you find him?"

"I did. Surprisingly, the internet had quite a bit of information on Robert Ulrich. The most recent entry on good 'ole Robert was his death record and a half-baked obituary. Between the two, I learned he was buried in the West Bainbridge Cemetery, had few relatives to speak of, where and when he was born, and that he'd died three years earlier." I lean over my knees, looking at the floor beneath my feet, the carpet stained and littered with tiny paper scraps. "All those years he was alive, and I might have met him…"

"I'm sorry," Donna offers, then, "Were you able to determine the cause of his death, or was age a factor?"

"No, his age was not the issue. He was only fifty-two at the time of his death. Robert Ulrich died in prison."

Donna is silent. I push off my knees and sit back in the chair again. I watch her, wondering about the thoughts, judgments, the suppositions running through her head. When I'm ready, I continue. "I'm sure it's probably in my file somewhere, but… Robert Ulrich was initially imprisoned for involuntary manslaughter as well as some other less severe crimes, mostly having to do with drugs."

Shaking her head no, Donna feels the need to clarify. "No, I'm not aware of that information."

I continue as if she hasn't spoken. "He should have been long out of prison by fifty-two, but while incarcerated, Robert Ulrich killed a prison guard. He was serving out his sentence for that felony when he was assaulted. The injuries were extensive. He didn't recover."

Donna scoots around in her chair again. The look on her face says she is searching for the right words. Condolences again, perhaps?

"Just don't," I say before she can come up with the appropriate response.

"Don't what?"

"Don't offer up any kind words or bullshit statements of understanding. I just want to move on with the facts."

Donna looks down, flipping through her notes, an action of procrastination as far as I can tell. She formulates her next inquiry and poses, "Did you confront Juniper with the information you learned about your paternity?"

"No. Like I said before, if I had wanted more lies, Donna, I would have confronted Juniper after the first DNA test came back listing Robert Ulrich as my father. Before I could present Juniper with the truth backed by factual information, I first had to answer why my DNA didn't link to Cherri's. I could deduce only two possibilities for the results as they were reported. Either Juniper and Cherri were not related, or Juniper and I weren't. Given Cherri's gypsy, free-love, drug-soaked youth, I was inclined to believe Cherri and Juniper weren't related."

CHAPTER FORTY-FOUR

Cherri

AUGUST ROLLS IN, and Juniper leaves for school. Cherri witnesses and understands how difficult it is for Juniper to drive away, to leave her infant. Juniper's eyes peer into the rearview mirror, tears racing down her cheeks. Cherri waves with one hand, cradling Roni with the other. Roni is not yet two months old, but Juniper is already completely enamored with her daughter.

In the weeks before her departure, Juniper cried and cried, begged and pleaded. She didn't want to leave Roni. Juniper claimed to have a terrible premonition that if she left Roni behind and went away to college, something awful would happen to her baby. Juniper could feel it in her bones. Cherri reassured Juniper that nothing would happen to Roni. Besides, it wouldn't be long—Cherri and Roni would be joining Juniper in Florida before Juniper could miss them, before anything bad could happen to Roni.

In order to convince Juniper to carry through with the plan they made, Cherri promised to move to Florida. There is no reason they can't all live in the same city while Juniper attends to her educational goals. Juniper is right about one thing—she and Roni need to be together, and Cherri no longer has ties in Brunswick to keep her there. Juniper finally concedes and counts the days until Cherri and Roni move to DeLand.

Juniper believes Cherri is making a sacrifice, packing up her life in Brunswick, leaving a job her mother has worked since they settled into the town. But Cherri has her own reasons for leaving, reasons other than simply moving so Juniper and Roni can live in the same town while Juniper attends school. No matter how pertinent the reason may be, though, Cherri knows the truth behind the matter—she is trying to control an uncontrollable situation.

True to her word, Cherri and Roni cross the Florida state line less than two months after Juniper's journey. Juniper has room and board on campus, but as soon as her mother and daughter move into the small home Cherri rented, Juniper makes the transition to live with them.

The early years are difficult. Cherri and Juniper share the responsibility of caring for Roni. The two work opposite hours, allowing one of them to always be home with Roni. Of course, Juniper has classes to attend and studying to complete when she isn't at her job, so naturally, more of Roni's care falls to Cherri. Cherri doesn't mind the extra work. She adores having her granddaughter at the center of her world, and Juniper is accomplishing her goals and dreams as planned.

Eventually, Juniper finishes school, obtaining her Master of Science in Finance. Cherri and Juniper stay so busy that the first six years of Roni's life seemingly fly by. Before they realize it, their precious girl is ready to start school herself.

Upon completing her degree, Juniper lands a job in Tampa with a sizeable financial firm, bringing in a salary the likes of neither she nor Cherri can believe. The three pack their belongings and relocate to Tampa. Settling into a nice-sized house, where each of them actually has their own room, the three fall into a routine. Juniper goes off to work each morning as Roni leaves for school, and Cherri spends her days taking care of their home, completing all the duties and errands of daily life. They are happy and ever thankful for their tight-knit trio, the Walder women.

Then along comes Alok.

Roni is fifteen, coming into her own, making plans for her adult life. Juniper has taken on Cherri's financial security, alleviating her need for a job. Cherri has made some friends and has some new hobbies to explore now that she no longer has to work. But this is the first time since her days in high school that Juniper has found something or someone other than school or work to keep her fulfilled. Juniper has poured all of her energies into her career and family. Therefore, the union comes as a surprise to all of them. Juniper and Alok are meant to be from the moment they meet, however. It is as if they had only been biding their time until the pact between the two could form.

Cherri is concerned about the relationship in the early days, but her unease subsides when she realizes how happy Alok makes Juniper. Alok fits nicely into their little family. He does not try to change the way they live, as Cherri feared he might. Alok is a man who believes in supporting family and is fine to start a life with Juniper, one that includes Cherri and Roni.

"You have jumped ahead in our review," Cherri's guardian spirit gently reminds, breaking Cherri from the process.

"Yes," Cherri admits reluctantly. "The memory of what I've done… well, I can't revisit that piece of my life just yet."

"We are to proceed with the life review chronologically. We discussed the process."

"Please. Just not right now. The memories are so lovely, with Alok, our family, the trips we took, the holidays, and special occasions we all shared. I'm not ready to darken them. I know I will not be able to skip over it, but… please."

"We can continue forward from this point, but we will return."

"If I can get to Juniper—if I can tell Juniper what I should have told her before I passed over—I'll be ready to visit that portion of my review."

"As we discussed, perhaps it was not—perhaps it is not—meant for you to relay this information to your daughter."

"But she has to know. I never should have kept it from her. I have to find some way to get to her. I have to find some way to tell her."

"This upsets you, I realize, but you must understand that perhaps the way things were left—the way they played out, so to speak—is the manner in which it all is meant to be."

"But I did it, so I was meant to fix it," Cherri insists.

"Your actions had residual effects that rippled across many lives, not only your loved ones. Others were impacted as well."

"Oh no," Cherri's thoughts fly through different scenarios of damning likelihoods. "I hadn't considered anyone else suffering the ramifications of what I did, but yes, you are right. What can I do? How do I rectify this?"

"What's done is done. All you can do now is review your actions and learn how you made others feel by having made the decisions you did."

"There has to be some way," Cherri muses. But even as she utters the words, Cherri realizes the lives of too many were impacted by her actions. She knows she'll never be able to make it right, even if she finally makes her wretched actions known to others.

CHAPTER FORTY-FIVE

Donna greets me the moment I walk through the doorway. "Good to see you, Roni. Let's get started, shall we?" She asks before I can get myself situated in the chair across from her.

"Anxious, or do you have more pressing matters to get to?"

"We're running out of time, Roni. Tick-tock, tick-tock," she chimes, pointing at her watch. This chipper charade is almost more grating than her humdrum schtick. "My report is coming due. At most, we have five sessions left before I need to hand over my findings to the review board."

Only five? Darn. "We can skip the remainder of our sessions if you prefer," I say in my own cheery voice. Please, someone put me out of this miserable, fucking situation. "I'm happy to help you draft the report, Donna. Lest you forget, I am qualified to do so."

"No, Roni. I have not forgotten. And, while I am aware you regard my professional demeanor as disparaging, I am quite capable of completing your assessment."

I feel the involuntary slump of my body in response, betraying me of the confidence I'm determined to present. Twisting in the seat, I pull myself straighter, deciding I will not acknowledge Donna's last comment. Why bother at this late point in the process? I've no doubt her ineptness will flow through the entirety of the report as it is. Furthermore, I think I'll take the lead today.

"Last session, we ended with the question of why my DNA did not match with Cherri's," I begin, a daring edge lacing the statement.

"I recall," Donna starts. "How did…"

Speaking over her, I move on, not allowing Donna to give words to her thoughts. "Getting Cherri's DNA tested without her knowledge was one thing. I remind you—I was her health proxy, so it was on the up and up. However, I could not use the same tactics on Juniper. That would indeed be illegal, as well as unethical. Asking Juniper about the test kit again wasn't an option either. We'd already had extensive conversations about the test and her reasons for not wanting to seek out the results of such. So, I decided the best way to get the answers I sought was to return to where it all started. Juniper had to have some association with Robert Ulrich, and both had connections to Bainbridge. I scheduled some vacation time and took a trip to Georgia."

"So, did you look for Robert Ulrich's family?" Donna asks. I don't bother to look at her, instead turning my focus to the window.

"High school," I begin.

"High school?"

I throw Donna a look that says she'd better shut the fuck up if she wants to hear this. Evidently, the message is conveyed and taken seriously. Donna changes the positioning of her legs, recrossing the bottom over the top, and waits.

"The town of Bainbridge is small, with only one public high school. That's where I began—at the school library."

She looks intrigued. I have her attention. Maybe I finally have her under control.

"I concocted a story about my mother having attended the school from '84 through '88. She owned only three of the four annuals from those years. I knew she was missing one, but I couldn't remember which. Maybe if I could see all of the books, I would recognize the three she had and figure out which one I needed to purchase to complete her collection—a surprise for her birthday."

"Why didn't you just search through Juniper's yearbook annuals? Why create such an elaborate story?"

"Because Juniper didn't have any yearbooks, Donna. Cherri didn't have the means to buy school annuals for three children," I say and move on quickly before she has the opportunity to interrupt me again.

"The school's librarian was eager to assist in my search. The woman fulfilled my request, then sat me down at a table where she could watch me, ensuring I didn't leave with the school's yearbook copy. I had no intention of stealing anything. Information was what I was after.

"All three of Cherri's children had passed through the high school, so all three should be pictured in the yearbooks. Of course, I had seen photos scattered about our home over the years, but how could I be sure the pictures weren't some sort of elaborate hoax?"

"Were they? The photos—a hoax?"

"No, they were all there—Dusk, Juniper, Luna. My aunt and uncle appeared exactly the same in the yearbooks as they had in all of Cherri's old photos. The three of them shared similar features; to me, there didn't seem to be a question of whether or not they were siblings. But that wasn't to say they all didn't belong to Dennis. What if Juniper had another mother? What if Cherri decided she was going to raise one of Dennis's strays and never told Juniper? No, I didn't have my answer, and there was still the question of Robert Ulrich looming.

"Once I had located my older family members, I searched through the books to find Robert Ulrich. Nothing. Nada. Whatever his connection to Juniper, it didn't seem to be from high school. Then I recalled Robert Ulrich was fifty-two when he died three years ago. Some simple math told me he would have been five years older than Juniper, closer in age to Juniper's brother, Dusk. Maybe it was Dusk who introduced Juniper to Robert.

"I headed back to the librarian's desk, sweet-talked her into perusing the annuals of the previous four years. 'My mother's older brother attended the high school during those years, and I never knew him because he passed away before I was born,' I explained. It wasn't the whole truth, but there were enough threads of fact to count.

"I found Dusk in the books from the previous years, but no evidence that Robert Ulrich had attended Bainbridge High School. I was losing hope.

"Looking to learn a bit more about Juniper—the woman who has lied to me my entire life—I slid the yearbook printed during Juniper's senior year back in view and randomly flipped through the pages. Juniper never spoke about her high school years, and Cherri sure didn't have anything to say about them. I always assumed the timeframe was off-limits for discussion because of Luna's fatal accident. If not for that reason, then maybe Juniper's high school years were as lackluster as most of the rest of us who have completed those horrible teen years. But that hypothesis didn't prove out. Juniper appeared all throughout the annual—various clubs, scholarships, and awards, looking well-rounded and rather popular.

I knew from stories throughout my life that Juniper was pregnant with me during her senior year, but to look at the photographs in the yearbook, you would never know it. Was she hiding her pregnancy? Was she even pregnant? She was painfully thin, almost sickly looking, even. I kept flipping pages, searching for a photo that would reflect Juniper was with child, and that's when I found it."

"Found what?" Donna asks, voice level dropping to almost a whisper. She's barely moved since I began.

"A full-page memorial to Christopher Adam Anderson from his loving parents, the Honorable James Anderson and Judith

Anderson. After all this time, I now had names for the people who I'd been *told* were my paternal grandparents."

"And your next step, I assume, was to seek them out."

"Indeed it was, Donna."

She waits, glued to my every word. If only she had been this responsive from the beginning, this bullshit mandate would have been much easier to complete.

"I had an address plugged into GPS within the hour. It took me longer to come up with an excuse for knocking on their door than it did to find the house."

I sit silently, sorting through the memories of what comes next in this tale. I've told no one this story. Of all people, the first person to hear it will be Dense-ass Donna.

"We can stop for the day if you like," Donna offers. Then, "But, I urge you to continue. We have such little…"

"For Christ's sake, Donna, learn to read a room. Jesus. I needed a moment, okay. All of this may be entertaining for you, but I have a lot of emotion wrapped up in these memories."

Across from me, Donna does her little unnerving, irritating, smarmy nod. It's difficult to imagine anyone taking this woman's professional opinion. Yet, someone wants it, and my future depends on finishing this process.

I pretend to have picked up on her signal to continue and peer directly at Donna now as I begin again. "The house was huge, in a historic neighborhood, a for-sale sign posted in the well-manicured yard. I parked at the curb and made my way up the front walk. The doorbell sounded inside, but I couldn't make out any movement. I waited and decided to ring again. As I lifted my finger, the door sprang open.

"Not often do I find myself at a loss for words, but standing there, I couldn't recall what I had planned to say. The situation was awkward at best. I expected an older man or woman, given that Chris, the Andersons' son, would have been Juniper's age if he had lived. The woman standing on the other side of the threshold, however, appeared to be my age. While I stood there dumbfounded, the woman finally asked if she could help me.

"I started with my name, then stated I was looking for the Anderson home. The woman informed me I was in the right place. At her confirmation, I jabbered on and on, spewing forth a rambling mess, confusing the woman who waited patiently for me to come to some point.

"When, at last, I quit speaking, the woman shook her head slightly, eyes bright with tears. Her brother, Chris, died before she was born, and her parents—the Andersons—had recently passed away, too. She lived in the house alone but was selling it because the memories were too much to bear.

"And there we were: two damaged women witnessing, sharing one another's pain. Then the woman invited me inside."

As I relay the interaction between Hannah and me to Donna, the anxiousness of that moment takes over now. I pick at the hangnail on my thumb. Bringing blood, I pop the thumb into my mouth. Donna sees her opening and can't help but take it.

"Was there anything familiar about the woman? Did she give you the feeling she was a family member? Several journal articles have been written on the subject of familial…"

"God, Donna. Do you not get what you're doing—leading me? You make it really hard for me to want to share this shit with you. Because, do not be confused, I would not be having this conversation with you if these sessions weren't required. I will get to the information you're dying to hear when I'm good and fucking ready."

"Of course, Roni. I apologize. Please take your time," she says, swinging her hand through the air as if she's some gracious host handing over the reins of the room.

"There is no reason to make this story longer than it needs to be, so I'll skip forward. We became friends."

"At great risk of suffering another of your profane lashings, let me stop you for a moment."

I feel my eyes narrow, brow drawing together.

"This meeting between you and the Andersons' daughter is at the crux of these appointed sessions. We've been moving slowly toward this moment for more time than initially allotted. Whether you agree or don't, I must insist we delve into this initial meeting between you and Miss Anderson."

Without words, without scorn, without emotion, I remain sitting, watching, waiting until I am ready.

"As soon as that door opened and revealed the woman on the other side, I had a feeling of familiarity. You know how you meet someone and think, I know this person—I've seen them somewhere? And then it hit me. I had just seen the picture of Chris Anderson in the yearbook photo. She could have been his twin—dark hair, square face, wide dark blue eyes.

"It was an instant connection, an electric feeling; seriously, I felt a surge of energy shoot straight through me. I didn't know what was happening. No idea still about who I was—my father, mother, other family members—but I knew who she was. And when she said her name, I knew I had never felt such a strong attraction as I was experiencing at that moment.

"Hannah and I were destined to be together."

CHAPTER FORTY-SIX

Juniper

THE FEAR IS DEBILITATING. I'm furious with myself for not fighting harder, but the terror is overwhelming. It is like nothing I've ever experienced before. In the past, I could talk myself out of dark places—push through challenges, take the next step forward, find a way out of disturbing circumstances.

Not this time.

There are too many questions, and I can't sort through them. I don't even know where to begin. Who's watching me? Who's trying to frighten me into submission? Is that what they want–or do they want something more? Why? No one is above suspicion. It is all I can think about, and when the answer doesn't present, I walk. Pacing the floors, going room to room, checking closets, peeking behind furniture, constantly searching for someone who is never there has proven more exhausting than my most punishing workouts.

This knowledge—that someone watches and knows where I go, who I talk to, what I eat and drink, reads through my private thoughts—makes me want to crawl into bed and hide beneath the covers. But then I remember: the watcher has already seen me sleeping. I get up and move to the sofa instead. Only one sensible, reasonable solution is clear. If I don't leave the confines of my apartment—if I keep every door secured—no one else can enter without my consent. No one can watch me. No one can follow me.

Curriers deliver necessities, leaving them outside my door. Three times a day, the dog walkers come to retrieve Boswell. Boswell's needs and my daily essentials are the only reasons I open my door. I haven't seen Noreen. Roni calls to check in now and then, but hasn't bothered to knock on my door. I tell Roni I'm fine, all is well—I know she's busy.

After losing the letter, I haven't been able to bring myself to tell anyone about it. How can I be certain there ever was a letter left at my door? And what better way to clue people into my obsessive neurosis than to tell them about a letter that doesn't exist? If I laid out my latest hysteria, Roni would need no further evidence to convince her to seek professional help on my behalf.

With all that has happened of late, I'm now questioning myself. How many times did Roni have to remind me of things I had forgotten, to clarify events, or words I had spoken? Is it possible I've contrived this whole letter scenario? What if it was just a dream that seemed real? I simply can't trust my thoughts anymore. I wholeheartedly believed the journal was a way around the forgetfulness. However, when I learned my words were further fodder for whoever is watching me, I quit recording the happenings of my days.

The isolation is depressing, disheartening. While I believe this is the best course of action for me at this time, I admit—my mental health suffers for it.

Alok calls—leaves lengthy voicemails, then sends emails—continuing to deny the affair, pleading for a discussion about our future. Noreen texts, knocks on my door, calls through from the hallway that she's concerned. I could use their company, but I worry. What if one of them is the one who is watching me? Am I paranoid? What if there is no one watching me? What if these are the same thoughts and feelings Cherri experienced as the sickness confiscated her mind?

I can't determine the answer to any of the questions popping forth for consideration. The only thing I'm sure of is that I do not want to live out the last of my days in the same manner Cherri did. I'd rather die than lose my mind.

CHAPTER FORTY-SEVEN

WHEN I STEP off the elevator, I see Clara, the concierge at the front desk. Boswell yanks forward, jerking the leash from my hold and tearing across the lobby toward Clara's post.

"Oh dear," I mutter, hurrying to catch up.

Clara reads the situation, scurrying through her door to the other side of the desk to intercept Boswell. "Boswell, you silly boy, are you running to see me?" Clara squats to pet Boswell, scratching behind his ears.

The young woman looks up as I come to stand beside her and retrieve my runaway charge. "Hello, Noreen. You must be on dog-walking duty for Boswell today."

"I am," I say, a bit too breathy for my liking. "He's usually not so rambunctious. I've never seen him give Juniper such a time." I accept the retractable leash from Clara, taking care to hold firmly to the handle. I hate to think of what might have happened had we been outside waiting to cross the street when he pulled such a trick.

"Mr. Boswell has had quite a few handlers lately, haven't you, boy? Maybe he's just testing you." She gives him one more rub across his head and stands. "Everyone seems to have a different technique."

"Handlers? I didn't realize Juniper was using dog walkers."

"Must be a new development. I only recently noticed—Juniper usually takes care of all Boswell's walks."

"Well, I'm taking Mr. Boz here for a playdate, but from now on, I'll be sure to keep a better hold on this little escape artist."

I tug slightly on the leash, summoning Boswell toward the front door of the building. Pushing through to the outside, a thick wave of humidity envelops me, draws my eye to the dark clouds rolling in from the south. Boswell and I wait for the traffic light to change, then cross the street. At the far end of the park, I spy Alok. Given the intensity of the conversation, he doesn't see us approaching. I hold Boswell back a bit, encouraging him to potty so I can get a better look at the woman Alok speaks with. The woman appears younger than Alok, rather fit, and tall (but not quite as tall as Juniper). Her long dark hair hangs in waves to mid-back.

While I'm busy snooping, Dash spots Boswell and begins to yap, giving our position away. Alok looks over the woman's head as she turns to view the commotion. He lifts a hand, waving me over. Boswell doesn't need to be encouraged once he's eyed Dash, but, for me, keeping up with the dog is another issue. Seeing me struggle to keep rein on Boswell, Alok hurries toward us, Dash in tow, but the closer Dash gets, the more difficult it is to control Boswell.

"My goodness," I say as Alok reaches to take Boswell's leash from me. "You'd think these two were excited to see one another."

"Best buds," Alok says, bending to give Boswell a rub hello. Alok stands, turning, waving the woman over. Alok swivels to address me. "Good to see you, Noreen. Sorry, Boswell's giving you such a hard time."

As the woman nears, I understand she is much older than I initially thought. She stops beside Alok, reaching down to pet the dogs. "Noreen, this is my assistant, Paula. Paula, my neighbor, Noreen." We shake hands, exchange pleasantries.

Alok proceeds. "Paula is new to the office but has caught on fast, not sure how I got by without her."

"You're far too kind, Alok," Paula says to him, then tells me. "He's a good boss—I'd do anything for him."

"And she has," Alok tells me. "Paula was the one who found the fire at our house. By remarkable coincidence, she was delivering documents and alerted the fire department early on. Otherwise, we might have lost the entire house."

"Oh my, wow, that is fortunate. Not the house fire, I mean, but, oh… You know," I stumble, my mind looping through the stories Juniper has relayed. Is Paula the dark-haired woman Juniper saw with Alok? Is this the woman she saw in bed with him? Not that I know Juniper's husband that well, but Paula doesn't strike me as Alok's type. Not to mention, she's much older than he is by the looks of it.

"Lucky too that Wellington hasn't been the victim of ransomware like West Palm Beach currently is," Paula says. "It's crazy how long this cyber attack has gone on."

I nod, listening as Alok continues.

"This mayor isn't budging. Says he's not giving in to hacking thugs," Alok tells us. "But at whose cost is it coming is what I want to know. The only thing this new guy is saving is his ego."

"He has definitely rubbed a few people in this town the wrong way," I add to the conversation. "But I have it from a reliable source that this is coming to an end very soon." The pair looks puzzled. "I would say more, but I'm under a non-disclosure agreement. Past employer. Anyway. I shouldn't have said that. But, well, I think this will be over soon."

"I hope you're right," Paula says, relieving me of my gaffe. She turns to address Alok. "I need to head back to the office before traffic gets moving down here." Paula looks in my direction to say, "Nice meeting you, Noreen."

"You as well, Paula."

Alok waves as Paula walks toward her parked car.

"She seems nice. And proficient. How long did you say Paula has worked for you, Alok?"

"Paula came on a few months ago, right when Juniper's mother, Cherri, took a turn for the worse. I was fortunate that Paula decided she wanted to come out of retirement."

"Out of retirement? She doesn't look old enough to retire."

"Paula is sixty-seven, believe it or not. It's the exercise that makes her look so young. She's been competing in bodybuilding competitions for the last ten years."

"Hmmm."

Alok loses interest in the conversation and shifts topics. "Well, thanks for bringing Boswell out. Did Juniper say when she wants me to deliver him back to her apartment?"

"I didn't speak with her. As a matter of fact, I haven't seen her. Juniper texted me earlier and asked if I could collect Boswell from her side patio. Said she would put him out there with his walking things."

"That's odd. Juniper doesn't normally do that, does she?" Alok asks.

"I'm not sure what Juniper is doing anymore." The statement falls out of my mouth before I can pull it back. "Don't take that the wrong way. I shouldn't have put it like that. It's just, well... I think something might be wrong with Juniper, and I'm not sure she would even want me to say anything to you."

"Here," Alok says, motioning me over to one of the park's benches to sit. We situate ourselves while the dogs continue to play around our feet.

Alok lays an arm over the back of the bench, angling his body toward me. "What's wrong with Juniper?" His forehead creases with concern.

"Like I said, I probably shouldn't raise concerns when I'm not positive. I realize we haven't been friends for all that long, but I already feel as if I know Juniper. I think something is off with her, Alok."

"How so?" Alok's voice crackles with worry.

"Juniper has been quite open about her feelings of grief—the loss of her mother and then you." I hold looking at Alok to be certain he's okay with me knowing personal details of his marriage. He nods, eyes cast downward. "Since our initial meeting, Juniper seems to have made progress toward moving forward, healing. Lately, though, it seems she is reverting."

Alok lifts his gaze to meet my eyes. "Reverting? You mean falling back into depression?"

I nod. "I think so, yes." I hurry on, offering examples of Juniper's latest activities to affirm my theory. "I don't think she has left her apartment for days. Juniper hasn't been walking Boswell. She's having her groceries delivered, and I haven't seen her go to the gym in over a week."

Alok removes his arm, sitting up, moving to lean his elbows on his knees. "Really? Juniper's not running?"

"No. I thought it was odd, too. Since I've known Juniper, she hasn't missed a workout. Juniper says it clears her head and helps with her anxiety."

Alok silently mulls over the details I've laid out as I reach down to run a hand over Boswell's head. He and Dash have settled and now rest by our feet.

"You're right," Alok says. "This is not like Juniper. She doesn't tell me much anymore—says she can't trust me—but I thought she was moving on?"

"I assumed the same. Juniper was taking control of her life and her health, being proactive with her physical and mental wellness. And forgive me if I'm overstepping here, but Juniper even appeared to be coming to terms with the fissures in your marriage."

"I'm not ready to accept that assessment, although I will say my last few conversations with Juniper have been much more civil. But then, I really haven't heard from Juniper lately either, other than a few curt text messages." Alok studies the ground, averting eye contact.

"So I'm not out of line here to be worried?" I ask Alok.

"No, Noreen. I think you have every right to be concerned. This doesn't sound like my wife at all."

CHAPTER FORTY-EIGHT

"I SPENT the remainder of my time in Bainbridge getting to know Hannah Anderson. I hadn't given up on my initial quest to learn the mystery of my parentage, but Hannah was so much more enthralling and worthy of my attention." I hold, taking in the surly expression Donna wears.

"You're looking at me as if I were obsessed, Donna. I wasn't. Hannah reciprocated my feelings. We both felt some greater force had brought us together."

Donna's hair is pulled back in a ponytail today—the gray streaking through the blonde showcases the dull appearance she wears daily. Although, to her benefit, the hairstyle pulls her eyes and forehead up in a faux-facelift kind of way. Though, upon closer inspection, nope—she looks a bit ghoulish, actually.

"Did you confide in Hannah?" Donna breaks into my thoughts, "Share with her your suspicions about the connection you believed there to be between the two families?"

"No. I told you I wasn't sure there was an association after what I learned from the DNA tests. For all I knew, Juniper got herself into a situation with someone, changed her mind about him, and then lied to the world about the real father of her baby."

"So you didn't have any qualms that you and Hannah might

be related? You were comfortable and confident about starting a relationship with her?"

I know what Donna is waiting for me to say, but that's not happening. Not now. Donna is going to have to wait until I'm ready.

"Hannah was like no one I had ever met. I never believed in that sappy, soulmate bullshit Alok and Juniper swore to, but I was sure Hannah was my other half. No way was I going to give up Hannah because of Juniper's *supposed* history with the Anderson family. Had Juniper dated Chris Anderson? Had she become pregnant with Chris Anderson's child? There was no proof. As a matter of fact, all the proof I did have, pointed to the likelihood that everything Juniper had told me was a crock of shit. According to three separate DNA tests, my father was Robert Ulrich—that was the only concrete evidence I had. So no. I was not going to give up Hannah for no good reason."

"And Hannah felt the same?"

"For fuck's sake, Donna, yes. Since you didn't hear me the first time, let me repeat it for you. *We. Were. Inseparable.* And the feelings were mutual."

Donna bats her eyelashes, puckers her lips, and nods, that ridiculous ponytail bobbing up and down. Not an attractive look, Donna. I'd tell her, but I don't think she gives a damn about how she looks. If she did, she sure as hell wouldn't be wearing that shapeless tunic.

I continue.

"The end of my trip loomed. I only had a few days before I had to get back to my job, get back to Cherri, who was getting frailer by the day. But for Hannah and me—*both* of us—the thought of being away from the other was more than we could stand. Before I left Bainbridge, we laid out a schedule of trips. I would return to Bainbridge, she would visit me in West Palm Beach, the two of us would meet in the middle. In those early days, we may not have been able to define what it was between us, but we were determined to make whatever it was work."

"Let me stop you there," Donna says, kicking her foot back and forth.

"What the fuck for now?"

"You took all that time off of work to learn who your father was, to learn why Cherri's DNA did not match yours. Am I to assume you let that search go to the wayside the moment you met Hannah?" She's doing it again, trying to rush me into saying what she wants to hear.

"You read the file, Donna. You know I didn't let it go."

"Then let's delve into the next actions you took in your quest for the truth."

This woman is too much, like a fucking scratched record— repeat, repeat, repeat—the same shit over and over. I know what Donna wants. She wants me to implicate myself. Maybe if I try a different tactic…

"I don't understand the point of this exercise, Donna. If you already have all the information laid out for you in the file, it seems to me that this is a waste of your valuable time. I do understand how thin they have you stretched."

"I appreciate your concern for my time constraints, Roni, but you know as well as I do, there is more to these sessions than uncovering or restating facts. We are here to explore the reasons behind *your* actions. Because it is *those* actions that led to the factual accounts laid out in the file." Donna tilts her head from one side to the other. Hoping to appear wise? Sympathetic? Nurturing? Whatever portrayal she's going for here, she fails— that limp ass, flaccid ponytail flopping to and fro.

"So what is it you want to know, Donna? Here's an idea. Maybe you should tell me verbatim what you want me to say. Save us both some time."

"I would like to hear what you told Hannah," Donna states, matter-of-factly, ignoring my last remark. "She must have had questions about how you came to be standing on her family's doorstep."

Leaning over my knees, I run fingers through my hair. It

needs to be washed. I push fingertips hard against my skull, trying to press out the headache building underneath my scalp. I sit upright, tuck the front strands behind my ears, then look Donna in the eye to deliver the answers she's asked for.

"I had no idea what Hannah's parents had told her about Chris's death. Tact was of utmost importance, especially since Hannah was grieving the loss of her parents.

"Hannah told me her mom had contracted pneumonia and couldn't battle the infection. Mrs. Anderson's death was sudden and unexpected. While planning his wife's funeral, Mr. Anderson experienced a severe heart attack and wound up following his wife to the grave. When I rang Hannah's doorbell, it had only been six months since their double funeral. She was still grappling with how to move forward without them. I didn't want to rush Hannah, but I didn't have much time before I had to get back to work.

"I expressed my condolences for her loss and carefully moved forward with my planned inquiries. I told Hannah I had hoped to speak with her parents about their son Chris. I asked if she would mind answering some questions for me instead. Hannah said she would tell me what she could, but her brother had died many years ago in a car accident.

"I told her my dad, Robert, had gone to school with Chris Anderson—that my dad died before I ever got to know him— that I was hoping to speak with someone who knew my father back when he was in high school. Not the whole truth, but pretty damn close.

"The more Hannah told me about her family, the more I allowed myself to believe fate had brought us together. I didn't know why Juniper would have lied about my father's identity, but it was clear Hannah was not to blame."

"But there was something," Donna starts, twirling that pen again, "some inkling that made you question yourself, was there not?"

"Why, Donna? Why the fuck can't you just let me have a

moment? It's childlike, you know? You, needing to drop these little info bombs before I have an opportunity to speak about my *own* life, my *own* actions."

Donna's eyes bore into mine. The look she gives declares I have hit a nerve. "I'm going to be as frank with you, Roni, as you are with me."

"By all means, Donna. A genuine statement from you would be quite fucking *refreshing*, as they say."

"You have regularly manipulated our sessions so as not to cover topics that are of the utmost importance to your case. One way or another, we will have to cover these issues. Given the way you conduct yourself during our time together, I'm inclined to believe that you might want to get this over with and done."

I mentally check myself, reeling in any non-verbal cues I might be portraying. I refuse to admit shit to this bitch, thereby wiping my facial expressions clean and ignoring her observation. Instead of responding to her, I begin again.

"Hannah and I grew closer, sharing more and more details of our lives, our upbringings."

"But you weren't as honest with Hannah as she was with you?"

"Donna," I mutter, shaking my head, biting the corner of my lip, knowing she's right, and hating her for it. "I wish I could have been completely upfront with Hannah, but there were so many questions still left to be answered. And also, I had no idea what Hannah's parents had told her about my family. If I had started with the full version of the story, Hannah might have been conflicted about answering those questions honestly.

"So, when I introduced myself, I used Cherri's maiden name as my surname. It wasn't a lie. My birth name is Veronica Barnes Walder. I couldn't tell Hannah I was a Walder, not at first. Cherri told me the Andersons blamed the Walders for the death of their son, that they wanted nothing to do with me. Cherri said it was one of the reasons we left Bainbridge, because they wanted us gone. If I had told Hannah I was Roni Walder instead of Roni

Barnes, she would have put two and two together and shut that door in my face the very day I met her. I could not let that happen."

"And as I understand it, you are currently awaiting the paperwork to be filed in the legal proceedings of having your name legally changed to Barnes?"

"Any day now, it should be official."

"And you did that specifically because of your relationship with Hannah?"

"Yes, and no. Yes, because I never wanted Hannah to learn I was part of the family who had taken Chris's life. No, because I no longer wanted to be a Walder. Juniper was Walder. She had lied to me, kept my identity from me, and I no longer trusted her or wanted to be associated with her. And yes, before you jump in, Donna, I'm aware Cherri was a Walder, but she was a Barnes first. By taking Cherri's last name, I could still honor her."

Donna stops me, "Did you tell Cherri or Juniper about your name change or about Hannah?"

I roll my eyes blatantly, obnoxiously, for Donna to see and note. She knows the answer to these questions, but is going to make me state them for the record anyway.

"I tried to tell Cherri—about deciding to change my name, about Hannah—but as one would expect, Cherri couldn't comprehend the significance of what I was relaying to her. Even if she did understand, Cherri couldn't put the words together to say such. I knew Cherri would be happy for me, though. My happiness was always so important to Cherri. So yes, I did try to tell her about Hannah. Whether Cherri understood or not, I wanted her to know."

"And Juniper? You withheld the information from her. You didn't think she had the right to know about the decision to change your name? Why not tell Juniper about Hannah? After all, Juniper had a relationship at one point with Chris, regardless of what the relationship status was."

"No. In my mind, Juniper hadn't earned the right to know

any of the details of my personal life. First, let me remind you that we weren't sure about Juniper's 'relationship status,' as you put it, with Chris, because she lied. You were listening, right, Donna? Juniper told me one man was my father and that he was dead. When in reality, my father, despite what he might have done, was alive. She stole my opportunity to know the man before he died. Secondly, for all my life, Juniper was a 'rule-follower,' and annoyingly so. One of her biggest pet peeves is people who don't obey rules. Juniper said those who break the rules believe they are better than everyone else. She never would have approved of my relationship with Hannah."

"Because it broke the rules?" The pen rolling between fingers, head tilting side to side. I have to close my eyes. The sight of the ridiculous woman sends my internal body temperature soaring.

I open my eyes and enunciate slowly, carefully, for Dense Donna's benefit. "Yes, Donna. It broke them all."

"Shall we expand on that?"

"Oh, for God's sake." It's never enough for this woman.

I scoot around in the seat, trying to find a more comfortable position. The more time I spend in this chair, the more confining it becomes, the less Donna seems to comprehend. "Let's try this again. I'll go slow. Juniper's little sister, Luna, killed Hannah's brother Chris, who, by the way, was Juniper's ex-boyfriend, or so Juniper said."

"I wouldn't deem any of the details you just rattled off as *rules broken*," Donna says.

"Well, I didn't ask for your viewpoint, did I, Donna?"

"As you wish, Roni."

"Don't do that bullshit, Donna."

"What do you mean by that statement, Roni?"

"You're patronizing me."

"Perhaps, but isn't that what you want?" When I refuse to justify her sarcasm, Donna continues. "I'm simply going to pose a different question. Maybe if I'm lucky, you'll decide to answer it."

"If we weren't so close, Donna…"

"And yet we are. Now, let's finish this session so we can both take a break from one another."

"By all means," I agree.

"I want to delve into the topic you have avoided for the last three sessions. We are running out of time, and the issue of the DNA test must be addressed."

"We've talked these freaking DNA tests to death, Donna. What more do you want to know?"

"You are well aware of what I want you to disclose, Roni. However, if it will make you feel better, I will…"

"Fine. We'll talk about Hannah's DNA test."

"You took such care to conceal your identity from Hannah, even going so far as to change your last name. Hannah had been blatantly honest with you about her past, her family."

"I know what you're getting at, Donna. I was dishonest with Hannah."

"Expand…"

"God. It fucking infuriates me when you say that."

"I'm sorry you feel that way, Roni, but we must delve deeper into this topic, and now that we are here, well, let's just get it over with."

"I didn't ask her permission. I took Hannah's DNA without her knowing and sent it off for the test results. Hannah had no knowledge of my actions."

"Yet, you were adamant about the fact that you were Cherri's health proxy and could seek her results legally, but you would not commit an unethical act to obtain Juniper's DNA results. What changed your mind about performing the illegal activity on Hannah, someone you claimed to love and care for so much?"

"Yes, Donna. You are right on all counts. Happy?"

"No, I'm not. I want to know why, Roni. You put your professional career in jeopardy for what reason?"

"I had to know. I needed to know before anyone else figured it out."

"And you did. You did find out when no one else had any idea about what was happening in the background of their lives, you knew, but then told no one. You kept it to yourself. Some people believe the omission of truth to be as bad as a lie."

"You are not here to judge me, to sit across from me and form opinions about my situation."

"I am not judging you or the situation, Roni. I simply don't have time to allow you to manipulate our sessions any longer. Our time is almost up. If you'd rather start over with another therapist, I can make that recommendation. Otherwise, you're going to have to deal with addressing the issues still at hand—and in a timely manner, I might add."

"I've told you how I felt about Hannah. I've informed you as to the lies I was fed all my life. I had two conflicting accounts. Juniper insisted she and Chris Anderson had a relationship. Hannah insisted Chris never dated anyone throughout high school. Juniper had lied to me about my father's identity, so perhaps Hannah's parents had lied to her, too. It was a hunch, and once I dug in, I couldn't rest until I found out the truth."

"This hunch, please talk about it."

"Hannah's parents told her Chris died before she was born, and no one could deny that Hannah and Chris favored one another as many siblings often do. The two were definitely related in some way, no question. What I found uncanny and disturbing, though, was how many of Juniper's mannerisms Hannah portrayed."

"So you were looking for a connection between Hannah's and Juniper's DNA?"

"Yes," I nod to confirm, hoping to end this conversation.

"What did you find, Roni?"

"You truly are a—I won't say it. No matter how much you goad me, I will not be that unprofessional."

"I'm waiting, Roni. What did you learn?"

"Hannah and Juniper were closely related, as in Juniper was Hannah's mother, not mine."

CHAPTER FORTY-NINE
Cherri

"And now, we will return to the portion of the review you skipped." Cherri's guardian spirit nudges her toward the postponed reflection.

She has been able to avoid it. If only her guardian spirit would end the life review here, at this point.

"We must go through all the moments. Ordinarily, it is done chronologically so you can determine and measure the growth of your soul over the reviewed lifetime. I have only allowed you to skip this one portion because it was clear how disturbed you are by the events that transpired."

"Isn't there some way of circumventing it?" Cherri implores. "I don't know if I can handle this part."

"You can. You must. We will begin in the spot where you began earlier, but then jumped over, so it may feel as though we are repeating pieces of the review. However, this time through, you must see the whole transaction. You will not be permitted to skip around and over situations you wish not to face. You will not be allowed to lie to yourself by omitting your transgressions."

Cherri offers a reluctant nod, still hesitant to face this period of her life. She so enjoyed visiting all the moments of Roni's upbringing, of the celebrations and holidays her family spent together, the vacations and trips Alok arranged for them to take. But the deal Cherri made with her guardian spirit has come to an end. It is time for her to face the portion of her life review—the segment certain to send her spiraling into the depths of the hell she constructed for herself during her years on the physical plane.

Oh, that little girl! She owns their hearts the minute she enters their world. Roni is born in June, just days before Juniper graduates high school and mere weeks before Juniper is due to begin college at Stetson University in DeLand, Florida.

It never dawned on Cherri that Juniper would become so attached to the baby—Juniper had shown no excitement during her pregnancy, no eager anticipation of the baby's arrival. But in the few short weeks Juniper spends with Roni, their bond swells.

Juniper began dropping hints in the days after Roni's birth that maybe she should wait to start her college education. Perhaps it is best if Juniper is at home to get Roni through her first year of life. Cherri and Juniper both know Juniper can't pass up the free ride she has earned at Stetson University. Giving up the full scholarship Juniper has worked hard to win would be tossing away the future Juniper has always dreamed about. Cherri simply must convince her of that.

Logic and rational arguments do little to persuade Juniper to carry on with their original plans. Juniper wants to be present for her daughter's early upbringing. And so, to appease all involved in the dilemma, Cherri presents another solution.

The perfect answer to all of their problems—Cherri will move to be near Juniper, bringing Roni up in DeLand rather than Brunswick. Juniper can attend classes while she takes care of Roni. Cherri has no attachments to Brunswick, only bad memories.

Cherri does not mention that, given the proximity, it is far more likely the Andersons will learn about the existence of their granddaughter. If that happens, Cherri and Juniper will have to share Roni with Chris's parents.

No. If Cherri has her way, the Andersons will never know about Roni.

And with all that in mind, she holds onto Roni, waving Juniper off to college with the promise of a reunion in the near future.

After Juniper leaves for DeLand, she begins the process of moving immediately. Unlike Cherri's gypsy days when she could throw a few things into a bag and head out, there is much to be done. Cherri finds she doesn't long for those traveling days of her youth anymore. From all the death in her life, Cherri has learned just how important family is. Cherri has promised Juniper that she and Roni will move to Florida within the next month and a half, two at most. The three of them—their little family—will be settled together in Florida before the holidays arrive, and Cherri is going to make sure of it, make sure nothing happens to her tiny family.

But then, the unthinkable befalls.

Cherri is working one of her last shifts at the bar. Tina, one of Juniper's closest friends, is looking after Roni while Cherri works. It is early in the evening when Cherri is summoned to the phone. She finishes up a drink order she is assembling, then hurries to take the call. On the other end of the line, Tina hastily begins by saying Roni is fine, not to worry, but Chris's parents, the Andersons, are there. They are demanding to see their grand-daughter. Tina doesn't know what to do. Tina told the Andersons she isn't allowed to let anyone inside while Cherri is out of the house. The Andersons will not listen to reason and refuse to leave without seeing their grandchild.

Cherri begs off work, rushing home to deal with the situation at hand, her mind running wild with terrible thoughts and chaotic scenarios. Chris was the nicest young man. Cherri couldn't have selected a finer boyfriend for Juniper—so thoughtful, considerate, well-mannered, and polite. However, the parents of this fine young man are polar opposites of their son. Maybe she can tell them Roni isn't Chris's baby. Perhaps Cherri can convince them she is the baby's mother, not Juniper; therefore, how could the baby belong to Chris?

Cherri finds them on the front porch, arms crossed, feet tapping, reddened faces. Their anger cannot be mollified. How could Cherri have even considered that it would be? During the most agreeable of times, the Andersons are hateful people. The things they had said about Juniper, about Cherri, not only after Chris's death but prior, were horrific. In the eyes of the Andersons, the Walders were nothing more than white trash.

The Andersons claimed to have heard the news from Juniper's friends that Juniper had given birth to Chris's baby. "*Gossips,*" Cherri throws out, then proceeds to spout off all the half-baked ideas she had come up with on the mad dash home. The Andersons buy none of them, of course. The pair will not entertain for even a brief moment that Roni is Cherri's child, declaring that while Cherri might have slept with two-thirds of Brunswick's men, she is quickly aging out of her childbearing years, demanding to see a birth certificate as proof instead. Roni was born at home, and Cherri hasn't gotten around to filing for the document. No matter, there will be a paternity test, but first, they will get a look at this baby for themselves. "*No more hearsay, no more cockamamie excuses, get the child.*"

Cherri has no other option than to allow the Andersons to see Roni. Cherri sends Tina home, pleading with her not to say anything about the visit to Juniper.

The minute the Andersons see her, it is as if Juniper has nothing at all to do with being Roni's mother. "*James, look at her! She looks just like Chris.*" Tears spill over their cheeks as they snatch up Cherri's grandchild and refuse to let go. Cherri hovers nearby, tears welling, knowing what is to come. She will have to call her daughter, tell Juniper that she and Roni will not be moving. Their worst nightmare has come true. The Andersons have found out about Roni. They will have to share custody of Roni with these awful people.

Oh, but it is so much worse.

If only Cherri had left town earlier… She should have moved to DeLand when Juniper did, not have waited. Loyalty to her boss—Cherri hadn't wanted to leave the woman in a lurch—is going to cost her family dearly.

They come at her slowly—teeth bared, slinking, skulking—evil hyenas boxing her in. For Juniper's sake, however, Cherri has to stand up to these awful people.

Chris's mother begins: *"You killed my son. You know it. I know it. Juniper knows it. The whole lot over at Bainbridge High School knows it. You were responsible for seeing that our Chris got home safely, and you couldn't. You are nothing but a pathetic lush. You probably MADE your underage daughter drive our son home. Whether or not you gave the directive, Chris would still be here if you hadn't been drunk that night."*

"I lost my daughter that night, too," Cherri reminds her.

"Irresponsible," Chris's father chimes in. *"Negligent. Yes, you killed our son and your daughter."*

In addition to being a man of great physical stature, Chris's father has an air of haughty authority. The man is a Superior Court Judge, in addition to being a very prominent, *very* well-respected man in their community. He frightens Cherri more than she cares to admit. *"You were plastered, weren't you?"*

"Any decent parent would have called the boy's parents to come to pick him up or even send him home in a cab," Chris's mother spat, backing Cherri into a dark corner, literally. *"But not you. You're not decent. You're not responsible. You're an alcoholic, and there is not a chance in hell that we will allow you to raise our granddaughter. You took our son. You owe us our granddaughter."*

Owe them? They can not have Roni. She is a baby, not a

knick-knack. Roni is a tiny human who belongs to Cherri's daughter. Cherri doesn't have the authority, much less the willingness, to give up the child to the Andersons. Cherri tries to tell them, to explain. *"Roni is not mine to give. Roni is Juniper's baby."* She can't possibly give them Juniper's baby.

"Juniper is unfit to be a mother. Case in point, she has already left her child in the care of another, an alcoholic other. Besides, Juniper is still a child herself. How can a child raise a child?"

Cherri's rebuttal is curt; Juniper will be eighteen in a matter of months. Until then, Cherri has guardianship over both her daughter and granddaughter. Cherri expects—well, perhaps hopes—the discussion is over. It will break Juniper's heart, but Cherri will concede and move forward to work out the details of sharing Roni's upbringing with the Andersons.

To Cherri's horror, however, the Andersons don't just want to share custody of the child. They want Roni all to themselves. Cherri and Juniper will give up all rights to the baby and have no future contact with the girl.

Ever.

Their demands are ridiculous and ludicrous. Cherri tries to reason. Cherri is sorry for keeping their granddaughter's birth from them, but they can all work something out. Cherri can't hand over Juniper's child.

Yes, she can, and yes, she will—unless Cherri is ready to go to prison. Cherri might not have been behind the wheel of that car the night it went over the bridge, but she had prior knowledge and probably even handed over the keys and the directive herself.

"We would have brought charges before." Chris's father hisses. *"Instead, we gave you the benefit of the doubt because your daughter died as well, but this child changes everything. It's called involuntary manslaughter. And I assure you, it won't be hard to prove."*

CHAPTER FIFTY

"I was running out of time," I reply to Donna's last inane query.

"How so? Are you saying in relation to Cherri's deteriorating condition?"

"No, Donna." I shake my head. "I mean, yes, Cherri's health was declining quickly, but I'm not talking about that, and you know it. You're trying to trip me up, and I don't fucking appreciate it."

"I'm not, though, Roni. I'm attempting to get an understanding of the mindset you were experiencing leading up to the tragedy."

I don't respond.

"Let's refresh." Donna slips her readers to perch on the tip of her nose, then begins skimming her notes. "I inquired as to why you felt the need to take such a lengthy leave of absence from your job. You replied that you were 'running out of time.'" Donna pulls the glasses from her face, looking directly into my eyes. "We've established that the concern for time was not the rapid progression of Cherri's illness. So what was the reason for your perceived time constraints?"

"Hannah."

"Hannah?"

"Are you going to let me talk, Donna?" She opens her mouth to respond, but I hurry on to keep from hearing her nasally voice. "I assure you, I want this over more than you do, Donna. So if you'll just shut the hell up for a second, I'll try to explain."

Donna shifts, scoots, crosses her legs. She pulls that tight-lipped pucker I've come to abhor—pen poised, her damn crinkled yellow pad perched atop her knee.

"Hannah and I had made plans for our future."

"Were these plans laid prior to the DNA results or after?"

"For Christ's sake. After. Not sure why that's important to you, but there you have it—the plans were made after I learned Hannah was Juniper's daughter."

"And at this point—after plans had been made—does Hannah know she is Juniper's daughter?"

"Honest to God, Donna. I don't know where to turn with you. You ask me one thing, and before I can answer, you want to know something else."

"You're right, Roni. I apologize. We simply have so much ground to cover that I'm anxious about missing details."

"Then act like a professional and jot down the *detail* you want to address when I'm finished spilling my guts over the last *detail* you ask about."

Donna makes a quick note on the legal pad, then returns her attention to me.

"You're ready now?" I ask. Condescendingly. Sarcastically. Yes. She deserves it.

Donna nods.

"I'm going to start where I want to start."

Donna nods. "By all means."

"From the DNA test results, I knew Hannah was Juniper's daughter and that she was somehow related to the Andersons. I was ninety-eight percent positive she was Chris's daughter—not his sister, as Hannah had always been led to believe. Here's the thing, though. Hannah was happy with the stories she had been led to believe—Chris was her brother, the Andersons her parents. Telling Hannah otherwise would have put her into a tailspin so soon after the death of her parents—or rather, grandparents."

"So you didn't reveal to Hannah what you learned because you were 'protecting' her?" She does that finger quote thing—almost loses her pen.

"Yes, Donna."

"And you didn't inform Juniper of what you had learned because she had lied to you?"

"Right again, Donna. Jesus. Do you just like to hear yourself talk?"

"Actually, Roni, I'm trying to convince you it is safe to reveal the true motivation behind your decision to withhold such important information from two people who supposedly meant so much to you."

"First, I've already told you how much Hannah meant to me, but I've never said anything about Juniper being *'near and dear, '*" I add sarcastically, mimicking Donna's finger quotes. "Don't go orchestrating thoughts and feelings for me. And, second, when I'm ready to be more open with you about my *motivation,* as you put it, I will do so."

Donna nods. She looks like a fucking bobblehead. God, I can't wait to be done with her.

"If it's okay with you, Donna, I will move on now to address your initial inquiry."

"By all means," she says, nodding.

In my mind's eye, I see Donna sitting on the dashboard of a car. Wobble, wobble. I would laugh, but Donna wouldn't understand the humor and would inevitably weave something negative into the report about an inappropriate emotional outburst.

"Hannah and I made plans for our future. To be honest, I wasn't entirely on board with all of them, but they made Hannah happy… excited. Hannah's happiness was all that mattered to me, so I went along with those plans as they were, even knowing things could go very wrong.

"When we met, Hannah's house was already on the market as she had previously decided she could not stay in a home so full of memories. I've told you how difficult it was for us to be apart, but commuting every weekend was taking its toll on us. It was Hannah's idea to move to West Palm Beach as soon as her house sold. She loved the thought of us living together, of sharing a life together, and I wanted that too. I just had to figure out how to make it happen."

"What do you mean by 'figure out how to make it happen?' People move to be closer to one another all the time."

"Yes, but, as I've already explained, I hadn't been entirely honest and forthright with Hannah."

"I thought we had already established that point. Not only were you keeping the secret of Hannah's parentage from her, but your true identity as well, even going so far as to change your last name from Walder to Barnes."

"I hadn't told Hannah a lot about my family. She knew my family was small and a bit unconventional, but not much else."

"You didn't tell Hannah about Cherri?"

"She was aware my grandmother was ill, and of course, I told her when Cherri passed away. Hannah wanted to come to the funeral, to be there for me. Honestly, it would have been easier to grieve with Hannah by my side, but..."

"But?"

"But, I didn't want to divulge too much about myself until I had come to terms with what Juniper had done."

"And yet you continued to believe it best not to confront Juniper? Why not simply ask her about Robert Urlich?"

"How many fucking times do I have to explain myself to you, Donna? The last thing I wanted was more goddamn lies."

"There's no reason to raise your voice, Roni. I was simply confirming we were sticking with that reasoning."

"*Sticking with that reasoning*? Are you for real? God bless you, Donna. Because only God knows how long your professional career will last with the actions you've portrayed here."

The lips pucker. The pen twirls. Legs crossed, the foot shakes back and forth. Donna does not reply.

"I thought I had plenty of time," I continue, "until Hannah's family home sold, I mean. The house was historical; rules and parameters had to be met for a sale to occur, the market was in a lull. People weren't exactly rushing to move to Bainbridge, Georgia. Neither of us could predict when it would sell. As it was, the house had already been on the market the entirety of our relationship—by that point, coming up on a year since Hannah initially listed it with a real estate agency. What hadn't crossed my mind was the possibility of Hannah scoring a job in West Palm Beach *before* the house sold. Hannah was thrilled and decided it would be best for her to go ahead with the move. "We can finally be together," she said. Hannah reasoned the commute was getting to both of us, the realtor could handle everything in Bainbridge, and we could get started on our life together in Florida."

"So she moved into the apartment building with you?"

"Yes."

"Was this before or after Juniper moved into The Grabell?"

I ignore Donna's questions and move forward as I wish. "Everything happened so fast. Once Hannah negotiated her new employment contract, she gave her current employer a month's notice. We figured one more month to commute wasn't that bad. Hannah was thrilled, but I still had so much to do—to get into place—before Hannah became a Floridian. As it happened, Cherri passed away three weeks after Hannah returned to Bainbridge to work out her notice. I had one week to get everything in order before Hannah returned to West Palm Beach to move in with me.

"The plan was in full motion, but like I said, I was running out of time. Not to mention how risky it was going to be having Juniper and Hannah living in the same building. I had no choice but to move forward; I'd already put in so much effort and paid a hefty chunk on renting the apartment to get the cameras and equipment all rigged and in place for Juniper's move-in date. I didn't have time to start over. There was barely enough time to carry out what I had in motion. The leave of absence from my job was necessary to give the plan the attention it needed."

"Roni."

"Yes, Donna."

"I realize this account and all the circumstantial, minute details that accompany it make perfect sense to you. And I am aware of how frustrated you are relaying it to me—Dense Donna, I believe, is how you refer to me. So, let me earn my nickname and ask for a bit of clarification with your timeline."

I close my eyes, wishing to be anywhere but here. (How did Donna know her nickname?) But this situation can't be wished away.

I comply.

"Of course, Cherri's diagnosis was devastating to all of us, but Juniper carried on in such a way that any outsider would have thought Juniper was the only one affected by it. When it became clear Cherri needed professional care on a daily/hourly basis, Juniper, Alok, and I began searching for a skilled nursing care facility. To hear Juniper during these tours go on and on about how her mother hates this, her mother loves that, you'd think I'd never even met Cherri. As always, there was Alok at Juniper's side, so concerned and caring and doting. God, her theatrics were disgusting. I couldn't stomach any more of Juniper's 'woe is me' routine. So, I took over the process."

"To clarify, this is where the animosity between you and Juniper started?"

"Yes, and it festered from that point forward. Once Cherri was settled into her care facility, I moved to downtown West Palm Beach to be closer to her. It was then I found out what kind of person Juniper really was. Not overnight, of course, but my knowledge of her subterfuge kept expanding, morphing until Juniper was this full-on monster. Dealing with Juniper's crap was too much, especially when I knew I had only a few days left with Cherri. "

"Have you considered that perhaps you began searching for your father's family as a means of 'replacing' Cherri?"

"Don't EVER accuse me of trying to replace Cherri."

"I apologize."

"I've told you that Cherri's psychobabble spurred me to search for them."

"Please." Donna bobs that head again. "Continue with the timeline of events."

"After Cherri's funeral, I knew it was then or never. It may not have been the timing I had long planned, but everything was falling into place. I had the cameras installed and working. The sound equipment wasn't in, but I figured I could work that out along the way. I rented one of the building's large storage units and set up my computers and monitors as my designated surveillance area. All that was left to do was convince Juniper to move downtown into the unit I had set up for her, and the sooner, the better. Hannah would be returning within a week."

"So you took a leave of absence from work? And you didn't share that information with Juniper or Hannah?"

"Work assumed it was grief I needed to work through. My bosses were understanding and compassionate. 'Take all the time you need, Roni.' And, no, I didn't tell anyone else about my sabbatical because I didn't want to have to explain my whereabouts or actions."

"You were confident Juniper would do as you directed and move into the building without Alok?"

"After discovering I had been stolen as an infant from my biological parents, I began assessing Juniper…"

Donna stops me.

"I realize you're anxious to continue with your story, but there are a few points we need to sum up for the report before we move forward."

Knowing I am imitating Donna's laughable action, I nod for

her to continue. At this point, I'll agree, do, say whatever to get this done and get her gone.

"Let's go in the order of your actions. First, we haven't discussed how you came to learn you were 'stolen,' as you have asserted."

"I hired a private detective. All I had to offer the woman to go on was Robert Ulrich's name, but she was good. The detective was able to link Robert Ulrich to Phoebe Daniels."

"Phoebe Daniels?"

"Cut the bullshit, Donna. It's in the fucking file. Phoebe Daniels was my biological mother. Note, I use the word *was* because she, too, is dead now."

"This Phoebe Daniels," Donna checks her yellow pad, "the cause of her death is not in the file. Would you please elaborate?" Donna cocks her head, eyeing me, waiting, finding my life *riveting*.

"According to the newspaper articles the private investigator found, in addition to the family members the detective interviewed, Phoebe and Robert were not married but conceived a child together in the fall of eighty-seven. Their child was born in the summer of eighty-eight—a girl. The couple—my biological parents—lived next door to Cherri and Juniper at the time of my birth. Not long after I was born, Robert was arrested. While Robert awaited trial, I disappeared into thin air. The official autopsy report stated Phoebe Daniels died of an accidental overdose. Phoebe's family, however, told the private eye they believed Phoebe's death was caused by grief and heartbreak—losing Robert and then her newborn baby."

"Still, you didn't confront Juniper once you learned this information, and you continued to withhold the truth from Hannah." Donna flicks that foot, staring at me. "Instead, you took matters into your own hands."

"Don't judge me, Donna. You are not here to form opinions and draw conclusions but to gather information. Right now, the only thing left for you to pull out of me is why. Let me assure you, my reasons are valid."

Donna nods. "According to my notes, that is in fact the next point we need to tackle. You've explained how you learned you were stolen, but we must also address the reasons you directed your anger at Juniper."

"She owed me."

"Juniper? Owed you?"

"Yep. Two parents and thirty-two years. Everything Juniper had stolen from me, I wanted back, but that was never going to happen."

"So instead…"

"So instead, I determined Juniper should lose everything as well, and by no means would she ever meet or know Hannah."

"But that wasn't enough for you, was it?"

"No. How many lives had Juniper ruined with her deceit? Think about it, Donna. Juniper gave Hannah up, leaving her own daughter to live a lie. Then Juniper destroyed Phoebe by stealing her child, causing Phoebe to take her life. And then there was the grief Juniper caused all the people who knew and loved Phoebe. Juniper deserved so much more than simply losing her husband to another woman, more than never knowing the child she discarded."

"What about Hannah?" Didn't Hannah have a right to know the truth about her mother?"

"Yes. I do harbor some regret about that decision, but I couldn't let Hannah find out. The truth would have broken her —would have destroyed our relationship. No, I didn't know the details of what transpired thirty-two years ago, but I knew for certain I could not live my life without Hannah. Not after I had experienced life with Hannah by my side."

I lower my gaze, running a finger over one eyebrow and then another, trying to smooth away some of the pain. The forced revelation is more difficult than I thought it would be—recalling how things were, holding them up against how things are now.

"We need to keep going," Donna prods.

"I thought about all the turmoil and angst Juniper had caused me and all those affected by her actions. Juniper needed to suffer in the manner she had made so many others suffer."

"Is that what you wanted? For Juniper to suffer?"

"No," I say, shaking my head. "Nope. I wanted more. I wanted her happiness. I wanted her memories. I wanted her misery. I wanted her life. In order for that to happen, Juniper had to go away. She needed to die."

Evidently, Donna didn't expect me to be so blunt, her eyes widening, mouth forming into an 'oh.' Donna quickly moves the pen to her mouth to mask her judgmental expressions, pretending to have some degree of professionalism. Too late, Donna.

"Don't look so shocked, Donna. You've known my feelings for Juniper all along."

"That's a lot of hate for someone you believed was your mother… for over thirty years, Roni." Donna's watching for some reaction, but I know what she's looking for and refuse to give her anything. "You wanted her dead," Donna states flatly, holding her expression hostage. Donna thinks she's perfected her poker face, but I know exactly what's going through her mind.

"But I couldn't kill anybody, Donna. And I *didn't* kill anybody."

"Yet, there was a devastating accident, spurred by your very actions."

"Fuck you, Donna," I state, matching her deadpan, impassive tone. "Our time is up for today."

CHAPTER FIFTY-ONE

Noreen

"Who's there?" I ask, although I can see perfectly well through my peephole who is knocking at my door. What I really want to know is what the fuck she wants and why she thinks she needs to bother me for it.

"It's your neighbor from seven-eleven," the woman says, aiming her words toward the tiny glass hole. All lips, tongue, and teeth. Does she know the difference between a peephole and a microphone? Jesus.

"Sorry to bother you. I won't take but a moment of your time."

I hold, wait. Maybe she'll go away.

"Hello. Please." And so it seems she won't.

I open the door, revealing myself to this small, older, meddlesome woman. Leaning into the doorframe, I block her from viewing inside my apartment.

"Hi there," she says, lifting her hand, shifting weight nervously between feet. "I'm your neighbor from seven-eleven."

"So you said," I reply through the crack of the open door.

"Oh, right. Yes, I did say that, didn't I? Sorry. I'm Noreen Flemming."

She waits, squeezing, wringing her hands. Seems Noreen expects me to introduce myself.

I don't.

"Okay, well, I was wondering if maybe you had seen my friend Juniper lately." Noreen holds once more, waiting to see how I will respond.

Again, I don't.

"She just—Juniper that is—lives right there." Noreen turns to indicate the door across the hall.

Although I know exactly who she is referring to, I look in the direction Noreen points. "Why would I see her?"

"Well, I thought, maybe, you might have seen, or perhaps heard even, Juniper coming or going out of her apartment."

Juniper hasn't gone anywhere in recent days.

"I mean, because you live right across the hall, that is," Noreen continues.

Juniper has been holed up in there for a while now.

"Sometimes, when I hear things in the hallway, I look through my peephole to see what is going on out there. Do you ever do that? Have you seen Juniper through your peephole, maybe?"

The woman—Noreen—won't shut up. I could tell her what I know, but I don't want to. I shouldn't. "Nope," I tell her instead, hoping she'll go away now.

"Are you sure? Has she had any company, maybe? Someone coming to see her?"

That dark-haired girl has been in and out—not saying that either. I shake my head. "Un-uh."

"And you haven't heard anything?" Noreen asks.

"Like I said," I continue to shake my head, no—meaning, get the hell outta here—but this broad will not let up.

"What about dog walkers? I know Juniper has had someone walking her dog. They don't come along the pool deck to pick up Boswell because if they did, I would see them, and I haven't seen anyone coming and going that way."

The dog walkers Juniper has been using are all punctual. If they aren't, she won't use them again.

"You're sure you don't see them enter and exit this way? You do have direct sight of her door."

Noreen is right. The walkers all come to the front door, knock gently, retrieve Boswell through a barely cracked opening, then return the dog, repeating the process. Juniper never shows her face.

"Ma'am," I begin.

"Noreen," she reminds me, wringing and twisting her hands again.

"Yeah, okay. I'm sorry I can't help you. Not everyone sits around and watches their peephole all day." I know how I sound. I know what I say is rude, but Noreen needs to move along; leave me be.

"All right. Well, sorry to have bothered you." Noreen makes a motion to turn, but then swivels back before I get the door closed. She holds out the palm of her hand to push the door open as I push the door shut. "Just one more thing. If you do see or hear anything out of the ordinary, would you please let me know?"

"Sure thing," I say, moving to close the woman out of my life.

As the door latches, I hear her call out from the other side, "Number seven-eleven."

"SHALL we begin by reviewing how you left our last session?" The question slaps me before I step through the threshold of the door.

"What a joy it is to be with you again, Donna."

"Thank you, Roni, but your pleasantry doesn't address the posed question."

"I wasn't going for pleasant, Donna. It's called sarcasm. Surely, you know it."

"I do, quite well, actually." Donna looks at the pad in her lap and mumbles, "Raised two teenagers."

"Now, can I get myself situated before you start lobbing out demands?"

"Of course," she says, looking up from her notes. Donna's head bobble starts as she twists both ends of her pen.

"Will you be calling the session short again today?" Donna asks. "If so, I'd like to order the topics of discussion by priority."

"How early we end this chat depends on you, Donna, not me."

"I see," Donna says, penning a note on that worn, wrinkled pad of hers. She's looking a bit haggard today, not that she doesn't normally, but her level of unkemptness is at a higher degree this afternoon.

"Humidity must be up out there."

Donna does that cocking of her head, pulling her face into a question mark. "And what spurs that observation, Roni?"

"Your hair. It's a frizzy mess."

The nod, the pursed lips, then, "Sure. Okay… yes. The air is quite heavy today."

I'm not going to bother with this anymore. I don't care for chitchat, much less with Donna, and I have more pressing issues to handle. "Let's get moving. We need to be wrapping this up. Surely your report must be close to complete."

"I would love to pass this case off to the appropriate handler, Roni, but your cooperation is a must in order to do so."

"I'm sitting right here, Donna, ready to do the work—get on with it already."

"Okay then," Donna says, dragging her readers into position, flipping the crinkled pages of her legal pad to find her last notes. "We had been discussing the urgency to carry forth your *plan*. You said, 'I was running out of time,'" Donna reads, dragging the capped tip of her pen down the page, scanning, searching. "Ah, yes. This is what I'm looking for. Later in the same session, you also stated, 'I wanted more. I wanted her happiness. I wanted her memories. I wanted her misery. I wanted her life. For that to happen, Juniper had to go away. She needed to die.'"

"I'm well aware of what I said, Donna. Your point?"

"We did not have the opportunity to delve into where this hatred for Juniper stemmed. If you recall, you ended the session before our time was up."

"Like I said, I don't have memory issues, but you do, Donna. I've been quite clear about how my feelings for Juniper evolved. It's hard to believe you've forgotten how many lives Juniper wrecked, mine being right up there at the top of the list. Tell me, Donna. Are they overworking you—putting too much on your plate?"

Ignoring the jab, Donna pushes on. "Juniper 'wrecked' your life, so you wanted her dead. You know, Roni, history presents a number of cases where daughters believe their mothers have ruined their lives, yet the accounts are not punctuated by the mother's death."

"Ah, but this one disproves your observation, does it not? Someone did indeed die in this particular mother-daughter relationship."

"You're referring to Phoebe Daniels, your biological mother."

"Yes, fucking Phoebe. I don't need to be reminded, Donna. I've lived through this story you now find so entertaining."

"I hardly find death entertaining, Roni."

"Nor do I, Donna, and for that matter, neither did my mother. Phoebe died of grief and heartache. Alone and broken. So too, Juniper would do the same."

Knowing Donna waits for the details, I sit staring out the window, understanding I cannot move forward without stepping back in time first.

"You know I've never been one of those people who check over their shoulder. I'm one of those who keep my focus on the future. I can't fix what's been done, but I have control over what's to come."

"So you took control."

"Yep. Juniper needed to be held accountable."

"Tell me how this plan for accountability formed."

"Do you have your phone?"

"Roni, it's best if we stay on track."

"Donna, do you have your fucking phone?"

"Yes, Roni, but I…"

"So you're recording this conversation?"

"Yes, Roni, you know I am. You know all our conversations have been recorded. We discussed this, went through the legal disclaimers, signed the consent forms prior to ever beginning our sessions."

"Yes, Roni, you know I am. You know all our conversations have been recorded. We discussed this, went through the legal disclaimers, signed the consent forms prior to ever beginning our sessions," I repeat in my best Donna voice.

"Excuse me," Donna says, cocking her head.

"Excuse me," I repeat, imitating her.

"Roni, I hardly see the point of this exercise. I do not appreciate being mocked. Please, let's not waste any more time."

"Roni, I hardly see the point of this exercise. I do not appreciate being mocked. Please, let's not waste any more time." Again, I parrot her words, mimicking her voice. "Now," I state using my own voice, "I want you to stop the recording function, scroll back, hit the play button, and listen to what just happened."

"Roni."

"Just fucking do it, Donna."

Donna follows instructions, listening to the two of us exchange the same statements. Donna shakes her head, her eyes narrow with confusion.

"Can you distinguish which one of those voices belongs to you?" I ask.

"Well," she begins, "I'm the first voice," Donna says, though not entirely certain of her claim.

"It's one of those strange talents. I have an uncanny ability to make my voice sound like someone other than me is speaking."

Donna sits silently, trying to make sense of what I am telling her.

"Obviously, women are easier to mimic, but I can imitate men too if they are altos."

Donna continues to deliver her wordless, dumbfounded stare.

"Okay, so, during my teen years, I realized I could make my voice sound like Cherri and Juniper. I would take their phone calls, pretending to be them when their friends, or work colleagues, or teachers from my school called. Alok would call home to speak to Juniper and never know it was me on the other end of the line—God, it pissed him off that he fell for it every last time. Cherri and Juniper eventually put a stop to it, made me promise to quit using the gift. I let them think I no longer practiced imitating. I used it when I needed it, though, and later in college, it was my party trick—mimicking our professors, coaches, friends."

"While I find this to be quite a clever skill, I fail to see how it is pertinent to our discussion."

Donna—poor, dense, dim-witted Donna. "I'm relaying the information you've requested."

Donna shakes her head, still not grasping what I am telling her.

Tension builds at the back of my neck. I rub a knot forming at the base, hoping for relief. "You asked about how the plan for Juniper's accountability began. I'm explaining that I can make my voice sound like another's."

"I'm still not following, Roni."

"The night of Cherri's funeral, the night Juniper saw Alok with another woman, the night she left me that frantic voicemail —that wasn't Juniper, it was me saying those things on the message. I'm the one who called my cell from Juniper's cell phone and pretended to be Juniper delivering a play-by-play of Alok's infidelity."

"You left the message? You're the one who saw Alok with another woman?"

"For God's sake, Donna, will you just listen? After Cherri's funeral, Juniper and Alok went home. Juniper wanted me to go with them, but I insisted on being alone in my apartment, told her I didn't feel like company. Later, when I knew it was safe to do so, I snuck inside their house, spiked Juniper's wine with a couple sleeping pills, and took her phone to plant the voicemail to myself."

"But you said Juniper recalled seeing Alok with another woman? That she finally remembered what had happened. How could she remember something that never took place, that she never saw?"

"Juniper only recalled what I *led* her to recall."

"I'm trying to follow here, Roni, but you are making this difficult."

"Surely you've read the psychology journals on memory hacking."

Donna tilts her head to the other side, eyes never leaving my face. "You're saying you modified Juniper's memories?"

"The memory is so fallible, don't you find?"

Donna sits across from me, staring, speechless—hands don't twirl the pen, the foot doesn't flick, the head doesn't bob.

"Before Cherri died, I tested the technique on Juniper to determine how receptive she was to suggestion. I knew once Juniper was grieving the loss of Cherri, manipulating her memory would be even easier."

Donna scoots around in her chair, resting an elbow on the chair arm, fingertips coming to her temple. This appears to be too much for her to comprehend. Perhaps I should have explained it more slowly. I should have known Dense Donna would require more time to process the workings of a complex mind.

"So let me get this straight," Donna begins, pen waving in time with her words. "You were controlling Juniper's memories, leading her to believe she was experiencing memory decline?"

"You asked for the plan's origins of formation. There you have it." She sits there, looking bewildered—hair wild, eyes wide. Donna seems stupefied, too obtuse to comprehend. Am I going to have to draw a goddamn diagram? Fuck.

"Let me simplify it for you, Donna; so you understand—the intention was to drive Juniper crazy with grief, with loss, lead her to believe her mind and health were failing, and then, Juniper would take her own life—the same as Phoebe had all those years ago."

Donna remains unmoving. She doesn't scribble on that pad. She doesn't shake her frizzy head or fiddle with her readers. It's obvious she's running back through what I've reported, trying to determine what to do with the information, to decide who should know the extent of my culpability. No doubt, Donna would be a terrible card partner—her facial expressions scream her inner thoughts for all to see.

"I don't need to remind you of the fact that our conversations are to be held in confidentiality, do I, Donna? You're required not to disclose the information I share with you in our therapy sessions." Donna stares on. "We discussed this," I say, *borrowing* Donna's voice, "went through the legal disclaimers, signed the consent forms prior to ever beginning our sessions." Donna narrows her eyes. Evidently, she doesn't enjoy hearing herself speak either.

"I'm well aware of the laws, Roni," Donna says, scooting around in her chair, shifting weight to the opposite hip. "And I would appreciate you never using my voice again—not in our sessions, not outside our sessions, never again."

"Jeez." I throw my hands up in surrender. "You're rather sensitive."

Donna seems fidgety with the facts, the laws—someone else being able to mimic her so convincingly. Watching her be so obviously agitated, I decide I would like to continue, go a bit more in-depth than I'd planned with the story.

"I remind you—I did not set out to ruin or take anyone's life. Initially, I only wanted to learn about my father's family. Simple enough. However, I learned that everything I'd ever been told about the man and his relatives was a lie. THEN, I discover my mother isn't my mother. *My* mother is dead because my *supposed* mother stole me as an infant, leaving my biological mother to take her own life out of heartbreak. All the new information was beyond disturbing. It was horrific. I'm nothing more than one of those milk carton kids from the late eighties. Everything you thought you knew becomes a new question when you discover something like that. How can you possibly believe anything someone tells you, knowing you've been a gullible idiot your entire life?

"Here's the thing, though—from all the deceit and all the deception, I found Hannah. Once I found Hannah, my whole outlook on life and family changed. Hannah was my world, my everything, and I was going to do whatever I had to do to make sure I didn't lose her."

"You formed your plan after you fell in love with Hannah?" Donna asks.

"Like I told you before, I didn't have a plan initially. Do you EVER fucking listen? I only wanted to learn more about my father. So, yes, I guess if I have to give you an answer. Yes. The plan was formed after I met Hannah. And when I established that Hannah was Juniper's daughter, I decided there was no way in hell I was sharing her with Juniper. Hannah was mine. Juniper gave her away. I've told you all this before. Check your shitty notes."

"But what about Hannah? Hannah didn't have the right to know her biological mother?"

"As far as Hannah was concerned, she grew up with her biological parents. Again. I've said this."

"And you didn't see the need to share this truth with Hannah?"

"I'm not answering that question for you again."

"A simple yes or no—you didn't see the need to share this truth with Hannah?"

"Fuck you. I told you if I relayed that information to Hannah, our relationship would have been over."

"Because of Hannah or because of Juniper?"

"Juniper." I'm done elaborating. Nothing gets through to this woman.

"So you began planting false memories, leading Juniper to believe she was losing her mind to disease, to dementia, the same as Cherri?"

"No."

"No, what? You didn't plant false memories? You weren't trying to make her think she was going crazy? Because I'm fairly certain you just told me you wanted her happiness, her misery, her memories."

"Yes, I planted the false memories. But, no, Cherri didn't have dementia."

"I'm going to need a more specific explanation, please," Donna says, an edge in her tone now.

"Juniper couldn't possibly have inherited the mutated gene for dementia, number one, because it so rarely happens, and two, Cherri didn't have dementia as it related to Alzheimer's disease. Cherri's medical diagnosis was Wernicke-Korsakoff syndrome."

Donna sits silently for a moment, mulling over this new piece of information. "So you're saying Cherri's alcoholism spurred this Wernicke-Korsakoff syndrome, which often has the appearance of dementia, given the memory issues the syndrome induces."

"Let's get you a cookie, Donna. Way to use that noggin of yours!"

"There is no reason to be condescending and patronizing, Roni. I find it offensive."

"Most people would."

"We are not getting sidetracked again. Moving on," Donna commands, perusing her notes. "How is it that Juniper, Cherri's next of kin, was not aware of the disease that claimed her mother's life?"

"I've answered that question as well."

"Then answer it again, please."

"I was Cherri's health proxy. Would you like me to spell it? You should write it down this time so you don't forget it again."

"Still, I would think the doctors would have spoken with Juniper about Cherri's condition."

"They might have if I had allowed Juniper to attend Cherri's doctor visits."

"Cherri's medical issues surfaced prior to you learning about your parentage. At that point, you had no idea of any 'deeep tion,' as you put it. Why not be honest with Juniper about her mother's health?"

"Because I didn't fucking want to. Juniper knew what Juniper needed to know. Cherri had entrusted me with that job, not Juniper."

"So it was a control issue for you?"

"Don't piss me off, Donna."

"I'd say it's too late for that, Roni." Donna stands, gathers her things, and leaves the room.

CHAPTER FIFTY-THREE

Cherri

THE ANDERSONS GAVE her a new name, made her legal, made her theirs and theirs alone. So as not to sully their dead son's reputation with the sordid mess of being involved with a Walder, they told their friends and family the baby girl had arrived via surrogate. After the sudden and tragic death of their only son, this child was a gift from God. Who would dare question their intentions or desires or means to obtain them? Cherri had been the one who made it all possible—the whole process so ridiculously seamless for them.

Cherri had never been one to follow the rules of society or even civil laws. She'd been a child of the sixties and proud of her free-thinking, free-spirited lifestyle. Cherri had delivered Roni in the basement of their rented home, telling Juniper they had plenty of time to file Roni's birth certificate and obtain a social security number.

But, in the days leading up to Juniper's departure for school, the hours were so full and hectic that Cherri had not gotten around to actually completing the tasks. She had not filed any of the proper paperwork proving Juniper was Roni's mother. Cherri had handed over her undocumented grandchild to a man who knew how to work the legal system. Every last trace of Roni having been born Juniper's child was gone quickly and efficiently and permanently. There was absolutely nothing but memory to claim that the baby now called Hannah Anderson was born Veronica Walder.

Juniper was off at school. Dusk was gone, doing whatever Dusk wanted to do. Luna was dead, and now, little Roni was gone. Cherri was devastated, but moreover, she couldn't fathom how she was going to tell Juniper. What would she say? How was she going to show up in Florida without Juniper's daughter?

"I was so disgusted with myself," Cherri relays to her guardian spirit.

"It was indeed a difficult situation. While this portion of your review is trying, take comfort in knowing you are close to completion."

"Trying? I don't call this trying. I call this torture. Making me witness, relive the horrible things I've done. Surely, I am one of the worst souls you've assisted in a review."

"Making judgments about another's actions during their lifetime is not something I do. My part is only to accompany a soul through this process."

Cherri forms her own judgment about her earthly experiences, and she does not approve of how she conducted herself over the lifetime. She will have much work to do in her next human life. She only hopes that she will learn from her unforgivable actions of this one and make better choices on the next go around.

"And that is exactly why we do the review," her guardian spirit says. "However, we still have to complete your review before we can move on."

Cherri turns back to the review before her, readying to witness the very worst deed she committed during her last lifetime.

◉

Cherri is sick… sick to death by what she has done. She moves through her days in a fog of denial and despair. Eating is impossible. The Andersons have taken Roni away with them, and the only thing that gives Cherri any comfort whatsoever is her drink.

In an attempt to keep busy in some way, to move forward somehow, Cherri continues packing for the move to Florida. She had phoned Juniper after the Andersons took Roni. Not because Cherri had the intention, much less the courage, to inform Juniper she had given Roni over to them, but to make sure Juniper wouldn't call her. The cowardice-fueled call was placed when Cherri knew Juniper would be in class. Cherri left a message with Juniper's dorm mate, relaying that she was disconnecting the phone to save a few dollars before the move. Please let Juniper know not to worry. Everything was going according to plan. If Juniper needed her mother, she should leave a message at Cherri's work, and Cherri would call her back.

Dazed, lonely, depressed, fearing—knowing—the worst is yet to come, Cherri roams the house, haphazardly tossing her things into boxes, unable to distinguish one day from the next. Ever present, in the distance, the sound of a crying baby. She knows it's impossible, but she believes the noise is coming from Roni. Her precious granddaughter is distraught and confused, relying on strangers for her care. No matter the volume of the television, or the radio, or how loudly she hums to herself, Cherri cannot clear the noise. She must be going crazy. This must be the punishment she deserves for handing over Juniper's child.

And then the police arrive.

Cherri knew the Andersons couldn't be trusted. They took Juniper's child and were now going to turn Cherri over to the authorities for killing their son. What proof do they have? There were no witnesses. Not only will Juniper have lost her baby, she will also lose her mother now, too. But the police do not climb the steps of Cherri's front porch. Instead, they bang on the door of the home next to her, demanding that the man who lives there come out.

Cherri has watched the couple next door for over a year, and while she knows the neighborhood thinks of her family as white trash, those two make Cherri's clan look like upstanding citizens.

The pair looks to be in their mid-thirties, though Cherri figures hard living has probably added a few years to their features. There's always a late-night party—questionable guests, loud exchanges. Cherri can't count the number of times she's seen suspicious behavior next door. Random people showing up on the couple's doorstep—a quick entrance, a quicker exit. Cherri has made claims on more than one occasion that drug deals must be going down in that house.

It turns out, Cherri's suspicions about her neighbors' nefarious activities are not unfounded. The police completely surround the house. The pounding at the door goes unanswered. Law enforcement enters with force. The man is handcuffed and led into a waiting patrol car. It is a scene out of a crime show that plays out before Cherri's eyes. The man is arrested not only for drug trafficking but is also charged with the indirect killing of one of his 'clients' as well.

The authorities instruct the woman next door to leave her home while they perform an extensive search. Cherri watches the woman—hair uncombed, scantily clothed, and barefoot—exit the house, struggling with an infant carrier, making her way into a friend's waiting vehicle. With all that had happened in Cherri's world, she had forgotten Juniper told her the woman was pregnant too, that the babies were due within days of each other. Cherri and Juniper had been so focused on Roni that neither even realized the neighbor had given birth to her baby as well. The crying baby has not been a figment of Cherri's overwrought mind. It has been coming from next door all along.

The police question Cherri about what she has observed over the last year. She answers their questions the best she can, which is not much help considering all she has suffered this past year.

Cherri hasn't had time to notice what has been going on in the house beside her, and when the crime scene tape comes down, Cherri forgets all about those people. She has other, more imperative concerns of her own to deal with.

As Cherri continues to pack, making her way through the last days in Brunswick, she hears the child's wails. The noise is infuriating. Cherri wants nothing more than to hold her granddaughter, and next door, there is a woman who does nothing but ignore and disregard her own infant. The baby doesn't seem to have one squall-free waking moment. It is always crying.

Cherri tries to ignore the noise, tries not to think about the neglected baby. She loads the moving truck she rented, preparing for her departure early the next day. Finally, Cherri will leave Georgia and all the terrible memories behind; she just has to keep working. Yet, Cherri finds it difficult to stay on track as the cries grow more urgent with each hour that passes. Yelps of hunger and distress. Her poor baby. Cherri realizes her own cheeks are wet, and the child isn't Cherri's baby or even Juniper's baby. She wipes away her tears and works harder, faster. Get it done. Get out of there.

Cherri walks to the backyard to grab the yard tools—the last of her things to go into the moving van—when she decides she can take it no more. She stops at the gate, turning toward her neighbor's home, viewing the open window, hearing the screams of the infant. Cherri steps closer to the open window. On tiptoes, she peers over the window ledge to see the baby flailing helplessly in a rickety crib, the door to the room closed. Temperatures have soared to ninety degrees this last day of September, yet Cherri can detect no noise from an air conditioning unit or portable fan to cool off the room. Where is the young woman? Why is she letting this poor child cry?

Cherri walks to the front of the house. She climbs the stairs to find the screen door pulled shut, but the front door wide open. Cherri's eyes sweep the room. The young woman is on the sofa, where she appears to be asleep.

Cherri determines that something is not right. No one could sleep through the pitiful wails the infant makes. She knocks at the door, calling inside to the woman lying on the couch. The woman makes no movement, no indication that she hears Cherri. Cherri pulls open the screen door and calls hello once more. When Cherri receives no recognition, she tiptoes closer to the woman. Cherri doesn't want to frighten her, to have her wake up and startle to find a stranger in her living room, but she needs to make sure the woman is okay.

Cherri moves closer to get a better look at the woman she has only ever seen from afar. Cherri has never been friendly with her neighbors—no cups of sugar borrowed, no stopping for chats at the mailbox. She leans over the woman to better assess the situation. The woman's coloring is sallow, hair matted and oily. Cherri nudges the woman's shoulder, trying to shake her awake. Limbs hanging limply over the sofa, the woman does not respond. Cherri checks to make sure the woman's chest moves with the action of taking in air. She's still breathing, although there is no telling what this woman has done to put herself in such a stupor. She very well could have overdosed on something, but Cherri's concern is for the baby. Cherri doesn't want to spend any more time on a woman who passes out on drugs while her newborn lies in a hot, closed room, starving and screaming for attention.

Cherri finds her way through the house, back to the bedroom where the infant lies abandoned. The closed-off room is stifling, making it difficult to breathe. Cherri hurries to the infant, the little face and body red and splotchy with heat and distress. Cherri lifts the baby out of the crib and pulls it to her chest, jostling and shushing, patting its little back, blowing air over the sweaty tuft of hair. She slips a hand around its tiny bottom to find the diaper soaked through. Dear God, this pitiful child. Cherri searches the room for supplies and finds changing items tossed onto the floor in the far corner.

She works quickly to get the baby out of the wet garments. A raw, blistering diaper rash covers the little girl's backside. The baby continues to cry, but the urgent tone subsides somewhat under Cherri's careful touch. Cherri can't understand how the neglectful woman is allowed to be a mother when their very own Roni has been stripped of her own doting mother and grandmother. It hardly seems fair. This child will never have a chance in life with a druggie for a mother and a convict for a father. Most likely, Cherri thinks sadly, the girl will end up in foster care, a ward of the state.

After Cherri has changed the child, she marches back through the house, not bothering to soften her steps or the wailing child. Cherri doesn't care if the mother wakes to find her going through the home—the baby is starving for sustenance and attention. The woman should be ashamed of herself. She doesn't deserve this sweet little girl.

Cherri finds bottles and formula in the kitchen, the bottles all filthy. Holding the baby firmly to her chest, she cleans a bottle and prepares the formula. The nipple barely grazes the little girl's lips before the baby finds it and sucks greedily.

Cherri walks the baby to the living room, settling into a chair across from the passed-out mother on the sofa. Cherri can't stand the sight of the woman and puts all of her focus on the baby, taking in her features as the infant gulps the milk. She looks so much like her little Roni. Cherri's heart aches, threatening to break in half. Her whole chest feels as if it will burst open under the pressure. The baby opens her eyes, staring intently, gratefully, into Cherri's; it's almost as if she knows Cherri is saving her at this very moment.

Cherri knows what she must do. She must protect the child. Cherri is unable to save Roni, but she can save this little girl. She can keep her from falling into the child welfare system, becoming a ward of the state, wondering all of her life why her parents couldn't have loved her and provided for her, all the heartache and years of self-doubt—Cherri can give this baby everything she can't give Roni.

Cherri's whole body tenses with the thought of rescuing the girl. She knows it is wrong, yet it seems right. The baby is in danger, and she looks so much like precious little Roni. Could she get away with it? The eyes are shaped a bit differently, but the child's hair is dark like Roni's. Besides, all infants look similar at birth. Juniper expects Roni to have grown, to have changed by the time she sees her daughter again. Yes. Cherri can pull it off. She can save this child from her neglectful, harmful family while saving her own child, Juniper, from the heartbreak of losing Roni.

Cherri looks at the unconscious woman splayed over the couch and back at the baby in her arms. It doesn't seem there is a decision to be made. Cherri stands, tightens her grip on the baby, and walks out of the house, the screen door slamming behind her.

"You see," Cherri implores her guardian spirit, "I must tell her. For the longest time, it was a secret—a horrendous, heavy secret —I carried because I didn't know how to tell Juniper what I had done. I always thought it would be my deathbed confession, but then I forgot. I forgot who I was. I forgot who Juniper was. I forgot who Roni was. But now I remember, and I have to tell her. Juniper deserves to know."

"What's done is done. Your time on the earthly plane has been completed. The events and their respective consequences have moved forth as planned."

"What do you mean? Juniper didn't plan to raise another woman's child."

"You've no idea what Juniper's soul contract for this lifetime is. Juniper made her plans for what she needed to learn in this physical experience, just as you did before you took on the body and identity of Cherri Walder."

"Don't you understand, though? I interfered with everyone's

plan, as well as my own plan. I had intended to tell Juniper before I passed on, and didn't. And now… now, Juniper's true Roni—Hannah Anderson—is old enough to know the truth without Chris's parents carrying out the initial threats they threw at me when they took her away from us."

"Have you considered Roni? How do you suppose Roni will feel when she learns you stole her from another family?"

"That will be difficult, yes," Cherri mumbles. "Yes, I admit, Roni will not handle the news well."

Cherri thinks back on all the times she counseled Roni through tantrums, unjustified hurt feelings, and manipulative actions. Roni always found someone else to blame for her aggressive and passive-aggressive mannerisms. Whenever she could get away with it, Cherri didn't share the school reports of Roni's bullying behaviors with Juniper, nor did she discuss the passive-aggressive attitude Roni used toward her teachers and friends. Cherri downplayed Roni's behavior with Juniper, who had worried excessively over Roni's belligerent actions. To Cherri's good fortune, Juniper believed Cherri to be a doting grandmother, making excuses for her grandchild, but Cherri had other reasons for not acknowledging Roni's issues.

None of Cherri's children ever acted in such a manner growing up, leading Cherri to conclude Roni's behavior was an inherited trait. To Cherri's knowledge, due to his uncontrollable rage, Roni's biological father continued to serve out a sentence for a murder he committed while incarcerated. It made sense to Cherri that Roni might have some of her father's undesirable tendencies. At least Roni didn't have her biological mother's desire for drugs. Cherri could coach Roni through anger issues, but addiction tendencies were another animal. Cherri knew far too much about addictions—except for how to overcome one.

"Roni has always had anger issues and tends to hold grudges —some unfounded, I dare say—when she believes she has been wronged," Cherri says.

Cherri studies her guardian spirit, her thoughts running wild with ominous outcomes should the truth be relayed, uncovered. Suddenly, Cherri understands. Her guardian spirit is right. The truth must remain hidden for the betterment of all involved.

Cherri wishes that just once more, she could forget. And she does, as she heads toward the loving, warm glow and embrace of her soul family.

CHAPTER FIFTY-FOUR

Hannah

After almost a year on the market, my parents' house sold. My new bosses were aware of the situation and graciously gave me the time off to wrap up the sale of my parents' estate. I left West Palm Beach on a Thursday, thinking I'd arrive in Bainbridge late in the evening, spend one last night in my childhood home, then rise early the next morning to begin packing up personal effects. The weekend was going to be long and difficult, but I had prepared myself for it and harbored no preconceived ideals of anything other than overwhelming sadness. Some moments must simply be endured.

Roni offered to come with and help me out. At the last minute, however, she had a work issue and couldn't leave town. While I reassured her of my understanding, I was inwardly disappointed. We had come to lean heavily on one another, and the truth was, I would have welcomed Roni's emotional support if nothing else.

Our relationship had progressed at breakneck speed. I'd never had anyone love me the way Roni loved me. When someone loves you that intensely, you begin to believe you're worthy of it, grow addicted to it. Roni and I shared our childhood upbringings, tales of our careers, stories of family, and past loves. We told one another our dreams, our fears, ambitions, and made plans for the future. Still, I couldn't shake the feeling that Roni was holding back. For all she gave, something was just beneath the surface, something she held onto fiercely. I assumed it was grief for her grandmother, but I did wonder why she didn't lean on her mother if indeed, mourning was the issue.

During several conversations, I inquired about Roni's family, but for one reason or another, we got off topic and wound up on another subject. We may not have spoken extensively about her mom, and I had yet to meet her—Roni said the timing wasn't right because her mother was going through a nasty divorce—but I got the impression Roni wasn't close with her mother. Still, I hoped one day Roni would feel comfortable enough to introduce me to her family.

Like me, Roni didn't have a lot of living family members, and although I continued to reiterate how important it was not to take family for granted, introductions were never made. I concluded I was most likely overreacting to Roni's slight because I was anxious to have people to call family again. Admittedly, I had fantasized that maybe Roni would share her mom with me, since mine was gone.

I missed my parents more than I thought possible, which made it more difficult to understand Roni's frustration and lack of interaction with her family. I couldn't help wondering if Roni's sudden backing out of this final trip had to do with some aversion to anything family-related. Then again, maybe Roni thought she'd be in the way, given how much there was to be done.

When I left Bainbridge to begin my new job in West Palm Beach and start my life with Roni, I left the Anderson Estate—so dubbed by the realtor to make the house sound more regal—exactly as it had been throughout my childhood and up until my parents passed. I hated the thought of selling off everything they had worked so hard for, but the maintenance on such an old, prominent place was more than I could afford. And too, I didn't want an *estate*. The term estate probably wasn't quite so ridiculous, I decided after spending a couple of weeks in Roni's apartment. The historic Victorian home was over 6,000 square feet, filled to the brim with antiques that my mother had collected throughout her life. Whether Roni came along to assist with the move or not, outside help was essential to pack up the lifetimes of my long-gone family members.

I had meticulously lined up all counterparts and outside purveyors who would handle the many details to achieve the goal of getting everything squared away in one weekend. As well, I had set forth a plan of attack for the hard tasks ahead of me. Keep the chores as clinical as possible. If I could remove my feelings from the sentimental purge, the move would go much smoother.

My father's office was first up. Rarely had my dad invited me into his private space. As an official of the court system, he set strict rules and consequences for all aspects of his life, but particularly for entering any of his domains in the old house. I'm not sure what I expected to find in Dad's home headquarters, but as it turned out, there was no point in wasting time on conjecture. Notes on old court rulings, bank statements, tax returns. Nothing proved to tell me more about the man than I already knew. I boxed up everything to go out for the shredding service and proceeded to my parents' bedroom.

All of their clothing and household linens would go to a charitable group. Once I finished in their room, the packers would come and box up everything for donation. I just needed to weed through Mom and Dad's personal items to determine what to keep. Really, there wasn't much that I wanted. My parents were older than most of my peers' parents. Our age differences were significant, and though I loved them dearly, the generational divide was real. The only thing I boxed up for myself was jewelry to go through at a later date. That task was one not to be rushed.

I moved on to the next room on my list, my mother's sitting room off of their shared bedroom. My mother was a self-proclaimed packrat and was proud to hold the title—the thought brought a sad smile. The woman saved everything, but to her credit, she had a diligent organizational process. Most everything in the sitting room was marked for trash. I saw no point in hanging onto dog-eared etiquette manuals, yellowed newspaper clippings, old magazines, polite correspondence, and thoughtful notes from her friends and fellow congregation members.

When I got to the small closet in my mother's private space, I found them. I had no idea my mother had been such a prolific writer throughout her life. She had a journal for every year, starting with the early ones, when she had just learned to read and write, it appeared. After thumbing through the diaries from her young girl years, I laid those aside. All the handwritten books were arranged chronologically. Some books were complete, no page left blank. Others had several pages unmarked. Without fail, however, she had begun a new book each New Year's Day.

The plan to start the packing process in the other rooms proved wise; once I found the journals, I couldn't bring myself to move on to another project. What a gift—my mother's thoughts and feelings and significant moments were there for me to read through, know her, understand her better. She wrote stories about my brother Chris that I'd never heard before. And then, I was in the year of his death. Reading through her feelings of the time, it's surprising she even made it through.

It was during that year that I was conceived. While I had heard the story of my miraculous birth on many occasions, I thought perhaps I might read some of my mother's private thoughts about those moments when she awaited my arrival.

I had always been under the impression that the news of my conception eased some of my mother's heartache. If it did, she wrote nothing of it. All my life, I had been told I was a miracle baby. I felt sure I would read through her feelings during the year prior to my birth, mixed as I'm sure they must have been at the time. Yet, the journals held no details of my arrival, first nights at home, or even preparation of the nursery.

Further into that year, I finally found my mother's first entry regarding my birth. To say I was unprepared for what I read would be a gross understatement. Reading, scanning, skimming, moving fast through the blurring words, I flipped page after handwritten page. It wasn't possible. This was not the account relayed throughout my childhood.

My parents always said they were having difficulty accepting the fact that Chris was preparing to leave home for college after high school graduation. The idea of being empty nesters was inconceivable, they declared. They wanted another child, even dreamed of perhaps having a girl the next time around. My mother was unable to carry to full term due to medical difficulties, however. Mom told me it was a decision that was not made lightly or easily, but my aunt, my mother's younger sister, agreed to be their surrogate. It was during the early days of the pregnancy that Chris was killed.

In that volume of my mother's life, I learned that my parents were not my biological parents, but instead my grandparents. Chris was not my brother, but instead my father. I was not born via surrogate but rather to a woman named Juniper Walder, Chris's girlfriend at the time of his death.

Juniper, an odd name, one I'd never heard before—until I met Roni. Roni never called her grandmother anything other than her name, Cherri. Likewise, Roni never called her mother anything but her name, Juniper. There just aren't coincidences that strange in life.

The more I read, the more I understood what must have taken place all those years ago. While Juniper was at school in Florida, my parents wrangled me away from Cherri. My mother was adamant that I was much better off being raised by them than I ever would have been with Juniper and Cherri. I was a gift from God. My parents had prayed and prayed, and though prayers wouldn't bring Chris back, they brought his daughter to them instead.

Is this true? Surely, my mother wouldn't have taken the time to record fictional stories in her journals. How could I be certain what I read was fact? How would I ever learn the truth? My mother and father had passed on. My aunt died ten years ago, having lost her battle with breast cancer. I have no other family members to consult—no other aunts or uncles or cousins.

My mind pleading to understand, I continued to read. As I flipped to the next page, several newspaper clippings fell out. Taking care not to damage the brittle, yellowing articles, my mother made a point of keeping, I unfolded each clipping and laid them out on the floor in front of me.

The story presented was one of a missing infant girl. The father was not a suspect as he, Robert Ulrich, was incarcerated at the time of the child's disappearance. The baby girl's mother, Phoebe Daniels, declined comment but, according to her friends, was inconsolable. All the clippings followed the search for the baby: personal details related to the missing child's parents, the time and place of the baby girl's birth, police interviews of all the neighbors. I skimmed each article for the reconciliation of mother and child, but never found that evidence. The child was simply gone, her disappearance never solved.

Why had my mother saved these clippings? What did these people and the missing baby have to do with my family? I returned the cuttings to the pages of the book. As I continued to read my mother's journals, I found the answers to my questions.

My mother had taken the time to put on paper her theory of what happened to the missing child. She speculated that Cherri (Juniper's alcoholic mother) had stolen the baby who lived next door to Cherri and Juniper. According to my mother's account, Cherri disappeared not long after my parents took me out of Cherri's care. My mother listed the facts laid out by the local police, the comments made by the child's relatives, and plotted the possibilities, coming up with her supposition.

My mother was convinced the stolen infant girl was Cherri's new Roni Walder, but Mom was determined to stay out of that investigation. My mother had what she wanted and didn't want to chance that she might have to give me up if she went to the authorities with what she knew.

Studying all the facts before me, my mother's conclusions make more sense than not. But why then is Roni's last name Barnes and not Walder or even Ulrich? Without alerting Roni to my suspicions, only one other person remains to be confronted for answers.

CHAPTER FIFTY-FIVE

Juniper

THE SUN IS LONG GONE. The moon hides tonight, taking the evening into a deeper level of darkness. Boswell sleeps tucked into my side, the two of us curled up on the sofa. I've been unable to sleep in my bed since finding the letter—the letter found on the door, the letter I left on the kitchen counter, the letter that then disappeared. It does make for long nights when you cannot sleep. Throughout the daylight hours, I doze a bit—fitful at best, but at least I am able to close my eyes.

As I shift to find a more comfortable position, Boswell rouses. He lifts his head to investigate, then drops his chin to rest on my leg when all checks out to his satisfaction. I twist my head from the window on my right to view the kitchen area on the left. The digital display on the oven relays we've moved into the two A.M. hour, ticking slowly towards three. At three, I'll check the doors again. I've gotten into the routine of making a loop through the apartment every other hour to be certain doors are locked and to break up the long night.

The hours might go faster if I read or watch television, but I can't. I can't risk that I may miss a noise, a movement, some tell-tale sign I'm not alone in my home. I need to stay alert. No distractions. That's exactly how I got into this position. Being distracted.

I lay my hand on Boswell's head, run my fingers through his fur. The act is comforting, soothing, a tad hypnotic if I'm honest. I think I could sleep—I'm so tired. Eyelids heavy, limbs deadweight, my body aches for good, solid rest.

Noise (although almost imperceptible) comes from the vicinity of the guest bedroom.

Eyes spring open, arms and legs seize in fright, my gaze flies toward the front of the apartment. I must have imagined it, I tell myself. At the last walkthrough, the room's sliding glass door leading to the pool deck was secure. I'm positive. I think I'm positive. I remember pulling on the handle, but was that at one A.M.—or am I recalling the eleven o'clock check?

Again. More noise. It comes from the direction of the guest room. This is happening. This is real. The familiar rhythm of fear dictates the beat throbbing inside my chest. Ears whoosh with the sound of blood pulsing in time with my heartbeat, making it difficult to determine the source of the noise.

Plastic clattering? A vertical blind knocking against the slat beside it? Maybe.

Inching upright, Boswell takes an alert stance as well. Focus on the far end of the apartment, we're both careful not to move, careful not to make any sounds that would give away our position.

Was that noise the rustle of clothing?

Slipping my hand underneath the sofa cushion, my fingers locate it—the cold, texturized metal of the pistol's grip. I carefully extract the weapon as I swing my legs over the sofa's edge.

Crouching low, I find my way to the kitchen. Boswell, obeying whispered commands, stays close at my heel. In my head, I run through the checklist of all I learned during my gun lessons. The gun's chamber has a bullet at the ready. I ease off the gun's safety, conscious of muffling the slight click.

Another sound. The racket is louder than the previous noises. Something falls to the ground. The noise, startling, I catch myself. Balancing. Listening. Is it the contents of a pill bottle rattling, rolling along the bare floor?

Maintaining my position, I obscure myself from view at the end of the kitchen counter. A footfall and then another. I do not imagine this. These noises are not in my head. Someone is in this apartment. It can only be the person watching me, following me. My head spins. Pressure builds in my chest. I force air into my lungs, trying not to gulp the missed breath.

In the bedroom, on the charger, that's where I left my phone. I turn my head to look behind me, reminding myself to pull more air into my body. The doorway to the room is unobstructed, only four feet away. I motion for Boswell to follow. Cocking his head to one side, Boswell stares, baffled by the command. I nudge him forward, shifting my own body in the same direction.

Inside the room, Boswell follows me around the end of the bed to retrieve the phone. I usher us into the deep recesses of the closet, fumbling to tap the phone icon. I think to call Roni, then recall she's in Miami tonight. Besides Roni, I have no one to call for help. Everyone else in my life has proved untrustworthy. The police. Of course, I should have thought of it before—my mind isn't working right.

Wait. Is the city still under cyber attack, or has the ransomware issue been resolved? If I call emergency services, will someone respond? If I have to speak to inform them of my emergency, will the intruder inside the apartment hear me?

I can text 911. I saw that somewhere.

Another noise. From the kitchen area?

The intruder is closing in, coming this way.

Fingers fly over my phone, tapping the wrong apps, hitting wrong numbers, errant links. I release the gun to the floor as I type out the plea for help. From the corner of my eye, I see Boswell creeping back through the closet door into the bedroom. I scamper in the direction he heads, reaching, grasping, trying to get hold of his leg, tail, something to pull him back inside the safety of the closet. He's gone before I can reach him. The gun is on the floor, somewhere behind me. The phone has fallen from my grip and is in the middle of the pitch-black closet. The screen has either gone dark, or I dropped it screen-side down. No light of any sort to help illuminate the space. Boswell is gone. My phone and weapon lay somewhere within the depths of the closet, within reach—but where?

Swallowed in silence, in darkness, nerve endings tingling, my heart pounds wildly. Breathing shallows. I need to think through solutions, plot out the best action plan.

If I call for Boswell, I'll give away my position. If I crawl out of the closet to look for Boswell, I risk a confrontation with the intruder. If I locate my phone, will an emergency text message get through to the authorities? But the lessons from my firearm instructor ring in my head. Before I make any decision, I must locate my gun. *Maintain control of your firearm. The most dangerous place for your weapon is in the hands of your attacker.*

On hands and knees, I move along the closet floor, running the palm of my hand over the carpet. I find the phone first and illuminate the screen to see the 911 message failed to send. Tapping at the screen furiously, I press harder as if the force will swish the message away into the ether faster. And then it's gone, but I have no idea where it went. Did it send the call for help to the emergency center? Did I accidentally erase the message?

I can't waste any more time. The screen of the phone brightens. I shine the light onto the closet floor. It's there just ahead of me. I hurry forward to retrieve it, listening for noises behind me.

Knocking?

Someone pounds on the front door of the apartment. It's not yet three A.M. Who would be knocking on the door at this hour?

It must be the police. They got here fast. Too fast. It can't be the police.

Do I stay where I am? Do I head to answer the door? Will the pounding avert the intruder?

Is there an intruder?

Yelling. Someone speaks loudly. Shouting. Even from outside the apartment, the voice carries through the rooms.

"Hello? Hello?" The voice calls. "I know you're in there. Open up, now," the voice commands.

Whoever is on the other side of the door is not from emergency services. But who is it? From the closet to the bed, I crawl. Holding the gun firmly in my right hand, I use the left one to grab the edge of the bed and pull upright.

Outside the bedroom threshold, Boswell stands near the sliding glass door, looking toward the kitchen. His tail wags as if he is watching someone in the distance, someone he knows and favors.

The pounding continues from the outside hallway. A crash from the kitchen—something falling from the counter to the floor. More banging, this time from inside my chest. On instinct, my hand flies to my breastbone, as if I can calm the fierce beating. I drop my gaze and find the gun resting against my chest. I yank it away, down to the side of my body.

"I know you're in there, and I know what you've done. You owe me an explanation," the voice in the hallway calls out.

No one answers. The silence is nerve-racking. A standoff.

Between who?

I tiptoe through the kitchen, making my way closer to the front door.

Another loud crash. From the office this time. The glass container holding my pens and pencils?

Back against the pantry cabinet, I crane my neck around the corner to see a figure emerge from the office. The front door handle jiggles. The intruder takes a step toward the apartment entrance. Who is it? Dark, boxy clothing hangs loosely from the shapeless form. Atop the head, a hat further disguises the figure.

The intruder turns toward the door.

Boswell races toward the intruder.

The whoosh of the intruder's clothing as the trespasser twists away from the door, pivoting to locate my position.

I close my eyes, willing myself to be strong, to do what I've trained for—to protect myself. The words of my instructor loop in my head: *If someone is in your house uninvited, that person is an intruder. If they didn't wait for an invitation, they sure as heck aren't going to offer up identification. Protect yourself. Protect your family.*

Gripping the stock with both hands, I raise the gun and pull the trigger.

CHAPTER FIFTY-SIX

"WHAT HAPPENS NOW?"

"You're all set to move forward. Your guardian spirit is waiting for you to finish up with me."

"This isn't how the process generally works, is it?"

"No. Typically, most souls are met by their guardian spirit after passing over."

"What happened with me? Why did we put in all that time together rehashing events if you already knew everything?"

"You thought you could fight it."

"Fight what?"

"Death."

"Fight death? You make it sound like I went twelve bouts with the Grim Reaper. Although—now that I think about how much time you and I have spent going round and round in this room, maybe the metaphor isn't so far off."

"I'm not sure I am comfortable being likened to the Grim Reaper, but in essence, yes, these interviews have been your version of that spectral entity."

"I don't follow."

"You felt more comfortable addressing your actions on the earthly plane in this manner… therapist to patient."

"I chose this bullshit process? Me? I elected to sit across from you time and time again?"

"Indeed." And there's the bobble. "Upon your demise, you decided that you were not ready to pass over. It is not that easy, however. In order to stay on the earthly plane, you had to plead your case. You needed to dive further into the reasoning for your behavior during this last lifetime."

"All this time, you let me believe this crap was mandated?"

"Well, you did want to go back to your life as Roni, and to do so, the meetings were a necessary step in your appeal."

Donna could have told me from the onset of our sessions what was going on. She could have explained that my body was clinically dead, that my efforts during our sessions would lead to the decision of whether I lived on or passed on.

"I don't understand, though. We've spent all this time together. Days. Weeks. Is my body in some sort of coma or something? Are doctors trying to revive me at this very moment? A lot of what I'm hearing from you sounds like bullshit, Donna."

"Time works differently on the astral plane. In this dimension, time—as it is measured in hours, days, and years on the earthly plane—does not exist."

"So… am I going back? Did I make a case for slipping back into Roni's lifetime?"

"No," Donna states, calmly, matter-of-factly, bluntly, no emotion, no solace, no compassion.

"No? Why the fuck not?"

"You have no regrets, no remorse. You still believe you had every right to take control of other souls, to manipulate what happened to them."

"And this is what your 'report' states?"

"It is."

"You're a bitch, Donna. You've known all along how you were going to *report* our sessions." Maybe if Donna had laid out all the details from the beginning, I could have made a stronger case for my return. Let's tick off yet another box delineating

Donna's ineptness. "Why let me suffer all the way through your dumb-ass questions when you knew you would be making this recommendation from the onset?"

Donna does not reply. She simply sits and watches and waits; I suppose she's waiting to pass me on to the next handler.

"So when this guardian spirit arrives, will I be meeting up with my family? Will I meet the mother and father I never knew during this lifetime?"

"No."

"What the hell? All those movies and books and church services—I thought when you passed over, all your long-dead family members greeted you, welcomed you home...blah, blah, blah."

"That information will be covered with your guardian spirit during your life review. Now that you are moving on to the astral plane, you will soon recall all you have forgotten while you were on the earthly plane."

"I don't know that I will *recall* why I am not to be reunited with my family. What... because I made some poor decisions while serving out this last lifetime, I'm to be punished by not meeting them?"

"The people you called your biological parents are not part of your soul family, Roni."

"How is that possible? I was their daughter. As an infant, I was stolen from them. I was the victim."

"As I said, it will all become quite clear as you go through your life review. What I can tell you, however, is that during your last reconciliation and preparation for this recent lifetime as Roni Walder, you chose this very situation."

"I chose it?"

"Indeed."

"Stop with the fucking 'indeed' shit, Donna. I highly doubt I would have picked this scenario to live out on the other plane. Who would choose to endure an ordeal like that messed-up situation?"

"Ah, but you did. We all do. Each soul chooses situations for which we will have the ability to garner the most knowledge, the opportunity to better ourselves, to understand the true meaning of love."

"So you're telling me that in this past lifetime I set up the whole twisted scenario before I was ever born to Phoebe Daniels and Robert Urlich? That I was never meant to have a relationship with Phoebe or Robert, even though they were my parents?"

"In…" Donna stops herself. "Correct," she says instead.

"So, will I see Cherri?"

"You will. Cherri is part of your soul family."

It hits—hard.

All I did to rectify the wrong done to me on the earthly plane only proved to work against me. I sabotaged my own spiritual growth by trying to manipulate fated happenings, happenings I planned prior to ever beginning the lifetime as Roni Walder. Something shifts with this knowledge. I feel a sense of peace move in as it pushes the anger away.

"So, do you know what happened?"

"Are you referring to the manner in which you died or how you left things on the earthly plane?"

"What happened with Juniper and Alok and Hannah? Do they know everything was done at my hand?"

"All are well and still following out their soul contracts."

"Life goes on for them," I say, half in statement, half in question.

"It does."

"As a family?"

"They have a lot to work through, to heal from, to learn from," is all Donna offers on that topic.

"Juniper and Alok reunited?" The two of them shared a love most people don't, and I tried to take that away from them—to break their bond.

"Why would they not? You fabricated the affair. Their separation was orchestrated at your hand. With the truth out in the open, they can move on, without further hindrances to their individual soul growth." Donna sits, taking me in, watching me for my reaction, I suppose. When I say nothing in response to her last statement, she adds, "Hopefully."

"You're so fucking diplomatic and compassionate, aren't you, Donna?" The anger seizes me once more. "Why don't you just say, 'Since you're out of the picture, Roni, they can finally live their lives happily?'"

"You need to let go, Roni. You'll soon realize there is no need for callousness."

"Are you kidding me, Donna? I would never tell a patient they were callous. You don't say that shit to a client."

"You're not a patient, Roni. More importantly, however, you need to understand you are not and have never been a victim."

"What the hell, Donna? You know I was a victim. We sat here for *how* long, going through all the details of all the shit I've been through? Did you listen to anything I said?"

"Indeed…"

"What did I say about using that damn condescending word, Donna?"

Dense as she is, Donna gets the question is rhetorical and doesn't bother to respond.

We sit in silence.

I wonder how much longer I have to endure Donna. I wonder if my guardian spirit will be more understanding and cerebral than this woman. I wonder what the next phase of this process, the life review, will hold. I wonder if Hannah is happier without me or if maybe she misses me.

I wonder what would have happened if I had chosen to react differently to everything that transpired during my lifetime as Roni Walder.

CHAPTER FIFTY-SEVEN

Juniper

THE REMODEL complete after the fire damage that occurred last summer, the house has a new look and feel to it. I guess the same can be said for us: Alok, Hannah, and me. In a sense, each of us had to be torn apart and rebuilt in order to come to some sort of acceptance regarding the events that occurred this last year. The difference is our scars can't be plastered over—they're still soft, still tender to the touch.

Tonight we put it all to the test. Will we manage to hold out for the gathering? Can we stand up to the task of socializing, of congregating with others, of moving forward? Will the house present well to neighbors and acquaintances we haven't seen in over a year? Will we?

Tonight, Hannah will be introduced to our guests as my daughter. Of course, they already know this, given the media attention surrounding the shooting investigation last year. However, this will be the first time many of them meet Hannah.

I met Hannah for the second time the night I shot Roni. It was Hannah pounding on the door, trying to get the truth from Roni. I wish Hannah had been able to get through to Roni. I wish Roni had answered Hannah instead of turning back and rushing at me that night. I wish I had not been so quick to react. I wish I had turned on the lights. I wish my 911 plea had been answered sooner. Each wish, however, proves more futile than the one it follows.

We thought Roni might pull through her injuries, but she didn't. I needed her to. I needed to understand why Roni did what she did, why she hated me so much. But those answers slipped away with her last breath.

I miss her, my daughter.

Between the police investigation, Hannah's account, and all the detailed plans and evidence found in Roni's secret storage unit, we've been able to piece together a conjectured motive. While it's plausible, it still isn't easy to accept. Then again, how does one come to terms with the fact that their child has orchestrated the demise of a parent—especially when that parental figure is you?

Given the situation, *bright sides* were hard to unearth, but I did get some answers I thought I'd never have. While many questions still loom, I now have a better understanding of some of the troubling issues from my past: Cherri's actions throughout Roni's upbringing, why Roni and I were complete opposites in so many ways, the reason I felt so disconnected to Roni whenever she and Cherri moved from Georgia to Florida to live with me while I attended school at Stetson.

When Roni was born, I felt a swell of attachment, thought I might explode with love and pride and happiness. She was mine —my girl. I didn't want to leave her. Cherri insisted: *We must go through with the plan.* I wasn't even eighteen, still grieving the loss of my sister and my baby's father. Overwhelmed, I did as I was told. Do I hold Cherri responsible? I can't answer that, not yet. I'm still working through the lies, the deceit, but that doesn't change my love for Cherri. Regardless of her actions, Cherri was my mother, and I hold to the belief she was doing the best she knew how to do.

Thankfully, I don't have to go through this alone. Alok has forgiven me for all the false accusations I've made, for how I've treated him. The affair and all the components of Alok's transgressions may have been masterminded by Roni, but I fell into the trap. Everything Roni told me, I believed. Although I could feel in my bones that it wasn't the truth, that Alok would never disrespect me in such a manner, I took Roni's word over Alok's. And my husband, being the man he is, does not begrudge me for taking the word of my daughter. Instead, Alok is patient and kind. He offers words of encouragement, of condolence, of sensibility, even after all I've done and said. The affair may have been planted into my head by Roni, but I was the first to hold Alok responsible for the city's cyberattack. I was the one who pegged that unethical, criminal behavior on my husband.

Noreen was the one who set that fallacy straight. She knew all along that one of her past employers on the island was responsible for the ransomware—a personal vendetta against the new mayor of West Palm Beach. Noreen couldn't say anything, however, because she had been bound by confidentiality agreements of long past.

Noreen has been a wonderful friend throughout the entire ordeal. She has been on hand and ready to help when one of us needs her. I try, but can't seem to thank her enough. According to Noreen, however, Alok, Hannah, and I are helping her. Noreen claims we've become the family she never had the chance to have, and now, we welcome her into ours.

It's Hannah I worry about. She has had so much to overcome: the heartbreak, the pain, the death. Hannah really has lost everything—the only identity she's ever known and the woman she believed she would grow old with. While Hannah and I slowly grow closer every day, I'm ever so grateful she allows me to help her through this, that Hannah doesn't hold any of what has happened against me, that she wants the two of us to have the relationship that was taken from us all those years ago.

As I move through the rooms of the house, waiting for our guests to arrive, I think about how much has changed in this house—from the drywall to the residents. I remember the dear, dear souls I've lost. I miss them, Cherri and Roni. Are they together again? Are Dusk and Luna with them? Will they be there for me when it's my turn to go?

I know I'm supposed to move on, to move forward with my life. I know it isn't supposed to be easy. I know we're supposed to make the most of our days on this plane. I know there are lessons to be learned. Some days I feel like I'm getting on pretty well. Yet, on others, I wonder if I'm doing what I should be, if I'm on track. Despite all my uncertainties, I believe everything is happening as it should. All the bad, all the good, I'm sure my day of reckoning will come round soon enough.

Never Miss a Book

You've reached the end of *When the Dead Remember*—but some stories stay with us long after the last page. If this one did, I'd be grateful if you shared your thoughts in a review and passed it along to a fellow suspense lover.

For updates on *When the Dead Remember*, news about upcoming releases, and exclusive offers, I'd love for you to join my reader list at Lcliaapiet.com

Also by Lelia A Piet

Fate Falls Hard

A pulse-pounding psychological thriller with a stunning twist

Perishing Hill

A gripping domestic suspense novel with a storm at its heart

About the Author

Raised in the shadowed woods of the deep South, Lelia A. Piet learned early that silence can be as dangerous as secrets. She spun her first twisted stories for her sisters while wandering the wild edges of Little River Canyon—and she hasn't stopped since.

She now calls Tennessee home, where she crafts psychological suspense that lingers in the gray space between memory and betrayal. Her novels pull readers into storm-swept settings and dark family reckonings—where no truth is safe from discovery.